Finding the Grain

Wynn Malone

Bywater Books

Bywater Books

Bywater Books First Edition: March 2014

Printed in the United States of America
on acid-free paper.

Cover designer: Bonnie Liss (Phoenix Graphics)

Bywater Books
PO Box 3671
Ann Arbor MI 48106-3671
www.bywaterbooks.com

ISBN: 978-1-61294-045-8

For Brantley, my rock and my sunshine

Your love is amazing

Prologue

Toward Grace

My aunt sat across the table from me, fiddling with her napkin. Her hesitation to speak worried me more than the deepening creases across her forehead. She stretched one arm across the red fiberglass booth at her back and looked down at her empty plate. "I didn't get good news from the bank today, Blue," Aunt Julie said. Though her face was turned down, I could see it had gone pale, almost as pale as the day she identified my parents' bodies. She looked up and locked her solemn gaze on me. "As you know, your dad borrowed a lot of money against the farm. I talked with the loan officer most of the afternoon. The only good option is to sell the farm to pay off the loans."

Julie paused and watched me for a moment. I wanted to be brave. I wanted to argue that I could find a way to work the farm and go to school. My mind only tumbled like it was falling into an endless well. "What about school?" I blurted out. "Is there enough money for college?" I hoped Julie didn't hear the helpless shaking in my voice.

"Don't worry about that. I'll pay for everything. I want you to start at Chapel Hill this fall."

What? Chapel Hill? Chapel Hill has nothing to do with me. Chapel Hill was where she went to college—at the University of North Carolina.

My thoughts suddenly caught hold and I glared at my aunt, Dr. Julie Riley, the woman I adored for all of her beautiful strength. Mom said she could be unmoving, though I had never seen it. With me she had always been forgiving, sometimes gentle to the point of tenderness, and often courageous, like a captain in a storm. Somehow, I had to stand up to her.

I straightened my back and willed my voice to be strong. "Julie,

1

you *know* I want to go to Auburn, like Dad did. I've dreamed about going to college there since I was a kid. I'll have a better chance to get into vet school if I go to Auburn for undergrad."

"I do know you want to go to Auburn." Julie laced her fingers together and leaned toward me, speaking with a soft firmness that delighted me when she used it on others. Now it pissed me off.

"You can go to vet school at Auburn if you want. Now isn't the right time. With everything that has happened, I want you closer to me. Starting college can be tough under the best circumstances."

I fell slack and turned away from her. How could she ask me to give up my dreams of going to Auburn? Hadn't I lost too much already? She had been there when the neighbors came to help us search for what was left of my life. She had been at my side when we dug through a pile of mangled debris and found my father's hat, the jagged sweat stains white against the John Deere logo; and later, when a neighbor from three miles down the road brought me the locket my mother had worn since I was a kid. Julie knew how hard the last six weeks had been.

"I don't see how I can be accepted to North Carolina when I haven't even applied," I said, my voice giving way and cracking a little. "Auburn has already accepted me and I have plenty of friends here in Alabama. Susan's parents will be close by if something happens."

Julie frowned and looked out the wall of windows at her shoulder. Birmingham traffic zoomed up and down the four-lane in front of the restaurant. I wanted to be in their current, driving somewhere far away from this conversation and the reality that trapped me in my aunt's decisions. I had to change her mind. She was the only relative I had left, and I would need her support to go to college. Julie turned back to me, her face now soft with compassion. "Your friend Susan and her parents have been a godsend for us, Blue. The fact is, we can't rely on them forever. When you start college there may be things that they're not equipped to handle. I'll be there for you, no matter what happens." She leaned forward to catch my eyes, still trying to pull me toward her will. "You've always liked North Carolina. We'll go fishing and camping in the mountains as much as my schedule will allow, okay? I need you to understand I only want what's best for you."

"What's best for me is to go to Auburn," I retorted. "I'll have friends there and I'll make more. I don't need you to be two minutes away every time I catch a cold."

Julie frowned and set her mouth, digging in. "Blue, this isn't about who's going to care for you when you catch a cold. This is about the support I can't give you from eight hours away. My schedule won't allow me to drop everything and run to Alabama at a moment's notice."

"I don't know why you would think you'd have to. I'm eighteen and I can take care of myself. Anyhow, I don't see how I'll be accepted to North Carolina. It's too late for me to be applying for fall semester."

"I'll get you in, Blue. I've already talked to the Dean of Admissions and explained your situation."

I turned away from her and covered my mouth with a fist. There was no use in continuing to argue. The file at Julie's hip was full of ledgers and bank accounts and facts that I couldn't change. Still I wanted to keep challenging her, to ask why I had to wait four years to get what I wanted. Hadn't I stayed out of trouble and made good grades? Hadn't I awakened at dawn every day to feed the calves and horses? Hadn't I mowed summer hay and harvested crops until dark? I had always been responsible.

A long, silent moment passed. The arguments I needed to persuade her wouldn't come. I could hardly think of tomorrow, much less the weeks ahead. I was weary from fighting for everything; for breath and the will to get out of bed. If I could just let go, maybe Julie would be my captain for a while. I loved the places we'd shared together. Maybe I could find refuge in her mountains and the landscapes I had come to love as much as my own.

"If I go to North Carolina now, I'm coming back here for vet school."

"If that's what you want," Julie replied.

"Can I come back here if I hate it?" I asked, trying to sound mature above my defeat.

"Give North Carolina three semesters, Blue. If you don't like it, you can come back to Alabama and go to school wherever you want," Julie said, her uncompromising expression remaining firmly in place.

Three semesters, a year and a half; it sounded like an eternity.

"Okay. It doesn't look like I have a choice anyway," I mumbled caustically.

Julie narrowed her sea-blue eyes on me, harsh for a moment. Maybe she was disappointed at my insolence. I didn't care. She grabbed her tea glass and tossed back the last swallow. "Are you ready to go?" she asked.

I pushed my empty plate aside and slid out of the booth. Outside in the parking lot was the one thing God hadn't taken away from me. Somehow my father's truck had survived the tornado with only a few dents, even though the trees around it were stripped of their bark. Tornados are strange that way.

We walked out to my truck in silence and stopped beside my door. We stood eye to eye. Still, I was no match for her strength. Julie stepped toward me and I let her wrap her arms around me. I leaned in and felt my body melt into her. She pulled me in tight and held on for a long time.

Part One

Hanging On

Fall 1980 – Summer 1981

1

Unexpected

Gone to the bank. Back in a few minutes. I taped the note to my apartment door and headed for my truck. Morning sun warmed my shoulders as I pulled the keys from my pocket and unlocked the driver's door. I looked up at the thin, wispy clouds scattered across the late September sky and imagined the next two days: the crackling of dry leaves under my feet; the scent of white pines and hemlocks growing stronger near the streams; the first spark of the campfire where Julie and I would warm our hands when the night air turned cool.

At Rosemary Street I turned right and spotted two sorority girls standing on the sidewalk beneath the bank sign. The girls bounced on their toes and held light-blue poster boards high above their heads. *Free Car Wash* arched across the posters in curled script.

"What kind of shit is this?" I muttered to myself.

"Free car wash," one of the girls yelled toward me when I turned into the bank entrance. She was a Delta Pi; the ΔΠ letters stitched across her ample breasts said so. I returned her wave and eased up to the drive-thru.

Three cars stacked the only open lane. I rolled down my window and watched a swarm of girls in cropped shirts and running shorts dance around a soapy green sedan at the far edge of the parking lot. My gaze swept from one girl to the next without pause. Sorority girls weren't my type, mostly because we didn't have anything in common except being undergrads at the University of North Carolina.

"Would you like a free car wash?" The question came with a knock at my passenger window.

I stopped writing my check and looked over, annoyed as hell at her nerve. She stood by my window, smiling. My body flushed warm with the sight of her. She stared back at me, and for a moment I couldn't move—or, at least, I didn't want to. Our eyes locked for an instant, and then she spun around and took a step away. I lunged for the window handle. "Are you taking donations for the car wash?" I asked, cranking frantically.

The girl turned around and smiled at me again. Her green eyes drew me in with intriguing promise. "Yes, I am," she said. She glanced down at the metal cash box she gripped between her tanned hands. "All of the donations go to our children's hospital charity. We wash your truck and you get to decide how much you want to pay."

"That sounds like a good deal. Can I catch up with you after I get cash?"

"Sure. Just pull over in the wash line and we'll take care of you." She glanced over at a couple of frat guys pulling up in a red Corvette, and then looked back at me. "See you in a few minutes." After a quick wave she turned for the 'Vette.

In my rearview mirror I watched her. She moved confidently, like a woman already comfortable taking risks. I kept watching as she bantered with the handsome frat boy in the passenger seat. He reached a green bill out the window toward her. She took it from him with a grateful smile, and then she gave an odd sort of curtsy and took a half step back. The guy smiled broadly, gesturing with one hand as he spoke. She laughed and pointed at him as if he were naughty. He tossed his head back, laughing harder as she walked away, as if he had gotten the better of her. I had an urge to kick his ass.

The orange VW bug ahead of me pulled away and I rolled up to the teller window. If I got my truck washed, I was probably screwed. Julie would be waiting by the time they finished, and she hated to be kept waiting. If I was lucky, she got caught in Raleigh traffic and I still had time. Regardless, I would explain that I couldn't drive away without talking to this girl again. Maybe Julie would still be pissed. The girl was worth the risk.

I swept my cash from the teller drawer and swung my truck around to the wash line. The girl now stood by one of her sorority sisters, the cash box still in her hands. She looked up and started toward me in a casual stroll. Her eyes narrowed and her eyebrows scrunched together as she drew closer.

"Have I seen you before?" she asked, her head cocked to one side.

I couldn't recall a previous meeting. If we had ever met, I would have remembered.

"I don't think so," I replied, feigning indifference. I reached into the front pocket of my Levis to fish out cash.

"Are you taking stats this semester?"

I nodded and pulled out a fold of two twenties. "Yeah, I've got Davis at nine."

"I thought so," she said. Our eyes met for a moment, and then her words suddenly became rushed. "I've got a class across campus at ten, so I sit in the back corner. I practically have to run to get to my next class on time. Some days I just skip."

"That's tough. Statistics is harder if you can't make class." I peeled off a twenty and held it out to her.

Across the parking lot a girl shrieked and we both looked over. Some shirtless guy in jeans had the hose on one of the Delta Pis. He laughed crazily as she squealed and hopped away. The girl with the cash box rolled her eyes and then looked back at me. She glanced down at the twenty and paused before she asked, "Would you mind writing a check instead? I'm running low on money to make change."

"At a bank?" I teased her.

She shuffled and her face flushed. "You're right. I just thought . . ."

"It's okay," I interjected, trying to make up for being a jerk. "The bank is really busy today, and I would need change. I'll get my checkbook."

I sensed her watching me reach into the glove box.

"Where are you from?" she asked as I opened my checkbook.

"Alabama. Not too far from Birmingham. How about you?"

"Virginia. Near Richmond."

"Ah, Virginia—I thought your accent was something Southern. It's a lot different than where I'm from. I like it. So, who do I make the check to?"

"Delta Pi, Gamma Upsilon Chapter."

I paused and looked up at her. "Or we can stamp it if you want," she said.

9

I tore out the check and handed it to her. "Good luck with stats. Look me up if you need help with notes or anything," I offered, though I knew her sorority status would give her access to ten years of notes and copies of tests from every statistics instructor in central North Carolina.

"I will," she said as she took the check and glanced at the amount. Her eyebrows arched and she smiled. "Thanks again for the donation. I'll see you in class?" I nodded and she looked at me as if she wanted to say something else, but she didn't. Her hand flew up in a quick wave and she spun around toward a waiting Chevrolet Blazer.

That night I stretched out under the stars and found the brilliant light of Venus. The evening star, my father told me one night. I had just turned twelve, the year that everything started changing inside me. He stood next to me in the back door of the barn, looking out to the twilight sky. He explained the orbit of Venus, and that sometimes Venus was the morning star and sometimes the evening star. He said that the next few years would be like that for me, sometimes I would feel one thing, and sometimes the opposite, but I would always be his girl. And he would always be proud of me.

I stared at Venus and wondered if the car-wash girl had ever noticed its arc across the night sky. Why was I even thinking of her? She was probably at some frat house chugging beer, no doubt with a date. She probably had a date every night she wanted. Maybe she had a steady boyfriend, and maybe it was serious. I could dream of the car-wash girl all I wanted, yet it wouldn't get me one minute of her time.

2

Grace

I had given up trying to talk to the carwash girl when I saw her in the hall. She waved to me once before class, but we hadn't spoken. She seemed too busy chatting with the other sorority girls to want to talk to me. I damn near fell out from shock when I looked out the window and saw her standing at my apartment door.

"Is that offer for your stats notes still good?" she asked the moment I opened the door. She regarded me calmly, as if I should have expected her.

"Yeah, sure, come on in." I stepped aside and held the door.

With charm-school footsteps she walked in and waited. I held up my hand and she moved to the middle of my one room apartment. The evening news report playing on my thirteen-inch television caught her attention. Walter Cronkite sat behind his news desk, his brows furrowed as he spoke in serious, chopped tones. Behind him the headline read: *Iranian Hostage Crisis, Day 340.*

"Is there anything new with the hostages?" she asked, her face etched with concern.

"No, it's just another horrible day for them."

I stood at her shoulder now. She was almost as tall as me. Her navy button-down was a fantastic contrast for her long blond ponytail, and her jeans were faded from wear and perfectly fit the slight curve of her hips.

"That's really a bad situation," she said, still watching Cronkite.

"Yes, it is," I said, trying to focus on the news. Everyone in Chapel Hill was keeping up with the Iranian hostage crisis, though I simply could not grasp that tonight I was watching with this girl.

11

Cronkite went to a commercial break and she glanced around. Her survey stopped on the poster tacked above my bed of the Justin Boots cowgirl in full gallop. She studied the poster for a moment, and then cut a curious glance at me.

I ignored the glance and turned for the kitchen, heat rising up my neck and burning my checks. "Do you want something to drink?" I called out as I crossed the room.

"Do you have a Coke?" she asked.

"Yeah. Do you want ice?"

"Yes, please."

"Have a seat if you like. I'll get your Coke." I held out my palm toward the table centered at the front window. She chose the chair facing the window and sat down straight and proper, keeping her back from slumping against the chair. I wondered why she felt the need for etiquette. She had seen my farm girl gait, my truck, the cowgirl poster over the bed; plenty of clues to know I was not Junior League.

I felt her watching as I dropped ice into two glasses. "Do you know who you're going to vote for?" she asked after a moment.

It seemed an odd question from a person so careful with manners, though perhaps not so much in a college town. In this election year, campaign zealots were willing to yell the same question at streams of students moving between classes. So long as the question was not "Have you been saved?", I was willing to answer.

"I'm not sure yet," I said. "I think Carter's smart, but he seems soft. Reagan's kinda scary. How about you?"

"My dad's a hardcore Democrat. He would disown me if I voted for a Republican." She smiled after she said it, though a trace of worry lingered when she looked away, as if she truly believed he would.

I watched the fizz settle in our Cokes and tried to think of something brilliant or thoughtful to say, though my mind seemed to be stuck on, *What the hell are you really doing here?* Even farm girls knew that was entirely inappropriate.

"Here's your Coke," I said, handing the glass to her.

"Thank you," she replied, looking up at me with a warm smile.

I wanted to run, though I wasn't sure why. Did I want to run away from her, or run to calm down? I knew only that the energy bouncing through my bones had to be harnessed before it gave me the shakes. I spun around and headed for my backpack. "So how did you find where I live? I don't recall even telling you my name."

"Let's just say I'm resourceful."

I looked up from my backpack and caught her smile, tauntingly playful. My thoughts became a logjam, all piled up at the mischievous glint in her gorgeous green eyes. "Oh!" I said when my mind finally remembered to think. "My check at the car wash."

"Bingo!" Her index finger shot upward.

I laughed and shuffled through my backpack for my notebook. When I turned back, her smile was changed. Could she possibly mean what I read in her face, a sort of interest that had nothing to do with statistics or politics? It was foolish to think such a thing. She was a Delta Pi, after all.

"Here ya go," I said. She took the notebook and looked over the cover. "Blue Riley. Is that a nickname? I thought your name was Augusta."

"My real name is Augusta, but most people call me Blue," I said as I sat down with her.

"I can see why. Your eyes are gorgeous."

"Well, it is not totally because of my eyes. My middle name is Blue. It's a family name."

She looked at me in the same curious way most people did when I told them Blue wasn't a nickname. "Blue was my great-grandmother's last name." She nodded and I looked at her with a brash smile. "Now you know my middle name and I don't even know your first."

"Oh, you're *right*," she said as her face flushed. She reached out her hand. "I'm Grace Lancaster."

"Nice to meet you, Grace Lancaster." The strength of her grip surprised me, and I held on a second longer than I intended. I loosened my grasp and she pulled her hand back, letting the tip of her finger trail across my palm.

Had she meant to do that? And if she did, what was I to make of it? The only thing I knew about Grace Lancaster was that she was a sorority girl, and that meant her life was tightly controlled by screwed-up conventions, like never drinking or smoking while standing up. I doubted that flirting with farm girls was on the list of acceptable behavior. Anyway, I'd never understood anything other than living by your own mind, and I sure didn't understand girls who would let their lives be ruled by quick, judgmental glances, whispers behind hands, and the postures of shunning.

I wanted to believe she could be different. Her captivating eyes— the golden green color of fall-ripe scuppernongs—seemed to take in everything with a curious intelligence. The last traces of a summer tan were still evident on her smooth skin, and her smile came easily. She sat at my table, vulnerable in coming here, but still sure of herself. Grace Lancaster intrigued me.

I leaned forward, close enough to catch her gaze. "So how are classes going?"

"Okay," Grace replied. She swept her palm across her brow and turned toward the parking lot, where a couple of guys tossed a football. "I could be doing better in stats." She frowned and watched a couple of tosses, then turned to me with a weary smile. "How about you?"

"Good for now." I took a sip of Coke, thinking for a brief moment about the exam I had in two days. "Bio-chem and physics are ass kickers, so I study a lot. I have to stay on the Dean's List to keep this apartment—my aunt's rules, and she's paying the rent. I moved here last year. I hated living in the dorm. Too much going on, you know?"

Grace nodded and looked at me curiously. "So are you a junior?"

"Yeah, I'm late taking stats. You're a sophomore?"

"Yes, I am. If I don't start doing better in stats, I may never see my junior year." Her weary smile came again.

I returned a hopeful grin. "You know, I don't have to study all the time, I have plenty of time to help you if you'd like. Is there anything in particular you are having problems with?"

Her face fell into a worried grimace. "I'm not doing so hot with standard deviations," she mumbled. She looked down at my notebook and let her fingertips slowly climb the wire rings.

"Standard deviations, huh? I've got a pretty good handle on that so far, and I bet I can teach you way better than Dr. Davis," I said, smiling.

She looked up and returned my smile.

"So when would you want to get together?" I asked.

"Do you have time now?"

"Yeah, I suppose so."

Grace pushed the notebook across the table and slid her chair next to mine. I flipped open my notebook and stared at the numbers and formulas, trying to concentrate on anything other than her light perfume.

3

Different

"Have you seen that *Elephant Man* movie?" Grace asked.

I dropped my backpack by my feet and plopped down at the table in the corner of the student union, where we had agreed to start meeting on Tuesdays. After the night she showed up at my apartment, I had thought of a thousand questions I wanted to ask her. *The Elephant Man* never crossed my mind, yet the movie about a grossly deformed man who was shunned by society was the first thing she asked me. I had no idea how to interpret her question. "No," I shrugged as I unzipped my backpack.

Grace turned to the students passing around us, some hustling through the atrium, some laughing as they strolled in packs of three or four. "It was sad, what happened to that man. People can be pretty awful to someone who is different." She looked over as I sorted through my notebooks. "Did you ever get any of that growing up? I mean, were people ever mean to you or anything?"

I froze and looked at her. Her toned body was covered by designer jeans and an azure blue sweatshirt with Greek letters stitched across the front. I doubted Grace Lancaster had ever been on the receiving end of schoolyard bullying, so I figured her question was all about me.

"I'm from a small town," I replied. "Most of us grew up together, so we weren't really mean to each other. I got some teasing and we played a few practical jokes, but nobody was ever mean to me. Why do you ask?"

She fidgeted and looked away. "I don't know. After I saw that movie, I wondered what it would be like to be ridiculed like that man was." Her eyes flew open and she looked at me, wide-eyed and flushed. "Not that I think *you* would ever be ridiculed. I mean look at you, you're good-looking, and smart, and built like a brick house. You'd probably kick their ass." Grace anxiously tapped her pen on her knee. More words rolled out in a rush. "Anyway, I like movies. And books, too, even literature. I love to read." She paused and looked at me, her face crimson. Our laughter burst out in the same instant.

"Well! That was awkward," Grace said when she caught her breath. She dabbed the tears from the corners of her eyes and playfully pushed her knee against mine. We looked at each other, and something seemed to give way. We started talking, at first about books and movies and then about the crazy things we did as kids, high school, our aspirations and a couple of regrets. Grace listened intently as I told her about the tornado. She watched me in a way that was lacking when I told most of my friends what had happened to my parents. She seemed more interested in my story than her own reaction to it, and I found myself talking about the funeral and the numb days that followed. I told her about selling the farm, and my plans to go to Auburn, and how my Aunt Julie had chosen Chapel Hill instead. Grace reached over and covered my hand. I looked up and met her eyes. "I'm glad you are here, Blue."

Any other time her touch would have sent my heart off like a pounding riptide. I only looked down and studied her hand. The clear polish on her thumbnail was chipped.

"I'll get a couple of sodas, okay?" Grace stood and fished a couple of dollars from the front pockets of her jeans. I watched her disappear down the hall. We were too different—worlds apart—and yet she had listened, and asked, as if she wanted to understand. I looked across the table to her notebook. A handwritten note on the margin of the page caught my eye, *Homecoming float—treasure chest.*

Homecoming floats. Maybe Grace was not really different from the other sorority girls. The evidence in her notebook said she had been spending her days thinking about things like homecoming floats, and probably, who her date would be for the weekend. I looked up to the ceiling. The huge atrium suddenly seemed smaller, constricting me into this alien reality. The three girls at the next table were talking again. They had become quiet when Grace reached for my hand, and they kept glancing over nervously until she stood and walked away from me. Now they debated going out for pizza or aerobics class. In the corner by the windows two guys thumped a folded paper football back and forth across their table, and over by a side door a cluster of jocks talked loudly and laughed.

After two years at Chapel Hill I had all of the categories figured out. Jocks, frat boys, sorority girls, GDIs (goddamn independents); I could put them all in their rightful categories with hardly a second look. Grace I couldn't figure. The only thing I knew for sure was that I didn't need her kind of distraction. When she returned to the table, I would suggest we discuss statistics and nothing else—and only for an hour on Tuesdays. Then I saw her returning with our Cokes. *Maybe we should make it two hours.*

Grace handed me a Coke and settled into her chair. "What are you doing this weekend?"

"I'm going camping and fishing with my aunt."

"I love to camp," she said, smiling. "Where are you going?"

"Over on the Pisgah, this side of Asheville. Why?"

"What if I wanted to go with you?" She cut her eyes at me and sipped her Coke, flirting in that subtle way some girls do, like it's all meant to be innocent.

"I don't think you would want to," I replied solemnly. Grace frowned and looked away. *Did I have to be such a jerk?* "Grace, it's not that I don't want you to go. I really don't think you'd want to. We're gonna backpack in a few miles." She glanced at me and I smiled. "The trail is straight up, both ways, and there may be lions and tigers and bears."

"Why do you think I wouldn't want to backpack?" Grace challenged.

"I just figured," I began.

Grace cut me off. "I've backpacked with my dad plenty of times. I even know how to cast—*and tie*—a dry fly."

"You're kidding," I replied, though the look on her face was dead serious.

"No, I'm not. I bet I can out-cast you." Grace looked at me with absolute certainty. She was actually taunting me, and I was not about to back down from the challenge of a sorority girl.

"You're on. I'll pick you up Friday afternoon. Can you be ready by two?"

"I can, but I don't have my backpack and gear here. You'll have to let me borrow."

"We'll scrape something up. Do you have waders?"

"Not here." Grace paused, the defiance in her face fading. She looked at me with a teasing grin. "I wanted to bring them, but there's really no place to hang waders in our sorority house."

Her smile felt like springtime sun on my face, warm and lively, and bringing life to places long gone dormant. In a way it scared me. It seemed too simple, and fragile, and dangerous. Still, I smiled back at her, like a goof who wanted to believe.

"No, I guess not," I said, looking at her with an undaunted smile. "We'll find some waders for you. No way I'm gonna to let a sorority girl out-cast me."

"We'll see," Grace replied. She shot me a cool, teasing glance and took a big swallow of Coke.

4

Holding Grace

The stillness of the woods enveloped me as soon as I stepped out of Julie's Jeep Cherokee. Between the crests of the mountains, night slowly crept over a day that had been so clear and crisp it seemed the air itself might shatter. I heard the creek rush a few hundred feet beyond us, and as I watched Grace swing out of the back seat, I was as contented as I had been in a long while.

I couldn't quite believe Grace was actually with us. I had expected a last-minute excuse. Instead the lie she told was to get out of a weekend packed with sorority socials, or steps, or whatever. I watched her as she stood and stretched, looking first to the sky, and then out to the surrounding forest. Julie caught me watching. She shook her head and smiled. "We'd better get going. It'll be dark as pitch in a couple of hours," she said, heading to the back of the Jeep for her gear.

We walked the narrow trail single file, climbing our way past the deep green of the rhododendrons and hemlocks and up to the yellow tapestry of poplar leaves covering the forest floor. Julie led us silently; the woods seemed too perfect for talking. I followed a few steps behind Grace, watching the easy way she moved up the steep grade, giving little notice to the weight of her pack. Her powerful gait conquered the slope in long strides, far less restrained than the way she moved on campus. I wondered if there were two Graces: the one who moved through the world without reservation, giving no thought to the opinions of those around her, and the one who constantly reined herself in, considering every move and every word before she made or spoke them. The thought unsettled me, and left me questioning which one was the true Grace. Surely it must be

20

the Grace that was with us tonight. After all, people lie only to cover up their true selves.

A couple of miles in, Julie veered off the trail and followed a faint path down to a campsite centered on a flat, natural bench about a hundred feet up from Steel's Creek. The gray of evening seeped through the woods as we slipped out of our pack straps. Grace leaned her pack on the beech tree next to mine. Without a word, she loosened the string bunched at the mesh pocket of my pack and pulled out the collapsible water jug and filter. Dry leaves crackled under her footsteps as she headed down the path to the creek.

Julie squatted down beside me. "How are your grades?" she asked, a hint of concern shadowing her voice.

"Good. A's so far," I said. I pulled out the tent Grace and I would share and rolled it out across the ground. The 7' x 6' tent never seemed so small when Julie and I slept in it.

"Keep it up," Julie said. She reached over for the tent poles and gathered them in her hand. "Don't let her distract you too much." She unfolded the poles and calmly popped them into place, as if she hadn't suggested I was mooning for a straight girl. Did Grace notice it, too?

"I may have trouble doing that." I dumped the small bag of aluminum stakes onto the ground and quickly counted them. "How do I keep my focus when she's all I think about?"

"That bad, huh?" Julie asked. I nodded. "Just remember there are always other women."

I looked over at my aunt. It was never her habit to be so cavalier. She had dated a string of women as far back as I could remember, yet I sensed she respected every one of them.

Julie shrugged and eased a pole into the end of the tent sleeve. Even in this her hands moved gracefully. "What I mean is that you've got a long life ahead of you, Blue. The most important thing you can do right now is get a good education. Relationships will come."

"I know. You've told me," I said as I walked around to the other side of the tent. I kneeled and pulled the pole through the sleeve. "I'm sure she's not even gay."

"All the more reason to keep it cool," Julie said.

A twig snapped at the edge of the campsite. Grace scurried into

21

the clearing, her arms wrapped around the sloshing water jug. Knees bent and elbows bowed out, she hustled over to the rock fire ring and kneeled to ease it down. "I saw some wood for a fire down by the creek," Grace said, breathing hard to catch her breath. She stood and slapped her wet hands across her pants with gusto I'd never seen from a sorority girl. "I'll get the fire started when I get back."

"Do you need help?" I asked.

"After you're done with the tents," Grace replied over her shoulder as she walked back into the woods.

Julie had finished threading the tent poles and now sat back on her heels, watching. She cocked a grin at me and said, "Come on, hotshot, let's get these tents up."

I scrambled to the far end of the tent and squatted down to push a pole into the corner tab. "Do you ever wish you were a man?" I asked Julie as the pole bent into an arc.

"Why, so I could pee standing up?" She said it as more of a statement than a question, like she had answered the same question a hundred times. She guided the end of the pole into the canopy tab and moved around the next. "I guess you're asking that question for a reason. What's on your mind?"

"I don't know," I said, keeping my eyes from her discerning gaze. "Sometimes I think it would make things easier. I mean, if were a man I could ask Grace out on a date. She would either say yes or no, and that would be that. I wouldn't have to wonder about her motivations all the time. I know she wants to hang out with me, but I'm not sure why. And it seems like she's flirting sometimes. If she's not gay, why would she do that?"

Julie made a final check of the tent poles and moved to her own tent. I scooted over to the opposite side. "All I can tell you is to be patient. If a physical relationship is what she wants, she'll find a way to let you know." We arched one pole into place and moved to the other. "It's always been that way for me. I don't let it distract me from my work, and neither should you."

"I know, I know. I got that part," I said as the tent took shape. Julie looked at me as if she wasn't so sure.

Grace reappeared from the tree line with a bundle of firewood wrapped under her arm. I jumped up to help. The bundle fell at my feet the moment I reached her. She looked up at me with a killer smile and tossed a small branch onto the top of the scattered pile. "I hope you have matches."

I pulled out a box of Fire Chief Matches from the pocket of my Levi's. "I don't go to the woods without them."

"Figures." Grace grinned and took the matchbox. She knelt by the fire ring and shot me a flirting glance. "Always prepared, like all good Girl Scouts."

I knelt beside her and grabbed a brittle branch to snap into starter. "I was in the 4-H, actually."

"I was in the debutantes." Grace looked at me under the hood of her eyebrows. Her lips turned into a slight smile. She was playing me—for what, I wasn't sure. I kept my gaze on the pyramid of needles and twigs in the center of the fire ring.

"Is that where you learned to build a fire?" I asked.

"I've always known how to build a fire," Grace replied, giving me that look again. I rocked back on my heels and watched her fish out a match and swipe it down the side of the box. Shielding the match with her palm she lowered it to the tinder and pushed it beneath the pile. Holding her hair aside, she leaned forward and gave a slow, even blow. In an instant the whole pile burst into flame.

At daybreak I crawled from our tent and looked around. Morning fog lingered in the woods, and I took in a deep breath as I stretched my arms toward the sky. *If only all of the world could be as peaceful as this,* I thought.

I finished lacing my boots and started toward a place I discovered when Julie and I camped here before. There was an American chestnut log close to the top of a ridge, and from there I could watch the sun rise.

Hunger turned in my belly as I climbed the hill to the log and untied my sweatshirt from my waist. I draped the shirt over the log to block the dew and sat down. I looked out over the woods at my feet and wondered how it all looked before the chestnut blight took out the American chestnut trees. Julie had told me of the blight on one of our backpacking trips when I was still in high school. She explained how it had changed the forests of these mountains. Later that year, I won a blue ribbon at the science fair for my project about the blight.

I reached into my back pocket for the leather pouch that held my dad's whittling kit. Through my science fair project I learned that chestnut wood is slow to rot. I figured it would be perfect for the letters I envisioned whittling for Grace, ΔΠ. I sat for a minute and let the sun warm my fingers as I studied the flow of the log's grain. My mind returned to last night; our dinner of spaghetti and marinara sauce and our late night conversation by the fire. Grace told Julie of her plans to get a degree in international business, which was what her parents wanted, though her real passion was to work with non-profits on socially worthy causes. She talked like an idealistic coed with dreams of changing the world. I may have sounded the same way as I waxed poetic about saving children's dogs and nursing a draft horse back to his sturdy feet. And then we put out the fire, and Grace crawled into our tent and burrowed into her sleeping bag, her body only inches from mine as I listened to the shudder of the trees and the scurry of a mouse, trying to harness the impulse to reach over and push the hair from her face and watch her eyes open, looking only at me.

I shook the thoughts away and pulled my Puma hunting knife from the sheath. Carefully I cut a small chunk from the end of the log. I turned the wood in my fingers, looking for the best place to start my cuts.

Bright sunlight streamed through the trees and warmed my back by the time I shaved away the last few slivers. I raised the carving toward the sun to check the dimensions. ΔΠ popped out from the wood in rough lines I would perfect later. I stuffed the chunk into my pocket and thanked my father for teaching me how to whittle.

A few hundred yards from camp I caught the first hint of campfire smoke. I remembered the look Grace gave me when she leaned down to blow the fire to life. My heart gave a jump that I tried to ignore. If Grace felt the same, she could have told me last night.

I walked on, my boots catching the dew of the morning. It was early yet; the birds were still busy with their morning calls. Through their chatter I heard the sounds of our campsite coming to life. Ahead in the clearing I spotted Julie stirring the eggs in her lightweight frying pan. Grace stood at the far edge of our campsite, tying a length of green fly-line between the branches of two white pines. I passed Julie with a quick good morning and walked over to Grace.

"Good morning," she said with a generous smile. Her hair was pulled back and tucked through the strap of a faded red Richmond Spiders baseball cap. She reached into her pocket and took out a tin of fly-line dressing.

"Good morning to you, too," I said. I walked over and picked up my fly rod.

"I've already done yours," Grace said, glancing toward me.

"Should I trust you?" I ran my fingers lightly over the line stretched along the length of my rod.

"You should do as you like," Grace said, her smile as teasing as mine. *No, I shouldn't.*

"Breakfast is ready. Eggs get cold fast," Julie called out from the fire ring.

Grace wiped her hands on a green hand towel she had draped over her belt. Together we walked to our log bench by the fire. Grace took the plate of scrambled eggs and instant grits Julie held out to her. Her manners still intact, she balanced her plate on her knees and waited for Julie to fill my plate, and then her own.

"So, Grace, last night you said you are from Virginia," Julie said. She settled onto her camp stool and scooped up steaming grits. "Your dad wouldn't happen to be Daniel Lancaster, would he?"

"Yeah, he is." Grace looked at Julie with a curious smile. "Do you know him?"

"No, I don't. I read an article about his work in the Democratic Party. He's in the military defense industry, right?"

"That's right," Grace replied.

"He's a smart man. I'm glad he's on our side."

I stuffed eggs into my mouth and stared at the smoke rising from the fire. I did not want to hear about Grace's father, or her home in Richmond, or anything else that reminded me of the impossible distance between me and Grace.

"Blue, are you going to fish the stretch of creek we found last summer?" Julie asked. Grace turned to me, curious and chewing.

"Yeah, I thought we'd give it a try. It may be tougher this time of year."

Julie nodded. "Bring back a couple for dinner if you can. It will be colder tonight. We could use the extra calories."

After breakfast we helped Julie tidy up camp and left her stretched out in a nylon hammock with a paperback. Midmorning sun warmed our backs on our hike down to the creek, fly rods in hand. A hundred feet from the creek, Grace crouched low and started a slow shuffle, like a bloodthirsty commando on a deadly mission. I stifled a laugh. Grace was *serious*.

At the edge of the bank we hunkered down behind a boulder and peeked over at the water's surface. "You know we look like a couple of thieves," I whispered, barely keeping laughter from my voice.

"If you don't want to fish, you can go back to the hammock," Grace whispered back. Her eyes focused on the rushing water, waiting and watching like a hungry grizzly. After a couple of minutes she turned to me. "I don't think they're feeding on top."

"Wet fly?" I asked, hushed.

Grace nodded.

"You take the waders first. When you've had enough, I'll show you how it's done."

"You wish." Grace grabbed the hip waders and crouched down behind the boulder. She looked at me with excited eyes and pushed a foot into the boot. "I'll be the one catching supper while you're busy daydreaming." She flipped the other boot over her toes. Her fingertips were stained from fire ash and dirt, which pleased me immensely. Her sorority sisters would never approve. "If you want to make yourself useful, you can tie the fly for me while I buckle these waders on," she said.

I grinned and opened my fly box. A North Carolina hatch chart lined the lid, and tiny flies were arranged into neat rows of dry and wet flies, the dry on top and the wet ones underneath. I picked out a gray midge and held it up to Grace. "Will this one work?"

Grace nodded and buckled the wader strap to her belt. I pulled the knot tight, checked it, and gave the rod to Grace. "Good luck."

"Who needs luck when you have skill?" Grace flashed a cocky grin and headed for the stream. I wondered if she knew how good her ass looked framed by those hip waders.

I settled against the boulder and watched Grace wade into the creek wearing my waders and carrying my favorite fly rod. Julie had been so right to suggest we share waders to keep the weight from our backpacks. Now there would be no competitor's rush, no need to outdo her at every moment. I could relax and memorize her, the way she looked walking through the stream, the way she worked a fly rod, efficient and assured.

Her second cast hit the water and the tip of the fly rod bent double. Instantly, green fishing line sliced through the water, jerking this way and that, zigging and zagging as Grace held on. Deep swirls in the stream and the widening of her eyes said the fish was a big one; I figured a brown trout. Grace pulled a stretch of line in and wrapped it once around her hand to keep it tight. The rod jerked to the left and she lifted it higher. Line cut through the water, zipping back and forth across the stream. And then it slowed. Grace eased her shoulders and slowly worked the line. The big brown swirled and jerked the rod one last time as the net came under it. Grace eased the hook from his mouth and slipped her fingers under the gills to hold him up to me. He looked to be at least two pounds.

"Two casts, Blue Riley! Two freakin' casts! How are you going to beat that?" Grace's smile beamed. She looked so beautiful and alive, standing there in the middle of the creek, the sunshine at her back, taunting me with a damn fish. She slipped the trout into her creel and looked at me again, her chin tilted up, still smiling. "Now that I've caught dinner, do you want to give it a go?"

I waved a dismissive hand toward her. "Nah, you go ahead. I'll show you how it's really done in a little while."

At that moment I couldn't have cared less about fishing.

Since sundown the temperature had dropped twenty degrees, and every hour was getting colder. Grace shivered hard and pulled her jacket in tighter across her chest. The campfire lit her face with an orange glow as she stared at the flames, frowning. She blinked against the smoke and pushed her hiking boots closer to the fire. I pushed back an urge to wrap her in my arms and hold her close.

"We'd better hit the sack soon," Julie said. "It'll be below freezing later tonight. We'll need all the body heat we can get in our tents." She stood and grabbed the hickory stick we'd used to stoke the fire. "You two go ahead and turn in. I'll take care of the fire."

Inside our tent Grace took off her boots and scurried to her sleeping bag, teeth chattering. She slid down into the cold lining and shivered hard. "Damn, it's freezing."

"You need to relax your muscles." I pulled off my boot and slid it under my sleeping bag. "Just relax and let the bag warm up."

Grace rolled to her side and hugged her sleeping bag close. Her miserable eyes peeked out and watched me take off my jeans and gloves and push them deep into my sleeping bag.

"You take things off to sleep," Grace said through a chattering breath. "Why aren't you freezing?"

"Body heat and a good sleeping bag." I wiggled down into my bag and rolled my knit cap over my neck. Determined not to shiver, I pulled the sleeping bag in tight to my chest.

"How about giving me some of that," Grace said.

"What, the body heat or the sleeping bag?"

"Both."

My heart took off like Casey's locomotive. I tried to think logically to simmer it down. It was possible Grace's proposition was innocent.

Maybe she simply wanted to get warm. But what if it was a prelude to something more? Either way, I knew my body could not keep secrets if Grace Lancaster was curled into it.

"Why don't you pull off your sweatshirt and hold it against your chest? You'll warm up," I suggested as innocently as I could muster.

"You're warm, so why don't you let me come over there with you?"

"It won't work if you leave the sweatshirt on," I said, certain the need to undress would dissuade her.

Grace sat up and pulled her sweatshirt over her head, stripping down to the tight thermal top she wore underneath. "Can I come over there now?"

I looked at her, trying to keep my stare from the fine shape of her tightly covered breasts. "All right then," I said, staying cool. I scooted to the edge of the bag and unzipped the side. Grace shoved out of her bag and crawled over. Her body pressed against me, working her way down until her back settled against my chest and her hips dipped into mine. I slid my arm under her neck, scarcely able to breathe as Grace settled into the crook of my elbow. For a moment we were still, and then Grace reached for my hand and pulled it between her breasts.

"This is much better." Grace rocked her hips and nestled against me. "Good night, Blue."

I lay perfectly still, wide-eyed and hoping my shallow breath did not give me away. Grace didn't seem to notice. Her shivering stopped quickly, and then her muscles begin to relax. In a few minutes, she grew heavy on my arm and I knew she was asleep.

The rest of the night I held her close, letting my heat flow into her body.

5

The Lights of Campus

"Come over Friday afternoon. I'll cook steaks," Julie whispered when she hugged me good-bye. She slipped a hundred-dollar bill into my pocket and looked at Grace with the kindest eyes, like she was remembering an old love. She stood in her driveway and watched us pull away, waving once before her hands returned to the pockets of her blue jeans.

Fifteen minutes down the road, I looked over at Grace. Her head rested against the passenger window, sleeping in the same way my mother slept on long drives home. Sometimes I would lean against Mom's shoulder and sleep so soundly I wouldn't hear the static-filled AM broadcast of the Atlanta Braves game my father listened to as he drove. I still sensed them when I drove my Dad's truck. Some days I'd catch a faint whiff of Mom's scent lingering in the cab, or find a flake of Dad's chewing tobacco nestled in the crevices of the driver's door.

Mom, Dad, this is Grace. I think you're going to like her. I smiled and settled under the steering wheel, heading west toward Chapel Hill.

Grace woke up when we hit the outskirts of town. Arms locked together and stretching toward the dashboard, she yawned and looked around with sleepy eyes. She didn't say anything, and for a moment it felt like we had made this trip a hundred times before, like we could drive on for miles without the need for conversation.

"Can we drive down Franklin before you drop me at the sorority house?" Grace asked. Her face brightened with her question, as if a switch had been flipped the moment she saw the lights of campus.

"Sure," I said, though I needed every minute to study for a physics quiz.

A sleek 1967 Oldsmobile Cutlass convertible pulled up beside us at the first traffic light. I looked over at the polished red Olds. Five preppy guys crammed the front and back seats with a couple of girls stretched across their laps. Ahead, Franklin Street lights illuminated glass store-fronts sprinkled with black Tar Heels and Greek letters accompanying lame slogans for the next big fraternity or sorority social.

"Chapel Hill. Yee-haw," I muttered.

"You don't like Chapel Hill?" Grace looked at me as if she couldn't imagine such a thing.

"There's nothing wrong with Chapel Hill itself. It's all the Greek shit that drives me nuts."

Grace rolled her eyes and folded her arms across her chest. "Well, I'll try to keep my Greek shit away from you, then." She said it so bluntly I believed her.

I reached over to touch her shoulder. "C'mon Grace, you know I don't mean *you*. It's the time of year that gets me: all these parties and socials and everybody running around like it all actually *means* something. To me it seems like a huge waste of time and energy."

Grace looked at me skeptically. "Oh lighten up, Blue. It's just a bit of fun."

"Sure, as long as you're invited to the party." I couldn't seem to stop myself from coaxing a stupid argument.

"Like you'd come if you were invited." Grace said, with a defiant tilt of her chin. "If you don't want to join, that's fine. I don't see why you've got to be so negative about it."

"It's not me I'm talking about, Grace. It's all the people who want to be at the party but can't even walk onto the lawn, much less get in the front door."

Grace looked at me curiously and turned away. In profile I could see her mouth twisted and her eyes locked in a contemplating stare. Laughing girls with ice cream cones passed by, and down the street couples walked close together and talked. The whole town seemed happy, infected by some Tar Heel spirit that promised a week of gorgeous October afternoons and a football win on Saturday. I glanced over at Grace and felt a sting of loneliness.

The traffic light turned, and I shifted to first. Grace said, pensively,

"I remember a girl who went through rush with me, my freshman year. Her name was Missy, and she wanted to be a Delta Pi so bad. It crushed her when she didn't make it—really crushed her. I thought about her for weeks after rush. It doesn't seem fair that I got in and she didn't. I would have switched places with her in a heartbeat if my Mom hadn't insisted on me pledging Delta Pi."

"Is your mom the only reason you went out for rush?"

"I don't know." Grace turned to me and shrugged. "I guess our sorority does some really good things for charity, and it's a good way to meet people and stay in touch after graduation. I think it's important to bond with people who share the same values, too. Don't you?"

I stared ahead and shifted to third. "Yeah, I suppose. But didn't we do that this weekend? I don't think joining a beauty club is necessary to share values," I said, attitude piercing my voice.

Grace's eyes narrowed on me. "What's up with you tonight? A sorority is not a beauty club."

"Ha!" I cut her a glance. "C'mon, Grace, you can't seriously tell me looks have absolutely nothing to do with getting into a sorority."

Grace turned and stared out the window. "I can't tell you anything," she said softly.

I had not expected the resignation in her voice. I wanted defiance, a reason to argue, an opening to ask why she was not the same woman under the lights of campus that I had seen reflected in the light of our campfire. Only an ass would push her now. I drove through the next traffic light, thankful it was green.

Silence built its barrier as we drove. I turned onto the drive of the Delta Pi house and followed Grace's gaze to the quiet lawn. She let out a sigh and looked toward the darkened windows, seeming to be relieved to find the house so quiet. I swung into a parking spot in the far corner and killed the engine.

Grace glanced around. Satisfied we were alone, she looked over at me with a quick, self-conscious smile. "Thanks for the weekend, Blue. I had a great time." She looked down at her folded hands, seemingly lost for the next words to say.

"We'll have to do it again sometime soon," I said, spewing out words to avoid uncomfortable silence. "Or maybe we could do something else. Maybe go to a movie or check out a band or something?"

"Maybe," Grace said vacantly. She looked out the window, though she didn't reach for the door handle or gather her purse. I had felt moments like this before, and the heavy silence that comes before something you don't want to hear. It felt like a guillotine above my head, ready to come down in an instant and announce the end. I pushed deep into my pocket for the chestnut carving.

"I made this for you," I said holding the carving out to her, too rushed and awkward.

Grace looked first at me and then down at the carving. She grasped it lightly between her fingers. "Wow. It's beautiful, Blue."

"It's American Chestnut. There's a fallen log not too far from where we camped. That's where I was Saturday morning—I cut a chunk out of the log to make that for you. I'll finish the letters and smooth it out later if you want. I guarantee no one else will have one like it."

Grace turned the wood in her fingers, smiling in a tender sort of way. She traced the letters with her index finger. "Delta Pi—I thought you didn't like sororities."

"I don't. I made it for you."

Grace glanced at me and looked back to the carving. I couldn't read the expression on her face, though I knew I had surprised her, maybe even scared her. It was too much, really. Why would anyone sneak off into the woods to carve a stupid block out of an ancient tree if they weren't hopelessly romanticizing? And there was the whole thing of Grace being a straight sorority girl.

"I love it," Grace said. She reached across the cab and covered my hand. "Thank you." I looked down at Grace's hand over mine. She followed my gaze to our interlinked fingers and pulled away, a bit too quickly.

"So, I'll see you on Tuesday?" I asked as our awkwardness returned.

"I can't this week. I volunteered to do a lot of stuff for the fall dance we have coming up this weekend." Grace's soft smile begged apology. "I'll catch you at class?"

"Sure." I shrugged, though I wanted to blurt out all I knew I couldn't say. I stuffed it all back and said, "I may try to get in one more fishing trip before it gets too cold. Do you want me to call if I do?"

Grace thought before she answered. "Look, Blue, I had a great time this weekend, and I loved being out in the woods with you and Julie, but I have a really busy schedule right now, you know? With school and all the other stuff going on, I don't have time for much else."

I forced a smile. "You mean you don't have time to give me another ass kicking like the one you gave me yesterday?"

Her green eyes danced with mischief. "Oh, I'll always take time to kick your ass."

I laughed and waited for her shoulders to square up the way they did when she was feeling cocky. Instead they fell slack as Grace turned away from me. Her voice was kind as she continued, "I don't want you waiting for me to do things."

Angry words screamed through my head: *Why don't you just say it? You don't want to be seen spending time with a butch farm girl. Someone may think you're queer!* Out loud I said, "Sure, I understand. Do you want to get together to study next week?"

"Maybe. I'll see you at class, okay?"

I nodded and watched her gather her things. She slid out of the truck, gave me a quick wave over her shoulder, and walked away. I watched until she disappeared through the back door of the house, just to make sure she was safe.

6

Did They Know?

Friday afternoon sun burned through my UNC t-shirt. I turned my face toward the sun and soaked in the rays as I walked beside Julie on the trail cut through an open field in the park. She reached over and cradled the base of my neck with her palm. She did that a lot now, like she wanted to protect me, or teach me something. "Blue, last weekend we didn't get a chance to finish our conversation about Grace. Let me tell you about something that happened to me when I was a few years older than you are right now."

I pushed my hands in my pockets and braced myself for the lecture. Julie felt me stiffen and gently massaged my neck with her fingertips before she continued. "My last year in med school, I fell crazy in love with a nurse who worked with me in the children's hospital. She was a few years older than I was, and married to a Marine officer serving in Vietnam. He came back to the States around Thanksgiving and told her that he wanted to start a family right away. Of course I was young and in love, so I asked her to leave him—begged her, actually. She thought about it for a while, but in the end she told me she owed it to him to stay." Julie fell silent and turned her eyes down to the path. Her mind seemed lost in the past.

"I thought the hurt was going to kill me," she said after a moment. "I went home for Christmas and moped around for a couple of days until it was time to go back to school. On the night before I left, I told your granddad that I was thinking of switching to family practice. I felt like I'd had the life ripped out of me, and I didn't have the fight left to stay in surgery. When I told him about my change in plans, he looked at me real hard, and then he took me to his bedroom for a talk.

35

We sat down on the bed and he opened up to me. He told me when he was in school he met this girl he wanted to marry. Turns out she wanted to go to New York to be an actress more than she wanted to stay in Alabama and marry a farmer. Your granddad said he actually thought about leaving, but in the end he knew where he belonged, so they broke it off. Within a year he met your grandmother, and he never looked back. He said by being true to himself he found the woman who was right for him."

I nodded and watched a heron glide into the edge of the lake, his him pick his way along the shoreline. I knew why Julie had told me her story. I just couldn't see why she didn't fight harder for what she wanted. Maybe that was why she was still single. "But what if the nurse was the one you were supposed to be with?"

"It didn't matter. Sacrifices always have to be made, especially when you're gay. We have to move on. What your granddad was saying is that you have to stay true to your purpose in life; that's the most important thing. You want to be a veterinarian. Stay focused on that, no matter what."

"What about what my mom said—that the Blue women only have one love per lifetime? Already Grace has me more twisted in knots than any girl I've ever met. I can't quit thinking about her. What if she's the one I'm supposed to be with?"

"You'll have to be patient enough to see what happens. In the meantime, remember there's plenty of Riley in you, too. You may fall in love many times."

Maybe Julie was right. I'd wanted to be a veterinarian for as long as I could remember. I would be helping animals every day, and it was a good profession, one that would allow me to easily support myself. If Dad were here, he would remind me of that, too. But what would Mom have said?

"Do you think Granddad knew you're gay?"

"We never talked about it, but he knew."

"Do you think Mom and Dad knew about me?"

"I don't know. Probably. Once, your mom asked me if I thought there was something going on with you and your friend Susan. I said I didn't know and asked her why she thought so. She said she noticed how comfortable you two were around each other, how close you stood . . . things like that."

"Did it sound like it bothered her?"

"You know your mom. If it bothered her it was because she never wanted anything to hurt you, even though she was willing to let you bang around and find your own way. She would have gotten over it if it upset her, and I think it would have."

"Because she wanted to protect me?"

"Yes, and I'm sure she heard the things people said about me, about gay people. She wouldn't want anyone to hurt you in that way. I'm sure she thought your life would be easier if you were straight."

I nodded and asked, "What about Dad?"

Julie chuckled. "Your dad never wanted to see you with any guy, even the ones you went out with for a while. He probably would have preferred you dating a woman."

We laughed, and then fell silent, longing for my father. Julie broke our silence. "Your dad always supported me, Blue, even when people were cruel. He would've fought for you in every way he knew how."

The knot that seemed always in my throat started to tighten. Most days I could swallow it back and keep the tears from coming, or the bleak hollow from taking over. I hoped today would be one of those days. I swallowed and said, "I miss them so much, Julie."

Julie wrapped her arm around my shoulder and pulled me to her side. "I know you do, Blue. I do, too."

7

Confession

On Monday morning Grace walked toward me in her body-hugging Gloria Vanderbilt jeans and her white, oxford Polo shirt; so typical sorority, I wanted to laugh. She stopped in front of me and returned my smile. "Can we get together tomorrow?"

I looked at her, all smiles and perfume. After blowing off nearly a solid week of classes, she wanted me to pull her ass through. "It's going to cost you," I said with a wry grin.

"Okay." She glanced away.

"Dinner Thursday night," I said. I brought my notebook around from my hip and held it in front of me as a sort of barrier between us, in case she said no.

She reached over and grasped the edge of my notebook. "You pick the place. And I'm paying." She smiled boldly and walked away. "See you tomorrow," she said, glancing over her shoulder.

Grace quick-stepped toward our table in the student union, steadying the soda she carried in each hand and leaning right to keep her backpack on her shoulder. "Hey, girl," she said, reaching my drink across the table. I grabbed it as her backpack slipped onto her elbow. She plopped down and asked, "How was class today?"

"Fine," I muttered.

Grace set her Coke on the table and looked at me, frowning at my mood. I watched her unzip her backpack and pull out her statistics notebook. "Grace, I need to ask you something."

"Okaaay," she replied, wary of the serious tone of my voice. She dropped her notebook on the table and stretched her backpack open to search for a pen or something, fiddling around to avoid my eyes.

"Why did you ask me to help you with stats? Couldn't your sorority sisters help you?"

Grace stopped her fiddling and looked at me. "I guess they could have, but I didn't want them to know how bad I was doing." Her face reddened and I wondered if she was embarrassed from the thought of her test scores, or if there was something more. After a moment she spilled the rest of it. "And I had heard you were the one who blew the curve on our first two tests, so I thought you'd know what you were doing."

I fell back and stared at her. She'd stung the shit out of me, and she spoke as if she didn't have a clue. Had she grown so accustomed to using people that she did not even know when she did it? Had she sought me out after the car wash because I was one of the smartest kids in the class, or spent the weekend backpacking with me to avoid a bad date? Had she crawled into my sleeping bag just to stay warm?

"So you didn't want your sorority sisters to know, but it was okay to take up my time tutoring you for free?" I asked.

Grace looked apologetic. "Yeah, I guess I never thought of it that way. I don't know why I thought I could take advantage of you like that. I've pissed you off again, haven't I?"

"You really have, Grace." I glanced around at tables full of students. "Let's go outside. We need to talk." I stood up and grabbed my notebook. "You coming?"

Grace riddled me with worried glances as she gathered her things. I spun around and walked across the atrium, staying a step ahead of her. I didn't want her beside me, where she could see the indecision on my face. She caught up on the sidewalk and crossed the lawn with me. Together we sat down under the shade of an ancient oak tree. She pulled her denim jacket tight across her chest and waited.

I looked straight into her eyes and said, "Grace, I think you should know I'm gay."

She nodded and turned away from me with the slightest knowing grin, like she had been expecting me to tell her. My anger, which had been pounding my heart like a jackhammer, began to fade, and the irksome *what ifs* that had haunted my sleep grew still and waited. Her silence felt like forever. "Well," she began, her mouth twisted into a little grin, "I thought you were either gay, or that cowgirl over your bed is a really close cousin."

Grace's smile broke wide across her face. I wanted to smile back, though it seemed too easy. I couldn't get past the realization that she *knew*, and had probably known since the day she came to my apartment, maybe even the day she took my check at the car wash.

"So is that why you thought it was okay to ask for my help?" I retorted, my expression a direct contrast to hers. "Because I was the gay girl who happened to be smart? Of course I would want to help you, right?"

Grace's face fell. "No, it wasn't like that at all," she replied, sweeping her hair away from her pensive eyes.

"Well, tell me how it was, then, Grace." I paused and waited for an answer. She turned her face away from me, so I leaned toward her. "My God, you crawled into my sleeping bag and asked me to hold you—do you know what that did to me? And now you tell me you knew all along."

"I suspected," she corrected weakly. "I didn't know until now."

"Oh, so that makes it okay, then!" My jackhammer heart started up again. "You're free to toy around all you want until the moment you know for sure." My sarcasm hung in the air between us.

Grace looked away and pulled her legs up to her chest. Her gaze drifted across the lawn to the circle of four guys bouncing a hacky sack from one foot to the next. In the silence I started thinking of the reasons Grace Lancaster really shouldn't matter to me. At reason three Grace looked at me and said, "When you offered to help me that day at the car wash, I thought it would be okay to take you up on it. I never meant to take advantage of you." The soft sincerity in her voice pulled me from my anger. "And I'm sorry I confused you, too, but I don't know how this is supposed to work. I know that's no excuse, but I hope you'll forgive me, 'cause I want us to keep being friends, Blue."

Friends. The word never sounded so freakin' hard—or cold. "So that's all you ever want from me? To be your friend?"

"Yes. I want to be your friend," Grace replied.

"*Why?* You have all your sorority friends, and I'm sure you have a date whenever you want. Why would you go out of your way to be friends with me?"

"Because you give me something most girls don't."

"Like what?"

"I don't know, Blue," she said, exasperation creeping into her voice. "I like you, and the truth is I could pay someone to tutor me in stats if I wanted. I happen to like being around you, and it doesn't matter that you're gay, *okay?*"

I nodded through a sudden, freakish urge to cry—an urge that started with the words. *It doesn't matter that you're gay.* I turned away from her, my mind swirling. I wanted to take off running and keep going until sweet endorphins flooded my brain. How could I feel these things for Grace and know them in my heart to be true, and yet for her they were not?

I stood up and brushed the leaves and grass from my pants and reached down to her. Without a word Grace grasped my hand and I pulled her up. She did not look at my face, or I at hers.

8

Inertia

My pencil rested idle against the page of my notebook. I stared at the five homework problems on the principles of inertia, one side of my brain shouting that the problems had to be done by tomorrow, and the other side still too pissed at Grace to focus.

I stood up and stretched, twisting my hips to get the juices flowing—until a glance of my cowgirl poster stopped me cold. The knot in my stomach tightened. Was it really the cowgirl poster that had tipped Grace off? It didn't matter. Grace knew now, and she wanted to be my friend. I, on the other hand, wanted to be that cowgirl, out on some ranch pitching hay bales; or swinging a sling blade through a patch of weeds until I was exhausted; or jumping on a horse and giving her the reins until we flew away from the bullshit and out to a place where the voices came in howls and whistles, and shrieks circling a thousand feet overhead. Out there, Grace Lancaster and all of her stupid games could kiss my ass.

I plopped down in front of my homework, staring again at the problems. How could I solve questions on inertia when my mind seemed to be spinning with thoughts of Grace? The formulas and notes I had written in my notebook weren't helping, and I had already run three miles to gather the focus to finish my bio-chem lab assignment. I needed another kind of diversion.

I went to the phone and punched in Trish Youngblood's number. Since the day I'd met Trish over a year ago, she always made me laugh. Her roommate Laney answered on the second ring.

"Hi, Laney. Is Trish around?" I asked.

"She's at work 'til seven," Laney replied. "After that she said she's going for a swim. You may be able to catch her at the pool."

"Thanks, Laney," I said.

"What are you doing tonight?" Laney asked before I could say good-bye.

"Trying to study. I think I need a break, though."

"You should come by here. We haven't seen you lately."

"I know," I replied. "I've been busy studying."

"Too much of that will warp your brain, you know," Laney teased. "We're gonna play some spades later on, and we've got beer left from the party last weekend."

"Thanks, I'll keep it in mind," I replied. "I'll see you around, okay?"

"Sure. You know where I'll be when you've had enough of that studying crap." Laney said good-bye with a flirtatious lilt. I smiled and hung up the phone. Laney was not the kind of diversion I needed.

The walk to the Bowen Gray Pool was only about ten minutes. Inside the pool building I gave the attendant my student ID and walked through the locker room to the pool. The place was mostly quiet. A couple of older-looking guys swam laps on the far side of the pool. I walked to the far lane away from them and looked out at the surface of the water, peaceful and waiting.

The first lap, I moved slowly, feeling my limbs stretch and unwind with every stroke. I touched the wall and turned, lazy as the water.

Can you even call her tonight?

Why couldn't I call Grace? She said she wanted to be my friend, for chrissakes. Friends talked on the phone, didn't they? Yet I knew she wouldn't like it if I called. Nosy roommates would ask questions. The whole situation was ridiculous.

I pushed hard from the wall and came up in a fury of strokes, pounding through the water until I thought my lungs would burst. Huffing for breath I grabbed the wall, and then I saw a pair of feet; small, thick feet attached to legs with calves as big as hams. I looked up to her freckled face and puckish smile, her thick little body covered by a black Speedo, her muscled arms crossed securely over her chest, and her full wave of blond hair. Trish looked down at me, smiling.

"Do you always swim like a Marine?" Trish kicked out a leg and dropped into the pool, her head going under and her arms waving forward until she blew out and surfaced through a flurry of bubbles. She swept back her hair and tiptoed over to grab the lane rope. "I called Laney before I left work. She said you might be here. I told her she was full of shit. I've been trying to get you to swim with me for over a year."

"Well, here I am," I replied.

"To what do I owe the honor?" Trish asked.

"Inertia."

She cocked her head back. "What is that supposed to mean?"

"Doesn't matter," I said, pushing myself up from the pool. I swung my hips around and sat on the edge. "I got sick of studying, so I took a break."

"I didn't think you ever got tired of studying." Trish shoved up to sit beside me. "Where have you been lately, anyway? I figured you'd crawled up into one of your books and died or something."

I grinned and said, "I've been around. The last two weekends I've been with Julie."

Trish leaned back on her hands. I couldn't see her face, but I figured there was a smart-assed grin aimed at my back. "That's a sweet deal you've got going there, Riley. Hang out with your cool aunt for few hours and then have the run of her house while she's at work. Not bad. You been going over to Raleigh alone?"

"Mmm," I hummed. Would Trish always be so obsessed with my love life? She seemed to want to know everything about everyone, which seemed a good enough reason to leave Grace out of the conversation.

"Well, that's too bad," Trish continued. "I hate to see talent go to waste."

I smiled again. "Is that what I am, talent?"

She leaned up and squared her shoulders beside me. "Well, I can't say for sure, but you had a few girls spinning around last year." I shot her a cross glance, and Trish grinned and nudged my arm. "You know I'm messing with you. I just get tired of women asking if I've seen you around lately. They think they're being all sly and shit, but I know what they want. And I know you'd kill me if I gave out your phone number."

"Yes, I would, but it's not like there's a bunch of women wanting to go out with me."

Trish swirled her feet in the water for a few moments before she responded. "There are a few, and I can't for the life of me understand why you don't give them a chance. They're nice girls, Blue. Good-looking, too."

Trish was right. I hadn't been out with anyone since September, the weekend before I saw Grace at the car wash. Maybe a few good dates with someone else would cure me of Grace.

I leaned toward Trish and bumped her shoulder. "So maybe you're right. Give me a call next time you guys are having a party. I promise I'll come this time."

Trish called the next afternoon. I leapt toward the phone the instant it rang, thinking it could be Grace. Before the receiver hit my ear, David Bowie's "Fame" drifted through the line. "Hey, Riley. This is Trish," she said, her voice nearly drowned out by Bowie's. "Hang on. Laney, turn that shit down!"

"Go into your bedroom!" a distant voice yelled back.

"Damn it, Laney!" A door closed and Bowie became a faded thump of bass. "Do you like lasagna?" Trish asked, like she was asking a question on "The Dating Game" or something.

What the hell? "Yeah," I replied, my tone questioning.

"Good. Laney said she wants to make dinner tonight after rowing practice. You should come over. There's a couple of new girls on the team you haven't met yet. You wanna come?"

"Sure, it sounds fun."

"Good. There'll be about ten of us, a little social, you know. You should be back home in time to study after we're done—unless you find something else to do."

9

Giant

Stats homework was probabilities and a discussion of dice; stuff I'd learned in high school that would come back easily. I pushed the book away and slid over the peach cobbler cooling at my elbow. My spoon crumbled through the flaky, warm crust, sending sweet peach scent rushing to my nostrils. I thought of my mother. She made the best peach cobbler in Shelby County, with blue ribbons to prove it. She'd probably freak out to see me eating the frozen stuff, but I didn't have a clue how to bake a cobbler. Anyway, it was the aroma that I craved most.

I scraped the cobbler from the sides of the bowl and held the last bite in my mouth, eyes closed and savoring. When I opened them, I caught a glimpse of Grace through the front window. She was almost to my door.

I grabbed my bowl and took it to the sink. The lasagna dinner, beers with Trish, a trip to the lake to watch Trish and Laney's crew team practice, and still Grace filled my thoughts. This morning I'd run four miles to get her out of my mind, which worked for about ten minutes. Now she shows up at my door again. Giving me space to work shit out didn't seem to be in her game plan.

"Come in. It's not locked," I said over my shoulder, loud enough for Grace to hear.

"Hi, Blue. I thought I'd better check on you since you missed class today," she said as she crossed the room. She settled her hips against the kitchen counter, facing me. "And you stood me up last Thursday night. I tried to call you all afternoon, but you didn't answer."

"I know, I forgot we were supposed to have dinner. I went over to a friend's house for lasagna," I replied, though I doubted Grace believed the part about forgetting our plans. "Today I had a bio-chem test. I skipped to study," I continued, which was another partial truth. The other part was that skipping meant I could go the day without seeing Grace.

"You can borrow my notes if you want," Grace said.

"So did you bring them over?" I asked tersely, avoiding her eyes by squeezing detergent into the bowl and cramming a dishcloth in it, scrubbing it as I felt my anger begin to grow inside me.

"No, I didn't actually," Grace crossed her arms tightly and rocked her hips against the counter. "I came over because I think we need to talk about our last conversation."

I stuck the bowl in the dish drainer and glared at her. "Alright, but I think we've already said everything we need to. I'm gay and you are not afraid to be my friend, so good for you. Maybe I can be your community service project: Be nice to the gay girl."

Her eyes snapped to defiance. "Is that all you really think of me?"

I didn't answer.

Grace planted her palm on my counter and leaned toward me, her eyes sharp and sure. "Blue, I'm not into you because you're gay, or because of what happened to your parents, or because you can make me understand statistics. I like you because of whatever it was that made you carve that piece of chestnut, and agree to tutor me just because I asked, and that you drive your father's truck when I know your aunt would buy you a Camaro, and that you have the most beautiful eyes I've ever seen and it scares me a little to look at them." She stopped and looked at me, as if astonished by her own words. She shook her head and turned away. "I shouldn't have said that, Blue." Frustration tensed the lines of her face and her hand curled into a tight fist. "The thing is, I only know how to be your friend." Her eyes squeezed tight and the corners of her mouth began to tremble.

I moved closer to her, still too guarded to risk a touch. "Grace, you scare me, too. I've tried to convince myself that I don't want you around, but the truth is, I'm not ready to let you go, either. Let's leave it be for a while, huh?"

Grace nodded. "Do you want to sit down for a bit?" I asked. "How about some cobbler, or maybe something to drink?"

"Do you have any wine?"

"Yeah, I think Julie left a bottle last time she was here."

Grace sat down at the table while I searched the refrigerator for wine. I found the unopened bottle and read the label. "Biltmore Chardonnay. Will that work?"

"Anything will work," Grace replied. She slid my statistics book over and vacantly studied the open page. "Thanks," she said, taking the glass with a thin smile.

I reached into the fridge for a beer. "So how was the fall dance?" The question felt as strange as the air between us.

"Busy. I'm glad it's over."

"So did you have fun?"

"Not really. My date was a total jerk," she said flatly.

"How so?"

"He got drunk and was all over me. I kept pushing him off, trying to be nice about it, but he started saying things real loud, like I was a frigid bitch and stuff. I finally had to give him a blow job to shut him up."

The thought of Grace going down on some arrogant frat boy made me want to puke. "He sounds like a fucking asshole," I said as I sat down at the table beside her. "I don't know why you want to go out with guys in the first place."

Grace offered a half smile and took a sip of wine. She looked out the window with unaffected eyes, as if she understood the world in a way I didn't. "Guys get drunk and do things they normally wouldn't. They usually feel bad about it later." She turned to me, her chin in a brave tilt. "Sometimes they even apologize."

"Did this guy apologize to you?" I asked.

"No, he didn't. I've been mostly avoiding him since the dance, trying to forget it ever happened." Outside my neighbor's grill flared from a reckless squirt of lighter fluid. Grace looked up, and I watched the fire-light blaze and die in her eyes. She raised her palm to her mouth and leaned into it. "I don't know why I can't shake it off. I've done that before with guys, but this time it felt different. I don't know, I told one of the senior sisters about it. Her advice was that I don't go out with him again."

Grace fell silent and turned away from me. Her mouth began to tremble and she sucked in a broken breath. "Damn it! I said I wouldn't cry about this." She dropped her head into her hands and drew in another ragged breath. "It's so stupid. I mean he didn't actually make me do anything, so why do I want to cry all the time?" She stilled for a moment, gathering herself again. She looked up and swept tears from her swollen eyes. "Shit!"

I reached over and rested my palm across her shoulder. "Grace, he manipulated you into doing something you didn't want to do. You have every right to be upset." I spoke calmly, though inside I was fighting the urge to hunt him down and kick his ass. More than that, I wanted to hold Grace until her crying stopped. All I could manage was to tighten my fingers on her shoulder and watch tears fill her eyes.

"I'm sorry, Blue." She blew her nose into the napkin I handed her. "I'm full of surprises tonight, huh?" She forced a chuckle and pinched back her tears.

I smiled tenderly, the way my mother did when she consoled me. "You've made my life interesting," I said. Grace looked at me, the corners of her mouth struggling to keep more tears from coming. She blew her nose again. "How about more wine?" Grace nodded and watched me refill her glass. "You want to watch TV for a while?"

Grace nodded again and picked up her wine glass. I followed with my beer and motioned Grace to my recliner. She sat back and pushed out the footrest, settling in as the worry lines on her face began to fade. I pulled over a kitchen chair and a step stool for my feet. We sat close, watching "Taxi" and "Soap," and each time Grace laughed I felt like a giant.

When the credits rolled on "Soap," Grace stood up. Her head weaved a bit and she reached back for the chair. "Are you okay?" I asked.

"Yeah. I think I stood up too fast."

"Or maybe drank too fast?" I offered.

"Maybe." Grace sat down and rubbed her forehead. "I didn't eat lunch today."

"I can fix you something—or take you home. You really shouldn't drive."

"Can you fix me something and let me stay here tonight?"

God help me. This woman is going to drive me insane. Motivations

49

raced through my head. Maybe it was the wine talking for Grace; or maybe she had somehow forgotten the part about me being gay and there was only one bed.

"I shouldn't have asked that," Grace said. She stood up, focused on her keys and the door, and took a couple of unsteady steps.

"No, it's okay." I hopped up and grabbed her arm. "Sit back down. I'll make you a turkey sandwich and find you something to sleep in. You should stay, Grace."

She ate the sandwich like she was famished, and asked for a bowl of cobbler after she finished it. I loaded a huge piece of cobbler into two bowls and gave one to Grace. We watched Ted Koppel discuss the Iranian hostages, turned off the TV, and crawled into bed. I stretched out, stiff as a corpse, though my mind raced. Grace restlessly shifted her long limbs beside me. She let out a couple of deep sighs and rolled toward the wall. The gay thing felt like an ice-blue void between us.

I stared into the dark room, wishing for some small hint of what to do, and then the weight of Grace's hand fell onto my shoulder, light as a dove. I turned toward her and pushed a shock of hair away from her face.

Grace looked at me for a moment and dropped her head onto my chest. She shuddered as I held her. A hot tear soaked through my t-shirt and Grace clutched onto my shoulders like she was drowning. This time, she seemed to be crying for a totally different reason.

"What are you doing this weekend?" Grace's cheerful voice came from my bathroom. Whatever she'd been crying about when I held her last night seemed forgotten. Wearing the pale blue boxer shorts and sleeveless white t-shirt I loaned her, she bent over to splash her face. I watched her tight butt slowly shift from side to side as water dripped from her chin. Figuring I'd surely lose it if I watched her a second longer, I rolled out of bed and padded to the kitchen. "I may go to Raleigh," I said, opening the refrigerator. "I'll know for sure tonight."

"Are you going to Julie's house?" Grace strolled from the bathroom and into the kitchen, patting her neck with a hand towel.

I took a couple of Hardees cartoon glasses from my cabinet and filled them with orange juice. "Yeah, I might go over to dog-sit. I hope it works out." I handed the Daffy Duck glass to Grace and kept Yosemite Sam for myself.

"Why won't you know until tonight?" Grace asked.

"Well, it seems my aunt Julie is having a hot affair with a surgical nurse from Charlotte. A married surgical nurse," I said with an uneasy glance at Grace. "Julie never knows until the last minute if her lover will be able to get away from her husband."

"Oh, I see." Grace looked at me with a conspirator's smirk and sipped her juice. When she put her glass down she looked at me thoughtfully. "Does it bother you that your aunt is having an affair with a married woman?"

"I don't know," I replied. "I've never met the woman she's seeing, so I don't know about her, but I've always thought my aunt practically hung the moon. I don't think Julie would have a fling with a married woman for fun. She's too serious a person for that. I guess the woman she's seeing wasn't getting what she wanted from her husband. Most marriages are for shit these days anyway," I said, though I didn't really mean it. My parent's marriage was anything but shit. I checked Grace's reaction to make sure she knew I didn't mean it. "I guess there's a part of me that thinks it's wrong, that you shouldn't get involved with married people. I don't think I would." I looked over at Grace and grinned. "Unless it was a woman as beautiful as you wearing my boxer shorts."

Grace looked at me with an easy smile. "I bet you say stuff like that to all the girls."

"No, not really." I grinned again and downed the last of my orange juice. "I've got to get ready for class," I said, heading for the bathroom.

"I want to go with you," Grace called across the room.

I stopped in the bathroom door and turned to her. "To class?" I teased.

"No, silly, I want to go to Raleigh with you."

I shrugged like I didn't care. "Sure, that's okay with me," I said, staying cool. "But don't you have a sorority thingy or a family shindig you need to go to?" I leaned against the door frame and hoped I looked adorable.

"No, smart-ass." Grace shot me a mocking smirk. "I don't have a sorority thingy to go to, and my mom and dad are in Europe this week. I can do whatever I want."

"Suit yourself," I shrugged. "But if you come with me you'll have to bring your own pajamas. I don't know if I can stand watching you walk around in my clothes all weekend." I smiled and ducked into the bathroom to start the shower.

I left off the hot water.

10

Glorious

A passing blur of autumn red maples and golden hickories framed Grace's face on the drive up the narrow road to Julie's house. Grace dropped her foot from my dashboard and sat up straight. She looked out toward residential lots thick with hardwood trees surrounding modern houses of gray, weathered wood and long, angular windows. "We should go for a hike tomorrow," she said.

"Maybe we'll take the dogs to the park." I leaned up to turn down The Pretenders cassette tape we had been listening to for the last fifteen miles. "There's a place up the road where Julie and I go sometimes. She taught me how to cast a fly on the lake the first summer I was here. I think I was ten or so."

"I'd love to see the lake." Grace looked at me with an adoring smile, as if imagining a spunky tomboy in rolled-up jeans skipping stones across the water. I wondered if she had been that same spunky tomboy when her dad first took her fishing, and if her smile was for the kid she imagined in me, or for the childhood she remembered.

"Maybe we can go fishing in the morning." I thought of her eyes filled with the light of the morning sun. I had gotten good at imagining Grace in my world.

We drove another half mile of climbing curves before I turned left onto the road that led to Julie's driveway. I rolled down the window to listen to the tumble of the stream that flowed alongside and spilled over a rock ledge down the hill. "You would never know this place is only a few miles from town," I said.

"I want to come with you every time you house-sit."

"What about your other obligations?"

Grace frowned and turned away.

I hadn't meant to taunt her, though she seemed to take it that way. "Grace, you know you can come with me anytime you want."

"What if you want to bring someone else?" she asked. I knew that she meant a date.

"I'll tell you."

She studied me for a moment, as if she wasn't sure I would. She still had questions. We both had questions neither of us dared to ask.

We turned into Julie's place and headed up the graveled drive. The sound of a basset hound's insistent baying drifted down the hill. His tenor vocals rang through the cool air like a good country ballad, full of sorrow with a twist of jest. I grinned and said, "That would be Barney. He's the boss. But wait till you see his sidekick."

I parked in front of Julie's garage and grabbed our bags from the bed of the truck. Inside the house a deep baritone added a three-count bark to Barney's clamor. Grace followed behind me and waited as I unlocked the door and pushed back a frenzy of churning legs and slobber. "Come on in," I said over my shoulder. Barney planted his paws on my thighs and threw his head back, his ears flopping out like clown shoes. I laughed and hooked my fingers around his ears. Then I spotted Ralph slipping around to plant his massive body in front of Grace. He cocked his head and stared at her. "That's Ralph. He's just a big baby." I sidestepped Barney and grabbed the Harlequin Great Dane by his collar and pulled him to my side. Barney now had his long snoot planted firmly at Grace's feet and ankles, sniffing like he had found the world's most fabulous cottontail. She kneeled in front of him and held his head in her palms. I watched her scratch his expansive ears and thought—God help me—that she would make a great vet's wife.

"I think you've won Barney's heart already," I said, pulling myself from my stupid daydream of me and Grace and a vet clinic at the edge of town. Grace stood and reached out for Ralph's shoulders. He stepped next to her and leaned his massive head against her hip. The daydream took off again.

"Come on to the kitchen. Let's see what Julie left us for the weekend," I said to the three of them.

Barney leapt in front and led us through the foyer, his long body swishing side to side as he trotted toward the kitchen, his tail straight up in the air like a guiding staff leading us through a corn maze. If Barney had been able to talk, he would have told us that the house was strictly modern with no formal living or dining room. The kitchen, his favorite of the three rooms downstairs, opened into a den, which featured fabulous cushy sofas and a nice, thick rug for stretching out on the floor. The tall narrow windows in the front and side of the den filtered in sunlight, creating an excellent environment for afternoon naps.

Barney flopped down on the rug in front of the sink and watched Grace as she walked around to perch on one of the stools at the counter between the kitchen and den. "This is such a cozy house," she said, her eyes scanning the gleaming white cabinets and ocean blue countertops.

"Julie's getting a hot tub next week." I plopped my elbows on the counter across from her and raised my brows with a suggestive smile. "Then it will be really cozy." I spun away before Grace could respond. On the counter across the kitchen I checked out the stash Julie left for us. There was the usual stuff, bags of pretzels and chips, and this time, to the side of the stash, a VCR tape. I picked up the tape and read the note on the top.

Good movie if you haven't seen it. Beer and wine in the fridge. Spaghetti sauce in the freezer. Have a good weekend.

I pulled the note off and read Julie's handwritten label. *Coming Home/Emmanuelle.* My face flushed with a mix of embarrassment and sexual possibility. *Emmanuelle* was nothing but sex wrapped around a lame plotline, and anyone over eighteen knew about the sex scene in *Coming Home.* I figured Julie hadn't been thinking about that when she left the tape for us. For her generation, *Coming Home* was about the consequences of war, and now I knew Julie had experienced the consequences of Vietnam in her own way. Grace and I had never talked about her father's military background, or whether he had seen any hard combat. I wondered if we could watch the movie and avoid talking about her father, or anything else that had to do with her family. I slipped the cassette behind the wine and grabbed the pretzels and chips. "How about spaghetti for supper?"

"That sounds great." Grace opened the chips and took a couple from the bag. "So you're gonna cook for me and teach me stats. What else are you planning to do for me?"

I looked at her dancing green eyes and teasing smile and thought of a hundred things I figured I'd better not say. "How about a glass of wine?" I offered.

The closing credits of *Coming Home* faded from the screen. I stared at the TV, trying to sort out the tragedy of the last scenes. Grace moved her foot from my hip and swung off the blanket stretched between us. She stood and stretched as she looked at me. "I've got to pee. Do you want another beer while I'm up?"

I shook my head and hit the stop button on the remote before *Emmanuelle* started. Grace had squirmed restlessly during the sex scenes in *Coming Home* and I figured she wasn't up for the erotic escapades of *Emmanuelle*.

"We should probably go to bed soon if you want to go fishing to-morrow morning." I flipped off the TV and stood for a long stretch. "Grab your stuff and I'll show you your room upstairs. There's a guest bathroom up there."

Grace looked at me, perplexed, as if she had not expected her own room. I opened my mouth to remind her we weren't at a sleepover, that I needed boundaries, or at least ground rules. "Yeah, I'm pretty sleepy," she said before I spoke.

With an expectant air between us we climbed the stairs towards the bedrooms, I turned right at the top of the stairs and held open the guest room door. Grace moved past me and I followed her in, moving about the room like I was merely a servant or innkeeper, wishing to avoid the conspicuous presence of the four-poster bed in the center of the room.

"Here you go," I said after checking the bathroom for soap and towels. "This room is all yours. Me and the boys will be down the hall in Julie's room. You know where the kitchen is if you want water or anything. If you need extra towels, they're in the linen closet across the hall."

I almost made it out of the room before Grace asked, "Are you going to sleep now?"

I stopped in the doorway and turned around. "I'll probably watch TV in bed for a while."

"Can I join you?"

I shrugged, like I didn't care. "Sure." Her smile stole a bit of air from my lungs. I sucked in an extra breath that I hoped she didn't notice.

"I'll put on my PJs and be there in a minute," she said.

I nodded and turned into the hallway. Barney looked up at me with his sagging hound-dog eyes. I wished to God he *could* talk. The old boy would probably have good advice about accepting all the love that was offered. He followed me into Julie's bedroom and sauntered over to his bed beside Ralph. I turned on the TV and grabbed my toothbrush and boxer shorts out of my bag. In the bathroom I flipped on the light and stared into the double vanity mirror.

What are you going to do about her? You can't keep this up forever.

I turned on the cold water to run across my wrists and then splashed my face. Water dripped off my chin as I stared at my reflection. *You're completely screwed either way. You'll love her and never completely have her, or you'll never love her at all.*

Right then I decided how I would love Grace. If I got the chance, I would love her on her terms, when she wanted and how she wanted. I would be happy for what she could give me. I would know that every minute she spent with me she was taking a risk, and she wouldn't take those risks if she didn't care about me. After losing my parents I'd realized that sometimes happiness comes on a daily basis, and loving Grace sometimes, on some days, would be better than never loving her at all.

I brushed my teeth, slipped out of my Levi's and pulled on my boxer shorts and a t-shirt. Maybe I was overreacting anyway. Maybe Grace actually wanted to watch TV and talk, like friends do. Maybe we should talk about boundaries and friendship and how for us, the two would always be intertwined. I nodded to my reflection and turned off the light, then scampered across cold hardwood floors for the king-sized warmth of my aunt's bed.

Ralph unfolded his lanky body when Grace walked in the room.

He sauntered over to greet her, and she cradled his massive head in her hands and kissed him between his finely crafted ears. I kept my eyes on him to avoid fixating on the outline of Grace's body pushing against silk pajamas.

"What you watching?" Grace crawled into bed and moved toward me. Without hesitating she nestled against my side and dropped her head onto my shoulder.

"Just the news right now," I replied. I reached across her shoulder and laced my fingers into her hair. *Screw the boundaries.* My fingers swept down the soft skin of her neck and I glanced down at her face. She had washed off her makeup, and her skin smelled like citrus. The inside of my chest made a flutter and then began to pound like a warrior's drum. I shifted down to keep Grace hearing it.

"'The Tonight Show' will be on in a few minutes. I think that David Letterman guy is guest hosting tonight. He cracks me up," I said casually.

Grace replied with a short sigh and nestled her head deeper onto my shoulder. I cradled her in the crook of my arm and held her there. In our silence the news anchor droned on, and then the sports guy gave a report on Tar Heel and Duke basketball. I hardly heard a word of it. My mind was stuck on the soft rhythm of her breathing and the warm weight of her body against me.

Flickering shadows from the TV faded into the dark, and then burst to life again with a blaring car commercial. I grabbed the remote and turned down the volume. Grace waited until I resettled and again dropped her head onto my shoulder. She shifted her foot across my ankle and then became very still.

Okay, time to talk about boundaries. I drew in a breath to begin my discourse.

"You know, you can kiss me if you want," Grace said softly.

I froze, even as my heart took off like a jet on a runway. Grace turned to face me. Her green, captivating eyes looked straight into mine. Her body fell heavy against me and her lips came to my mouth.

The length of my body filled with a glow that seemed to come from someplace else; someplace unfamiliar. Grace was not my first lover, nor my second, yet the touch of her lips took me over. How long had I wanted this? All of the moments I never dared to touch her, and now Grace was on top of me, her lips on mine, then her tongue, tentatively dipping into my mouth, and then rushing in, like a flood after a breech.

Our kiss broke and I opened my eyes. Grace straddled me, her fingers turning the top button of her pajamas. She had never done this before. I could tell by the uncertain look in her eyes. I had to keep my wits. This night had to mean something to her. She would have to remember, even when she didn't want to. I grasped her hips and watched her hands part the seams of her shirt. Her arms slid free and she shook back her hair. She looked at me with certainty now, her eyes pulling me in like an invitation.

I held her gaze and moved my fingers across her body, the soft skin still tanned from the summer, the traces of muscle in her arms and chest, the curve of her hips. I had imagined Grace's body in a hundred dreams, and like a dream, I feared this night would be fleeting. I wanted her to remember it as I would. I sat up and pulled off my t-shirt. Our bodies met; skin against skin. Grace clutched me, her mouth at my neck and her hair falling against my shoulder. Heat and blood rushed through me, but I had to stay in control. I slowed my kisses and pulled Grace down, savoring the taste of her lips and the way she looked up at me as I rolled on top. She closed her eyes and held me loosely, her body arching to the slow path of my lips. The tip of my tongue reached her nipple and circled it. Grace drew in a sharp breath and tightened her arms, and I knew she wouldn't push me away.

I moved my lips slowly, wanting every inch of her. Light moaning came quicker as my fingers moved up her thigh. Warm wetness met my fingertips, and the scent of her exploded around us. Pressing and sweeping I moved to what she wanted most, my fingers responding with the quickening of her breath and the reflex of her hips against my hand. Grace opened her legs, her fingers digging into my skin. My own body pounding and aching, I pushed inside her. Her soft cry rang in my ear and she clutched my back. The world seemed nothing to me now. There was only Grace.

Her breath fired through my body, and inside she opened up to me. Together we moved in a rhythm that pushed and bonded. Grace grasped the sheets and shuddered, her mouth opened without sound, and then it came, sharp in my ear. She constricted, her power meeting mine as a cry rose from somewhere deep inside her, a place I knew she had never been, and then she fell back, her body still shuddering beneath me. She buried her face in my neck and clutched me to her chest, spent and gasping for breath.

I pulled her close and waited for her breath to slow. *Glorious.*

Grace's arms grew heavy against me. I had wanted this particular moment since the first time I held her; this untroubled moment when I knew it hadn't been crazy to want her. Softly she traced two fingers across my back.

"You were the first, Blue," she whispered, her breath in my ear. I pushed up to look at her. "I've never had anyone inside before."

I smiled and studied the mystery in her eyes. "You've been saving yourself?"

"Yep," Grace pushed my hair from my face and she kissed me. "And you were definitely worth the wait." She rolled me onto my back and draped a leg across my hip. "And now I want to do something else for the first time."

Her hand moved down the line of my stomach and slowly teased up my thigh. Fingers swept across me and I sucked in a breath.

Glorious indeed.

11

All Things Equal

Two blocks from Trish's house, I still couldn't find a place to park. If I hadn't promised Trish I would come to her Homecoming party, I wouldn't have bothered stopping. After all, I had physics to study for, and Grace had said she would try to come by my apartment later on.

At a spot on a corner three blocks away, I parked and pulled on my jacket. For November it was a warm night, warm enough to keep the dykes outside and unfolding their drama along the rows of cars; a small group sharing a joint; a couple fighting; a friend comforting another because of the indiscretion of some girl named Donna. At least I didn't have to share Grace with this world. Our secret belonged only to us, and that alone was enough to make it shine.

I turned at the pecan tree that anchored the edge of Trish's yard and headed toward her house. Donna Summer's "Bad Girls" boomed and faded into the night as a flow of women moved in and out the back door. In the carport a small group watched four women furiously working a foosball table. Trish stood close, watching the game like she had money on it. She looked up and spotted me halfway up the drive.

"Blue Riley!" Trish dropped her arm from the foot taller woman beside her and started toward me. In her right hand she held her Tar Heels glass, which I figured contained a mix of more Jack than Coke. Her free hand slipped around my waist and pulled me close. "Damn if you aren't sober." Her hand slipped to the small of my back as she led me toward the door. "I was beginning to wonder if you were coming. You've gotta meet some of these women. There's women here from Charlotte and Raleigh and some Army chicks from Fayetteville. I don't know who invited them, but I don't give a shit."

I grinned and opened the door. Donna Summer blasted at us from two-foot speakers suspended from the ceiling. I blinked hard and stepped into the faint light of a den filled with women standing shoulder to shoulder or dancing hip to hip. It seemed like I had walked into the Promised Land. Trish's hand inched toward my ass. I stepped around and leaned close to her ear. "I'm sorry it didn't work out with your girlfriend."

Trish shrugged. "Just as well—now I can chase after you." She popped my butt and spun away, grinning. I stood alone at the edge of the den. Tonight the room was in party mode. The couch and chairs were pushed against walls to make room for dancing, and over the fireplace was a Michelob Light sign lit up in blue and gold. Cigarette smoke hung in the air, thick as an Appalachian morning fog. I scanned through the crowd and didn't see anyone I knew. Eyes burning, I headed for the beer keg in the kitchen.

At the door my gaze stopped dead still on a dark-haired woman standing by the keg. She looked back at me and the length of my body stirred. With each step I took, her dark brown eyes grew bolder. I stopped next to the keg and pulled a Tar Heel blue cup from the stack on the counter.

"Would you like one?" I asked, tilting the cup toward her.

"No thanks, I have one," she replied. She leaned in, her cleavage spilling from her red sweater like a dare. "I'm Anna," she said into my ear, loud enough to be heard over Stevie Nicks.

I pushed the tap and leaned toward her, my lips brushing the edge of her thick black hair. "Most people call me Blue."

Anna's gaze moved over me, her eyes a mix of curiosity and seduction. I flipped off the tap and leaned toward her. "Are you a friend of Trish's?" I asked.

"Trish is my sister's roommate."

"So you're Maria's sister?" It had to be Maria. She looked very much like her, only more predatory.

"Yeah, I'm staying here until Maria gets done with classes. Then we're flying out to Aspen for Thanksgiving." She looked at me like I should be impressed. I wasn't.

"Are you in school?" I asked.

"I'm working on my master's at Miami." Anna paused and looked at me with eyes that devoured whatever she wanted, and for now they were set on me. "But I'll be here for the next ten days."

Every flirtatious movement of her body suggested we could make the most of those ten days. There would be no waiting for her to come by after a date with some guy, or imaginings of what she was doing in the upstairs room of a frat party.

"Are you here with anyone?" I asked.

"No. Not yet anyway," she replied. She dropped her hand onto my thigh and slid it inward. Heat pulsed through me and settled between my legs.

"Tell me you don't have a girlfriend," she said.

"I kinda do," I replied, though at the moment I wasn't exactly sure.

"Kind of?!" Anna snorted. She pulled her hand away and looked at me with a haughty smile. "She must be straight."

"Well, not entirely, is she?" I said, smiling.

Anna looked down at my boots, and then up to my eyes. She smirked and turned away. "Keep telling yourself that, cowgirl." Most girls would piss me off with the arrogant smile that creased her lips, but then most girls didn't look like Anna. Her tongue swept her lip. "When you get tired of her shit, give me a call. You know how to find me."

She gave me her empty beer cup and walked away, grabbing a girl on her way to the dance floor.

My apartment was quiet when I walked in. I shed smoke-filled clothes on the way to the bathroom and stepped into a hot shower. I stood under the stream of water, letting it wash away the smell of smoke that infiltrated my pores the way that thoughts of Anna crept into my brain. I didn't want her there. I grabbed the soap and remembered the morning at Julie's when Grace pulled me toward the shower. Soon thoughts of Anna melted away and there was only Grace.

Refreshed and clean, I pulled on my sweats and grabbed Tolstoy's *The Cossacks*, the required reading for my lit class. I read the second page for the third time and tossed the book aside, looking for some other distraction. "Saturday Night Live" was still on. I flipped on the TV and settled in to wait for Grace.

By one-thirty I knew she wasn't coming. I turned off the TV and watched the light fade from the screen. It should have been easy for Grace to sneak away from a huge Homecoming party. Maybe she hadn't even tried.

I crawled into bed determined to think only of Anna; her face and eyes, the smell of her perfume and the round breasts that swelled up from her low-cut sweater. Maybe tomorrow I would call her. Maybe by tomorrow night she would be in my bed and I would be pulling her sweater over her head to take in the beauty of those round breasts. I rested my hand on my thigh and imagined it, Anna straddling my chest, Anna bending to kiss me, Anna's breast in my mouth, Anna rocking into my fingers, Anna climaxing and falling breathless against me.

But Grace wouldn't allow it. All of my imaginings flew back to her, the way her morning hair fell wildly in all directions, the way her soft moaning turned to insistent cries when her body opened up to me, the smell and taste of her skin, the way she mastered languages but struggled with simple statistics. I rolled to my side and punched my pillow. I couldn't will myself to fantasize about another woman. Grace inhabited me.

"Goodnight, Grace," I said out loud. Somehow, the sound of her name on my tongue slowed my thoughts, and I drifted off into sound sleep.

Rapid pounding jolted me awake. Stumbling out of bed, I pulled on a sweatshirt and rubbed my eyes open as I crossed the room. I peeked around the heavy curtain at the window. There was Grace, pulling her jacket close as the swirling wind blew her hair across her face. I swung the door open and she flew past me. She grabbed my hand and pulled me toward the bathroom. "Let's get in the shower. I need to wake you up. I've been waiting all night for this."

12

Grace and Truth

Trish tapped the end of the cards on my table, flipped halfway through, and shuffled them for the third time. "God, I'm glad I'm done with finals," she said. She tapped the cards sharply and zipped them into another shuffle. Her habit of exactly ten shuffles per deal was making me crazy. I went to the refrigerator for a new round of Michelob Lights.

Outside, lightning flashed through pouring rain, sending some poor guy sprinting across the parking lot in a *come-to-Jesus* frenzy. I watched him duck under the roofline and shake off the rain as I twisted off beer caps.

"Are you coming to the 'Thank God It's Over' party tomorrow night?" Trish asked over shuffle number eight. "We're getting a keg and *you know* there'll be a lot of good-looking women there. Anna's coming to stay with Maria again before they leave for Christmas holidays. She's been asking about you." Trish grabbed her beer and looked up at me with a devilish grin.

I swung my leg over the back of my chair and sat down. "I doubt I'll come. I may have other plans."

"Other plans! I know everybody you know and they're all coming to the party. You can't have other plans," Trish said over shuffle number nine.

"Trish, you don't know everyone I know," I said flatly, hoping for a moment to dampen Trish's brash confidence in all things gay, including me. I watched her hands flex through the motions of shuffle ten. Outside a sharp bolt of lightning cracked the air, followed immediately by floor-shaking thunder. Trish looked out, shook off a shiver, and tossed the top card across the table.

"I really do have plans with someone else," I said.

"So who is this mystery woman?" Trish held the cards still and looked up at me. "It isn't someone I know, is it? 'Cause if you're dating someone I know and I don't know about it . . . well, that just isn't right."

I brought my beer to my lips and held it there for a moment, long enough to watch Trish's fretful eyes grow more worried that she might not know every bit of gay gossip in Chapel Hill. "It isn't anyone you know," I said with a half-cocked grin.

"I knew it!" Trish hopped up and spun around like she had just won the "Price Is Right" showcase. Still grinning, she sat down and looked at me with her brash confidence. "I knew there was a reason you weren't going for Anna!"

"Anna is tempting," I said casually.

Trish leaned toward me, chin propped on her palm, looking at me with shining intensity, like I was the most fascinating person in the world. After a moment, she fell back and eyed me curiously. "But someone else has you *wrapped*—and I don't even know who it is. Is she married or something?"

"No! She's not married. Do you think I'm crazy?" Married might have been easier. At least I would know to never expect more. "I haven't told you because I didn't want you running your mouth about it. She's a Delta Pi," I said calmly.

"Oh my freaking God!" Trish looked at me as if I were a god. "You're doing a Delta Pi? First, let me say that's freaking *awesome*. Second, *have you lost your ever-loving mind?*"

"Okay, Trish, for starters, I'm not *doing* anybody. I'm seeing someone who's pretty special to me, and aren't you getting a little too much in my business? Sometimes your curiosity about my love life seems a bit obsessive."

"I tell you, no good will come from it," Trish said. She shook her head with certainty, as if she had seen it happen a hundred times, and always with the same results. "Sorority girls are trouble. She'll rip your heart out and stomp it flat."

"I know that can happen, Trish," I replied. She nodded like she didn't believe me and went back to dealing the cards. "I'm keeping my eyes wide open, believe me. You can't always choose who you fall for, can you?"

Trish didn't answer. She seemed more interested in keeping up her lecture than in philosophical discussions about love and choice. "I should have known it was something like this," she said. She popped the last card onto her stack and babbled on, "I mean, you keep half the rowing team in a stir about you. Bitches always asking me, 'What about Blue? What about Blue? Who's she going out with?' Bugging me every time I turn around. Now I know what you're up to and you won't let me tell anyone. That's just great." Trish pursed her lips like a scorned old woman and picked up the stack of cards in front of her. I wanted to laugh, but I thought it would get her more pissed—and irrational. I turned over the top card on my stack; the three of hearts. Trish turned the eight of clubs and swept up the cards. Then, we both turned a jack.

"Battle!" Trish demanded. Quick as a cat, she smacked two cards down on the table and turned the third on top.

I stacked two cards and paused. Trish's eyes were locked on me, dancing with defiance. "Trish, why are you so pissed about this?"

"'Cause we always get the leftovers." Trish cocked her head and looked straight at me, as if her explanation made perfect sense.

"What the hell are you talking about?"

"You know, gay people, we always get the leftovers."

"Leftover what?"

"Well, not that *you* are leftovers or anything. You're a long way from a leftover."

Here we go again. Now we were off on some nonsensical babble about leftovers, although I had learned if I stayed with her long enough, somehow Trish *would* make sense. "And neither are you, but go on and make your point," I said.

"What I mean is there aren't many gay women around. So when somebody like you comes onto the scene, women get a little excited, like they might have a shot. See, we want you to be on our team, dating one of us. Now I find out we've lost something else to the straight world—you."

"I don't think Grace is exactly straight."

"Well, she's not willing to live in our world either, is she?" Trish scoffed. "We can't even have the satisfaction of knowing you're stealing a little something from all those straight asshole guys. You won't let me tell anybody, so how will they know what you're up to?"

"Okay, I understand that part, but I don't see what this has to do with leftovers."

"That's what the breeders think *lesbians* are. They think we're just a bunch of women left over from the straight world; women too butch, or too athletic, or too shy, or too whatever to get to ride in the front of the bus with the straight people. They don't respect us, Blue. They think all us leftovers should get together and sit in the back."

"So you think Grace and I are supposed to get you to the front of the bus?"

"No, that's not what I mean." Trish let out a long, heavy breath and paused for a moment. "The thing is, if people saw you two together, they'd see it's not so bad sitting in the back."

"Well, with any luck maybe Grace will decide to ride in the back with us," I replied, turning my battle card up.

"Don't count on it, my friend," Trish said as she swept the hand. "I'll save you a seat—'cause Grace will end up in the front."

Grace's hurried knock rapped again on my apartment door. I turned down the TV and glanced over at the clock. *Oh yeah—you escaped.*

Eight-thirty and already she had slipped out of the Delta Pi Christmas party. I hustled over to the door and unlocked it. Grace threw it open and rushed in. Without taking her eyes from me, she quickly locked it. I grabbed her hips and crashed full into her body, my mouth meeting her hard kiss. Her legs opened to my thigh as her back hit the wall. I pushed against her, reaching around for the button of her skirt, then the zipper. Her breath came in gasps, hot against my neck. The black skirt hit the floor at her feet. My hand pushed into her crotch, reckless and dire.

"You've been thinking about me?" My fingers swept her wet clit.

Grace grabbed my hand to move it farther down. I pushed two

fingers inside her. Her nails dug into my shoulder and sharp gasps rushed into my ear as she rocked against me. "God, I've been waiting for that," Grace said, her voice low and her breath on my neck. "Let's get out of these fucking clothes."

On my bed Grace's arms tightened. I pushed into her, against her. Her hand moved past my hips and found the spot that was begging for her touch. My back arched, muscles converged, and then—pow! Thick liquid shot out of me and covered Grace's belly. Panting and sucking air, I rolled to my side and stared at the clear juice covering Grace's skin. "Jesus, Mary and Joseph! What the hell was that?"

Grace laughed and looked down at her stomach, smiling. "I don't know baby. I think you like me."

I dropped my head onto her shoulder, still gasping for air. "As soon as I can move again, I'll show you how much."

Grace tightened her arms around me and kissed the top of my head. "I'll take you up on that," she said, fingering my hair as I caught my breath. "But let me take a shower first."

"Yeah, I can see why you'd want to." Embarrassed heat surged up my neck. "That's never happened to me before. I'm really sorry."

"No, silly, I loved whatever *that* was," Grace wrapped her arms around me and pulled me down. "It's not that at all. My hair smells like nasty smoke."

I gathered a lock of it and held it to my nose. "Yeah, it kinda does."

Grace kissed me and got up. "Don't you ever worry about spraying me with your love juice, baby," she said as she walked toward the bathroom. She stopped in the door and grinned. "Maybe one day you'll get me pregnant."

I smiled and closed my eyes. Content and loose, I fell into a light slumber. The lavender scent of her freshly washed skin woke me a few minutes later. Grace got into bed and stretched her leg across mine. She settled against my body, her head resting on my shoulder. "Three days of nothing but me and you. How does that sound?"

"It's a start." I traced the curve of her shoulder with my fingertip. "I don't see why you have to go home for Christmas. You can stay with me, you know."

"Don't I wish! Let's be thankful for three days. My mother wanted me to come home today. I told her I needed to do some shopping in Raleigh."

"Shopping? Is that what you call it?" I smiled and looked into her eyes.

"Sure. Shopping is the acquisition of wanted goods, right?" Grace ran her fingers along my ribs. Her touch aroused me again. "Well, you are wanted, and you are *good*."

13

Magic Days

December rain fell outside; a gray drizzle of fine mist hung in the air between short, lazy showers. Grace sat cross-legged on the floor in front of the stereo, flipping through a stack of Julie's albums. Beside her, Ralph rested his head near the crook of her hip. The familiar tug of loneliness pulled at me as I watched them. Grace would be going home soon, and she would be careful, so careful that no one would suspect I even existed.

The past three days we'd spent in Julie's house held a kind of magic: simple, electric, promising, amazing—and dark. Some moments felt so good I could feel the cells beneath my skin dancing the cha-cha-cha. Then the moment would turn, and our lives again seemed out of control, totally ruled by outside forces.

Yesterday afternoon Grace had called home to beg two more days. Her breathing became shallow and her voice shook a bit as she explained to her mother that she would see her family only a few short hours before they left for New York, so why not just stay in Raleigh with her friends for a couple more days? I listened and wondered if her mother detected the edge of panic as Grace flew through the logic of her request.

"Oh, I love this album." Grace pulled out a white album cover from the middle of the stack.

I looked over. "Poco's *Legend;* that's actually mine. Julie borrowed it to record."

Grace slid the vinyl disc out and flipped both sides to check the song list. She chose side one and popped up onto her knees to place it on the turntable. I watched her drop the needle on the edge of the vinyl, and then she turned to me with a look so tender it stole the breath from my lungs.

"Come over here," I said.

Smiling, she grabbed the album cover and shuffled across the room on her knees. I took the cover from her as she crawled onto the couch and nestled against me. "Let me see the cover," she said, leaning into my chest.

"Don't know how much I can take, I can't stand another break," Grace sang out loud. She swung her foot to the beat of the bass as she read through the song titles. "'Heart of the Night' makes me want to go to New Orleans every time I hear it," she chirped. "I love that place. Have you ever been there?"

I tightened my arms along the curve of her ribs. "No, I've always kinda wanted to go, though."

She dropped the cover onto the floor and flipped around to face me, smiling like a kid. "We should go during spring break. I'll pay."

I swept her hair over her shoulder. "You mean your father will pay."

Her smile faded and she looked away. "Whatever," she said as she twisted around to resettle against my chest.

I squeezed an apology against her sides and tried to shake my mood. From the moment Grace hung up last night, I had felt the dread of things not being said. She had smiled and thrown her arms around me when she said she could stay, yet I saw the shadow of worry in her eyes when she took my hand and led me from the phone up to the bedroom. The rest of the night she couldn't quite look me in the eye.

Grace trailed her finger in a circle around my knee and asked, "If you could have three wishes, what would they be?"

The music changed to the easy mood of "Spellbound." I moved my hands to her belly and dropped my head against the arm of the couch. "I don't know, baby. What would you wish for?"

"I'd wish I had my BMW back."

I chuckled and lowered my chin to the curve of her shoulder. "Figures," I teased, with an edge of sarcasm shadowing my voice. Her shoulders fell and she let out a sigh. I hoped she knew it was class warfare I resented. After all, who wouldn't rather drive a BMW than the used Volkswagen Grace's father gave her after she'd wrecked her Beamer last spring? And Grace, for all of her designer clothes and sorority balls, had never laughed at my boots or called me a cowgirl. In fact, I'd never heard her say anything bad about anyone. "What about your second wish?" I asked. I nuzzled the soft skin of her neck and breathed in her clean citrus scent.

She thought for a moment. "I'd wish I could meet your parents," she said, her voice light as a whisper.

The air in the room suddenly collapsed around me. My parents—for the last three days I hadn't really missed them, not in the hollow, vacant way I usually did. I had passed pictures on the walls and the mantel of Julie's house and for once I had not become lost in the fact that I couldn't call them; that I could never tell them about the loves I would have or the things I would do, whether good or bad. I would have wanted Mom and Dad to know Grace. I, too, wished they could have met her. I leaned close to Grace's ear and said, "You mean that, don't you?"

"Yes, I do. I think they must have been really amazing people. I'd bet they were totally different from my parents."

I let out a caustic laugh. "*That's* a safe bet. Maybe one day I'll meet your parents and I can tell you for sure."

Grace shrunk and pulled her elbows away from my knees. I was pushing my luck, and I knew I'd better back off. I slipped my arms around her waist and started a slow rock. "What about your third wish?" I asked sweetly.

Grace flipped around to face me. Mischief flashed in her eyes, "I'd wish for three more wishes."

"Oh! You're going to pull that one, huh?" I smiled and watched joy fill her face.

"Why doesn't everyone say that? Isn't it brilliant?" Her smile glowed.

"Yes, Miss Lancaster, you are indeed brilliant. We'll get out the memo." I laughed and wrapped my legs around her ankles. "Now what about your fourth wish?"

Grace's face grew serious and she looked at me for a moment before she answered. "I'd wish I could live with you, somewhere up in the mountains, in a little farm house with a garden in the back and a creek running right down the hill."

I nodded coolly while my heart began to pound. Grace dreamed of the same life I wanted: to live in a world surrounded by the things we both loved. I believed she meant it, though as the moments passed, the timid, hopeful voice in my head turned cruel and began to shout it was never going to happen. "Wouldn't you miss your riding stables?" I asked with a smile as thin as my hope.

"We'd have horses," Grace replied, undaunted. "You would be a veterinarian, so we'd have all kinds of animals. We'd have two horses and a donkey and a bunch of goats and chickens—but no pigs. I wouldn't want pigs." Grace paused for a moment. "Well, maybe we could have one pig. If it was like that pig on "Green Acres"— Arnold—maybe we could have a pig like Arnold."

"Uh-huh. So only smart pigs," I laughed and watched her smile— amazing, promising magic.

"Yes! All of our animals would be smart, just like our kids."

Kids! Now Grace really was talking a fantasy world, though for the moment I wanted to hold onto the magic. "And what would you be doing while I'm taking care of all these animals?"

"Making you happy."

"What about making *you* happy?"

"That would be your job, too," Grace teased. "Now what would you wish for, besides three more wishes?"

I thought for a minute. "I think I'd wish I was a man."

"What!" Grace shot up and looked at me. "Why in the *hell* would you want to be a man? You've never said anything about wanting to be a man before!"

I reached for her hand. "Don't get your panties in a twist, Grace," I said with a guarded smile. Maybe part of me was itching for a fight, though I had no idea why. "You know I don't mean it like that. It's just that if I were a man we could have the life we want."

Grace slowly shook her head. "That's not what I want, Blue. If you were a man you wouldn't be the person you are and I would never have been attracted to you in the first place."

"Why not? I don't think I would be that different."

"Maybe you wouldn't be, but that's not the point. If you were a man you wouldn't be the beautiful woman that you are, and I wouldn't want you every time I think of you. In case you haven't noticed, I'm gay."

"I think you're bisexual." I tried to smile like it didn't matter. "You go out with guys all the time."

"Because I *have* to. When I'm out with a guy all I think about is that I'd rather be with you."

"Then why don't you quit *faking* it?" I snapped at her. She tried to pull her hand away but I held on. I swallowed back rising anger and rubbed an apology into her palm with my thumb. "Grace, why can't you move in with me?"

"In your tiny apartment?"

Her clever grin set me off again. "Of course not in my apartment," I said tersely. In her eyes I saw enough hurt to stop my angry tirade at the brink of takeoff. "We could find a place together," I finished hopefully.

She turned and looked out at the gray mist hanging in the morning air. I could sense her drawing inward, and it scared me.

"What do you think, Grace?" I sat up next to her.

"That's not how it works, Blue. You know that." She looked at me with an expression I read as defeated.

"Because *you* don't want it to. I'm sick to death of all these unspoken rules and the fact that *I* have to live by them." I leaned close to her, close enough to hear her angry, rapid breath. "It could work however we decide we want it to!"

Grace's eyes pierced through me. "So you think I should simply quit school and move in with you." I hated her sarcasm, mostly because it held too much truth. I stared back and said nothing. "I'll get a job down at the mall while you finish your degree," she said, the sarcasm still there.

"I didn't say that," I replied sourly.

She shoved up from the couch. Her angry footsteps hammered across the room. I sat still, soaking in misery until it felt like I would go under. I forced myself to look at her, standing at the window, her arms crossed tightly over her chest, staring out at the gray. She looked as lonely as a ghost.

I got up and slowly walked over to her, stopping behind her shoulder. Grace glanced at me and looked back into the mist. The fear that she might reject my touch left me timid. I stood awkwardly until I couldn't stand our poison silence a moment longer. "Look, baby, I don't want to make things harder for you than they already are. I want every day to be like the last three. If we lived together, it could be like that."

She shook her head. "If we moved in together, my family would want to know everything about you." She kept her gaze out the window and spoke in a soft, firm voice. "They would insist on knowing where you came from, who your family is, why you're not in a sorority. Eventually they would want to know why I'm spending so much time with you, and you would have to watch me go out on dates and that would drive you crazy."

I gently grasped her arm. "Grace, we can work it all out as it happens. It's up to us to figure out how to do this."

"My family will never leave it up to us." She finally turned to me. The color had left her face. She forced a weak smile. "Those are the rules I live by."

I nodded, though I hated what she was saying. "If you knew that, why didn't you just leave me alone? Why did you come to my apartment that day?" I asked.

She shrugged and swept her hand up to rest on her shoulder. "After I saw you at that stupid car wash I couldn't get you out of my head. I kept wondering what you were doing, where you had gone, who you hung out with. Every time I saw you, it got worse. After a few days, I figured I was being stupid and I'd just go find you. You know what happened after that. I promise I didn't fall for you to spite my parents."

"I know." I stepped next to her and wrapped my arms around her. I pulled her tight. "I'm sorry I pushed you."

She relaxed as I held her, yet I felt powerless, unable to give her what she wanted. Could it be that my love for Grace was inferior somehow to the love she would someday pretend—or maybe had pretended—for a man? I tightened my arms again to drive the question from my mind. She leaned into me with a heavy sigh. We stood there staring out at the dark day, stuck in the reality that every good thing we felt would eventually lead nowhere.

The rest of the day we spoke only careful words and touched with timid gestures. It wasn't until that night in the dark quiet of Julie's bedroom that I reached out for Grace and she flew to me.

At daybreak we woke and made love desperately, as though if we touched and kissed and fucked enough we could make everything alright. Grace fell against me after she came. Our bodies pressed together seemed primitive and bare, sacred between us, never to be open to the evaluation of others, much less to their judgment. But it would be, and there was nothing I could do about it. Grace would go home to Virginia and I would spend the next three weeks just waiting for her to call, hoping that when she came back she would find me worth her trouble.

Grace's orange Volkswagen Beetle appeared and disappeared in and out of the tree line until she rounded a curve that took her from my sight. I stood in Julie's driveway, listening to the whine of the Beetle engine winding its way through the road's curves, pausing for a second as Grace shifted through the gears. The high pitch of the engine drifted through the crisp morning air for another minute or so, and then it was gone. I went inside to call Trish.

"Hey, you want to come to Raleigh for a few days?" I asked after Trish's hello. "Julie's coming home, but she'll be working late this week. We'll have the house mostly to ourselves."

"Grace must be gone."

I imagined the sarcastic smile that accompanied Trish's clever voice. "She left this morning, smart-ass. It's fine if you don't want to come over. I thought you might want to get away from your parents for a while."

Trish was silent for a moment. "Yeah, okay. It's already boring around here. Do you want me to come today?"

"Yeah, if you can. And bring the Jack Daniels, I feel like getting drunk."

Trish laughed. "Wow, Blue Riley wants to get drunk! Grace must have done you in. I think Anna will be back in town soon. I'm sure she'd like to see you," Trish said, the insinuation in her voice taunting me.

"Grace and I are fine," I said with more certainty than I felt. "I just want to get drunk, okay?"

"Yeah, okay. I'll be there in a few hours."

A few minutes after one, Trish's car horn beeped into the chatter of "The Donahue Show." Barney and I unfurled our lazy bodies from the couch and walked outside. Trish hopped out of her blue Nissan 280-Z with a half empty Tar Heels glass in one hand and her Jack Daniels bottle in the other.

"Don't you think it's a little early for that?" I said, pointing at the whiskey bottle as I walked toward her, Barney at my heel.

"Get my bag, whiner," Trish smiled.

I grabbed her duffle from the front seat and put my arm across her shoulder. She looked up at me with a hint of whiskey drifting in her breath. "So you want to get drunk, huh?" Trish said, more as a statement than question.

"I think I do."

"I had a couple on the way over to get a head start on you. Two drinks and you'll be smashed . . . fuckin' lightweight."

Barney's nose pressed against Trish's Levi's, sniffing up to her knee and back down to her stark white Adidas tennis shoes. Trish looked down at Barney. "Sorry, buddy, I'm not Grace."

I watched him work his way around her pants cuff. "I think he knows that. Ralph has been in mourning all day. He wouldn't even get up when I came outside."

"And I had to come all the way from Asheville to work on you," Trish said as she walked into the house. "This Grace woman must be something else."

"Yep, she is."

In the kitchen, I pulled a highball glass out of the cabinet and handed it to Trish. She filled it with ice and poured in two fingers of whiskey. "Does that look like enough?" she asked, holding the glass up to me.

My eyebrows shot up. "I definitely think that will do." I sat down on a stool and watched Trish top off the whiskey with Coke. "Why does life have to suck so much?"

Trish looked up, a bit startled. "Whoa there, cowgirl." She walked around and handed me my drink. "I thought you said it was all good with Grace."

I shot her a sour glance. "It is all good with Grace. That's just it.

Things are great, and now I've got to go three weeks without seeing her."

"You can't go up there?" Trish asked.

"Not likely. Her parents will be home sometime soon. I don't think she wants to introduce me to them. Not yet, anyway."

Trish hmm-ed.

"I know. You can say you told me so."

Trish shook her head. "No, my friend, saying I told you so won't help a thing."

"So what will?" I asked dully.

"A road trip." Trish looked at me as if there were really no other answers.

"A road trip? A road trip to where?"

"Virginia, dumbass. Where else?"

"We can't just go up to Virginia and barge into her parents' house."

"Good God, Blue Riley!" Trish jumped up from her stool and shot an annoyed glare on me. She strutted to the kitchen with her chest puffed out like a rooster. "You are one sad-assed dyke." She grabbed the whiskey from the counter and tipped in a good measure to freshen up her drink, then spun around to the freezer for more ice. She looked thoughtful as she poured more Coke into the mix. "Do you want this woman or not?" she asked as the Coke settled.

"Of course I do," I grumbled.

"Well, then, you've got to show her you aren't going to let all this bullshit get in your way." Trish grabbed her drink and again started a cock-of-the-walk strut. "Now, you know I have friends all over the place, so I'll make some calls tonight to make sure we've got a place to stay if we need it. Then it's up to you. The way I see it, you've got to be a little crazy for her. Show her that you aren't gonna let anybody or anything stop you from seeing her, including her rich-bitch parents."

Trish now stood right in front of me, one hand on a hip, looking at me with the determination of a pregame coach. I had to laugh. Beneath her bravado Trish was actually making sense. "You're right, my friend. Tomorrow, we'll go to Virginia!"

Trish grinned. "Good! Now get the cards out and let's get drunk."

14

Mercy

A quarter mile of white board fence passed at forty-five miles an hour. Trish slowed her car, down-shifted into second, and turned right at the sign for Lee Oaks Farm.

"Jesus, Blue, look at this place."

Eyes wide, I hunkered down like an animal at prey. An alley of thick-trunked oaks arched over an asphalt driveway. At the top of the hill the Lancaster mansion loomed with the hair-raising bluster of a waiting battalion. My fingers rolled into nervous fists and I swallowed hard.

"Are you sure Grace is here alone?" Trish asked. Her gaze darted about as she crept up the driveway. The fact that Trish was in awe of the place worried me even more. I figured she had seen plenty of haughty spreads in her lifetime.

"That's what she said. Her parents and sister are in New York and her brother is still in school. No one is supposed to be here but the caretaker and his family."

Lee Oaks Farm looked like a tourist postcard under the day's pale blue sky. Every few hundred yards the white horizontal lines of a three-board fence curled into separate pastures. Saddlebreds covered by forest green blankets bent their muzzles to the ground and grazed near a grand gambrel barn set a couple of hundred yards east of the house. Oak trees scattered about the pastures reached bare limbs toward the sun, at rest until spring. There was nothing sinister in sight to cause the quickening of my pulse, yet it was off like I was being chased. In a way, I felt I was.

"Did you bring the Jack?" I asked.

"It's in my bag," Trish said. Her bugged-out eyes were locked on the Federalist-style brick manor. "I don't know what to make of you wanting to drink two days in a row."

"Who said anything about wanting to? I felt like shit this morning."

"So you're looking for a little liquid courage, huh?" Trish pushed my shoulder and grinned. I wanted to punch her arm, but she held the keys to the escape car.

"I can't wait to see the inside of this monster," she said when we topped the hill. She pulled up next to the entrance walkway and reached for the parking brake. "I wonder if it has an indoor pool."

I stared at the immense frame of the black door, expecting to be greeted by something grand or frightening; maybe a butler, or a barrel-chested man wearing mirror shades and a frown, or a frothing dog charging toward us. The door swung open and there was Grace, standing in the doorway in shorts and a baggy cotton sweatshirt, her hair pulled back in a ponytail and her freshly tanned skin glowing in the early afternoon sun. I swung out of the car with an unbridled grin.

"You must be Grace Lancaster," Trish said. She bounced around the long hood of her car with her hand held out.

"And you're Trish Youngblood. I've heard so much about you," Grace said politely. She took Trish's hand. "Blue adores you, you know."

Trish drew back her head and looked at me with a self-pleased grin.

"'Adore' would be a strong word for it," I said bluntly, and then broke into an easy smile.

Trish waved a dismissive hand toward me and turned her attention back to Grace. "I see already I'm gonna like you."

Grace smiled and slipped her arm inside the crook of Trish's. She walked by me with a promising glance. "Blue didn't tell me her friends were so charming. I need to keep an eye on her."

"You probably should," Trish said as they walked together through the front door. "Blue Riley is only the hottest dyke in Chapel Hill right now." Trish cut her eyes back at me and grinned. I suppose she thought she was helping me, though I hoped Grace and I were past the need to rely on jealousy to keep us going.

My first step onto the marble floor of the entryway echoed

through the cavernous walls of the first floor. Why in the hell I had worn cowboy boots? "Should I take off my boots, Grace?"

"Not yet," she replied with a devilish smile. She turned her attention back to Trish and led her up the hallway. Grace was so fuckin' good at this stuff, making Trish feel special because later on we would be leaving her alone for a long while. She kept her arm looped into Trish's as they turned left into a massive sitting room covered by rich, red, gold, and blue tapestry wallpaper.

"This house is well over a hundred years old, so it has some interesting features," Grace said.

"Ghosts?" Trish asked.

"My parents won't allow that."

"Good thing, I'd hate to end up in the bed with you and Blue tonight."

"*I* wouldn't allow that," Grace said, laughing.

"Me either," I added. I stayed a couple of steps behind them to give Trish all of Grace's attention. Plus, I needed a few moments to take the place in, to try to imagine a childhood growing up in this house full of irreplaceable relics. There must have been rules, and expected behavior so proper that even smiles were only allowed at the appropriate time. Was Grace using me to break away from those rules?

The Christmas tree situated between the sitting room's two doors looked to be at least ten feet tall. We stopped there and I looked up at the sweet face of the angel perched on top. Her grace-filled eyes seemed to be looking right at me. *Mercy.*

"Do you play?" Trish asked, making her way to the baby grand piano in the far corner of the room. She sat down on the leather bench and lightly touched middle C and D.

"A little. The piano is mostly for my parents' parties. They always hire somebody to play." Grace grabbed my hand with a look that told me not to even ask for a song. "Come on, I'll show you the rest of the house." She laced her fingers in mine and pulled me out of the room.

Her hand grew warm as she led us through the library, lined floor to ceiling with hardback books and record albums, then into a smaller sitting room behind the library, a billiards room, and finally into the formal dining room. The mahogany inlay table looked like it could easily seat thirty guests. A short stack of dry logs waited beside the marble mantel of the fireplace. Grace dropped my hand and leaned against an intricately carved chair at the corner of the table. "So that's the formal part of the house." She glanced around the room and then looked at Trish. "We don't use any of those rooms except for holidays and special occasions. My parents like to entertain, so we have lots of dinner parties and stuff down here. Come on upstairs and I'll show you where we actually live."

Trish and I fell in behind Grace as she started up the stairs. I noticed Trish's eyes set on Grace's ass. I thought again about punching her, until I looked up at Grace's firm bare legs. I couldn't blame Trish.

"My mother and father decided to modernize this floor when they moved in," Grace said when we reached the top of the stairs. She swung to her left and then turned into the first bedroom. "This will be your room, Trish."

I rocked back on my heels and looked around. I'd seen rooms like this before, in magazines like *Southern Living* or one of those decorator monthlies. A light golden spread covered the four-poster bed, the spread a shade darker than the sheer curtains, and a perfect match for the floor-length drapes. By the window was a built-in bookcase filled with hardbacks. A rocking chair sat by the corner fireplace.

"Wow, I may not want to leave," Trish said. She walked over and picked up the TV remote from the bedside table.

"My room is on the other side of the bathroom across the hall." Grace lifted her thumb toward her room. "Come on, I'll show you guys the game room."

Grace led us to the end of the hall and into the only carpeted room in the house. My feet sank into the plush, cobalt blue carpet that stretched between pine-paneled walls. Unlike the formal and stuffy downstairs, this whole room said, "Play." There was an arcade-size pool table, a custom entertainment center, and the biggest television I had ever seen. In the far corner the lights of a pinball and Space Invaders machine flashed into the sunlight pouring through the windows. A red neon Maker's Mark sign hung on the wall behind the bar.

"Do you mind if we leave you for a while?" Grace asked Trish. "I need to take a shower, and I want to take Blue with me."

"Hell no, I don't mind," Trish replied. "I could stay in this room for days. I think Donahue is gonna have transvestites on his show today. That should be a blast. What time does it come on here?"

"I think at three," Grace said. She looked at Trish with an amused grin, like she was watching a puppy. In an entirely different manner she turned to my eyes. "Come with me?"

Oh yeah . . .

Grace took my hand as we walked down the hall. Wordlessly she closed her bedroom door and wrapped her arms around my shoulders. "Baby, are you okay? You haven't said much."

"I've never been in a place like this, at least not that anybody still lived in." I tightened my arms around her back and brushed my cheek against the soft skin of her neck.

She lowered her head to my shoulder. "But you knew I lived in a really big house, right? I've never hidden that from you."

"Knowing it and seeing it are two different things." I leaned back to look into her eyes.

She held my gaze. "I know where I'm from, Blue, and I know I want you." Moving her hands to caress my face she kissed me with the certainty I needed.

"Lie down on the bed," she said when our lips parted. "And take your shirt off."

I glanced around, still uneasy in her parents' house. "Grace, I don't know if we—"

"Don't be silly. My family's going to a show tonight, so you don't have to worry about them coming home early. Now lie down on your stomach and relax. I promise you won't be sorry."

"Can I take my boots off now?" I grinned as I walked toward her bed.

She cupped her chin in her hand and hummed. "I guess," she replied with a wicked smile.

I grinned and launched myself onto her bed and wrestled my boots off. My shirt came next, and I flopped face down in only my Levi's. With a satisfied sigh I closed my eyes. I heard her footsteps moving around the bed, and then there was the sound of an opening drawer, some shuffling through items, and the drawer closing. A match scratched into flame and then came the crackling of a candle wick.

Grace's knee sunk onto the bed beside me. She swung a leg over to straddle my back.

"I love this soft blonde hair," she said. She gathered my ponytail in her fingers and moved it away from my shoulder. "And I love that you keep it long."

"Like Samson in the Bible," I muttered against my pillow.

"The Bible, huh? I wonder what the Bible would say about this." She nibbled her way down my spine, her warm breath teasing my skin.

Holy . . .

I squirmed and considered flipping over to pull her to me, though her teasing seemed too magic to stop. She pulled her lips away right before I completely lost it. "This was supposed to be a Christmas present, but I'm giving it to you early." She shifted to perch on my butt. I heard the top of a plastic tube break open, a pause, and then top closed and her hands rubbed together. Her fingers gripped my shoulders and squeezed hard. Liquid heat seeped into my skin.

"You are so tight; try to relax, baby." Her thumbs dug into the muscles at the base of my neck where most of my worry seemed to gather. The room became still as she squeezed and kneaded my shoulders, my neck, and down the center of my back. Somewhere in the glorious haze I lost my Levi's and Grace lost her sweatshirt. When her hands stopped I felt I could hardly move. My body seemed liquid and loose, like I could melt into the bed. She kissed my cheek and lowered her body full onto mine. She reached for my hands and wrapped her fingers around my palms. "Wanna take a shower with me?"

"Sure," I mumbled, though I doubted my muscles would remember how to move. Eyes half open, I watched her roll off the bed and stroll into the bathroom. Through the doorframe, I saw her shorts and panties fall to the floor. Suddenly I felt like moving. I shoved myself up from the bed and hustled into the bathroom. Grace only smiled as she stepped behind me and closed the door.

"Does Trish ride horses?" Grace asked. She wrapped her bath towel around her hair and reached for her robe.

"Yeah, I think she rides some." I flipped a plush beige towel over my head and started drying my hair.

"Good. Tomorrow morning I want to show you two around the farm, and riding horses is the best way to see it all."

"All?" I asked.

"It's only a few hundred acres. My mom inherited most of the land and the house."

"So your mom's family is rich, too?" I hung the towel on a hook and grabbed a hairbrush.

"That's the way it works." Grace flashed a smile over her shoulder and walked out.

Maybe that was the way it worked in her world. My world had different rules. How long could we keep playing our impossible game? I watched her get dressed and hoped it could be forever.

The first few flakes of snow hit the windshield as Trish pushed her car's gears from reverse to first. I stared at Grace, standing in her front door in blue jeans and a blue sweater. I thought I might cry from the wanting of her. If her parents weren't on the way home, I would still be wrapped in her arms.

"Did you tell her you love her?" Trish asked as we rounded the first curve of the drive.

"She knows."

"But you didn't tell her, did you? You spent two days with her and you didn't tell her."

"No, I didn't tell her. She knows I do, and besides, we could tell each other for a hundred years and it wouldn't change anything, would it?"

"You should tell her."

"I'll think on it." I slumped down and closed my eyes and tried to ignore the hollow growing in my belly.

15

Grace and Granite

Christmas night I sat on the couch with Barney curled up at my feet and Ralph on the floor beside me, all three of us waiting for Julie to come home from a string of emergency surgeries that started right after breakfast. On television Julie Andrews charged up a mountain meadow, her singing as beautiful as the snow-covered Alps. My mind drifted back to the first time I saw *The Sound of Music.* I went with my mom to the theater in Birmingham where it first ran, before everyone knew it as a classic. When we left the movie my mom looked strangely starry-eyed. She kept the same expression through our dinner of hot dogs and a milk shake at the glass-front diner we went to after the movie. I burrowed under my blanket and remembered Mom's smile.

By the time Mother Superior belted out "Climb Every Mountain," I couldn't stand it any longer. I grabbed the phone from the end table and dialed Grace's number. "Merry Christmas, Grace," I said. Conversation and laughter roared in the background. Grace had said there would be more than fifty relatives floating around their house for most of the night.

"Merry Christmas, Blue. Are you alright?" Despite my best effort, Grace seemed to have caught the crack of my voice.

"Sure. I'm fine," I said after I'd steeled myself. "I just called to wish you a Merry Christmas. I'm glad you were the one to answer."

"Is Julie there?" Grace asked, concern in her voice.

"Not yet. She said she'd be home around ten. She's bringing turkey and dressing from the cafeteria."

"That's just sad," Grace said with a chuckle. I imagined her smile and knew she was doing her best to cheer me up.

"It is, isn't it?" I had to laugh, too. Trying to pull off any semblance of Christmas tradition over a Styrofoam box at the kitchen counter seemed rather silly.

"Do you want me to come down there?" Grace asked. I heard enough sincerity in her voice to know she really meant it.

"You're supposed to be at home until after New Year's."

"I'll figure something out if you want," Grace said. An edgy silence fell between us while I considered my answer.

"Never mind, I'll be there late Saturday morning," Grace said.

Grace pulled a potato chip from the Pringles stacked on her paper plate. She popped it in her mouth and watched me take another bite of the homemade pimento cheese sandwich she had made for me.

"How long has it been since you were in Alabama?" Her eyes narrowed and her mouth twisted slightly, the expression she often wore when she was being cautious with me.

I stopped mid-chew and looked over at her. "Last spring. Why?"

"How would you feel about going there for a couple of days? We can go through Auburn and look around, maybe find the bookstore. I'll buy you a sweatshirt for Christmas."

"You already gave me too much for Christmas, and six hours is a long drive for a sweatshirt. Auburn will be dead anyway. They're on break like we are."

Grace frowned and was silent for a moment. She walked over to wrap her hands across my shoulders. "There is another reason I think you need to go to Alabama," she said as she lightly squeezed the base of my neck. I closed my eyes and leaned my head against her chest. Grace continued, her voice growing softer as her touch became lighter. "I've been here for two days now and you've been restless the whole time. Sometimes when I'm talking it seems you're not even listening, and that's not like you, baby. I think I know what's on your mind, and I only know one way to fix it."

"So how's going to Alabama gonna fix this . . . whatever?" I leaned forward, away from her hands, and picked up my sandwich.

"We'll go to see your parents."

My sandwich hit the plate. Fuck Grace! What did she know about what I was feeling, what I had been feeling since we drove away from her parents' mansion? What did she know of waving good-bye to your mom one morning, and coming home the next day to nothing? She had never had to pick out a coffin, or shake hands with hundreds of people who could only say, "I'm so sorry."

Grace swung around to stand in front of me. She kneeled down and tried to catch my gaze. Hesitantly she reached for my hand. I let her take it, though I turned away from her. How could she ask me to go there? What if I lost it when I looked at their names chiseled into matching granite headstones? Would Grace see the depth of my emptiness? Would she still want me? I swallowed against the knot tightening in my throat. "It's been hard this year. I'm not sure I want to go there right now."

"Okay. We don't have to go to the cemetery. How about we visit a couple of your old friends? Maybe Susan and some of your old teammates?"

Susan. I needed to see Susan. Susan had held me all those nights, and let me make love to her when it was all we knew to do. I could talk to Susan, and cry and curse and scream until I was again strong enough for Grace. I would tell Susan everything. She would understand.

I looked at Grace and nodded.

"We'll leave in the morning, huh?" she said. She stood up and moved her arms up to cradle my head. I pulled her in to keep me from the abyss.

Grace stood on the shore and watched me push the pontoon boat away from the pier. The morning frost had melted a couple of hours ago, and now the Alabama sun beamed from directly overhead. Susan sat at the helm of the boat. She clicked the engine into gear and we slowly moved away. Grace waved and headed back for the cabin.

The outboard engine hummed softly as we cut across glass-smooth water. I knew where Susan was headed. There was a small cove nearby that had somehow escaped lakeshore development.

Susan turned into the tree-lined cove and killed the engine. She scanned the shoreline, her face content. A breeze blew into the cove and caught the dark hair trailing from underneath her wool cap. For a moment I wondered what would have happened if I'd never left Alabama. "Do you remember this place?"

"Oh yeah, especially that time we swam under the pontoon." I raised my eyebrows suggestively.

"Hot August nights," she smiled. "I remember them well."

We were silent for a moment. I remembered those nights, too, and the night I first kissed Susan. We were on this lake, talking into the night after swiping a few of her father's beers. I had leaned toward her face, and she didn't lean away. It seemed my body exploded when our lips met.

"How are you, Blue?" she asked, pulling me back from my memories.

"I'm good," I replied. "I got A's again this semester, and Grace left her folks' house early to spend time with me. I've got my apartment and I spend a lot of time at Julie's. Life is pretty good right now."

"So why are you here?" By the solemn look on Susan's face, I knew she wouldn't allow any of my bullshit.

I shoved my hands into the pockets of my down jacket and shrugged. "I think I needed to see home."

She nodded. "Are you taking Grace to see the farm? The Taylors bought the piece up by the pond. They're building a couple of houses there."

I was glad to hear it. If anyone should have the pond where Dad taught me to fish, it might as well be the Taylors. "No, actually, I don't think we'll go by there. Maybe after they finish building, I'll stop by. It won't look quite the same as when I left."

She nodded again. "Grace said you're going by the cemetery tomorrow. Have you been by there since we went with Mom?"

"No, I haven't. I haven't been back to Alabama since then."

"Mom and I took some flowers by on your mom's birthday. Everything looked real nice."

"Thanks for doing that," I replied. I couldn't muster much more.

"We miss them around here, Blue." Susan paused for a long moment, and then continued in a gentle voice, "We miss you, too." She turned her eyes away before I could look at them.

I watched her for a moment, studying the face I knew so well, the face that had given me strength all the times I thought I was about to lose it. "It's you I miss the most," I said.

Susan did not look at me. She kept her eyes toward a forgotten bobber and fishing line that had become tangled in fallen tree limbs near the shore.

"I know I should call and write more than I do," I continued. "I want you to know that I think of you a lot. I haven't forgotten what you mean to me. That will never change."

She looked at me with a strained smile. "What I meant to you, you mean. I think you've gotten along okay without me."

"It may look that way." I said. I moved closer to her and leaned against the rail of the boat. "When I said I wanted to come home, I meant I wanted to see you. I can't think of the farm as home. It's all gone now. You're the one who I know I can count on."

"What about Grace? Where does she fit into all of this?"

"I want more than anything to know I can count on Grace. I love her so much it scares me."

"Why does it scare you?"

"Grace is different from us. She's from this big deal family up in Virginia. I don't see them ever welcoming me into the fold."

"Well, no matter what happens with Grace, you will live through it, Blue. You've survived one of the worst things that could happen to someone. Always remember how strong you are."

"If I'm strong, it's because you helped me get through it."

"And I will again if you need me to. I love you, Blue Eyes."

I stood up and pulled her into my arms, holding her in a tight hug. She rested her head against my shoulder. She felt so familiar; settling, even. Still, I knew something we once had was slipping away.

"So what did you think of Susan?" I draped my wrist over the steering wheel and turned my attention to the stretch of Interstate 65 that would take us to Calera.

"She's nice," Grace said. She hesitated before she added, "and pretty." I glanced over to see her eyebrows furrowed and her gaze fixed straight ahead. "I have to admit I got a little concerned when you guys were out on the boat for so long."

"Concerned?"

"Yeah. I mean, you and Susan were really close, right?"

"Yes, we were. We still are, but you don't need to worry. I love Susan, but not in the way I love you." There, I said it out loud. The look on Grace's face tempted me to pull off the interstate and find the nearest abandoned dirt road. Instead I leaned up and cradled the steering wheel. "So now you know how I feel when you go out on a date with a guy."

She looked straight ahead. "That's different."

"Oh!" I said with a caustic laugh. "How is it different?"

"The guys I go out with aren't pretty." She flashed a seductive grin. She reached across the cab and ran her hand along my thigh. Grace was quickly learning how to turn my moods. I laced my fingers into hers and moved our hands to rest on the truck seat. We kept them there until the Calera exit, our fingers gliding over and around.

I looked up at the English ivy trailing down from the white wrought-iron arch over the cemetery gate. The sky above the arch seemed such a delicate shade of blue, as if in condolence to those milling about, placing flowers and wreaths and dragging fallen tree limbs away from headstones. I pulled into a parking space and switched off the engine. The truck door squeaked when I swung it closed. The door had never squeaked before, and I had a crazy thought that the truck was trying to say hello to my dad. I shook the thought from my head and reached into the bed of the truck for the holly wreaths we bought at a Christmas tree stand a few miles from the cemetery.

"Come on, let's go do this. I'm ready to get to Birmingham." I regretted the tone of my words as soon as I said them, yet the whole idea of what we were doing seemed like a waste of time. Mom and

Dad were gone, and a thousand visits would not bring them back—at least that was what I had forced myself to accept. Grace frowned and said nothing as we walked up the hill to the graves.

"Here we are," I said as we drew close. Grace stopped a few feet back and handed me the wreath she carried. I walked up to Dad's headstone and leaned the wreath against the black granite. The other wreath I leaned against Mom's. In the shine of the granite was the worst day of my life: May 5, 1978—the day of the tornado. I kneeled there, staring at that date, too empty and numb to be angry. I wanted anger. At least anger felt alive.

A minute or so passed before I heard Grace's footsteps. She kneeled down beside me and pushed a few errant sprigs back into the wreaths. I stood up and waited. "Mom was a botanist," I said as I watched Grace work the holly. "She would tell you that the wreaths are made of American holly, and if you showed interest, she would go on to tell you the range of where it grows, and why it's important for birds, then she'd tell you why we use holly to decorate in winter. She liked to teach me the names of things and why they're important. She said the more you know about something, the more likely you are to take care of it."

Grace nodded. "I would have liked that about her." She pushed the last sprig into the deep green leaves and sat back on her heels to look over her work. Satisfied, she reached up for my hand. I pulled her up, and for a moment we stood there until, strangely, I became aware that I had made no introduction.

"Mom and Dad," I said, talking to them for the first time since the day they died, "I want you to meet Grace Lancaster. I go to school with her at Chapel Hill."

"Your daughter is amazing," Grace said when I had become too quiet. "She's smart, and beautiful, and she pulled me through statistics, which was not easy. You would be proud of her. Her aunt Julie is good for her, too." Grace reached up and rested her hand on my back. "Now if you don't mind, I'm going to let your daughter talk to you alone."

She stepped away and I stood very still, staring at my mother's name. I wanted to tell her so much. I wanted to tell her of all of the things I had been thinking and feeling since she left. I hardly knew where to start.

"Mom, do you remember telling me that I wouldn't fall in love but once? Well, I think Grace may be the one. I know I'm in love with her. The problem is she's from a rich family. She's in a sorority, can you believe that?" I let out a short laugh and continued, "Me with a sorority girl; I know you're probably laughing." Then I remembered my mom didn't *know*. Julie said she probably suspected, but she didn't *know*.

"I don't know how you would feel about me being with a girl. I think you knew I might be headed that way, and I know how you and Dad felt about Aunt Julie. I want to be like her, Mom. She's well respected in Raleigh, and I want that, too. I know it can happen if I do the right things, so don't worry, okay?"

I looked over at Dad's name. Dad had loved his sister fiercely. More than once, I overheard him defending Julie to a close-minded classmate or a fellow church member.

When I spoke again, I talked to both of them. "Grace sees me in a different way than anyone ever has. It's like we've known each other for a long time, even though it has been only a few months. She seems to know what's going on inside when I get down. We've got an amazing connection. It's a little scary too, you know. I don't know what will happen with us. But it's okay because I know she's good for me now. She talked me into coming here, so you can thank her for that."

A gust of wind rushed across the cemetery, sending clusters of long-forgotten flowers tumbling across the grass. I bent down to catch a clutch of plastic poinsettias and sat down on the ground next to Mom and Dad. I grasped the flowers between my hands as I told them about school, my grades, the mountains, Grace's fly-fishing skills, my friends. I must have talked for twenty minutes or so. Finally, I felt I'd said enough. I stood, dusted the dirt and grass from my pants and looked up to the soft blue sky.

"Tomorrow's New Year's Day. Nineteen eighty-one. There's a new president coming in: Ronald Reagan, if you can believe that."

I turned to Grace. She smiled and started toward me. Her arm slipped around my waist, and together we looked at their headstones. "Well, we better go now," I said after a long moment. "I miss you every day. I'll come by again soon, okay?"

16

Silver

Grace rolled over on top of me and pinned my arms down with her knees. "What'd you get me for Valentine's?" she demanded, her smile eager and growing.

I looked up at her bare chest and wildly tossed hair, wondering how she still had the energy to move after the last two hours. Five minutes ago she had drained my body for the fourth time. The last orgasm, I came so long and hard I thought I'd passed through heaven's gates. "Don't you think what we did this afternoon is enough?" I teased. "How many ways do I need to show you that I love you?"

"Oh, I don't think you've even started," Grace chuckled. She rolled off my chest and pushed her body against mine, settling her head on my shoulder. "But, I'll give you thirty minutes to rest if you'll give me a hint of what you got me."

I moved my hand to the curve of her hip. "It's silver," I said.

She wiggled in closer. "Silver, huh? It better not be anything expensive. We said nothing over ten dollars."

"It was a dollar-fifty," I replied.

She trailed her fingers across my breastbone, her brows furrowed in thought. "A dollar-fifty. It's not anything tacky, is it?"

"Nope, nothing tacky about it." I slipped from under her and leaned up on an elbow. "I'll go get it," I said after a quick kiss to her forehead. I crossed the room to my dresser and pulled out the red envelope hidden underneath my socks.

"Ah ha!" Grace said, laughing. "I knew you had a card around here somewhere. Give it to me," she said, her hands beckoning me toward her.

I leapt into the bed and crawled next to her, triumph beaming across my face. "Here you go," I said. She reached for the envelope and I playfully pulled it away. "Wait, let me make sure I didn't get this one mixed up with the one for my other girlfriend."

Grace popped my arm. "Like you could handle another girlfriend," she teased. She grabbed the envelope, her face becoming curious at the weight of it. "What's in here?" she asked, pulling at the seal. The silver key fell onto her belly and bounced off onto the bed. She reached for it, her smile growing.

"It's for my apartment," I said. "You should be able to come over anytime you want. I made some room in one of my drawers for you, too."

Grace threw her arms around me, the key clutched in her fist. "Thank you, Blue. I love it, and I love you, too."

I pulled her to me and said, "I never get tired of hearing that."

"I never get tired of saying it," she replied.

"Just be sure I'm the only one you say it to."

She settled again against my side. "You're the only one, outside of my family. I promise."

"Your family: my only competition."

I meant to tease her, though as the words settled over us, I felt the truth of it. I knew I didn't have any competition from the boys she dated. As much as I hated the thought of her having to kiss them, or do things I could not allow myself to think about, I knew she didn't love them. Some of them she barely even liked. Her parents were another story. Helen and Daniel Lancaster were used to getting what they wanted.

"Speaking of your family, what does your mom think about you not going to the Valentine's Dance?"

Grace grimaced and shifted her knee across my leg. "Let's just say the phone line got *really* quiet when I told her I wasn't going. Then I said it was because I didn't have a steady boyfriend, and she got better. I could tell she still didn't like it."

"Do you think she knows about us?" I asked.

Grace let out a nervous chuckle. "I sure haven't told her."

"I didn't think you would," I said, smiling to keep things light. "But, no matter what happens with your family, I'll be right here with you."

"Good." She lifted her head from my shoulder and looked at my face. "What's all this talk, anyway? I think you're stalling," she said as her fingertips slowly moved up my thigh.

I stood beside Trish in her backyard, taking a break from our Spades game and giving Laney and her new girlfriend Beth a few minutes alone. "God dang it, the moon is pretty tonight," Trish said, her breath streaming out white into the cold night air. She lifted her glass skyward in a toast to the gods. "Take care of my friend Blue Riley. She's got it bad for a beautiful woman, and you know how that goes."

"Hey, what does that mean?" I protested.

Trish turned to me and grinned. "Oh, nothing. I've only been watching you fidget all night. I bet you don't even know what the score of the game is right now."

"We're up by three, and Al Wood has twelve at the half," I replied. "And you and I are up on Laney and Beth by 120 points."

Trish nodded, though she still had that "Trish knows all" look on her face. For the life of me, some days I couldn't figure out why I hung out with her so much. She harassed me like we were sisters or something. "We're up by 120 because I keep pulling your ass out of the fire. I swear, when you threw down that queen of spades I thought I was gonna have to kill you. You'd better tell me you were thinking about Grace when you did that, 'cause if you weren't, I'm gonna need a new spades partner."

"That was pretty stupid, wasn't it?" I said. I tipped back my beer and took a long swallow. "I have been thinking about Grace tonight." I shoved my free hand deep in my pocket to keep it warm. "She's out on a date with some new guy. I hate it when a new one comes on the scene. Guys she's dated a few times I know a little about. She tells me what she thinks about them so I don't worry, but every new guy is something else to worry about."

"I don't see how you do it. I wouldn't have the patience to share Grace with anyone."

I shivered, though I wasn't sure if it was from the cold or from the thought of sharing Grace with a man, a man who was clueless about me, or for that matter, a man who was clueless about Grace. The poor guys probably spent the entire date trying to impress Grace, and all she wanted was to get away from him and back to me. *Totally fucked up.*

I peered over at Trish with a clever smile. "I won't have to share her when we go to New Orleans."

Trish whipped around and looked at me. "New Orleans? What the hell are you talking about?"

My smile grew. "Me and Grace are going to New Orleans over spring break."

"New Orleans? Why New Orleans? Nobody goes to New Orleans on spring break. Besides, aren't you supposed to go with us to Florida?"

"I was going with you guys until Grace asked me to go to New Orleans. We're going there because it's a cool city, and like you said, nobody goes to New Orleans on spring break. We'll have the whole town to ourselves."

Trish stared at me, her mouth gaping open in total awe. "That is pure genius, Blue Riley. You guys may find a way to make it after all."

"God, I hope so," I replied.

17

Prodigal

Grace rested heavy on my arm, breathing slow and easy. I kissed her on the shoulder, momentarily savoring the slight taste of salt that lingered on her skin. Careful not to wake her, I slid out of bed and walked to the hotel window.

Outside, the Quarter was coming to life. In the doorway of the pub across Royal Street a drunk bumped into the morning cook and stumbled down the sidewalk, passing a family dressed for Sunday Mass. On the corner a fortune-teller in her shimmering gold jacket crossed the street and headed toward Jackson Square carrying her purple, glittered sign and her card table.

New Orleans. Prodigal City.

Grace let out a soft moan and turned in our bed. She settled and again became still. I folded into the crook of the window seat in our room and watched her sleep, remembering last night. We'd danced at Charlene's Club until sweat and smoke covered our bodies, and then caught a cab back to Bourbon Street, where we walked hand in hand, teasing the boys on the way to our room. Grace had closed the door and come to me, and we made love to the steady beat pounding into our room from the streets below.

She opened her eyes and blinked hard, her face buried deep into her pillow as she looked at me. "Good morning."

"Morning, beautiful. Are you ready for coffee and beignets?"

She groaned and rolled into her pillow. "Are you always hungry?"

"Are you always so lazy?" I settled next to her and swept my fingers through her hair. "We have to pack up and leave soon, you know."

She rolled onto her side and traced my arm with her fingertip.

"What if we stay another day? We can change our flight to tomorrow."

"We'd be cutting it close for classes. Remember I have an eight o'clock on Tuesday."

"I know, but we don't have to be back until then. I want to spend a perfect day with you, and maybe this could be the day."

"What was wrong with yesterday?" I leaned down and kissed her cheek.

"I can do better," she whispered.

I popped the last bite of beignet into my mouth and licked powdered sugar from each fingertip. Grace grinned and sat back, settling her shoulders against a wrought-iron patio chair.

"We should go to Europe someday," she said. Her eyes skimmed the crowded tables of the Café Du Monde. "We could hike the countryside and stay in little cottages and sip wine in cafés and drive on the wrong side of the road."

"Hmmm, sounds tempting, especially the driving part." I smiled and watched the Mississippi River wind blow her hair away from her face.

"Would you want to go, though? Seriously, if you could go, would you want to?" She held her gaze on me now, her expression more questioning than hypothetical.

I shrugged. "I don't know. Europe seems so confining to me."

Grace frowned and reached over to rest her hand next to mine. With two fingertips she brushed my thumb. "So, if you could go anywhere you want, where would you go?"

"I'd like to go to Australia someday." I watched her fingertips slide across the stretch of my hand.

"Why Australia?"

"My dad had this book about it. It was mostly pictures, maybe a *National Geographic* book or something. There were photographs of these great beaches, and the Opera House, and aborigines, and brilliant red sunsets on the Outback. On rainy Sunday afternoons I would sit in front of my father's chair, looking at that book and dreaming about going there to see all of those things. If I got the chance, that's where I'd want to go."

Grace must have noticed the distant look growing in my eyes. Until that moment I had forgotten about my dad's book. "Hey, maybe one day we'll go there together." Her palm covered my hand, gentle as the morning. "But today we're not going to think about that, okay? We're going to think about being in New Orleans and buying a painting and listening to jazz and watching the Mississippi roll its muddy self to the Gulf."

"That sounds great." I returned her easy smile and looked up to her eyes, set with kind determination, yet so ready to dance with joy. Today I wanted another day of joy. I turned my fingers into hers. "Have I told you today that I love you?"

"You have now," she said. She squeezed my fingers, the joy now spreading across her face. "Now let's get out of here. You've got a painting to pick out."

Grace held onto my hand and pulled me toward Jackson Square, to the paintings and the tourist carriages and the sprawling live oaks and the street performers. We walked arm in arm, shopping the canvases that hung on the black wrought-iron fence surrounding the Square. We wanted them all: bright reds and yellows surrounding black silhouettes of jazz men with their saxophones leaned out from their chests; ghostly gray scenes of deep-shaded Louisiana bayous; muted watercolors of the old homes of the Garden District. We circled the perimeter twice before settling on a jazz man playing to a bright red, bleeding heart dripping from the top corner of the canvas.

Grace pulled out two twenties to pay the gap-toothed artist. He grinned when he gave me the canvas he had wrapped with plain brown paper. We both thanked him with a promise to cherish his work and headed through the center of the Square. In the shadow of Jackson's statue I caught the eye of the gold-jacketed fortune teller I had seen from the hotel window. She looked at me, her guarded stare and deep-set frown seeming to warn, *Child, if you only knew.*

My heart pounded at the pull of her gaze. I turned away from her stare and picked up our pace. What could she know, anyway? She was just a hustler trying to make a few bucks off tourists and sailors. At least, that is what I told myself as we turned north for Preservation Hall. Her grave eyes kept haunting me, even as we stood along the plain walls of the Hall to watch weathered hands pulling out jazz from instruments that seemed as old as the Mississippi River itself.

Thunder rolled against our window. In the next burst of lightning, I saw Grace's content eyes and the ease of her mouth. I pulled her closer to my side and waited for the next flash to light her face. Perfect.

"Let's not go back," she said.

"I've got to," I replied as I moved my fingers down to stroke her arm. "My Micro prof takes attendance and I've already missed once. I think you were involved in that decision."

"I don't mean don't go back tomorrow." She shifted and leaned on an elbow. She smiled at me and said, "Let's not go back at all. We can live here in New Orleans. You can be a wrestler in one of those bars on Bourbon Street and I can study to be a fortune-teller."

I laughed. "As tempting as that sounds, I think I'd rather finish school. I'd prefer to stay out of the shady lady wrestling ring." I reached up for the softness of her hair. "After school we can come back here to live if we want. How does that sound?"

Grace dropped her head to my chest and let out a long sigh. She didn't say a word. The easiness of the room slowly vanished as silent seconds clicked by. I lay still and stroked my fingers through her hair, sinking in the dread of things we couldn't change.

18

Falling from Grace

In the brilliant sunlight pouring through my apartment door I saw the squint of Grace's red, swollen eyes. Beside her empty wine glass a couple of crumpled tissues littered the occasional table. I tossed my daypack onto a kitchen chair and walked over to kneel in front of her. "Hey sweetheart, what's up with the crying? Were finals that bad?"

Grace shook her head and looked down, saying nothing. I took her hands and waited for something, any clue. Her palms turned into mine and she opened her mouth. Nothing came out. A tear streaked down and caught at the corner of her chin. Her mouth closed as another tear spilled from her eyes.

I inched toward her and tightened my fingers around her hands. "Look, baby, I know you're going to Germany for a few months, but you'll be back before you know it. I'll be right here waiting for you." Her gaze dodged mine as I searched her face. "Tomorrow we're going to the mountains, just you and me. You and your fly rod can kick my ass for the tenth time."

She sucked in a broken breath and tried to smile.

"Grace, what is it? Did something happen to your family? Just tell me what's wrong." I swallowed hard as panic started to pound in my head. She couldn't be sick; we were too young. I knew Grace's body; healthy and perfect. I looked it over; clear, tan skin, strong shoulders, firm breasts, flat stomach. I stopped cold and stared at her belly. What if?

"Grace, you're not pregnant," I said with a quiver of panic breaking my voice.

She shot an indignant glare at me and bolted from the chair. She stopped in the middle of my apartment and wrapped her arms across her chest. "I meant it when I said you would be the only one."

I exhaled a silent thank God. "Okay, fine, we can play twenty questions all day if you want, or you can just tell me what the hell is going on. If this is about you going to Europe, you're selling us short. It's only for the summer."

"It's not only for the summer." Grace's hoarse voice hung in the air like choking poison.

"What?" I shook my head and tried to absorb what she had said.

"It's not just for the summer, Blue." She turned around to look at me. Tears spilled even as her eyes grew calm.

I stepped back when she came toward me. "Grace, what are you saying?"

She stood in front of me now, close enough to reach out for me, but she didn't. "I'm saying I'll be in Europe longer than the summer. My father lined up a job for me near Rome. I'm supposed to go there right after I finish in West Berlin. It will be more than a year before I'm back to finish school."

"That's not a problem, Grace. I'll apply to vet school at NC State. I don't have to go to Auburn. I'll still be a—"

"Blue, stop! Please!" She took a step toward me. The anger and confusion in my eyes stopped her short. "It's not that simple. My parents won't—"

"Grace, I've always known I'd have to fight for us. I'll graduate next summer and get a job here."

"I'm not keeping you from going to vet school; no way." She shook her head like a determined coward.

"I don't have to go to vet school. In a year I'll have my degree. I can get a good job and support both of us. Easily. I could."

"*Blue, you're not hearing me!*" She grabbed my wrist and stepped closer to me, her face inches from mine.

I fell silent and stared into her frantic eyes. Slowly, the corners of her mouth turned into a gentle smile, and at that moment I knew it was over.

"Blue, on the day I was born my parents started the invitation list for my wedding. We've always known they're not going to let me live my life with another woman—ever." Grace touched my arm. It felt like sin.

"You don't *know* what they'll let you do."

"I know my parents, Blue. I know what they expect." Her hands moved to the top of my arms. I let them stay there.

"Do you have to do everything they expect, Grace? Or have I just been some sort of lark for you?!"

"No, I love you more than anything." Her fingers dug into my shoulders. "That's why I want to protect you. My father may do things."

I threw my arms out to get her hands off me. "Oh! So now this is all about protecting me. Is *that* how you've rationalized this to yourself?! What bullshit!"

She looked at me fiercely but said nothing. A few apartments down, some asshole cranked up his stereo. Bass thumped against the apartment walls like the pounding in my brain. I spun away from Grace and slammed my hand against the wall. Hadn't I known this was coming? But it was supposed to be later, after she graduated. By then we could figure a way out of it—together.

"Do you want me to leave?" she asked.

I turned around and looked at her. She stood behind my chair, her face now ghostly pale. Maybe she was scared of what I'd do. Maybe she should be. I could do things, too. Hit the Lancasters back—hard. No, they would only take it out on Grace. I couldn't let them hurt her. I pinched the tears from my face and walked over to my bed. I sat down and forced myself to look at her. "How long have you known about this?"

Grace dropped into my recliner. She kept her face straight ahead, too much of a coward to look directly at me. "I've known about it for a while. My dad told me about the job after we got back from New Orleans. I've been trying to get out of it since then. This morning Dad called and said if I didn't take the job he would take it to mean I didn't care about my education, and I would have to find a way to pay for school."

"So you've known for, what, six weeks or so? And all that time you were lying to me?"

"I've never lied to you."

"You didn't tell me about this."

"But I did not lie to you."

"Oh!" I jumped up and paced to the wall. "So if you don't say it out loud it's not a lie?" I spun around to face her. She had no response. "I should have known, Grace. You lie to everyone about us. Somehow I thought you wouldn't lie to me."

She shook her head and turned her eyes to the floor. Her hair fell forward to hide her face. Grace was so good at hiding. For an instant I considered the misery of living like that, until my anger again rose like a demon inside me.

"Blue, I don't want us to end like this," she said as I paced past her. "Can we stay together until I have to go?"

I turned to her. She had to be fucking kidding me. But as much as I wanted her out of my sight, I could not bear to watch her walk out the door. In that instant, she would become another one I lost forever, and I couldn't bear it. My shoulders dropped as I shook away a coat of rage. "Just give me a few hours. I need to go for a run," I said.

Grace wiped the tears from her face and stood up, her back straight. Without another word she was gone.

I stared at the clock as it clicked from 3:59 to 4:00 a.m. Grace lay folded into my body, her hips molded against mine and her back resting against my chest. The bed still held the strong aroma of her, of us. I breathed in deep and remembered the desperation of the last few hours, how we moved, together but unconnected, each of us searching for something to take the pain away. Grace let out a single, soft whimper. She would be awake soon, and I knew I had to be the one to go.

I slipped out of bed and dressed in the dark. Shoeless I walked to the door and picked up my running shoes. In the dim light from the breezeway I found my keys.

"Where are you going?" Grace's voice came out in a hesitant whisper.

I froze and stood silent for a long moment, battling my insane urge to go back to her. "Julie's," I said as soon as I found the breath for words. I picked up my keys and held them in my fist. "Leave your key on the table."

Early morning glare streamed into my eyes as I turned into Julie's driveway. At the end of the drive I set the parking brake and looked over at the house. I'd been driving for hours to avoid the moment I had to walk through the door and face her. I'd have to say the words that had been swirling though my mind since I walked out of my apartment. *Grace and I broke up.* I knew the knot filling my throat would burst open and the tears would finally come. I refused to be a sobbing wasteland in front of anyone, especially Julie.

Barney and Ralph were in full chorus by the time I got out of the truck. Before the end of the doorbell chime, Julie opened the door. She looked at me with tired but kind eyes and turned away without a word. I followed her and the boys toward the strong smell of coffee.

"Barney and Ralph heard you drive up. By the look on your face, I'm guessing this has something to do with Grace," Julie said.

I grabbed a cup and poured my coffee. "Yep."

"How bad?" she asked.

"As bad as it gets," I answered, pouring cream into my coffee, staying cool as John Wayne. "We broke up." My throat tightened.

"Why?" Julie's steady voice felt like ballast.

"She's going to Europe this summer. She's not coming back for a year."

"And?"

I turned around to face Julie. She looked back at me, patient and clinical, giving me time. Maybe she knew the importance of giving a person enough space to hold tears in check. She'd had years to practice. I met her gaze and replied, "And her parents will be expecting a wedding in the next couple of years."

Julie nodded and picked up her coffee mug. She looked at me over the rim as she took a sip.

"I want to leave here for the summer," I said before I lost my nerve.

Julie set her mug on the counter and crossed her arms loosely. She swung her shoulders slightly and studied her feet. I knew that posture. It meant she didn't like what she was hearing. "Where do you want to go?"

"I was thinking I'd try Kentucky. Maybe see if I can get a job at one of the horse farms around Lexington. Mucking stalls sounds pretty good to me right now."

She shook her head. "Three years of education at Chapel Hill and you want to go muck stalls?"

"I can make contacts in the horse industry there. I'll need recommendations for vet school and there's a strong connection between Auburn and Kentucky. Most of the vets up there graduated from Auburn," I said, using the logic I'd rehearsed in early morning hours of driving. Truthfully, I only wanted to do something mindless and physical.

She raised a skeptical eyebrow. "What about the VCAT?"

"I'll study for it. I can take it up there, or maybe come back here for it. It doesn't matter."

"Just be sure you study." She picked up her mug and pressed it against her palm. "So, where do you plan to muck stalls?" Her haughty expression said she already knew the answer. Still, she wanted to hear it from me.

"I don't know. I'll figure it out when I get up there."

"That's not gonna work, Blue. No one is going to trust you around million-dollar horses without a recommendation. I've got a colleague over at Duke who has thoroughbreds up around Lexington. I'll give him a call."

I wanted to argue that I didn't always need her help, but I was too beat for another fight. "Just tell him I know horses. I can shovel shit without a Ph.D."

She grimaced and looked down into her coffee. "There's something else I want to talk to you about," she said. She looked up at me, her eyes keen. "You know I've always wanted you to make your own career choices—so long as it's not shoveling shit for the rest of your life. Over the summer I'd like for you to give serious thought to medical school. You may be selling yourself short if you settle for vet school."

Julie had never mentioned medical school. How long could she have been thinking about this? She wanted to control me, like always. "I wouldn't consider it selling myself short," I snapped. "I'd consider it doing what I want to do. And right now I don't like people very much."

Julie looked at me, unfazed. "You don't have to like people. You only have to like medicine."

"Vet school is medicine," I replied.

She shot me an aggravated glare. She put down her coffee and grabbed a loaf of bread. "I'll make you toast and eggs, and then you need to get some rest. When I get to work I'll call Dr. Pennington about a job at Calumet Farms."

I watched her pop a couple of slices of bread into the toaster. My head was pounding from lack of sleep, but I couldn't go back to my apartment. Ralph stood at my hip, nuzzling for my hand. I looked down and took his head in my hands. He looked up at me, his eyes understanding. Eat, sleep, feed and water the animals. Like my father said, it was the work of the earth that would get a person through.

19

Hit Me with Your Best Shot

Eastern Kentucky stretched out in front of me. The rough, jagged edges of the hills and the clamor of coal trucks seemed to taunt, "Are you tough enough for this?" After eight hours of driving I felt tough enough for anything. I slipped Pat Benatar into the cassette deck and sat back with my arm draped over the steering wheel, feeling untethered and slightly dangerous. Privilege is a fucking hard mistress, I told myself as I drove. My aunt's money and status were putting me through school, making connections for jobs, and maybe one day they would help me get into vet school. But privilege would only go so far. She would never let me reach as far as the Lancasters. She would never let me reach as far as Grace.

Privilege made Grace lie to me. Grace had known for weeks that she would be leaving for a year. Her father, with all of his graces, convinced her she would have no life without his privileges. Julie had been right. Trish had been right. People like us would never ride in the front of the bus, and people like Grace would never ride in the back. I had been a fool refusing to believe it. I would never be that naïve again.

Five miles south of Lexington, I pulled into a Waffle House for supper. At the newspaper box by the door I bought a *Lexington Herald* and walked on in. Two guys sitting at the bar in muddy jeans and sweaty t-shirts locked their horn-dog eyes on me. I gave them a cross glance and slipped into a booth on the back wall.

Somehow, every Waffle House in America looked the same as this one. The razor-thin waitress behind the bar lowered her cigarette to the ashtray and sauntered to my booth. She looked at me with a tired smile. "What can I get you, sweetie?" She sounded as if the life had been sucked out of her deep, raspy voice years ago. She flipped her order pad and focused on it while she waited.

"I'd like a cheeseburger, all the way," I said.

"Hash browns?" she asked without looking up from her pad.

"Yeah, hash browns and sweet tea."

"Cheeseburger, hash browns, and sweet tea," she repeated. She looked up and eyed me curiously. She opened her mouth to say something but seemed to think better of it and walked away.

I watched her slip my order under the clip above the cook, and go through the spiritless motions of pulling a glass from the rack and filling it with ice, like she had probably done for the past thirty years. I shuddered at the thought of such a life and opened up the *Lexington Herald* to the Rentals Want Ad section.

"Where you from, honey?" the waitress asked, setting my iced tea on the table.

I was never quite sure how to answer that question anymore. "Originally I'm from Alabama." I folded the rentals section into quarter size and put it down on the bench beside me. "I'm going to college in North Carolina right now."

She nodded and slipped one hand into the pocket of her black-trimmed apron. "You plan on staying in Kentucky for a while?"

"I've got a summer job working at Calumet Farms. I want to go to vet school after I graduate."

Her eyebrows arched and she nodded. "Well, good luck with school, honey," she said kindly. "There ain't no good jobs for women unless they got a college degree." She winked with a click of her tongue and turned away.

I watched her walk back to the grill. She was right. Without my aunt's money I would probably be just like her, stuck in some crappy job with long hours and little pay.

Privilege was a fucking hard mistress.

Two guys dressed in three-piece suits walked into The Huntsman Restaurant ahead of me. I'd figured my jeans might not meet dress code, yet I hadn't been able to bring myself to spend any of the three hundred dollars in my wallet on an acceptable pair of slacks. Before leaving the Motel 6, I'd pressed creases in my yellow button-down oxford. My least faded jeans would have to do for slacks. I sucked in a nervous breath and pushed through the revolving door.

The maitre d' looked up from his reservation book and frowned. "I'm here to meet the Wells party," I said. I swallowed and tried to smile at him. He was at least six inches shorter than me, yet his cold brown eyes made me feel small. He turned with a smirk and started toward the main dining room. I squared my shoulders and followed him.

Everything about the restaurant said money, from the sturdy walnut maitre d' stand, to the fox and hound décor, to the rich wood paneling and the brass railing leading to the bar. The waiters wore shiny black waistcoats as they flowed through the restaurant looking purposeful and efficient.

The maitre d' stopped beside a black leather booth in the far corner. Two young women sitting at the table stopped their conversation and looked up at me. In an instant the one in the blue blazer and khakis swung out from the booth and stood up, facing me with an eager smile. Perfect white teeth beamed from her eerily tanned face. "Hello, you must be Augusta Riley," she said. She thrust her hand toward me and I shook it. "I'm Rhonda Wells, the woman you spoke with on the phone this morning."

Rhonda tightened her grip and looked directly into my eyes. She had nice eyes. In the dim yellow light they appeared a deep shade of amber. She kept them opened a bit too wide, as if she were on guard for some impending calamity. "Nice to meet you, Rhonda. Most people call me Blue."

Rhonda cocked her head and her eyes narrowed. She pulled her hand from mine and turned it toward the woman sitting in the booth. "This is my roommate, Lilly Carter."

I looked at Lilly. Her eyes, calm to the point of seductiveness, leveled onto mine. Her lips turned up slightly when she reached for my hand. I clasped her soft palm and felt my face flush. "Blue Riley," I said, like a dork.

"Nice to meet you, Blue." Lilly looked at me with a patient smile, like a woman abiding the flirtations of a twelve-year-old boy. I glanced away and slid across the leather bench opposite her.

"So what do you think of Lexington?" Rhonda scooted next to Lilly and continued without waiting for my reply. "It's a great city, still small, but Louisville is not far, and Cincinnati is only about an hour. We go down to Lake Cumberland almost every weekend. I bought a boat last summer. What a beautiful lake, right, Lil?"

Lilly looked at Rhonda with an indulgent smile that seemed to ask, *Are you through?* She turned to me and said, "Yes, Lake Cumberland is great. Maybe you'll go with us sometime."

"Thank you," I replied. "I'll see how the summer goes." My eyes lingered on her. *Striking* seemed the best word to describe Lilly Carter. Thick chestnut hair fell in loose curls down to delicate collarbones that framed the shallow dip at the base of her throat. Her deep-set green eyes held on to everything—and everyone—for an unnerving extra second, and for the moment they were set on me.

Rhonda opened her menu and chattered on as she read. "I recommend one of the seafood selections. They have it flown in. So, Lilly, Blue tells me she has a job over at Calumet. She's going to school at the University of North Carolina. Coming up on her senior year, she says. She wants to be a vet."

I looked at Rhonda and then Lilly. Neither of them seemed to notice the incongruity of Rhonda's ramblings. "I see," Lilly said calmly.

"A little yard work won't bother you, will it, Blue?" I didn't get a chance to answer before she rambled on. "So, vet school is pretty ambitious. Have you applied?"

"No, not yet. I'll be applying this summer."

"Do you plan to go to vet school in North Carolina?"

"Maybe. My first choice is Auburn."

Rhonda looked up from her menu and smiled. "Oh, why is that?" She lifted a goading elbow into Lilly's ribs. "Did you hear that, Lil? Auburn."

I glanced from Rhonda to Lilly and back to Rhonda before I answered. The notion that I wanted to go to Auburn obviously made Rhonda happy. "I'm from Alabama," I said. "I've always wanted to go to Auburn, but my aunt wanted me to—well, I won't get into that right now. Anyway, I ended up at UNC."

Rhonda leaned toward me, as if to speak in confidence. "Lilly is a huge 'Bama fan. Starting in July, all I hear about is Bear Bryant and 'Bama football."

"She exaggerates," Lilly said. I could almost hear her finishing, *about everything.* Lilly paused and moved her sinewy hands to her lap. She looked at me with the calmness that Rhonda seemed to lack. "I graduated from The University."

"Hospital administration," Rhonda interjected. I nodded.

"I work at a nursing home," Lilly said. I nodded again.

A stocky, redheaded waiter in a black waistcoat now stood beside our table. He had moved in so unassumingly I hadn't noticed him until he stood beside us. With an elegance I did not expect from such a heavily muscled man, the waiter folded his hands and recited the chef's specials. He listened to each of our orders in turn, acknowledging each with a single nod and shift of his eyes. Lilly ordered last. I listened to the southern rhythm of her soft voice and imagined the frustration of the old guys at the nursing home. After Lilly ordered, the waiter disappeared as quietly as he had arrived.

Rhonda looked across the table and studied me for a moment, as if she wanted to tell me something, but she wasn't sure she should. She tapped a couple of fingers on the table and leaned forward on her elbows. "Look, Blue, I'm going to be straight up with you. We put that ad in the paper for a summer roommate because I have to spend a lot of time helping my mother. She's got health problems and I work long hours at the office. I don't have time to help Lilly keep the yard and the house up, so I agreed to give this a try. We'll take it a week at a time and see how it works out."

She looked at me and waited for my reply. I glanced over at Lilly. Her eyes were on me, too. I couldn't quite believe my luck. A room in a house with two professionals would beat a crappy apartment any day. "That sounds fair. I'd really like to give it a try," I said.

"Good," Rhonda said with a satisfied rap on the table. "I had my secretary call the references you gave me this morning. Everything checked out, so you're good to move in whenever you like."

I smiled agreeably. "I'll be happy to help with any kind of work you guys need." I looked at Lilly and smiled again, maybe for a bit too long.

Rhonda cut her eyes over at Lilly and then looked directly at me. "Is there anything else you need to tell us about yourself?"

I fidgeted with my napkin, considering whether the time was right to bring it up. They had given me enough clues to know they were a couple. Still, it was wrecking my nerves to make the first move. I leaned closer to them and said in a low voice, "I think you should know I'm gay. If that's a problem I'll look for another place to live."

Lilly smiled. "That's far less of an offense than being an Auburn fan," she teased. Our eyes met and held for a moment, and my face flushed with heat.

Rhonda's smile had faded. She cut her eyes at Lilly and then looked directly at me. "I've been through seven football seasons with Lilly. She didn't want to leave Alabama, but I got her to move up here right after she graduated. Obviously the gay thing won't be a problem. The Auburn thing I can't say." Rhonda's smile returned as quickly as it had left.

Lilly placed a bowl of black-eyed peas on the table of their breakfast nook and returned to the stove for the skillet of cornbread. Already she had brought over the plate of fried chicken and fried green tomatoes, and I stared at it all like a hungry kid.

"I'm glad you're here to eat dinner with me," she said as she crossed the kitchen with the cornbread. "Rhonda doesn't like a lot of country cooking, and I don't want to cook if it's only me." She sat down and settled into her chair. The food smelled so good I could forgive her Crimson Tide t-shirt.

I grabbed the bowl of peas and winced, my hands still sore from three days of being wrapped around a muck rake. "Rhonda's crazy to pass up this cooking," I said, smiling.

"Cooking reminds me of my grandmother. I used to go over to her house all the time when I was growing up. We'd can all kinds of vegetables and make jellies and things. I don't get to see her much anymore. It's too far to go home on weekends." We ate a couple of bites before Lilly said, "So, did you have a girlfriend back in North Carolina?"

I swallowed hard and nodded. "I did. We broke up right before I came here."

"I'm sorry," Lilly said. "Do you mind me asking what happened?"

"Her parents," I replied.

"Oh," Lilly said, nodding. She pushed her fork through her peas, contemplative for a moment. "I know all about that. Rhonda's mother barely speaks to me. It makes things hard sometimes."

"At least you're still together." I took a bite of cornbread to keep from having to say anything more. Grace and I could still be together if only she had the faith that Lilly had in Rhonda. If only Grace could tell her mother that all the cold shoulders and threats of ostracizing her from the family were not going to work. If only she could tell her father that she didn't need his money or his connections. If only, if, if, if—all the ifs I could name weren't going to bring Grace back. I figured there was only one way to get Grace out of my system, and that was to find the right distraction.

"Is there a gay bar in town?" I asked after a long swallow of iced tea.

Lilly glanced at me with a thin smile. "There is, actually. It's a new place downtown called The Bar, if you can believe that. Rhonda won't go, so I haven't been there. I've heard it's nice."

"Rhonda probably wouldn't approve if you went with me," I said, grinning.

Lilly's brows went up and she chuckled. "Probably not." She pushed her knife through the butter and spread it across a slice of cornbread. "But we can eat dinner together if you like. Rhonda usually doesn't eat at home during the week."

"I'd like that." I bit through the warm crust of my fried chicken and savored the tangy juice spreading through my mouth.

"Good. I was thinking I'd make a peach cobbler later tonight. I have some Chilton County peaches in the freezer I need to use."

Memories of my mother rushed in, though when I looked at Lilly, I felt we shared a similar longing for what we'd left behind in

Alabama. "Have I told you what happened to my parents?" I began.

Calumet Farms seemed to spread out forever. I slowed at the gate and turned in, still a quarter mile away from the stables. I breathed in the scent of an organic mixture of oiled leather, fresh grass and musty manure that tangled and drifted in from the west wind. As far as I was concerned, Calumet at daybreak was a picture of heaven. Today an orange-yellow sun brought first light to rolling green pastures that seemed to rise and vanish under the morning haze. Along the white-board fence young foals stood close to their mothers, their bobbed tails twitching about like nervous squirrels. I watched them graze, imagining in three years one of the foals would be thundering down the homestretch of Churchill Downs, the roar of the crowd in his frenzied ears, stretching and straining every muscle of his sleek body in an all-out sprint to the finish line; and then a blanket of roses in the winner's circle. The thought of it made my skin tingle.

I got out of my truck and walked toward the gleaming white stable next to the exercise track. Katie Logan was waiting for me. She leaned against the red trim of the door, staring at me with eyes loaded with piss and vinegar. Katie was good with looks like that. I had already been hit by them more times than I cared to recall. We had been dating for a couple of weeks—or, more like, leaving The Bar together and going to her apartment for sex. Last night I'd cut out early on her, before she could get me in bed again. It wasn't that the sex was bad. She had skills, but after a few nights I realized that even good sex with Katie was nothing like holding Grace while we slept.

Katie kept her eyes on me, arms crossed tight over her chest, like she had some reason to be mad, like I had promised her something. Her face was almost as red as the ponytail gathered beneath her riding helmet. She waited until I got close, gave me a smirk, and stormed off, leaving puffs of dust behind her angry footsteps. I watched her tight butt as she strutted to the far end of the barn. She stopped beside a prancing black thoroughbred and spoke briefly with the trainer.

117

With a leg up Katie popped onto the slip of a saddle draped across the thoroughbred's withers. She settled in and pulled the reins toward the track. Her small frame became a beautiful silhouette against the glare of morning sun. The sight of her taking control of the fiery thoroughbred stirred my body.

I watched her ride away and decided to find her at lunch. I would make a quick apology and promise to meet her tonight at The Bar.

The house was dark when I turned into Lilly and Rhonda's drive. Quietly I slipped in the back door to keep from waking Lilly. I turned into the den and found her stretched out on the couch watching a silent television. She looked over at me but didn't say anything. I sat down on the far end of the couch and turned toward the television. David Letterman grinned and snapped his fingers over some quip we didn't hear. Lilly frowned and reached over for her pack of cigarettes. I watched her tap one out and got up for a glass of water.

She glanced at me through a stream of smoke when I came back. "You're home early for a Friday night. I thought you had a date."

"She got drunk and passed out." I downed a couple of gulps of water and felt the cool seep through my chest. "When did you take up smoking?" I asked, keeping my gaze on the television.

"It keeps me awake."

"Where's Rhonda?"

"At the hospital. Her mother had another heart attack."

I swung around to face her, "*Another* heart attack?"

Lilly kept an unaffected gaze on David Letterman. "Yep. This is number two." She took a drag from her cigarette. I watched the smoke drift out of her mouth and I pushed my knee against her outstretched foot. "You okay?"

"Yep," she said through tight lips.

"Nope," I countered.

"What do you care? You'll just go find another girl to fuck."

I fell back and stared at her. "Whoa, now, what the hell is that about?"

Lilly turned to me, her jaw clenched tight. "Today I left work and went straight to the hospital. When I got there Rhonda had me wait out in the public waiting room, like I was nobody. She said it might raise suspicions if I waited with her in the family room."

I reached over and rubbed the top of her foot. "Suspicions? Whose?"

"Her brother, if he showed up. Her mother's preacher. Preacherman waited with Rhonda while I spent the day in a noisy room with fifty strangers. Seven years with that woman and she leaves me in the *public waiting room?*"

After my date with Katie, I wasn't in the mood for more drama. I gently squeezed the bridge of Lilly's foot, which was about all the compassion I could muster. "So, I guess everything's okay with Rhonda's mother?"

Lilly gave a sarcastic chuckle. "It will never be okay with Rhonda's mother."

"But, she made it through the heart thing okay?"

"Yeah, unfortunately she did."

I pulled my hand away from Lilly's foot. She seemed too proud of her words.

She swung around and leaned up to catch my gaze. "I'm so sorry, Blue. You know I didn't mean that."

"I didn't figure you did," I muttered.

She reached for my shoulder, but I wouldn't look at her. If she wanted a savior from her anger, I could not be it tonight. She leaned closer and trailed the back of her fingers down the side of my neck. I cut a warning glance at her and shook my head. She pulled her hand away and brought two fingers to her lips, watching me for a moment. From the corner of my eye I could see her eyes were apologetic. "Can I tell you about Rhonda's mother and me?" she asked.

Letterman went to a commercial and I stared at Mr. Whipple squeezing Charmin. Tonight I did not want to hear about parents, or disappointment, or breaches of respect, or facing the end. I did not want to hear about cowards at love or people who passed. Or think about Grace in West Berlin. And yet Grace was there, in every day and with every woman I kissed. Always, there was Grace. I would not change that by turning myself away from people who needed me. I looked at Lilly for moment before I answered. "If it will help, go ahead."

She grabbed a burgundy throw pillow from the back of the couch and clutched it against her chest. "I love Rhonda, but her mother hates me. I mean she really *hates* me."

"*Hate* is a strong word."

She dropped the pillow to her lap and slowly ran her fingers across the fabric, as if pulling her thoughts from it. "I don't know if she hates me. I know she blames me for Rhonda being gay, and she hates that for sure."

"Why does her mother blame you? Rhonda seems totally gay to me."

Lilly looked up, eyes wide. "She *is* totally gay. Her mother refuses to see it. She found out about us a couple of weeks before her first heart attack, and now Rhonda blames herself for that. I can't convince Rhonda that her mother's two-pack-a-day habit is what caused it, not finding out her daughter is gay."

"Rhonda's a smart woman. She can't really believe it only took two weeks for her mother to work herself into a heart attack."

"Rhonda says women don't have heart attacks unless something shocks them into it."

"*Come on,* she has to know better than that."

"Rhonda *wants* to feel guilty about being gay. Her mother gives her a great outlet to push all that neurosis into."

"So Rhonda's not comfortable with being gay?"

Lilly looked at me as if considering the concept for the first time. "Are you?"

"Yeah, I am. I don't feel guilty about being with a woman, if that's what you mean."

"I think Rhonda does." Lilly reached up to run her slender fingers through the thick curls of her hair. She spoke thoughtfully, as much to herself as to me. "I can feel it sometimes. I know she loves me and everything, but she always seems to be holding back. I think it's the guilt she feels. One of these days I want to be with a woman who doesn't feel guilty about loving me."

"Maybe one day Rhonda will get there."

"Or maybe one day I'll find someone else," Lilly replied, too quickly. She looked at me and her face flushed.

For a moment we sat stone still and stared at each other cautiously, as if we suddenly found ourselves at the edge of a cliff and had to back away slowly to keep from falling off.

20

Born to Run

Rhonda stood beside me at the edge of her lawn, holding a set of landscaping plans between her outstretched arms. She'd had the plans drawn up a couple of summers ago and still hadn't gotten around to getting the work done. Last night she had shown me the plans and asked if I could do the labor.

"If you're sure you want to do this, I'll pay you well," Rhonda said. "It will save me the trouble of dealing with a contractor, but I can wait until next summer if you don't want to fool with it."

"I'd really like to do it," I replied. "If you're good with it, I can get started this weekend."

Rhonda dropped the plans to her side and looked out across the thick carpet of Kentucky bluegrass covering her yard. A trickle of sweat ran down from her temple and caught at her chin. She handed the plans over to me. "I'm a little concerned about the maintenance after you're gone, but yeah, I think Lilly and I can handle it for a few weeks. I'll set up an account at the nursery so you can buy the supplies."

"Great," I said as I rolled the plans into a tight cylinder. Rhonda watched me, though her mind seemed elsewhere.

"Blue, I want to ask if you could do something for me. It has to do with Lilly."

Her expression worried me. I slipped the rubber band off my wrist and rolled it onto the plans, careful to avoid her eyes.

"The thing is, Lilly needs some kind of outlet. When we went through this heart thing with my mom a few years ago, she was alone almost the whole summer. It was hard on her since she was new in town and she had all the work at home to do. That's been better with you around to help. I'm still worried about her getting bored. Last night when I told her you might do the landscaping, she said she'd like to help you. Would you mind? She needs to stay busy, and you can show her how to do the maintenance."

I looked up at her and shrugged. "Sure, that's fine."

"With everything going on with my mother, I wouldn't worry as much if Lilly was busy helping you."

"I understand. I'll be glad to have her help." I glanced at the house. I needed a beer.

"Look, Blue," Rhonda stepped around in front of me and spoke discreetly, though there wasn't anyone around to hear. "I know what I've got with Lilly. I mean look at her, she's sexy as all hell. I don't want to mess it up with her. The thing is, I need time to deal with my mom, and Lilly shouldn't have to stay home drinking wine and smoking cigarettes every night." Rhonda stepped closer. "She might get restless, you know?"

I nodded. I definitely knew.

Rhonda continued to make her case. I wasn't sure why she went on; maybe to convince herself as much as me, or maybe because she scarcely knew when to quit talking. "I know Lilly is the right woman for me. She keeps me sane, but I've got to take care of my mother. I don't think Mom will live much longer, especially if she doesn't quit smoking."

What was it with these women and their death wish for Mrs. Wells? Rhonda sounded as if her mother were a burden. I couldn't imagine the luxury of having such a thought. "You never know. You should hope."

Rhonda nodded heartily. "You're right. I hope my mom lives forever." She rubbed the back of her neck and looked up to the towering summer clouds. Worry lines creased her forehead. "Something's gotta give, though, Blue. My mother doesn't like Lilly, and vice versa."

"Lilly mentioned something to that effect," I replied.

"See, that's why I need help." She looked at me intently and raised her hands to plead her case. "If you can keep Lilly happy for the rest of the summer, I should have something worked out for Mom by the time you leave for school."

"I may be able to keep her busy for a while, but you're the one who makes her happy."

Rhonda smiled. "She sure makes me happy. I'd do anything for Lilly."

Except stand up for her, I thought.

"*This* is where you've been going lately?" Lilly asked in a voice that questioned my sanity.

I pushed away a couple of canebrake stalks and held them back for her. "Yep, this is it." I grinned as she passed by me. Lilly turned her lip up in a teasing smirk and ducked under another leaning stalk. At the edge of the canebrake, Lilly swatted the gnats swarming around her face. She looked back as if she hated me. I wanted to laugh. She was so unlike Grace.

"Keep moving," I said in a prison guard voice.

Lilly straightened and marched forward through the patch of foot-high grass that grew beyond the canebrake. After the grass was a long stretch of sun-bleached river shoal—poor man's beach as my dad would have called it. It wasn't a fancy boat on Lake Cumberland or a weekend get-away to Myrtle Beach, but I hoped it was good enough for a hot July afternoon.

Lilly walked out onto the shoal and turned her face towards the sun. She looked over at me with a smile that lingered.

"Anywhere you like," I said, nodding toward the stretch of sand ahead of us.

She kicked off her sandals and strolled across the shoal. At a spot of white sand ten feet or so from the water's edge, she stopped and glanced up and down the river. Her beach bag dropped and she started unbuttoning her baggy, white cover-up.

My mother had taught me not to stare, but as Lilly's cover-up dropped past her shoulders I couldn't stop myself. I stared. I stared at her supple, tanned back, bare except for the string tied below her shoulder blades. Her ass got most of my attention. The roundness of it seemed to have been molded from a form of the perfect ass. My blood rushed when she bent over to spread her crimson and white beach towel over the sand.

Lilly didn't seem to notice. She kneeled at the edge of her towel and looked up at me. "You coming?"

Not quite. "Yeah, sure." I tossed my towel next to hers. It took all of my willpower not to stare at the two fine breasts barely hiding beneath the shining black fabric of her string bikini.

She crawled onto her belly and held out her suntan lotion. "Put some on my back?"

I used every distraction I could find to take my mind from the feel of her skin underneath my palms. At her shoulders I watched the swarm of yellow butterflies swirling about at the edge of the river. As I rubbed the small of her back and moved down to the line of her bikini bottom, I looked up and searched the sky for some curiosity in the shapes of the clouds. It wasn't working. I slid my hand around the curve of her hip to cover the final spot and jumped to my feet.

"Where are you going?" Lilly asked without opening her eyes.

"I need a quick swim to cool off," I said without thinking.

One eye opened and she looked at me with her suggestive little half-grin. My face flushed hotter than the sand beneath my feet. I turned away and peeled off my shorts and t-shirt. Headlong, I jumped into the water and started swimming upstream.

Alabama girls. Beautiful pains in the ass.

I had not expected this shift between us when I brought Lilly here. Yet, I felt it as certainly as the river flowing around me. Out here it was only me and Lilly—no Rhonda, no Katie Logan, no girls from the dance floor or the pool tables of The Bar. God help me, for today I wanted it that way.

Dripping wet I walked back to our towels. Sweat beaded across Lilly's top lip. I wanted to wipe it away and taste the salty skin of her mouth. I grabbed a Bud Lite from the cooler. "Don't you want to get in the water?"

"I told you there are snakes," she muttered.

I sat down with my beer and slipped it into my UNC hugger. On the far side of the river, curious turtles poked their heads out of the water. Lilly would freak if she saw them. "You swim in the lake, don't you?"

"Only the deep parts," she replied. Leaning on her elbows, she squinted in the sun. "It's so freakin' hot. Will you get me some ice?"

"The river will cool you off quicker than a drip of ice. You can jump in and come right back to your towel. I'll stay right beside you if you want."

She thought for a moment. "You'll keep the snakes away?"

"I promise." I stood up and offered my hand.

At the edge of the river Lilly slipped her arm into mine and tiptoed a few steps in. Shin deep, she teetered and grabbed my shoulder to pull her mud-covered foot out of the water. Her face scrunched at the sight of it. "This is really gross."

I had to agree with her. Organic brown mess slid down her foot and dripped into the water. "Yeah, I guess it is. You can ride on my back. I'm used to it." I swung around and offered my back to jump on.

"Maybe I'll stay here and watch you."

"Come on and try it, chicken shit," I said over my shoulder.

She cocked her head back and looked at me. "Oh, is that how it is? All right then missy, let's go." She grabbed my shoulders and jumped up on my hips. Toned legs quickly wrapped around my thighs. "Ha-ya, mule!" she said, playfully kicking my legs.

I waded deeper into the current, her arms and legs clamping tighter. Loose strands of her hair brushed across my neck, rousing me in a way that I had not felt since Grace. I pulled my arms in closer to my hips. I liked that Lilly wasn't as sure as Grace, and that she needed me to keep her safe.

The current flowed at my chest when I stopped. Lilly relaxed and leaned against me, her lazy arms dangling from my shoulders and her fingers trailing in the water. After a moment she tightened her arms and nestled her chin against my neck. Her lips close to my ear, she said, "Thank you for this."

God help me, I wanted it this way.

Katie Logan barely looked at me when I passed by her. That was okay by me. We hadn't spoken since our last date weeks ago. I hung my muck rake in the supply room and headed for my truck. It made no sense that I was pissed. I'd been fuming since Rhonda called at lunch to ask if I could make myself scarce for the evening. I knew what that meant. She wanted to spend time in bed with Lilly.

I turned out of Calumet and headed for the river. Hauling ass down the blacktop, I cranked up Pat Benatar. What the hell was wrong with me? I wasn't in love with Lilly and I knew I didn't want her to leave Rhonda, especially not for me. But I'd meant something to Lilly. In the evenings we sat on their deck and drank beer and wine and talked about Alabama and God and how it felt when integration came and parents grew silent and suspicions began. She'd made lemonade when we took a break from the landscaping and eagerly hopped in my truck for every trip to the river.

At the end of the river road I parked the truck and hustled through the canebrake. Peeling off sweat-covered work clothes, I crossed the sandy shoal and stormed out to the river's edge. I launched myself up-stream and started swimming, pounding the water in angry strokes. My arms ached and burned when I finally stopped. I rolled to my back and looked up at the afternoon sky. Overhead a red-tailed hawk sailed on steady afternoon winds. I watch her bank against the waning sun, circling for prey, alone, like me.

I could not expect Lilly to change that.

August sun beat down on my back like a demon. I pounded the final shaft of rebar through the timbers of the last flowerbed and rocked back on my heels to look it over. Tomorrow I would plant some annuals and be done.

Lilly pulled into the drive and got out with a bag of groceries. She headed for the front door without a wave or hello, and that was fine with me. For the last week she'd been sniping, lobbing shots from the next room or launching some cutting remark from the couch as I passed through the den. I didn't know what the hell was eating at her, but she was not my problem. Lilly was Rhonda's problem, though Rhonda had hardly been home to notice her mood.

I dusted my knees and stood up to gather the tools strewn across the yard. I hadn't figured out how to tell Rhonda I was leaving early.

So long as I finished the landscaping, I figured she wouldn't much care.

The house was quiet when I went inside. I pried my dirt-covered hiking boots off at the door and walked into the kitchen. The groceries were put away, and Lilly's purse and keys were on the table of the breakfast nook. I went over to the kitchen sink and flipped on the cold water to splash my face.

"You never quit, do you?" Lilly's charged voice raised the hair on my neck.

I glanced over my shoulder. Drab green scrubs draped loosely over Lilly's willowy torso, and her wet hair was combed back. The scent of her shower soap drifted across the room and clashed sharply with my odor of dirt and sweat.

"Actually I'm almost through. I'll plant the annuals tomorrow." I pulled the bandana from my pocket and wet it down to wash my arms and neck. Facing the window I wiped my skin cool.

"I'm not talking about planting flowers," Lilly said in a voice so determined I knew she was not going away. "I'm talking about you, standing there in those faded out Levi's, wearing that silly cowboy shirt with the sleeves cut out, acting like you're all cool and innocent."

I looked over my shoulder. Her eyes were locked on me, moving closer. She stopped at my back, close enough to feel her breath. "You've been avoiding me, Blue." She reached up to grab my bare shoulders. Her fingers squeezed once and slowly moved down my arms.

Desire surged through me. I kept my back to her and wished to God she would go away. Or maybe that she wouldn't. "I've been here every night, Lilly. Right outside if you hadn't noticed. You could've been helping me if you wanted."

She leaned against my ass and pinned me to the counter. "I'm not talking about digging in the dirt."

I froze as my instincts battled for control. *Don't turn around. Turn around. Do not turn around!*

Lilly didn't wait. Her chest pressed into my back and her hands moved to my hips. Fingers slipped under my Levi's. "Isn't this what you really want from me?" she whispered, her breath teasing my skin.

I pressed my hips harder against the kitchen counter, as if I could push my way to freedom. "It doesn't matter what I want, Lilly. You're with Rhonda, and I don't do this kind of shit."

Her fingers crept inward and I closed my eyes. "Who says you don't do this? No one is going to know. You're leaving soon and I know you want this like I do." Her hands moved under my shirt, inching toward my chest.

I grabbed her wrists and squeezed them hard. Lilly breathed in deep.

My hands flew under her scrubs the moment I turned around. Her lips were exactly as soft and full as I had imagined them to be, though in our fury we kissed too hard and I felt the hard edge of her mouth. I jerked her ass into my hips and she sucked in a sharp breath. My fingers were inside her so quickly that for a moment, for an instant, it felt like Grace.

Shirts dropped along our stumbling course to my bedroom. At the edge of my bed I pushed down Lilly's scrubs. I looked down at the trimmed patch between her legs, glistening wet. I was on top of her as soon as I shed my Levi's. Her breath drummed in my ear and I reached down to stroke her. Hips rocked against my hand and I pushed inside.

"Goddammit," Lilly groaned. Her legs opened wider, fingers digging into my skin, hips thrusting, wanting more. Another finger slid in and my thumb swirled at her clit. Her moans became high-pitched gasps, driving me to the edge. I rocked against her, my own faint cries joining hers. Inside, I found the rough edge waiting for my touch. Eyes shut, her body shook and then gathered. Her mouth flew open with no sound, and then it came.

I fell against her as we gasped for breath. I had done it. I had done what I thought I would never do, and all I wanted was to be inside her again.

It was dark outside when I finally became aware of time. Lilly napped on my shoulder and I reached down to stroke her hair. She opened her eyes and looked up at me. Desire rushed back and I reached for her hand and pulled her to the shower.

I held her up when she came, and we dried each other off and moved to my bed again. After midnight I finally dozed off cradling her in my arms.

We never mentioned Rhonda's name.

At daybreak I woke and looked over at Lilly sleeping naked in my bed. Splintered sunlight fell across her face and highlighted the hint of auburn that tangled through her hair. I wanted to reach for her again. Knowing that she would let me, I knew I had to leave.

I slipped out of bed and tiptoed to their bathroom for a shower. Rhonda's things were everywhere. My stomach suddenly burned and my head began to pound. I wanted to blame Lilly, but I was the fucking asshole who had given in so easily. Her scent on my hands made me ill. I turned on hot water and showered as fast as I could.

Quietly I slipped back into my bedroom. Lilly snored softly. I grabbed my bags and started packing, moving about the room like the thief that I was. I had taken something from Rhonda that could never be given back. My only hope was that she would never find out. I stuffed the last of my clothes into my duffle and slipped out the door.

Their quiet neighborhood was unusually still when I walked outside; or maybe it was that I had something to hide. I tossed my duffle and suitcase across the seat and slid the key into the ignition. Three blocks down, I turned left toward New Circle Road. I wasn't sure where I was going yet; Julie wasn't expecting me home for another two weeks. Maybe I would backpack for a few days to get my head together.

I shifted into second gear and glanced up in the rearview mirror. Fuck!

Rhonda's car turned right, heading home. *Fuck, fuck, FUCK!* My ears roared with the force of a hurricane. In a couple of minutes Rhonda would be walking into her house. She'd look for Lilly in their bedroom, and not finding her there, she would come to ask me. I imagined Rhonda's face, her eyes wide and her face pale as she stared at Lilly lying naked in my bed. I slammed my hand against the steering wheel and tried to think.

There had to be a way out, some way I could get to Lilly first. The closest pay phone was a half-mile away. I floored the gas to get there. No use. Rhonda would be turning into her driveway by now.

Blind panic flooded through my mind and shook my body. My hands trembled wildly, fumbling through my cassette box to find something to anchor the firestorm in my head. Emmylou Harris, "Born to Run." With shaking hands, I pushed the tape into the deck and twisted the volume up.

"*Living as dangerous as dynamite, sure makes you feel nervous but it makes you feel alright,*" Emmylou's sweet, defiant voice sounded so strong. I blew out an anxious breath and gripped the wheel to steady my hands.

Dangerous living, what the hell was that? I had always done as I was supposed to do, got good grades, said yes ma'am and no sir, and never messed around with anyone else's girlfriend. Those were my rules—until last night. Sleeping with Lilly was a total fuck-up. I was a total fuck-up.

"*Just to feel free,*" I sang along with Emmylou.

Just to feel free; that's what I wanted—like the way I felt last night when Lilly and I moved together. Had it really been so wrong? Lilly and Rhonda were never going to last anyway. I could change my rules. I just needed a change of scenery, a place to figure it all out, and then I could go back to Chapel Hill and get on with my life. Maybe out west; maybe I could backpack the Rockies for a few days. Out on the wind-blown ridges, a thousand miles from anyone I knew.

I lowered myself deep into my seat and drove away from the rising sun.

21

Hanging On

I drove west out of Kentucky, building as many miles as I could between me and Lilly. I kept going as the sun made its arch from behind me, to high overhead, and down again to set with its glare in my eyes. At a west Kansas truck stop I stretched out in my front seat and napped for a few hours, and then kept going through the windy Midwest farmlands and into Colorado. The rise and fall of guilt and all-night radio kept me awake as I drove.

The moment I saw the peaks of the Rocky Mountains, I sat up straight and let out a low whistle. The Rockies were different from the mountains I knew back home. My Appalachian Mountains were old, and slow, and thick. These Rocky Mountains seemed young and bold, alive and inviting. I wanted to be up in their snowcapped peaks. I wanted to hike through their forests and sleep in their meadows, closer than I had ever been to the stars. Maybe in the freshness of these mountains I could shake off Grace, and Lilly, and the pain of the last three years. I'd heard there was a vet school not far from Denver, at Colorado State University in Fort Collins.

My eyes were closing for two-second naps by the time I reached Fort Collins. I took the Mulberry Street exit and headed west towards the mountains. Holding my chin in my hand, I propped myself against the truck door. Fort Collins was everything I loved in a town. Broad-faced cows grazed in pastures wedged between gas stations and liquor stores. Downtown streets were lined with huge cottonwoods and blue-green spruce. Graffiti-covered railroad cars silently waited for the pull of a locomotive.

At the outskirts of town I pulled into a sporting goods store called

JAX. I went inside to buy a few things for camping. I figured I would stay for a few days, at least long enough to clear my head.

"Go up Poudre Canyon if you are looking for a nice place to rest," the sales clerk said. He flashed a sympathetic smile at my bloodshot eyes and checked the prices of the stove and tent on the counter. "It's a great place. If you've never been up there, just go to one of the Forest Service campgrounds or find a trailhead to pull off. Everything's right on the river."

I paid for the gear, thanked the guy for the information, and walked out to a parking lot scattered with pickups, duallies, and hard-scrabble sedans covered in dust. "Not much farther, old girl," I said as I crawled back into my truck, "then we can both rest."

My stomach burned from the acid of too much truck-stop coffee, buffered only by the day-old donut I'd had for breakfast. I drove past the bone-dry landscapes of western cattle ranches on my way to the canyon, wondering how I had ended up so far from home. All I knew for sure was that I felt like shit, and Julie was going to kill me when she found out I was in Colorado. Soon I would have to go back to North Carolina. I didn't have the strength to convince Julie I could make it here.

My mind changed when I turned left and headed toward the Poudre River. Exhilaration swept through my body, jolting me awake. A midmorning breeze swept the tall grass at the mouth of Poudre Canyon into waves of sage and gold. Up another mile the canyon surrounded me with its rust-colored cliffs, the tumbling echo of the white-water river, and the cool, crisp air of an August mountain morning. I leaned forward to check the cloudless sky and imagined Grace next to me, window down, her hair blowing like the tall grass, smiling as we drove upstream. We would listen to the rush of the river becoming louder as the canyon narrowed, and then fading as the cliffs opened to Tar Heel blue skies.

"Fucking useless daydreams," I mumbled out loud. Grace was gone from my life forever, so I might as well get used to it. I turned up Fleetwood Mac to push it all from my mind.

A few miles up the winding canyon road, I turned beside the entrance sign for Ansel Watrous Campground. Along the banks of the river, tents of yellow, blue, and green billowed in the breeze. The campground was mostly deserted. I figured most folks were out for the day. At the end of the campground I found an empty site and parked under the shade of a cluster of cottonwoods. I climbed into the bed of my truck and rolled out my ground pad and sleeping bag. Beside me the Poudre River hummed like a lullaby from heaven. Finally, I slept.

"What the hell are you doing?!" Julie demanded. I held the phone away from my ear and imagined her jaw clenched tight and her nimble fingers drumming her kitchen counter. "You need to get your butt back to Chapel Hill, *pronto*. You *are* going to graduate if I have to come out there and drag your ass back myself."

"I'm going to graduate." My whining voice betrayed me. I had planned my whole speech out and rehearsed exactly what I was going to say to her, but Julie bore in and left me in tatters the moment I said I wouldn't be home on Sunday. I sat up straight and summoned the calm-headedness of my father. "I plan to work for a year to save some money. I'll finish undergrad next year. CSU has a great vet school, so I can apply here."

"You'd damn sure better. And don't count on any money from me until you are back in school, understood?"

"I won't. I've got some money left from this summer, and I've got a bunch of job applications in all over town."

"Where are you staying?"

"I've been camping mostly. I met some people, too. A bunch of them live in a house in town. They said I could sleep on their couch 'til I find a place. You want the phone number?"

Julie took the number. "Do any of your new friends go to CSU?"

"A couple do."

"So, most don't."

"No, they mostly work in Fort Collins." I winced and imagined her blue eyes staring at me in piercing disappointment.

"What kind of jobs?"

"Oh, this and that," I said, haltingly. "One works for the rec. department, one works in an office, one's a bartender . . . stuff like that."

134

"Do any of them smoke pot?"

"A few do."

"Shit." A long silence fell between us. Julie drew in a deep breath and I dropped my head into my hand to brace for the lecture I figured to be coming.

"Okay, Blue, here's how I see it. You're about to make a big mistake, and I don't help people make mistakes. When you're ready to come back to reality, give me a call. Until then, good luck and call me at Christmas."

She hung up and left me with the dial tone.

Sitting on the banks of the Poudre River, I stared up at the dome of stars above me. Most nights, the stars felt like old friends. Tonight was different. Tonight even the stars in the constellations seemed lonely. I couldn't blame it on the stars. I had brought it all on myself. Julie was the one sure thing I had in the world, and now I was gambling with losing her. I blew out a heavy breath and chunked a stone into the river. Maybe I should pack up and head home. If I left by morning I could be in class before the middle of the week, fall back in line, and get on with my life.

Fall back in line.

Fall back in line? To live in a world of *should* and *should nots*—the world that demanded Grace turn her back on me? Fall back in line to finish school in the requisite four years, jump straight into the vet school pressure cooker, and grind out a professional life? Fall back in line and never know these mountains, never know life without a safety net?

Living in the world of expectations had fucked me over. I'd thought if I tried hard enough, somehow it would work out. Now I knew it wouldn't. Grace took the easy road and walked out, and the friendship I'd had with Lilly was now conquered by guilt.

"Screw that," I said out loud. I jumped up and jerked off my boots and socks, and then my jeans and shirt. I tossed them in the back of the truck and headed for the river. Frigid water swirled at my feet as I waded out. I stopped in the middle and kneeled. My limbs numbing, I sucked in a couple of deep breaths and fell backward. Pain shot

135

everywhere at once, stabbing into my brain and taking the breath from my lungs. I sprung up and gasped for air.

"Jesus! Jesus!" I bent over, laughing between deep breaths. "Oh man." Freezing cold water dripped from my hair and trickled down my back in frigid lines. Shivering like a half frozen lunatic, I glanced around to see if there had been any witnesses to my insane, icy baptism. Thankfully, I was alone with a sky full of brilliant stars, shining down like old friends. Maybe I was crazy to immerse my naked body in freezing cold water, and maybe I was crazy to drop out of school, but I was still freakin' alive, in spite of everything the bastards had thrown at me.

I didn't have to fall into anyone's line.

Part Two

Untethered

Summer 1982 – Summer 1983

22

The Road to Laramie

"Does this shuttle go to Laramie?" The woman's voice came from the back of a small pack of passengers huddled around me buying tickets for the airport shuttle.

"Yeah. It's $35 instead of $20." I answered over the roar of jet engines. I finished writing a receipt to the mustached cowboy standing at my side and tore it from my book.

"Yes, I expected it would be more," the woman said from behind me. I turned around to find her standing close, holding one hand on the handle of her suitcase and the other at her forehead to shade her almond-colored eyes. In the shadow of her palm I saw her curious expression as she looked at me. She reached into her jacket pocket and pulled out two twenties, gave them to me, and walked away without change.

My mind stayed on her as I closed the van doors and walked around to the driver's door. A fit, thirty-something businessman waited in the passenger seat with his blue suit coat draped across his lap. He watched me step up and settle behind the steering wheel. "Am I okay here?" he asked with an unassuming smile.

"Sure," I replied. I wrote down the number of passengers in my log and pulled my seat belt over my shoulder.

"How long have you lived in Colorado?" the businessman asked as I pulled out from the airport terminal.

"Not long. A little less than a year," I said cheerfully, angling for a good tip. "How 'bout you?" I glanced to the rearview and caught the Laramie woman watching my reflection. The businessman yakked away as we cleared Denver traffic and headed north. I nodded and agreed at the appropriate times, though my mind was stuck on the woman behind me. Her glances flashed into my rearview mirror as the businessman's voice droned on in my ear. I tried to concentrate on the road ahead, on the businessman, on the eighteen-wheeler merging in front of the van, on anything but the reflection of her eyes watching me.

The businessman yawned and closed his eyes. I took the moment to study her. She stared out her window now, and in the mirror's reflection her face appeared too long, though her dark hair fell in perfectly coiffed layers against amazing olive skin. How could anyone's skin not have a single flaw?

"Thanks, and have a good night." I dropped two suitcases at the front door of my last Fort Collins passenger and took his tip. The woman stood by the passenger door, arching her back in a long stretch. A breeze from the north blew her blue, gypsy skirt against her legs. I noticed for the first time that she wore light tan cowboy boots stitched with blue and yellow swallowtail birds. She relaxed from her stretch and watched me walk toward the van.

"So, Laramie?" I asked, stepping up into the van. I pulled out my driver's log and fumbled with the pen.

"Yes," the woman said. She clicked her seat belt and looked at me with amused eyes. Her slightly pursed lips seemed to be holding back a smile. "I'll give you the address when we get close to town."

I nodded and picked up the radio mic to call in. "Shuttle 3, leaving Fort Collins with one passenger to Laramie."

"Where are you from, originally?" the woman asked as I pushed the mic back into the dashboard clip.

"Alabama; just south of Birmingham."

"Perfect," I heard her whisper.

I glanced over. She stared straight ahead with an intimidating air of indifference. She seemed too old to be playing games with me, yet I couldn't figure out any other motive for the glances, the whisper, or her sudden air of indifference. If she was into games, I had forty-five minutes to play along. I turned onto College Street and headed toward Laramie.

"So, do you work or anything?" I asked before our silence became awkward.

"I'm a writer," she said candidly.

My eyes flew open like I had just met Katharine Hepburn. "Wow! That's wild. So do you write books?" I glanced over in time to catch her patient smile.

"Yes, I write books; grand fiction novels about human suffering and decadence. The critics eat them up." The jaded edge in her voice implied it was simply a game she had learned to play, and that I should not be overly impressed by her success.

"Do you mind me asking your name?" I wanted to ask if she was rich, though my father had taught me better.

"I don't mind at all. My name is Cecelia Rose Thornton. As an author I'm known as C. R. Thornton." She turned and looked at me. For a fleeting moment she looked vulnerable. "My publisher thinks Cecelia Rose is too lyrical to be taken seriously."

"Are you serious?"

Cecelia chuckled. "Yes, I am serious."

"That's too bad. Cecelia Rose is a beautiful name."

She nodded, smiling. "Thank you. I like it too. As it turns out, my name doesn't appear on my work at all."

"Thornton's not your name?"

"Thornton is my husband's name."

"Oh." I glanced over at her hand resting on her left thigh. A thick band of gold circled her ring finger, one of those hand-crafted bands meant to signify some great, soul-defining bond between the wearers. Knowing that she was married made her all the more intriguing somehow. I looked away from her and watched the road, searching for something adequate to say. Ahead of us a dually pickup pulling a livestock trailer struggled up the hill. His trailer fishtailed wildly in the forty-mile-per-hour winds blowing across the plains. I couldn't risk a two-lane pass and the passing lanes were several miles ahead. I fell in behind the trailer and tried to ignore the thick smell of manure drifting into the van.

"So, your books. How do you create the stories?" I asked after a silent mile.

Cecelia turned to me. Her face seemed more attractive each time I looked at her. "Stories are everywhere," she said. "My work is to pick the right ones to tell."

"And how do you do that?"

"I observe, then I assume, then I project."

"What do you mean?"

"I mean that stories are most appealing when readers relate to them. People everywhere have an interesting story to tell. I've learned that, with a few questions and a few assumptions, I can write their stories, and be at least seventy percent correct." She looked at me with suggestive eyes. "I'd say you have an interesting story."

Her voice sounded determined underneath her quiet tone. I had the feeling of a moth caught in an intricate web, though the prospect of danger sparked a thrill inside of me. "Well, we've got a ways before we get to Laramie, so if you've got questions for me, fire away."

"OK," Cecelia began. "Do you have any family in this area?"

"No."

"Are you going to school?"

"No."

"Did you go to college?"

"Yes."

"Did you graduate?"

"No."

"Have you lost any of your immediate family members?"

"Yes, both parents."

I felt her studying me closely before she began. I tried not to fidget under her warm gaze.

"You're an orphan from the South and now you're working in Colorado. You are driving an airport shuttle to support yourself; therefore you did not come here for employment reasons. You're not in school and you don't have a family here. You went to college but didn't graduate. So, I think you came to Colorado to get away from something, maybe to start over. I'm guessing there is a relationship involved. You are an attractive young woman who doesn't wear makeup, even though you were raised in the South. You have short nails and you walk with more of a swagger than a swish, not to mention the way you've been looking at me, so I think you are gay. Your hiking boots are worn and scuffed, indicating you're really into the outdoors."

The wind whistling against the van pushed us toward a tumble of boulders near the road's shoulder. I tightened my grip and slowed down.

"So here's your story as I would tell it," Cecelia continued. "You came to Colorado to escape, to outrun a broken heart. You love being in the mountains, and you expect to go back to school someday. You think you'll stay here because you really don't have any reason to be anywhere else. Your parents died in an accident and you've been on your own for several years, though until recently you were doing exactly what they would have expected you to do. Being out here, away from the South, has changed that. Every day that passes is a step further away from the life you thought you'd have."

I flinched with the sting of her accuracy. "It was a tornado."

"Your parents died in a tornado?" I nodded. "I'm sorry." Her voice was gentle with apology.

"Do you mind if I try?" I asked quickly, wanting to avoid the subject of my parents. I did not want to think of them now, not with the thoughts running through my mind about the married woman sitting beside me.

"Sure, why not?" Cecelia said.

Now, I wanted to be the weaver of the web. "So here's what I know so far," I began. "You are a successful writer who lives in Laramie, so I'm assuming your husband works there. From your wedding band and the fact that you use his name professionally, I deduce you love him, or you once did, but you've been toying with me since we left Denver. For some reason you are interested in me. You're perceptive and confident, and at least a little bit cynical." She silently nodded.

"Now can I ask a few questions?" I asked.

"Sure," Cecelia replied. Her voice sounded less assured than it had been, and seemed crowded with secrets.

"Do you have children?"

"No."

"Do you like girls?"

"Yes. And women too," she teased, like she was calling my bluff. *So coy.*

"Can you support yourself financially?"

"Yes, easily."

"Are you originally from the West?"

"No."

"Do you go to church regularly?"

"No."

"So in the story I would write, you and your husband are a professional couple who met somewhere back East and came here for his job. Since there are no major industries in Laramie, I'd guess your husband is a professor at the University of Wyoming. You and your husband are both liberals, but you fit in well in Laramie, and you are currently trying to decide whether to try to adopt a child."

"Not bad," Cecelia said with a satisfied lilt in her voice, which left me wanting to know her secrets all the more. Up ahead I saw the white farmhouse that anchored the edge of Laramie. That meant my time with her was running out.

"I still can't figure out why you're interested in me," I blurted out. Instantly, I regretted saying it. Though the question had been running through my mind since Denver, it seemed wrong, somehow, to ask it out loud.

Cecelia looked at me, smiling, I supposed, at my impetuousness. "Your accent. It's still pure."

My accent; I had long grown weary of it. "Thanks. I guess," I said. I sank down in my seat and slowed down as we drove into the outskirts of town. "So you only wanted to hear me talk?"

"No, actually it's more than that. I'm writing about a young girl from Alabama and I'm using quite a bit of dialect. It's important to get it right, so I was thinking of asking for your help."

"Aren't you supposed to write what you know?" I asked, and instantly hoped she would forgive the belligerence of my tone.

Cecelia smiled, undaunted. "I enjoy a challenge," she said, her voice rich with insinuation. I stupidly nodded. The woman was playing me exactly as she wanted.

"It's up here on the right." Cecelia looked toward a row of brick houses lining one side of an open field. "Spring Creek Drive." I turned onto her street and she pointed to the sixth house on the left, a typical three-bedroom, white-brick ranch situated along a row of similarly unspectacular architecture. I swung into the drive and parked. "I'll get your luggage," I said as I slid out.

144

Cecelia walked around to the side of the house and unlocked the door. She looked over and waved me inside. I carried her tapestry suitcase into the kitchen and looked around. There was nothing noteworthy about the neatly organized room. She dropped her keys into an engraved pottery bowl at the end of the counter and looked over her shoulder at me. "Bring my bag if you don't mind," she said as she started down a narrow hall.

I picked up her suitcase and carried it past the Frederick Remington reproductions hanging along paneled walls. I turned into the bedroom door and stopped in my tracks. Cecelia stood across the room, looking directly at me as she took off her suede jacket. She slipped the jacket from her arms and glanced at the bed, just long enough for me to catch it. "You can put it down there," she said, pointing to the foot of the bed.

I put the suitcase where she wanted and took a step back. She watched me intently, still playing her game. I gave her my I-may-be-from-Alabama-but-I'm-not-a-stupid-hick smile and turned to walk out.

Cecelia caught up with me in the kitchen. She grabbed her purse and reached in for her wallet. I waited while she shuffled through her cash. "So would you be willing to help me with the dialect for my novel? I'll be happy to pay for your mileage and your time." She held out a ten-dollar bill, her expression now completely business.

I took the ten and stuffed it in my shirt pocket. "Call me at work. I'm willing to help you with the writing, but just so we're clear, this ain't about nothin' but my Alabama accent." I looked at her with a smart-assed grin and walked out.

23

Far from Grace

"Riley, it's for you." Rob, the shuttle shift manager, held the phone receiver out to me and turned his attention back to his schedule book. "Third time she's called today. She must want you bad." His blasé voice held an edge of inference. Rob was an ass, but he gave me all the shifts I wanted. Mostly I ignored him. I took the receiver and stretched it across the room, as far away from Rob as I could get.

"This is Blue."

"Hello, lover. You were quite something last weekend." Cecelia's low, seductive voice flowed as thick as honey. I closed my eyes and remembered the moonlit night in the bedroom of her mountain cabin, Cecelia straddling my hips, her fingers teasing the strap of her satin negligee over her shoulder. Everything about the woman stirred me now.

We had not started out that way. My first two sessions with Cecelia were mundane afternoons spent on her patio drinking ginger ale while she explained the plot points and character development for her novel. After reading a few pages of draft dialog, I sat down beside her, looked her in the eye, and boldly told her I thought her main characters were off the mark, too often veering off into a distorted mix of Bo and Luke Duke and Rhett Butler. I suggested she set her story in another place. Cecelia's reply came with a cagey smile. She assured me she knew her story better than I, and I should just take the easy money she had to offer.

"Likewise," I said into the phone. Rob stirred and coughed, for an instant taking my mind from the memory of Cecelia's rapid breath in my ear.

"Can you meet me at the cabin this Saturday?" Cecelia asked. "I have more dialog to work on. I'll make dinner and we'll work after. I want you to stay the night, too."

I grinned as my blood rushed. "I've got a morning shift Saturday. I can come up after I'm done. I'm off all day Sunday."

"Good. I hope you'll spend it with me."

"If you want," I replied coolly, even though images of my hands on her body fired through my mind.

"I wouldn't ask you if it were not what I wanted. I'll see you Saturday evening?"

"I'll be there."

"Good. We'll be having elk steaks for dinner if you want to bring wine." She said good-bye and hung up.

I brought the receiver over and handed it to Rob. He put it back in the cradle, tore the top sheet from his schedule book, and handed it to me with a knowing look. "Last run for today. Keep your mind on driving."

Cecelia glanced up when I walked into the cabin. She sat across the room in her chaise lounge, her pencil resting against her lips and her yellow legal pad against her bended knee. She returned her attention to the legal pad, her eyes narrowed in concentration, "Give me a minute."

I nodded and stepped back onto the porch. I wouldn't have figured Cecelia to be the kind of woman for a place like this. The closest neighbor was likely five miles away. My first night here, Cecelia told me she bought the place with the royalties from her second book. She said she liked the quiet of it, and that her husband Kenneth rarely came here. A routed sign over the cabin door read "Rose."

A smattering of snow remained on the mountain peaks to the north. Cecelia said another month in the summer sun would render them bare. In the meadow across the road Indian paintbrushes colored the grass with splashes of red. I'd been in Colorado almost a year now, and I hadn't found a place as peaceful as this.

Cecelia's Australian Shepherd emerged from the woods by the

meadow and ran full out towards the porch. Her tail wagged wildly as she hopped up the stairs, panting heavily as if she had been chasing deer all afternoon. I kneeled down and let her come to me. "Hey, Emma," I said, rubbing her chest. She licked my chin with a high-pitched whimper. "It looks like we have time for a walk if you want."

Emma yelped and jumped away. Her eyes gleaming, she hunkered down and looked up at me. Keeping her belly close to the floor, she crept a few steps back and barked. "Just like Lassie," I said with a chuckle. Emma barked again and spun around toward the steps. I followed her off the porch and out across the meadow behind the cabin.

In the meadow I breathed in the rosin-laden air and watched Emma dart back and forth, sniffing out clues from the latest passes of the mule deer or moose that hung around the cabin. She stopped where the meadow met the woods and turned back to wait. "I'm coming," I said. Dry needles crunched beneath our feet as Emma led me along a path running beneath a thick canopy of ponderosa pine. Up ahead I heard the gentle flow of a stream.

Emma gingerly picked her way along a jagged line of rocks and down into the shallow pool of the stream. I watched her lap up a long drink and thought of Grace. She had described this place once, when we were at Julie's house on a December day, dreaming of the life she said she wanted. For a moment I wondered what Grace would think of me being here with a married woman. My choices would be none of her concern, now.

Emma leaped out of the stream and trotted up beside me. She lay down on her belly and surveyed the woods around her, as if it were all her kingdom. I plopped down beside her and rubbed the top of her head. "Thanks for bringing me here, Emma. It's nice," I said. The black tips of her ears suddenly perked up. A few seconds later, I heard it too. The flow of Cecelia's skirt caught my eye first, and then her sandaled feet. She sat down beside me and settled her skirt around her legs. She leaned back on her elbows and said, "Do you like it here?"

I chuckled, "Yeah, I do. I was just telling Emma I did."

"We can have a good summer here, Blue." Cecelia looked at me with an easy smile.

"Only the summer?" I teased.

Her smile dropped and she looked at me for a moment. Her pensive expression worried me. Who was I to presume more than a summer? After all, I was only a college kid who had spent one night with her—a famous author with contacts in New York and London. She could easily have me out of her life with a single, explicitly phrased sentence I would never forget.

Cecelia sat up and crossed her legs. "Come over here," she said, patting the taut fabric stretched across her lap. I eased my head down into the sling of her skirt. "How would you describe a woman's orgasm?" she asked plainly.

My face flushed and I grinned up at her. "You're the writer."

"Obviously, I am." She looked at me with a gentle smile and reached down to sweep her fingers along the length of my forehead. "I'm interested in how people describe their pleasures. A woman's orgasm is a pleasure for you, both giving and receiving, is it not?"

I folded my hands over my chest and looked up to the sunset sky, thinking. "A woman's orgasm is like a stream, isn't it?" I began. "I mean, it starts out high in the watershed, really no more than a trace of possibility." I raised my hands up, rolling one over the other as I spoke. "Then the stream begins to roll, it seeps and gathers, until it becomes this life-giving force. It builds energy and gains strength and power as it flows. It pounds on, deeper and wider, bold and reckless, like this inevitable churning. It rages on until it reaches a ledge, and then—" my hands flew out like fireworks "—it explodes like a waterfall, all of that energy falling down, forceful and beautiful. Then the waterfall flows into the water below, still churning, but not for long. The stream stills, becoming a serene pool. And then it flows on, just waiting for the next waterfall."

Cecelia looked down at me, not saying anything. I wanted her to say something, or roll her eyes, or raise her eyebrows appreciatively, or anything that would give me a clue as to what she was thinking. She kept her eyes on me, her face unchanged. Her look was making me crazy. I didn't know if she was building some new storyline in her head or if she thought I was a naïve kid. "Was that the kind of description you are looking for?" I asked her.

"You surprise me," she said, though her face looked more clinical than surprised. Her expression softened and she reached for my hair. "I like to be surprised by people."

I wasn't sure exactly how I surprised her. Maybe I didn't want to know all of the assumptions Cecelia projected onto me. I didn't want complications. "You surprised me, too," I said.

"Oh? How so?"

I reached up and grasped her knee. "Well, for starters, I didn't figure you to be a woman who would buy a mountain cabin in the middle of No Damn Where, Wyoming."

Cecelia smiled. "The clean air clears my thinking."

"I think there's more to it than that," I replied.

She looked out toward the stream, her face content. "Yeah, maybe," she said with a placid smile.

Had there been other women, or maybe other men, that Cecelia brought here—away from Kenneth, away from neighbors and crappy hotels? I doubted I was the only one. The notion that there may have been others who shared this same place, this dog, this woman, left me feeling out of sorts. I shifted uneasily and took my hand from her knee. "So what else do you writers do to clear your thinking?" I asked.

"Well, if you mean my creative process, I always spend at least a couple of weeks in the place I'm writing about. I need for my senses to be engulfed in order to write about a place authentically. In fact, I want to go to Alabama before the summer is out, and I want you to go with me."

Reality zoomed in, taking me from this beautiful place and Cecelia's attentive eyes. I didn't want to go back there, not now, not when the pull of my roots was finally loosening its grasp. "Cecelia, I don't think—" I began, but then the right words wouldn't come.

"It's okay if you don't want to go with me, Blue. I've traveled the world by myself. I think I can handle Alabama."

"Have you ever *been* there?" I joked. If I told her how I dreaded going back to Alabama, she might find me weak and lacking. I sat up and gathered her hands in mine. "I would be happy to accompany you to Alabama, Cecelia. After all, I know the language," I said, grinning.

She laughed and stood up. "Come on, I put bread in the oven. I know you must be hungry." She grabbed my hand to lift me up, and led me back to the cabin.

24

Hot August Nights

Cecelia took a sip of Long Island iced tea and methodically lowered the glass onto her cocktail napkin. I wasn't sure what she was pissed about, but I damn sure knew it had something to do with me. I avoided her glare, watching her pink nails tap the side of her glass. "Why don't you tell me who you're looking for? Maybe I can help you find them," she said, her voice curt and pointed.

I looked out toward the passengers and flight crews hustling through Terminal C of the Atlanta airport. If she hadn't insisted on flying into Birmingham, we wouldn't be stuck here waiting for our connector flight, and I wouldn't be searching the crowds for the off chance of spotting Grace. "Nobody in particular," I mumbled. I realized I hadn't spoken a full sentence to Cecelia since we landed in Atlanta almost an hour ago. "It's just being back in the South. You never know who you might see."

Screw the South. Could I not come here without looking for her? What would I say to her anyway? Thanks for fucking up my life?

"Where will we be staying in Birmingham?" I asked in a lame attempt to make conversation.

"At the Hyatt Regency."

I forced a smile. "Sounds nice."

Cecelia sat back and settled her hands in her lap. I had learned over the last few months that this was the pose she garnered when she wanted to set boundaries, to be the unflappable bitch in charge. She looked at me and said, "It will be, if you don't spend all of your time looking for her. The South is a big place, Augusta. There are probably, what, a few million people here? Do you think she'll suddenly appear and ask if you can please run away with her?"

"It's not like that."

"Tell me what it's like, then," Cecelia said. I couldn't stand the haughty look on her face. I had seen it before, when she dipped from intellect to spite.

Not like anything you'll ever know.

I grabbed my beer and tipped it back for a long swallow. I didn't want to fight with her. For the next week all I had to do was show her around, introduce her to some people, and help her understand. And there would be sex; pull-off-the-road sex, all-night-in-our-bed sex, her-cries-in-my-ear sex. Cecelia's only requirement was that I looked at her when I talked.

I lowered my beer. "It's a little weird for me, okay. I haven't been back to Alabama in a couple of years, and now I'm here with you."

"Do you have a problem with that?"

I looked over at the guy who had been eyeing us from the bar for the past ten minutes. He slipped off his stool and straightened the belt beneath his overlapping stomach before he started toward us, his gaze drifting from Cecelia to me. She cut her eyes toward him in an unmistakable warning. He pulled off a save with a turn toward the bathroom.

"Maybe I shouldn't have cut him off," Cecelia said, a cynical grin curling on her lips. "It would have been interesting to see which one of us he went for."

I smiled. "I don't think there's any doubt he would have started with you," I said with a glance toward the cleavage rising from her yellow, scoop-neck blouse. "After you chewed him up and spit him out, I would have ended up talking to him about football." She laughed, and I watched her eyes brighten. She raised her glass and tilted it toward me, "To clueless men."

I lifted my longneck to the height of her glass, "And beautiful women." I kept my eyes on her as I downed a healthy swallow. Thank God she really didn't want to fight, either.

The white and amber lights of Birmingham filtered through the sheer curtain of our hotel room window. Cecelia came to our bed, her movements a silhouette in the shadows of our room. I lifted the covers for her to move in next to me. Her body was warm from her shower and she carried the subtle scent of the wildflower lotion she had smoothed into her skin. The naked length of her felt familiar to me now. We had made love on so many mornings and nights, and again a few hours ago, and yet our appetites for each other had not waned. I was developing a taste for forbidden fruit.

Cecelia propped up on an elbow and reached over to trace the line of my jaw. Her fingers stopped at my chin and she looked at me with alluring eyes. "Tonight I want you to fuck me like a Southern girl."

I smiled. Two of my fingers trailed down her chest and stopped at the rise of her breast. "A Southern girl I love, or a Southern girl I just fuck?"

Cecelia looked at me for a moment. "A Southern girl you love," she said softly.

I hadn't expected the sincerity in her eyes. They held me in, and my heart began pounding as wildly as if she were a new lover. I took her in my arms and kissed her, kissed her like I had once kissed Grace. Her fingers laced into my hair as my lips moved down the length of her neck and settled on the soft skin at the base of her throat, the place where Grace would draw in a sharp breath and arch in anticipation. Cecelia's hands swept down my back and around to my ass. Grabbing my cheeks she pushed my hips against her thigh to coax my legs open. Grace never did that. I lifted my gaze to Cecelia's face. Her eyes opened in lazy blinks. She looked as beautiful as ever. How could I suddenly not want her? She looked at me strangely, confused and maybe a little bit pissed. I kissed her once on her breastbone and reached for her hand. "Baby, I really want to do this right," I said softly. "It's been a long day, so why don't we get some rest tonight? We've got the whole week together." I trailed my fingertip between her breasts and hoped like hell she wouldn't see the deceit in my eyes.

Cecelia shifted away. "You don't lie well, Blue, and you should never fool yourself into believing I'm in love with you. We both know what this is about." She turned her shoulder to me and moved across the bed.

In the shadow-filled room I stared at the sweep of her dark hair falling away from the curve of her neck. I did love Cecelia, if love meant that I wanted to be with her; if love meant that I respected her intelligence and her confidence, and that I reveled in the way she watched me. Maybe there were different ways to love someone, and just because I didn't love her the way I loved Grace, that didn't mean I didn't love her at all. Did it? I rolled to my back and stared at the ceiling, listening to the hum of the air conditioner taking the heat from another hot August night.

In the morning I opened my eyes and gazed across the room. Cecelia sat lengthwise in the love seat by the window, her feet tucked under a blanket and her writing tablet resting against her knees. The hotel's complimentary robe opened loosely at her chest.

We both know what this is about.

"Mornin'," I mumbled.

Cecelia stopped writing and looked over at me, too stern for this early in the morning. "Good morning, Blue." She lowered her pencil and put her writing tablet on the coffee table in front of the love seat. "I want you to take the car today," she said, sitting up to face me. "Go wherever you need to go and stay as long as you need. When you come back, we'll do what we came here to do."

I propped up on my elbow. I needed coffee for this. "What are you going to do without the car?"

Cecelia glanced at the Birmingham visitor information book on the coffee table. "I'll spend the day in the city, seeing things the mayor wants me to see. After that I'll come back here to write."

I nodded and got out of bed. "I think I'll go to Calera to catch up with some friends," I said as I walked to the bathroom.

"Call if you decide to stay out for the night. After I dress, I'm going to breakfast," I heard Cecelia say as I closed the bathroom door.

Azaleas lined the circle driveway of the last house on the right. I looked down at my notepad to check the address. When I called Susan's mother to get the phone number, she mentioned Susan had started graduate school. There weren't enough student loans in the world to afford this place.

Susan opened the front door of the sprawling, stone and cedar-sided contemporary house and stepped out onto the walkway. Her smile grew as she walked toward me. "I can't believe you're here," she said, her voice pitched high.

I wrapped my arms around her and pulled her close. "My God, it's good to see you," I replied.

She leaned back in my arms and looked at me with her playful, crooked smile. "I was beginning to think you were trying to avoid me."

"No way." I pulled her in again and rocked her in my arms. The scent of her suntan lotion took me back to our days at the lake, and long boat rides, and how we used to talk on the pier.

Susan hooked her arm in mine and turned me toward the front door. "This place is beautiful," I said, looking across the landscaped yard. "I can just imagine what it looks like when those azaleas are in bloom."

"I'm a lucky girl."

"It looks like you are," I replied as we walked through the front door. I stopped in the foyer and glanced across the rich blue textiles and wood décor in the sunken den ahead of us. Rows of planters filled with caladiums, English ivy, Joseph's coat, ferns, and ficus plants added their color throughout the room. Three skylights scattered sunlight onto the golden hardwood floors of the house. "Beautiful house," I said.

Susan smiled proudly. "Thank you. I wish I could say I had more to do with it. Cory designed and built it a couple of years before we met. I knew I was in love the minute I walked through the door."

"Cory is a . . . ?" I asked. Last time we'd talked, Susan was beginning to question whether she would ever get over the adolescent phase her mother had assured her was at the root of Susan's attraction to women. I had tried to assure her otherwise.

"Cory is an architect and a woman." Her smile grew as I looked at her.

"I knew it!" I hugged her tight enough to lift her off her feet. "What's she like? Are you happy?"

"I am happy, Blue." Susan's eyes gleamed. She grabbed my hand

and led me down two steps into the den. "Have a seat if you like." She pointed toward their couch. "Do you want a beer or a Coke? I can make tea," she said, walking toward the kitchen.

"A beer sounds great." I walked over to the entertainment center and the family pictures there. There was one of Susan, her head tilted toward a slightly older woman with short, wavy blonde hair, lightly freckled skin, and a generous smile. I studied the woman's eyes and the way she held her shoulders—relaxed and confident. "I assume this is Cory beside you in this picture."

Susan leaned back from the refrigerator and looked. "Yep, that's her. How'd I do?"

"Pretty damn good, I'd say. Where did you meet her?"

"In Pensacola. This past spring break, actually." Susan walked toward me with a couple of Bud Lights. She handed me one as she continued, "Cory was doing a consulting job on a condo next to our hotel. I saw her a couple of times at this bar and grill on the beach. One night I drank enough to get the courage to speak to her. I told her my girlfriends and I felt like dancing, and I asked if she knew where the dance bar was. Fortunately, Cory guessed what I meant and wrote down the name of the gay bar on her business card. I looked down at the card and saw the 205 area code. We started talking and next thing I know, I'm walking into this house and falling in love."

"I'm really happy for you," I said, calculating the time since her last spring break. It could only have been four months or so.

Susan nodded and studied my face for a moment. I knew her well enough to know she had questions. I looked outside to avoid them. "Show me your pool?"

"Sure," she replied.

She led me out to the edge of the pool and we sat down at the deep end, where the water would be coolest. Our feet lazily flipped back and forth beside each other. I had forgotten how safe it felt to be with her. "Did you go to see your parents?" she asked.

I nodded and looked out to the red blooms of the crepe myrtles defining one edge of their yard. "Yeah, this morning I took some flowers over and sat with them for a while. The heat finally ran me off." I turned to her sweet, understanding face. "What about your folks?" I asked. "Your mother was nice on the phone, but something seemed off. Are they doing okay?"

She shifted uneasily. "Yeah, they're okay. We've had some issues." The sun broke from behind an afternoon cloud and bore down on us. Susan squinted, though her eyes seemed as etched by worry as by the searing light. Haltingly, she said, "Blue, at the end of my sophomore year I had an abortion. My parents found out I was pregnant, and they wanted me to get married. They really liked the guy. I did, too, but the thing is, I didn't love him, and I knew I never would. So I went to a clinic in Birmingham and did what I thought I needed to do." She looked up and stared into the distance, for the moment tattered and alone.

I put my arm around her shoulder. "Why didn't you call me?"

She shrugged and looked down at her feet swirling in the pool. "I don't know. You were all the way in North Carolina, and I knew you would come, even if I didn't want you to. I didn't want you to miss school."

"Susan, I'm so sorry." *Sorry* seemed inadequate, it always did. What else was there to say?

"I had no idea it would still be so hard, Blue. Cory's really helped me a lot, especially with things being so tough with my parents. She reminds me of you in some ways. I've always felt at ease with her."

I pulled Susan closer. "I'm glad you found her. It's funny how things are turning out. In high school we thought I would be the homebody, and you would be the one off on adventures."

"I know. Ironic, isn't it?" Susan rested her hand on my knee. She seemed one part broken and two parts hopeful. "I know it may seem like I'm moving too fast with Cory, but when you find the one you want, you have to believe you can make it, you know?"

I nodded. I knew about believing, and how it felt to find out I was wrong. I turned away from Susan's gaze and took a swallow of beer. A jet roared in the distance, and I wished to be on it, flying away. I looked at my feet, at a wren by the diving board, up to the sky. Susan took her hand from my knee, giving me my space. "You're thinking about Grace, aren't you?"

Nodding was all I could force out of myself.

"Blue, I've been worried about you. We've hardly talked since you left Chapel Hill."

"I know. There's really not much to talk about. Right now I'm driving an airport shuttle for a living and having an affair with a married writer."

The worry lines returned to Susan's face. "Wow." She thought for a moment before she spoke again. "That actually sounds like a lot to talk about. Are you planning to stay in Colorado?"

"I don't know. I really like it there, so I guess I'll stay. For a while, at least."

"What about school?"

"I plan to finish at Colorado State. They've got a vet school. If I'm lucky I'll get in there."

"So you'll be back in school this fall?"

"I don't think so. I haven't registered."

"Why not? If it's money, I can get Cory to help you with a loan. She's in with her father's practice and they're doing really well."

"It's not money. Julie will pay for school." Should I tell Susan the truth? That the dreams I once had now seemed too cloudy, and in truth I held more passion for being the young lover of a big deal writer than for the rigors of professional school?

"It's the woman you're here with, isn't it?" Susan asked, so gentle it felt like a caress. Somehow she always knew, and she never judged.

"Yeah, it is," I said.

"So she's married, which complicates things. Do you love her?"

I turned away and watched the wren again. Another bird joined him, and they flittered and quarreled in rapid chirps. "Cecelia is an amazingly interesting woman," I said, keeping my gaze on the birds. "She challenges me, and I like that about her."

"But how does she make you feel?"

I thought for a moment, "Important," I said, turning to Susan. "Cecelia makes me feel important. Like I matter, you know?"

"You've always mattered, Blue, to me and a lot of other people."

"You might not be so sure if you knew how things have turned out."

"Try me," Susan said, her gaze steadying me.

I nodded and said, "Last summer I went to Kentucky to work on a horse farm. While I was there, I ended up sleeping with this girl who had a girlfriend. They'd been together for seven years, and toward the end of the summer she came on to me. The next thing I knew we were in bed together. When I woke up, I didn't even have the guts to stick around."

"So did her girlfriend find out?"

"I don't know, probably. I was outta there the next morning before Lilly woke up. When I was driving out of the neighborhood, I saw her girlfriend coming home, unexpectedly, of course. Unless Lilly happened to wake up, she was still in my bed. Naked."

"But you said this Lilly girl came on to you, right?"

"Yeah, but it doesn't matter. I don't do that shit. Or at least I didn't do that shit before."

"Why do you think it happened that time?"

"I don't know. I knew I was attracted to Lilly. When she came on to me I was just being stupid, I guess."

"Is that what you're doing with this writer, being stupid?"

"No, I know what I'm doing with Cecelia. A year ago I wouldn't have been with her, but I'm living by different rules now. I like trying things out to see where they go. Cecelia and I are good together, and I don't want any big commitments, anyway."

Susan looked at me, unconvinced. She said, "Blue, I don't know anything about Cecelia, and it's not for me to say whether you should have an affair with her or not. What I do know is you've got a lot going for you. Be sure you don't go too far from where you need to be."

I wished I could promise her, though I couldn't. Nothing seemed certain now.

"I had forgotten how green it is here," I said to Cecelia. We passed a field of soybeans as we rolled along Highway 25, the two-lane leading to Calera. Out here in the country, the entire mosaic of crop fields, cow pastures, and loblolly pine plantations was covered with the deep green of summer. It seemed the whole South was a tangle of green; a tangle of green that hid and nurtured.

Cecelia glanced over and gave me a quick smile. "What was it like growing up here?"

I knew she wasn't asking about childhood memories of happy Christmases and learning to ride a horse. She wanted my memories of the South, of Alabama. I looked out at the endless ribbon of gray asphalt ahead and remembered the first time I drove this road with my dad. The memory took me back to the years before he was gone, when life seemed simple. "Every person you knew went to church, and we swam a lot in the summer. George Wallace was always governor, or his wife was. The nightly news headlined with a body count from Vietnam. Then things started changing, and people got angry."

"What do you mean, people got angry?" Cecelia asked after a long moment. Her hands twisted on the steering wheel, like she was anxious or agitated, or something.

"All of that stuff going on in the 60s. It made people angry," I answered evenly.

"People you knew got angry?" Cecelia asked, her voice ramping up.

"Yeah, some people I knew were angry. My dad said people just don't like change, and a lot of things were changing really fast. Like on the farm, a black man and a white man may have been working together for years and suddenly it was there, these things they saw on the news—civil rights marches, school integration, issues with the draft, things like that. It was in the air between them, and I guess a lot of people became uncertain. They felt like somebody from somewhere else was telling them what to do, so they got mad."

Cecelia looked over at me as if she was suddenly uncertain, and I knew the inquisition was on. She checked the road and looked at me again, her eyes narrowed and shrewd, as if trying to flush out any racism I might be harboring.

"There's still a lot of anger here," I said. I looked out the window, away from her critical eyes. Maybe coming here with her was a waste of time. She would never begin to understand this culture in a week, maybe not in a lifetime. After a few minutes, I couldn't take the silence anymore. I turned to Cecelia's smug face. This time I wasn't about to back down. "You can't write a book about this place until you stop being so goddamn critical. For once in your life, you need to stop all of your projecting and really listen to people. You might actually learn something from them."

Cecelia's cheeks rushed with color and her jaw clenched tight. I figured I was in for it. "You're full of audacity for this early in the morning," she said brusquely. She pushed the accelerator down and we took off like a bootlegger. I wanted to laugh. I had never seen Cecelia lose control. I glanced over at her shoulders all squared up and her eyes squinting tight, mad as all hell. A quarter mile ahead a John Deere bounced down the road, his bush hog jacked up behind the tractor. Cecelia barreled toward it, her foot still pressed hard on the accelerator. A line of cars was coming from the other direction, leaving no room to pass. We flew closer and closer to the tractor, close enough now to see the orange safety triangle. Cecelia's foot hadn't left the accelerator. The tractor had nowhere to go. The ditches were too steep. Bush hog blades hung right in front of us. My foot pressed hard against the floorboard, like I could stop the car if I pushed hard enough. *For chrissakes, slow down!*

The force of locked brakes hurled me toward the windshield. "Fucking farmers," I heard Cecelia say with contempt.

I fell back into my seat and looked up at the guy on the tractor. His wide eyes stared back at us, and then he turned away, shaking his head. I could only imagine his tight-lipped cussing. "Is that Ned?" I asked, referring to one of Cecelia's favorite characters, a poor farmer who hid his homosexuality in his devotion to the illnesses of his mother.

Cecelia relaxed and looked at me with a hint of a smile. "Okay, that was stupid, and you're right, I don't know a damn thing about life in the South." She rested her head in her hand and stared at the tractor she had almost wiped out. We settled behind it, barely creeping along. After a moment, she said, "I just don't understand why people couldn't see life from another person's perspective. Like this white man you say worked right beside a black man for years, and never once did it occur to him to challenge the injustice?"

I nodded and said, "I've thought about that a lot in the last few years, especially now that I live with injustice myself. But, for some reason I'm still drawn to the South, even though I run from it. There's so much more to it than all the bad things people say."

"This place fascinates me, Blue. Maybe that's why I'm compelled to write a story set here. With all of its heat and conflict and bare-knuckled survival, there really isn't a better setting than the South." She reached over and grasped my forearm. "You know I need you for this."

I took her hand and laced our fingers together. "Of course I do, and you are right, we should talk to some black people about the way they see the South. We'll go to see a couple of men who worked for my father, and maybe look up my high school history teacher, too. He was one of the first black students at the University of Alabama. He told us a few things about his college experiences when we were in high school. I would bet he has plenty more stories to tell."

Cecelia's face brightened. "I would love to talk to him. Do you think he would be willing?"

"I think so," I replied. "He was the head of our Beta Club, so he knows me."

"Will he wonder why you're here with me?"

"Maybe, but we could try telling the truth. We don't have to mention the part about sleeping together."

She smiled. "No, I guess not. Thank you again for doing this, Blue."

I squeezed her fingers in mine. "I'm with you till the end, Rose."

I switched off the light on the bedside table and curled my body around Cecelia. My hand wandered up her thigh, across her hip, and stopped to rest on her stomach. She pushed her hips against me and ran her palm gently across my arm. Our flight back to Denver wasn't until noon tomorrow. We had the time to make love for hours, though all I wanted was to sleep with my body wrapped around hers.

For the last five days, it had seemed as if Cecelia were mine. We met my high school teacher for lunch at Ollie's Bar-b-que, drove Highway 80 from Selma to Montgomery, swam in Lake Martin, and bought Cokes and crackers at country stores while we chatted with the owners, most of whom lived in a house behind the store. We drove back roads and dirt roads, talked on the porch with a couple of my dad's old farmhands, ate homegrown tomato sandwiches and fried chicken lunches at small town cafes, and napped during the heat of the afternoon. One night, I butched Cecelia up in blue jeans and one of my t-shirts and took her to shoot pool at a dive near Talladega. We had done everything I could think of to give Cecelia my sense of Alabama in seven whirlwind days. I couldn't get her to go to church, though, even though I promised no Baptists.

"I'm thinking of divorcing Kenneth," Cecelia said so casually she may as well have been telling me she wanted eggs for breakfast. "It doesn't seem a good omen for our marriage when we're both in bed thinking of other women."

I stiffened. Did she plan to leave Kenneth for me? I wasn't ready for that; didn't want it—ever.

"Don't panic; it's not because of you. Kenneth's been having an affair with a woman in Canada for years, and I've discovered I prefer women—crave them, in fact."

I moved my hand up and let it rest between her breasts. "So what do you want to do?"

She rolled over and trailed a finger across my cheek. "If you mean about us, I think we should simply enjoy each other until one of us wants to leave."

Carrying on an affair with a married woman never sounded so simple. What did I have to lose?

25

Losing and Finding

Julie laid her book on the couch beside her lap and picked up her glass of merlot. A sharp glare from the late afternoon sun reflected off the snow slopes rising from the base of our condo. I lowered the shades on the massive window at her back and sat down on the easy chair across from her. A rumble of hunger passed through my stomach and I thought about the steak restaurant where we had reservations for dinner. She cradled her wine glass in her palm and looked at me. "I took the liberty of reading your VCAT scores, Blue. They were high enough to get you into most any vet school in the country."

The suddenness of the topic hit me with a jolt. Julie had rented this condo in Vail for a weekend of skiing, she had told me. Now, on our last night here, we were getting to the truth of why she had come. "You read my VCAT scores?" I asked incredulously.

She looked at me, unfazed. "They came in a few weeks after you took off and came out here. They've been sitting on my desk since. You didn't seem interested, so I opened them. Sue me if you want. Just remember: I paid for your education."

"As if you'll ever let me forget," I muttered loud enough for her to hear. I stood up and walked to the window. Julie's money paid for a lot of things, like lift tickets and everything I needed for spending three kick-ass days with her in Vail. I didn't need any of it, though. I hadn't asked anything of Julie since I left Kentucky. "I haven't asked about my VCAT scores because I don't want to go back to school right now," I said. "I like living out here and I'm making my own way."

Julie's hardened expression said she disagreed. "So tell me about making your own way, Blue. Tell me how driving a shuttle is helping you build a future." Her sarcastic tone tightened the growing knot in my stomach.

I turned away from her and watched gliding skiers make their day's last run. The sun behind them dipped below the crest of the mountain and the room got darker. "I'm not just driving a shuttle. I'm helping someone write a novel."

"How? By having an affair with her?"

I whipped around and met Julie's gaze. "What's wrong with having an affair? You do it."

Julie's calm eyes cooled to ice. "That's right. I have had a couple of affairs, but I built my career, so I've *earned* the right to live my life as I want."

Earned the right. What the hell was she implying? That respect was all about a fancy career? That only a fat bank account would gain me license to do in the world as I chose? If that was what my aunt believed, she was no different than Grace's parents. "I've earned the right to live as I want—just like you have."

"We both know that's not true. The difference between you and me is that I'm not a dropout. You're wasting your life, Blue. You've got the intelligence to make something real out of your life. Until recently, I thought you had the discipline and the common sense you need, too. With all this shuttle-driving nonsense, I'm not so sure anymore."

I'd had enough of her condescending crap. "It's not about driving a damn shuttle," I argued. "It's about living my own fucking life, without your interference or jumping my ass to get back in school!" Julie stood up, her face drawn and her mouth tight. I knew I was pushing her, but I wasn't going to fall back in line. Not now. I stormed toward my bedroom, away from her angry glare. "I should have known when you came out here it wasn't all about skiing and fucking hot chocolate!"

My still-drying clothes hung everywhere in the bedroom. I grabbed my duffle bag and started stuffing them in. Why couldn't Julie see that driving the shuttle wasn't about a future? It was about making a few bucks so I could be free to live as I wanted; free to go to the mountains to escape the pain of my own thoughts; free to escape to Cecelia, the woman who I ran to because she demanded nothing.

I finished stuffing my duffle and zipped it closed. I heard Julie in the kitchen, probably pouring more wine. To get out the door, I would have to face her one more time. I threw my duffle over my shoulder and steeled myself to face her. I caught a glimpse of her in the kitchen and kept moving toward the door. "I can tell you right now I'm not going back to school next semester. So I'm gonna cut your losses and leave right now."

"We're not finished, Blue," I heard her say as I jerked open the door.

I closed the door behind me and headed for my snow-covered truck.

26

Back to Blue

The March wind roared against the walls of Cecelia's cabin and clamored down the chimney. Emma looked up from her nap by the fire and listened for a moment. She looked at me until her eyes again grew calm, and she laid her head back down. I pulled the Pendleton blanket across my hips and picked up the stack of typed pages of Cecelia's first draft. A dog-eared page marked the place where I stopped for dinner. I flipped to the page and started reading again.

Cecelia strolled out from the kitchen with a mug of coffee in each hand. She lowered them onto the coffee table and walked around beside me. "It looks like you're almost done with the reading," she said, motioning for me to sit up and let her scoot under.

I waited for her to settle in and lowered my head into her lap. "Does finishing the book mean we're done, too?" I asked with an easy smile.

She caressed my face and looked down into my eyes, "If you want."

I reached for her hand. "You know nothing makes me want you more than telling me I'm free to go."

Cecelia smiled. "You've always been free to go."

"And I've always wanted you." I kissed her wrist and she drew in a deep breath. I twisted around to avoid the look in her eyes. "I know we have to end this someday," I said. She didn't respond, so I figured she didn't want to talk about it.

"I've been thinking about quitting the shuttle," I said after a moment. "I want to do something that feels like it matters, but I can't go back to school right now. I'm not ready to be that confined again."

Cecelia swept my hair back from my neck and trailed her fingers along the base of my ear. "What do you have in mind?"

"I've been thinking about getting into firefighting. I met this guy on the shuttle who worked for the Forest Service out of Fort Collins. He said they're starting to hire women now."

"Why firefighting? It seems dangerous."

"Yeah, it probably is. I think I could do it, though. Maybe Julie wouldn't think I was wasting my life if I was a firefighter."

"That fight you two had in Vail is still bothering you, isn't it?"

I turned around to Cecelia's understanding face. "I don't want to disappoint her, Cecelia. I can't seem to make myself do what she wants, either. I've got to find a way to keep her off my ass 'til I figure some shit out."

You're wasting your life, Blue. Julie's admonishment from six weeks ago still sounded as clear in my mind as the night she had said it. The clinking noise coming from under my truck's hood seemed to drive home her point. I slowed to a crawl as the clinking got louder. What did Julie know? Just because I had spent the last year and seven months driving an airport shuttle, it didn't mean my whole life was wasted. At least I didn't owe anybody anything. If my parents could have said the same thing, I might have more than this overheating truck to show for all their years of sweat and worry.

My dashboard temperature gauge crept up another notch, now only a quarter peg from the top of the scale. I leaned up to check for steam. A faint stream drifted up from the front grill, and I knew I was fucked. If only I could squeeze out one more mile I would be in Pinedale, Wyoming. Maybe it wouldn't cost too much to get to the truck fixed. The last thing I needed was to have to call Julie for money.

Steam billowed out from under the hood as I limped into town. I pulled into the first gas station and parked beside the open garage bay. "Can I help you, ma'am?" A lanky mechanic in blue coveralls wiped his hands with a rag as he walked toward me. The blue stitching on his white shoulder patch said his name was Bill.

"I hope so," I said. "The temperature gauge was reading high and then it started boiling over. I figure it's a leak in the radiator or something." I pulled my bandana out of my pocket to cover my hand and opened the hood latch.

"Yeah, it looks like you've got a leak," Bill said. Steam poured against his scrunched up face. He leaned into the heat and snaked his head around the length of the radiator. "There's where it's coming from," he pointed.

I followed his finger. "Yeah, I see it. Can you fix it?"

"I can, but it'll be tomorrow. I've got one on the rack to finish by five." He rocked back on his heels and glanced down at my plates, then turned to me with squinted eyes. "You're from Colorado?"

"Yeah, Fort Collins."

"You'll need to stay the night if you leave it with me. There's a hotel a couple of blocks up on Fremont that's not too pricey this time of year. Tell them your rig broke down and they'll give you a deal."

"Do I need to get all my stuff out?" There was enough camping gear in the bed to last a week.

"Don't worry about it. I'll lock your truck up in the garage."

I grabbed my duffle bag and handed Bill the keys. "Thanks a lot, Bill. I'll be back to check on it tomorrow." He nodded and I started walking. To the west, the Wind River Range rose into a cloudless blue sky, as beautiful as a whispered promise. I could hardly wait to get up there and spend a few nights staring up at the stars and figuring out what the hell I wanted to do with my life.

A gray-haired clerk at The Inn looked up and smiled when I walked into the lobby. "Bill sent you?" she asked. I grinned and nodded. "I give ten percent off to Bill's breakdowns." She flipped a pen out of her burgundy, pearl-buttoned cowboy shirt and grabbed a key from a pigeonhole on the shelf behind her. "I need a driver's license and thirty dollars," she said as she handed me the pen and pushed a registration form across the counter.

"Is thirty the discount rate?" I asked as I started writing.

The clerk straightened her shoulders and looked at me with an expression that landed somewhere between a smile and a smirk. Her erect posture said she was no-nonsense. I figured ex-military. "Yep," she said, her pale-blue eyes on me with a stare that could go from friendly to fire-breathing in a nanosecond. "It's usually thirty-four this time of year. I rounded it down for you."

"Great," I said cheerfully. I reached into my pocket for a small clutch of folded bills and peeled off a twenty and a ten. "Here ya go."

She opened her cash drawer and stashed away the money. "You're from the South?"

"Yes, ma'am. I'm originally from Alabama."

"Alabama, huh?" She tilted her head back and looked at me over the tip of her nose. "I spent some time in Alabama when I was in the service. Fort McClellan."

"Near Anniston," I said.

"Yep, that's the one." She leaned toward me and rested her elbows on the counter. "Listen, if you need a place to eat tonight, the Double D has good food and cold beer." She pointed her pen northward. "It's a block on up that way."

"Great. Thanks." I liked this woman. She reminded me, in some ways, of my mother. "Room 105," I asked, looking down at my key fob.

"Yep." She smiled in a proud sort of way. "It's a nice room; right next to my apartment."

"Okay, maybe I'll see you later," I said. She lifted a three-finger wave and I headed down the hall, one room past the door with the brass plate that read, *Manager*. Maybe she gave me the room next to her apartment because her years in the military had given her a taste of how it felt to be a single woman in a strange town. Maybe the difference between her and me was that I liked it.

The Double D looked like a lot of western saloons: round tables and spindle-back chairs scattered across the front room and a handcrafted bar centered on one side. Behind the bar a huge, vintage mirror spanned several feet in each direction. I walked over to the bar and

170

settled onto a stool. The bartender, a sinewy, deeply tanned guy with a thick brown mustache, broke from his conversation with a trio of locals and sauntered over to me. He turned his head to listen to my order, then swung around to the cooler, grabbed a Bud Light, and set it in front of me. "You by yourself?" he asked as he pried the bottle top.

"Yep," I replied, hoping to dissuade further conversation—from him or any of the three watching us from the end of the bar.

"You won't be for long," he said with a glance past my shoulder. He took my two dollars for the beer and headed for the cash register.

The sound of heavy boots pounded toward me and stopped. I looked into the bar mirror and saw a six foot hunk of swaggering muscle standing at my right shoulder. I watched him as he reached into his front pocket and stepped up next to me. His thick forearms rested against the bar and he leaned forward, a ten-dollar bill creased between two fingers. "I need some more quarters, Mick," he said. A shock of blonde hair fell across his forehead when he turned to face me. "Welcome to Pinedale. Can I buy you a drink?" he asked in a low grumble.

I lifted my Bud Light, "I've got one. Thanks." I gave him a quick smile and returned my focus to my beer.

"Suit yourself." He took his quarters from Mick and swung around to me. "A few of us are shootin' some Eight Ball in the back. You can join us if you want."

He walked away before I had a chance to again tell him I wasn't interested. I watched him leave, and glancing back at the pool tables, I saw her: taking aim over the cue ball, about five-eight, with shaggy, shoulder-length blonde hair, and arms like Martina. I quickly looked away, though I wanted to stare. I knew I couldn't. She could kick my ass if she wanted; I could tell that with one look at her. Yet, I couldn't stop myself from stealing glances. Her body looked like a power-house—long, thick legs that could chew up mountainsides, wide shoulders framing her tight butt, and the way she moved, with as much swagger as grace. How in the hell could I ignore a woman like her?

171

"Here you are, ma'am." Mick set my hamburger and a basket of fries in front of me and planted his hands on the edge of the bar. "That'll be four-fifty." He watched me reach into my pocket for my wallet. "If you've looking for a way to pass the time tonight, that's a good bunch of kids back there."

"Thanks, man," I said.

I ate slowly, all the while contemplating how to introduce myself to her and avoid too much attention from the guys. I swallowed my last bite and glanced at them again. She was walking my way. She stopped at my elbow and raised a couple of empty Budweiser bottles at Mick. He nodded and started for the cooler.

"I've got a bet with those guys that I can bring you back to the tables with me," she said. Her smile, half-cocked and brazen, seemed more playful than arrogant.

"Why would I want to?"

"Because you'd help me win ten bucks."

"And what would I get out of it?"

"A beer—and a chance to hang out with some good guys for a while. I'll make sure they behave." She looked at me with a wry smile.

I chuckled and held out my hand. "You've got a deal," I said. I looked into her hazel eyes and tried not to wince from the tight squeeze of her grip. "I'm Blue Riley."

"You can call me Beck," she said as she loosened her grip. "Beck Long. You can call me either Beck or Rebecca. If you ever call me Becky, I'll take out your knee." She grinned and reached for her fresh beers.

"So who are your buddies back there?" I asked.

"Sorry-assed firefighters," Beck said with her eyes toward the pool tables. "They're worthless, but they're my buds. We start gearing up for fire season next week. We're just hanging out 'til then."

"So you're a firefighter?"

"Yep, we're all firefighters."

"I've been thinking about trying to get on with you guys. I came up from Fort Collins to talk to the ranger about an opening I saw posted near CSU."

She flashed a skeptical grin. "It won't hurt to try. The competition is tough, but they're looking for women these days. Somebody has to knock some sense into these knuckleheads." She reached over and planted her free hand on my shoulder. "Come on back with me. I'll introduce you to these horny bastards."

I slid off the bar stool and grabbed my beer. "They'll be wasting their time."

Beck glanced back and grinned.

The sky above us held a few passing clouds, the ones to the west illuminated by a moon so full they shone like satin. Beck pulled out her ChapStick, swept it across her lips, and popped it back in her pocket. Behind us an outdoor heater glowed bright orange. The heat didn't quite reach my toes, so I wiggled them in my hiking boots to fight back the cold. Beck stretched her legs out on the lounge chair beside mine and rested her beer on top of her belly. The faint voice of Rosanne Cash drifted through the walls of the bar and mixed with an occasional rustle of wind flowing down from the mountains. I couldn't quite believe how completely relaxed I felt around this woman I'd just met. I folded my arm behind my head and watched the passing clouds.

"It's so freaking beautiful out on the fire line at night," Beck said. She raised her beer and slowly waved it in the air, as if to orchestrate her thoughts, "The sky's as clear as a coyote's howl, and the stars, like a dome of diamonds, just doing their thing, all these thousands of tiny little pinpricks of light, millions of miles away. You can see the fire burning up on the ridge, like this orange glow, hanging close to the ground. The stars and the mountain, all on fire, and in the valley is the sharp smell of smoke. And you smell like that, too. Your body is covered with smoke and your own layers of sweat; and you're so freaking tired all you want to do is sleep, but you don't want to miss the beauty around you. So you lie there, close your eyes, and go to sleep with the sound of the wind, sweeping across the ridge, feeding and starving that fire as it goes. The next morning, you wake up and convince your tired body into moving. You get up and do it all again, and as much as it hurts sometimes, you love it. Firefighting gets in your blood.

When it does, you can't shake it." She turned to me. She must have seen the dumbass fascination in my eyes. She grinned and tipped back her Budweiser. "The money doesn't suck, either."

I watched the easy smile that seemed to light up her face. Beck was more handsome than beautiful. The lines around her eyes hinted of long days spent in the sun, though her skin seemed well suited for it. Her full lips turned up slightly at the edges, so a constant smile seemed always on her mouth. Mostly I liked her eyes. They held a kind of intelligence, like a patient watcher.

"So, why do you want to be a firefighter?" she asked.

"After what you just told me, why do you even ask?"

She chuckled. "Like I said, the competition for a firefighter job is tough. A lot of us got on by working a summer or two as a seasonal and then applied for a firefighter job. It helps if the ranger knows you already."

My hopes sank. A seasonal job wouldn't impress Julie, or make her believe I was getting my shit together. "If I do get on as a seasonal worker, what are the chances I could get on as a firefighter next year?"

"It depends. Most seasonals get training so they can help out when we're stretched thin. If you show promise, you'll be more likely to get picked up as a firefighter the next year."

"So how can I get a seasonal job?"

"The ranger is taking applications now. Talk to him when you go in tomorrow. You can still put in for a fire job, too. You're more likely to get on as a seasonal, but he'll know you're interested in firefighting."

I nodded and took a sip of beer.

"So why do you really want to be a firefighter?" Beck asked.

"I want to do something important, you know? My aunt has been on my ass to go back to school, and I know I should. But I don't want to be that tied down right now."

"Your aunt has been on your ass?" Beck asked. I heard the question she didn't ask, too, like why my aunt would care more than my parents.

"Yeah, she's the only family I have now. My parents died about five years ago."

"Wow. I'm sorry to hear that." The kindness in her voice said she meant it. "So you used to be in school, and now you aren't. You're here

174

looking for a firefighter job in a new town, and your aunt stays on your ass. This sounds like a story I'd like to hear, if you don't mind telling it."

"You want all the gory details?"

"I do." She looked at me and waited.

I started with the farm, and my parents. I told her about my dreams of being a veterinarian, of my love of the mountains, and how Grace had left me. Beck asked attentive questions, and I kept talking. I told her about Lilly, and how much Lilly had changed me, so much so that I was allowing myself to have a long-term affair with a married woman. I told her I had left Cecelia's cabin just this morning, and there had been so little guilt, about the staying or the leaving.

When I finished, Beck's expression seemed intrigued rather than harsh. "So it sounds like you've done some living, Blue Riley. Did you commit any crimes while you were doing all that living?"

"Well, sodomy laws." I grinned and waited to be sure she would smile back. "Probably in most every state I've been in, and adultery, if that's illegal in Wyoming."

Beck laughed. "I wouldn't tell the ranger about that, although I'm sure half the people in Wyoming would be guilty of the big A."

The side door leading from the bar opened and Mick walked out. He lit a cigarette and leaned against the wall. A string of perfectly formed smoke rings popped from his lips. For a long moment we watched him. "After I finish this smoke, I'm closing down," Mick said, seemingly to no one. "Your guys left about an hour ago, Beck."

She shrugged and sat up, straddling the lounge chair. I wanted to ask if she was up for another beer somewhere—anywhere she wanted. Instead I downed the last of my beer and grabbed the empty bottle beside me.

Beck waited and we walked across the deck. At the door she wrapped her arm across my shoulder. "By the way, in case you're wondering, I'm not gay. I'm too into guys to swing the other way."

With a little time, maybe I could change that.

27

Earning It

The Grand Teton relief map on the wall of the Pinedale District Ranger's Office held my attention for the moment. Feeling as flighty as a thoroughbred, I studied the names of the peaks and streams as I waited to talk to the district ranger.

"Good morning," a commanding yet friendly voice sounded from behind me.

I spun around. The guy walking toward me was short and stocky rather than the tall, Clint Eastwood figure I'd conjured up in my head. "I'm Dave Brennan, district FMO. I mean, district Fire Management Officer. Sorry, we use a lot of acronyms." His walrus mustache turned up at the corners in what appeared to be a smile.

"I'm Augusta Riley," I said, meeting his gaze like my dad taught me. My fingers wrapped around his wide, meaty hand with a firm grip. "Most people call me Blue." With Dave standing across from me, I realized that without his boots he was probably an inch or so shorter than me. That, along with his round glasses and the rumpled look of his thinning, sandy blonde hair, calmed my nerves.

"Beck Long tells me you're here to see the ranger about a seasonal job," he said.

"Yes, sir, I am. I'm interested in firefighting, too."

"That's what Beck tells me. Come on back and I'll introduce you to the ranger."

I followed him down a hallway lined with maps, and photographs of fire on mountains and logs on trucks. A cluster of black and white photos of serious-faced men hung near the ranger's office. Dave tapped on the open door and waited. "A young lady is here to see you about a seasonal job," he said after a moment.

"Tell her to come in," I heard a deep voice grumble.

Dave turned to me. "Go on in." I felt him looking me over as I passed by him, though it seemed he was checking me out more like a horse on an auction block than a potential woman to date.

The ranger got up to greet me. "Good morning," he said, standing behind a simple wooden desk. "I'm John Walters, District Ranger."

I hustled over to take his hand. He was the tall version I had expected. He wore his dark hair in a crew cut, like most of the men in the pictures outside his door. "I'm Augusta Riley."

He pointed to a chair across from his desk and we sat down together. "So you're here about a seasonal job?"

I nodded. "Yes, sir."

"I'll have my clerk get you an application. Have you ever worked for this outfit before?"

"No, sir," I replied. I quickly added, "I grew up on a farm, so I've worked outside most of my life. I can drive a tractor, ride a horse, work with cattle, and mend a fence. I also backpack and fish if that will do you any good."

The ranger cocked his head back and looked at me an amused smile. "Fishing always does me good," he said. He picked up the pen from a stack of papers and rolled it in his fingers. "Our seasonal jobs are only for a few months and they aren't the kind of work everyone enjoys. How do you feel about cleaning shitters?"

Cleaning shitters—Julie would love that. I swallowed hard and replied, "Well, it wouldn't be honest to say I would like to clean shitters, but if that's what you need me to do, I'm willing to do it. I guess it wouldn't be too much different from mucking stalls."

"It may be a little different," he said with a full out grin. "Though, I do appreciate your honesty, Miss Riley. I find it encouraging." He stood up and I followed his lead. "My clerk's office is next door. Stop by and get an application."

Like a goof, I reached over to shake his hand again. Our hands clasped and I said, "Thank you, sir. If you have any openings for a firefighter job, I'd be interested in that, too."

"Most of you kids are," he replied with a halfhearted smile.

My cheeks rushed with heat as I turned and left. The clerk had my application waiting. "Here's the application for you to fill out. Have it back by close of business on Friday." She seemed nice enough, though I couldn't wait to get out the door. I nodded and mumbled a thank you and took off down the hall. When I turned for the entry door, I saw Beck reaching to pull it open.

Great, now I have to tell her I made a fool of myself.

"How did it go?" Beck asked when I stepped outside.

"I totally blew it. Mr. Walters asked me if I'd ever worked for the Forest Service and I ended up telling him I liked to fish."

She grinned. "He likes to fish, too. Don't let it bother you. Do a good job on your application and see where it goes."

She stood across from me in her green pants and yellow firefighter shirt and the coolest boots I'd ever seen. Her confidence filled the air between us, and I latched onto it like a soul searching for faith. I straightened and said, "I'll do that. I'll see you around, okay?"

"You bet." She grasped my shoulder and gave it a gentle squeeze.

I turned away from her and walked to my truck, still feeling the weight of her hand.

Part of me hoped Julie wouldn't answer. I listened through the series of phone rings, my mind rehearsing the right words to tell her about my new job with the Forest Service. No matter how I said it, I figured she wouldn't be pleased. The new job meant I would be farther away from Fort Collins and the pull of a university.

She answered on the fifth ring. "Hi, Julie," I said, starting off with enthusiasm.

"You sound happy. What's up?" I knew by the tone of her voice she wasn't buying my shtick.

"I just got a job with the Forest Service."

"The Forest Service," she replied, her voice covered in doubt. "Doing what?"

"All kinds of things, I think. We'll be doing wildlife stuff and helping out in their campgrounds. The ranger said I'll be trained for firefighting, too."

"Uh, huh," Julie said. "Is this job in Fort Collins?"

My heart began to pound. "No, it's in Pinedale, Wyoming. I'll be living in a bunkhouse."

"Why are you doing this, Blue? Do you need more money?"

I hesitated for a long moment before I answered. "I want you to be proud of me," I began. "I hope getting on with the Forest Service will lead to a firefighting job. I figured you wouldn't think I was wasting my life if I was doing something important like that."

It seemed an eternity before she replied. "You've got to grow up sometime, Blue, and maybe this summer job will help you understand that a life of hard labor is difficult. I want you to start thinking about the long-term ramifications of these decisions you're making."

"I will," I replied, though I knew I wouldn't.

"Do you have any friends in Pinedale?"

My heart calmed and I smiled into the phone. "Yeah, I've hung out with a few people up there, mostly with this girl named Beck Long. Her parents have a ranch not too far from Pinedale. You want their number?"

Julie took all the numbers, of Beck's parents, the bunkhouse, the ranger's office, and even the Double D. Before she hung up, she asked me one more question. "Is this what you really want to do?"

The gentle sincerity in her voice caught me off guard, and I actually found myself thinking about it for a moment. "Yes, it is what I want."

Beck flopped down in the grass beside me. A thin coat of sweat covered her face and moistened the edges of her hairline. After five miles of running, she barely seemed fazed. I could hardly move my legs. Running at eight thousand feet was far different from running at five thousand feet, and Beck insisted we do it at least once a week.

She reached down and retied her running shoe. "That last hill was a bitch," she said, between deep, steady breaths. I hadn't regained enough air to speak. She stretched out and propped up on her elbows, surveying the mountain on the horizon. "You'll thank me for this later, when you're up there working your ass off all day."

"I hope so," I said as I sucked in breaths. "I'd hate to know you are torturing me like this for nothing."

She chuckled. "We'll have more fire starts soon. With this drought, you'll get in on some good action before long."

I followed her gaze out to the steep mountainsides of the Wind River Range. Did I want all of that beauty to be ablaze? Were we being selfish to want the adrenaline rush of chasing smoke? Or were we merely accepting the fiery course of Mother Nature, and wanting to protect her from herself? All I knew was that I longed to be out there, fighting fires with the others. "Man, I'm so ready," I said.

"I think you are ready," Beck replied. "I'm hearing good things from the guys who work with you. That's important."

"Do you think there's any chance I can get on the fire crew next year?" I asked.

She thought for a moment. "If you do well being around fire and Dave Brennan likes the work you do, I'd say you have a really good chance."

"I know some of the guys don't think women should be firefighters. They haven't said anything, but I can sense it when I talk about wanting to get into fire. They get real quiet or change the subject. They don't seem to mind that you're a firefighter, though."

Beck sat up and turned to me, her eyes squinted in the evening sun. "I had to work hard to earn their respect, and some of the guys have known me since we were kids. It's gonna be harder for you, but I know you can do it if you really want. I don't think you'd be running five miles in this altitude if you didn't."

Dave Brennan called the crew up to the engine and spread a topographic map across the hood. "After lunch we'll do a hose lay along this line," he said, his finger trailing along a pencil line drawn on the map. "Winds will be southwest and relatively calm this afternoon. We should be able to get the hose done by midafternoon." He folded up the map and looked up at us. "Go get your lunch and be back here in thirty."

Beck and I headed down the dirt road, bone-dry dust rising around our thick-soled boots. She had talked me into shelling out two hundred bucks for the pair of White's boots I wore, and I was glad she had. I'd walked several hundred miles in them since fires started popping in mid-July. Most of our other work had been put on hold while we chased fire from one start to the next.

Beck angled away from the road and scrambled down the embankment toward a narrow stream. At a cluster of rocks near the water's edge, she propped her boot up and started unhooking the laces. I settled onto the flat surface of a boulder and watched her strip down to bare feet. Gingerly, she tiptoed into the stream and picked her way toward a shallow pool.

"Fuckin' glorious," she said, standing in chin deep water. "My feet were burning up walking in that shit."

I took an apple from my daypack and shrugged, as if her morning walking over hot, burned-over ground was really no big deal.

"Oh screw you, Riley." Her hands moved to her hips and for a moment I thought she was actually pissed. "You're going to pay for that attitude. I'll make sure you pull hose up that damn hill for the rest of the day."

"Yeah, and you'll be right behind me." I pulled out an orange from her lunch bag and tossed it to her. She waded out of the water and sat down beside me, then propped her feet up on a rock to dry, and sank the edge of her thumbnail into the orange. "Do you think we could get on with the hotshots next season?" I asked.

Beck stopped in mid-peel and cut her eyes over at me. "Don't you think you should start by getting on as a regular firefighter?"

I bit into my apple, undaunted by the skeptical look on her face. "I would be a regular firefighter, only better trained and better paid. You could be, too. We'd go all over the place, and we'd make enough money to last all year."

Beck gathered her orange peels and stacked them on the rock beside her. "I have been thinking about applying for the hotshots.

Eventually I want to get into a job like Dave Brennan's. A season or two as a hotshot would look good on an application."

"It wouldn't hurt me, either. Maybe my aunt would finally have something she could brag to her doctor friends about."

Beck grinned. "She's still on your ass, huh? Are you going back to North Carolina after the summer?"

"I'm not sure yet. I may try to get on at a ski resort or something."

Beck reached into her bag and pulled out a turkey sandwich. The sandwich looked the same as every day, thinly sliced meat slopping out of smashed bread. She frowned and lifted the edge of the wrapping. "You could winter at the ranch if you want. We couldn't pay you much, but you'd have a place to stay. My mom's a pretty good cook, too. Way better than this stuff." She wadded up the plastic wrap and bit into her sandwich, grimacing as she chewed.

"What do you think your mom and dad would say? It seems like a lot to ask."

Beck swallowed and said, "I've already asked them. Mom said as long as you were willing to work, she would be happy to have you."

"I don't know, Beck. I mean, she doesn't know I'm—"

She cut me off. "Yeah, she does know because I told her. I didn't want you to have to dodge questions about boys all winter. She said she didn't see how that would matter, so long as you know how to work."

28

As Close As I Could Get

Beck stood outside our tent, looking out to the spiraling column of smoke rising from the ridge to the north. The unease on her face worried me. "I hope we're not flying today," she muttered, seemingly as much to herself as to me.

I finished lacing my boot and stood up beside her. "You feeling okay, bud?" She had to be sick; Beck loved to fly, especially in helicopters.

"Yeah, I'm fine. I didn't sleep well is all," she replied in a voice too shallow to be convincing. She reached over and touched my back. "I'll see you after briefing."

"I'll get your water for you," I said to her back as she walked away. "You want one Gatorade?"

"Yeah," she answered over her shoulder. I watched her walk away, as purposeful as ever. I wasn't buying her confidence. For the past couple of days something seemed to be nagging at her, though I couldn't figure what it was, and she hadn't told me. When I'd asked, she said she was fine, in a not-really-fine kind of way.

I crawled back into the tent to gather our water bottles. The acrid smell of sweat and wood smoke filled our nylon dome with a constant fog of funk. The odor seemed everywhere, in the creases of our sleeping bags, our clothes, and even our skin. Maybe Beck was itching to get home. We had been on our assignment in Oregon for almost three weeks, sleeping in tents and freezing our asses off at night. We were all ready to get home, sleep in a real bed, and take a decent shower.

Home. I couldn't be sure where that was anymore. The obvious answer was Julie's house, though it had begun to seem less so in the two years that had passed since I left North Carolina. At least Julie and I hadn't been fighting as much lately. I'd called her a couple of weeks ago to tell her I was in Oregon on a firefighting assignment, and I was certain I'd caught a hint of pride in her voice.

At least for the coming winter my home would be at the Longs' ranch. After spending a few weekends there, Beck's mom, JoAnne, started calling me her "flatland daughter from Alabama."

The first time I saw JoAnne, it seemed I was seeing an older version of Beck. She walked out of the ranch house with Beck's purposeful gait, headed straight for her daughter and threw her arms around her with such gusto I thought she'd knock her down. When JoAnne turned to me she held onto Beck's shoulder. "You must be Blue Riley," she said. She shook my hand and looked at both of us. "You girls ready to do some riding? We've got a few head we need to check up in the summer pasture."

I followed them to the barn and we saddled the horses, grabbed lunch, and headed up the trail to the high country. Though it had been a while since I'd been on a horse, I rode well enough to convince Mrs. Long I could earn my keep at the ranch. That night we sat down together in the kitchen of their sprawling ranch house to eat dinner. I nodded for the blessing and ate until my huge hunger was quenched. Our conversation flowed effortlessly through dinner and on to dessert, and although the table was bigger and the conversation louder, I felt as settled as I'd been years ago, in the days before the tornado came.

I don't know why I looked up at the exact moment I did. The lean started at the top of the tree, angling toward Beck and picking up momentum. "Beck, run!" I yelled.

She turned to me, frozen in her tracks. "Run!" I yelled at the same goddamn moment the tree started its eerie groan. She glanced up, her eyes wide with terror, the mammoth tree hurtling toward her, time for only two giant strides, and then came the crash. Dust and ash flew through a tower of shuddering branches, and then it all grew still.

"Beck!" I yelled, sprinting toward her, my heart slamming against my chest. "Beck!" Tree branches scraped and popped against my face.

Limbs stabbing at my legs, I shoved my way into the massive tree, searching desperately for a sign of her yellow shirt. "Beck!"

"Here." Her weak voice came from somewhere I couldn't see. I spun around and stumbled out of the tangle of branches and sprinted around the end of the tree. Beck's body lay sprawled against the ground, unmoving except the index finger of her hand. Blood soaked the right side of her pants and colored the rock at her knee.

"Don't move, Beck," I said, kneeling beside her. I scanned her back for bleeding and dropped to the ground to check her face.

"I think it broke my fuckin' leg," she groaned between clenched teeth.

"Blue!" Jim Parker's voice rang through the woods at the far side of the tree.

"Over here!" I yelled back.

"You hear that, Beck?" I said close to her ear. "Jim is on his way. He'll fix you right up." She closed her eyes. We both knew EMT kits wouldn't be enough to fix the blood pouring from her knee.

Jim scrambled over the trunk of the fallen tree resting beside us. I grabbed Beck's hand and sat up. Quickly Jim checked Beck's back and neck and moved down to her knee. "Hold onto her, Blue." He pulled out his first aid kit and got the scissors. "We need to stop that bleeding first." Gently, he put his scissors to the cuff of Beck's pants and began to cut, every slice revealing more bruising and blood. "Call Gus and tell him we'll need an airlift," Jim said.

Beck squeezed my hand and groaned.

I watched her blood soak through the gauze bandage Jim held against the gash and wondered if my skin looked as pale as hers. Between winces of pain, her eyes searched my face for clues of how bad it was. "He's almost got it, Beck," I said, looking confidently into her eyes. The rest of the squad surrounded us now. They knew to keep their mouths shut.

"You ready for a ride out of here?" Gus asked after we loaded her into the emergency litter.

Beck looked up at our crew boss and tried to smile. "Beats walkin'," she said.

Gus smiled back and pulled the litter strap tight over her chest.

He turned to me after he gave the strap a final tug. "I want you to go with her, Blue. Bill will meet you at the hospital with the paperwork to get her admitted. You just take care of her until the Longs get there." He grabbed my shoulder and gently squeezed it. "You did good today, Blue."

The shrill start-up of the helicopter engine rang in my ears. I crawled in next to Beck, strapped in, and gave my thumbs up to the pilot. The ship lifted off the ground, climbing slowly above the tree line. In the distance our crew formed a straight line of yellow shirts, all the guys facing the ship. We flew toward them, and all at once they lifted a hand into the air. I waved as we passed, and watched them scatter to get back to work.

Beck's eyes struggled to open. She blinked at me for a moment, trying to focus. Her weakness startled me. I had never seen her look so vulnerable. "Hey there, Blue Riley." She glanced around and resettled her gaze on me. "Where are we?" she asked, her voice barely above a whisper.

I took her hand and held it loosely. "We're in a hospital in Bend, Oregon. Your mom and dad are on the way. How're you feeling?"

"Okay." Beck's leg jerked and she winced with pain. She tightened her grip on my hand, still weak as a child. "What the hell happened to me?"

"You were attacked by a tree," I teased her.

"Shit." Beck tried to smile. "Who won?"

"Well, the tree is dead, and you're still alive, so I'd say you won."

Beck managed a weak smile. "Damn right I did," she said, and closed her eyes again.

I pulled the guest chair close to her bed and cradled her hand in mine. For a long while I watched her sleep. They had cleaned up the blood and soot and sweat from her body, and I had bummed a shower from the hospital. Still, the smell of smoke and blood hung heavy in the air, a constant reminder that she had almost died nine hours ago. My mind flashed through images of that tree that had looked sound and the lean that started toward her, and the sound of my voice yelling her name, the thunder of the tree crashing, and my heart, pounding. The fear wouldn't leave me, yet I had to push it away, to stay strong for Beck.

Beck's Jeep sat alone in front of the Longs' ranch house. I parked beside it and hopped out of the truck. I'd missed Beck every moment of the six weeks since the accident. The few calls I had made from fire camps were no match for seeing the confidence of her cockeyed smile, or the hours of conversation we had in our tent or under the stars.

I let myself in and called out to her as I walked through the kitchen carrying the huge, stuffed Smokey Bear I bought for her at the ranger's office. "In here!" Beck called back from the den. Her eyes lit up when I walked in. She dropped her book in her lap and held her arms open to me. "It's about time, Blue Riley!" she said with a huge mile.

I tossed Smokey on the recliner and hustled over. Beck pulled me close, her muscled shoulders and back as firm as ever, and her hair falling against my face, soft again from days out of the sun. "Sit down, girl," she said when her arms grew slack.

I scooted to the end of the couch and scrunched into the space beside the tower of pillows supporting her leg. Neat rows of white scars crossed over the jagged red line below her knee. I figured the heavy black brace that surrounded her leg hid the surgery scar. "How's rehab going?" I asked.

"Better. It hurt like hell when I first started. Can you believe they made me bend it right after surgery?" I shook my head. "I suppose it paid off. My physical therapist says I'm ahead of where I should be."

I grinned and wrapped my hand across her toes. "So does that mean you're gonna be ready for the hotshots next season?"

Beck frowned and pushed herself up to sit straighter. She worked her fingers into her hair and twisted her mouth the way she did when she had to tell me something she knew I wouldn't like. "I don't think so, Blue. I think I'm done with firefighting."

"Oh, no way," I said with a smirk. Beck had to be joking. Firefighting was in her blood. She said so herself.

"Yep, I'm afraid I am," she said, looking away from me.

I still thought she was shittin' me. Beck Long did not quit, especially something she loved. There had to be a reason. "Come on, girl, I know you can get strong enough if you try. I'll be here all winter to help you with rehab."

"Blue, you know my mom and dad want you to stay here on the ranch this winter, and I want that too, but you gotta know no amount of rehab is going to change the fact that this knee is shot. It's time for me to hang up my boots." She pushed against my thigh with her good leg and looked at me with a hesitant smile. "It's a good thing I trained you to take my place."

I grinned and rubbed her foot. She could still have a career in firefighting. There was always dispatch, or maybe a tanker base, or helicopters. "So what will you do? I know you can't stay away from fire."

Her smile faded. She picked up her book and gripped it between the palms of her hands, stalling. "Well, I have been giving it some thought," she began slowly. She looked up at me, her eyes apologetic. "As much as I want to stay in fire, I think I need to focus on getting back in school. I'd like to graduate before I'm eighty years old."

My mind drifted away from her next words, and soon her voice droned in my ears without comprehension. We were supposed to apply for the hotshot crew next season, and I was certain with our experience we could make the cut. Now she wanted to go back to school? That left me nowhere.

"Earth to Blue, you still here?" Beck's firm voice jerked me back from my thoughts.

I shook out of my fog and looked at her. "So, are you going back to Idaho to finish school?"

She looked away. "I'm not sure." She thought for a moment and returned her gaze to me. "I think I'm going to stay around here, Blue. I met this guy at the rehab center. He's a physical therapist for brain injury patients. He's a terrific guy, and, well, I think I'm falling in love with him."

Falling in love? When did this happen? She hadn't even mentioned a guy last time we talked.

"So what's his name? And why haven't you mentioned him before now?" I asked, swallowing back the hurt that began tightening my throat.

Beck smiled. "His name is Jared Anderson. And I haven't told you about him because we've hardly had a chance to talk since Jared and I met. Besides, I wanted to hear how you guys were doing with the fires."

"So tell me about Jared," I said, faking interest.

Beck looked at me skeptically. She knew me well enough to see I didn't really want to hear about Jared Anderson just yet. "How about we eat first? I'm starving."

"At least that hasn't changed since last time I saw you."

"Neither have you, you stupid rookie."

I grinned and watched her face brighten. "So you want a sandwich or something?"

"I'd love one. Ham and pepperjack with mayo and mustard. I think we have lettuce, too."

"You got it." I stood up and Beck reached out her hand. I held it loosely and swung it side to side, as if we really were alright. "You're an asshole for not telling me about Jared, you know that?"

"Yep, but I knew you'd get over it," she replied. I gave her the slow grin I knew she expected. I would get over it. She was right about that. I dropped her hand and headed for the kitchen.

"So are you planning to stay here tonight?" she asked as I walked away.

I had planned to stay before I knew about Jared Anderson, and Beck giving up on her dream of a career in firefighting. "No, not tonight. I promised my Fort Collins buddies we'd go camping before it gets too cold. I'm heading down this afternoon."

She probably knew I was lying. Lies like that were one of the things friends did to spare each other's feelings, like making sandwiches was one of the things friends did to show they still cared. At least that was what I reasoned as I pulled the bread from the aluminum box on the counter. I took the mayonnaise and mustard, cheese, ham, and lettuce from the refrigerator and piled it on the counter by the bread. My fingers slid in toward the middle of the loaf and pulled out two pieces. Beck always wanted the softest bread. I knew that about her. I had heard her complain day after day about the sandwiches we ate in the field. I wondered if Jared knew Beck hated hard bread. In only a few weeks, what could he know about her?

It didn't matter. If he was lucky, Jared would have his whole life to learn about Beck. For me, there would only be less. Less time to spend with her; less daydreams to share; less nights under the stars; less importance in her life; less, less, less, until one day there was nothing. I knew the day would come, just like it had with most people I loved.

Beck bit into her sandwich and closed her eyes with a satisfied smile. "This is a damn good sandwich," she said before her second bite.

"Just one of the many services I provide," I replied.

"Like staying beside me in the hospital?" Her face was serious as she chewed.

"Yeah, that too."

She returned my smile. "So tell me everything that happened after I got hurt."

"Well, we came back to Pinedale for a few days of R&R, and then we got called up to a big fire in California, not too far from Yosemite. It was okay. We got lots of hours, but the food sucked and we couldn't get many supplies. The scenery was incredible, though. I want to go back there when it isn't on fire."

"God, I'm gonna miss firefighting," Beck said wistfully. "The day they told me that my knee would never be stable enough for firefighting, I came home and cried all afternoon." She looked down at her knee brace and grimaced. "Mom and I had a long talk after that. I decided it would be better to do something totally different than to sit on the sidelines being frustrated I couldn't go on the fire line." She took another bite from her sandwich and chewed it slowly. Her thoughts seemed to be lost in the world of what could have been.

I couldn't help thinking that people who say things happen for a reason are jacked-up liars. There was no reason for that tree to fall on Beck, or for that tornado to kill my parents. The world was totally random. Anything else would be inexplicably cruel. "I'm sorry I wasn't here when you went through that. It had to be tough."

Beck shrugged. "You were where you needed to be. Besides, I met Jared soon after they told me about my knee. He's great to talk to. Some days we go down to the river for the afternoon and then go to the Double D to hang out for a while. It helps me get over what I'm missing with the fire crew."

"He sounds like a neat guy," I replied. I couldn't bring myself to say I was looking forward to meeting him. He would be the one taking Beck in her new direction, and I would be sitting around watching it all unfold. I imagined nights of Jared coming by to pick Beck up for dates, late night phone calls, and stopping by on Sunday for lunch at the Longs' kitchen table. There didn't seem much room for me in all that was to come, except maybe as a bridesmaid, which was something I'd never aspired to be.

I swallowed the last bite of my sandwich and picked up Beck's plate on my way to the kitchen. "So I guess I'd better get going," I said. "It's a long drive back to Fort Collins."

"Yes, it is. Have fun camping."

I set our dishes in the sink and went back to the den. "Okay, I'll see you around," I said.

Beck opened her arms again. I pulled her close and held on for a long moment. When I stood up straight, I held onto her hand. "Call me," she said.

"I will." I dropped her hand and took off without looking back. No way was I going to let Beck Long see me cry.

I got to my truck and looked around the corrals and outbuildings of the Longs' ranch. I'd hoped to spend the winter here, learning to hunt for elk and waiting for Christmas, watching football games and slinging hay and watching the weather—right beside Beck. And then we'd get on with the hotshots and go all over the place, helping people and earning good money. Julie would see I wasn't fucking up anymore.

The whole of it would never happen now. There was no use in staying around in hopes that it would. I backed the truck around and drove to the end of the driveway. The dry, dusty road waited to take me wherever I wanted to go.

I wasn't JoAnne's daughter or Beck's sister. I was an orphan in the world. It was time I accepted that. I turned right and headed for the West Coast, as close as I could get to oblivion.

Part Three

Staying

Spring 2001 – Spring 2004

29

Calling the Prodigal

Rebecca L. Anderson. The name neatly printed on the upper left of the envelope caught my attention first. Beck's still awesome, I thought as I pulled the stack out of my mailbox. On the back of the purple envelope, she'd written a note. *Do you know how hard it is to keep up with you?* I smiled and remembered the first time she tracked me down. She had gotten my phone number from Julie and called me on a Sunday afternoon. "You're an asshole, Blue Riley," she said as soon as I got out "Hello." Then she proceeded to give me a thorough tongue-lashing for leaving without saying a word. By the time she was through with me, I had apologized profusely and promised to come to her wedding, so long as I didn't have to wear a pastel dress.

I leaned against the wall next to the bank of apartment mailboxes to open her card. The Anderson family photograph fell out and landed at my feet. I picked it up. The background this year was a waterfall, I figured maybe Yellowstone. Jacob now stood almost as tall as his dad, and Lowry came up to Beck's shoulder. Abby wore a ball cap and a ponytail, and looked more like Beck than she had the year before. Jared and Beck looked as fit as ever.

I tucked the rest of my mail under my arm and climbed the stairs to my apartment. Inside, I flipped through the stack of bills and junk mail. Underneath the flap of one of the grocery flyers, I noticed the edge of a letter. I pulled it out and read the return address label. "Oh hell," I whispered into the empty room. Julie rarely wrote letters, and when she did, she was on a mission.

One hand holding Julie's letter and the other gripping my lowball glass, I dropped into my recliner. The sting of bourbon seeped down my throat as I unfolded the single page. Julie's handwriting was as precise as her scalpel.

Dear Blue,

I trust this letter will find you well. As for me, I am the same as when we last spoke.

It recently occurred to me that you are approaching your 41st birthday. By the time you read this letter, it may in fact have arrived. I hope you will have a good day, but more than that, I want to encourage you to take the day as an opportunity to reflect on what you will do with the rest of your life.

Although you have certainly had your adventures over the last twenty years, I continue to find your lack of direction to be troublesome. While I fully acknowledge that it is your life to live, I feel that in many ways I have failed you. Your talents and intelligence are substantial, and perhaps my lack of proper guidance allowed them to go untapped. You are now in what should be the most productive years of your life, and I want you to spend them well. I am proposing you return to North Carolina, where my resources to help you find meaningful work are more readily available. At this point I am no longer advocating for a university education, although I do believe you are still quite capable of earning a degree. There are a number of nonprofit organizations and charities in need of assistance, and in this way you would be able to make a significant contribution to society. Admittedly the pay is not good, so I am willing to assist you in buying a home.

I want you to consider that we are both aging, and as the only living relative to each other it will be wise to live in closer proximity. Again, returning to North Carolina seems to be most sensible, but I would understand if you choose another area to live. There are a number of attractive choices in the South, and I feel a return to your homeland would help you find the direction you need. I understand your attraction to the beauty of the West Coast, and particularly the Pacific Northwest, but I happen to believe the great expanse of the West has contributed in some ways to your lack of grounding. Although Portland is a beautiful city, I think you would agree that the two jobs you have held while living there in the last two years have not served you well. It seems there is nothing substantial to keep you on the West Coast, and because of this I have little trouble asking you to return closer to home.

Give my proposal some thought in the coming days. I will call you soon to discuss it further.

Enjoy your birthday. I am enclosing a check for dinner on me.

Love,

Julie

"Drama queen," I mumbled as I folded the letter back into the envelope. I sat back in my recliner and looked around my one bedroom apartment. On the mantel was a short stack of hardbacks, a cluster of animal figures I had whittled somewhere along the way, and a couple of candles I lit only when the electricity went out. In the corner across from my faded-out recliner, a red wool blanket draped the leather rocker I picked up in Alaska. Other than my bicycle and kayak, the rocker was the only thing in the entire apartment I cared about. The notion that Julie could be right pissed me off as much as her audacity in sending me the letter.

I tossed the letter onto the coffee table and grabbed my cell phone. I hit the button for Julie's number and walked out onto my balcony.

"Hello, Blue. Happy Birthday," she said when she answered. Sometimes I hated caller ID.

"Thanks, I got your letter. Don't you think a nice card would have been better?"

Julie took a deep breath. "I'm sure you think so, but I wrote that letter for a reason. After you get over being angry, you should think about it."

"If you want us to be closer, why don't you move out here?" Instantly, I regretted asking such an asinine question.

"You don't want me to answer that, do you?" Julie replied.

"No, of course not." For a moment I listened to her silence, though I knew she would wait me out. "The thing is I like it here. I can't see coming back to the South," I said.

"Why not?"

"It's too conservative for one thing."

Julie answered as if she'd been anticipating that lame reply. "Some of my friends in Raleigh are very liberal. Not everyone here voted for George W. Bush, you know."

"The majority did."

"Are you afraid to come back to the South?"

"Afraid? Why would I be afraid?" I replied.

"Because you might have to face a few demons if you come back. Like maybe the ones you keep running from."

I started pacing, my anger again flaring. "So now you're trying to psychoanalyze me over the phone?"

"I'm not trying to psychoanalyze you, Blue. I'm asking you to give some thought as to why you have been living your life the way you have for the past twenty years. You can begin by asking yourself why you change jobs and girlfriends every few months. When did you start thinking that was the way you want to live?"

"I didn't think about it. It's just the way it's happened, that's all. And I don't see why it matters to you so much. It's not like I'm asking you for anything."

"You're not asking anything from yourself, either."

"Okay, are you trying to get me to go to a therapist or something? 'Cause that would sure be easier than moving back to North Carolina."

"Except you would still be a five-day drive away from here."

"That's what they make airplanes for."

"That's not the point." Julie paused, and I knew we were done debating. She never hesitated when she was busy making her point. I heard her take in a ticked-off breath, and then she asked, "What are you doing for your birthday?"

"I'm not sure. The woman I'm dating made all the plans."

"Is this woman someone new? Last time we talked, you weren't dating anyone."

"We've been going out for a few weeks. Her name is Rachel."

"Anything serious?"

"I doubt it. I like her in a lot of ways, but she wants to go faster than I do."

I could almost hear Julie thinking, *so what's new about that?* She spared me the sarcasm. "I see. Well, let Rachel treat you to a nice night."

"I will. Thanks."

"You have it in you to be a great person, Blue. I want you to think about that."

Julie said good-bye and hung up. I hit the end call button on my cell phone and stood in the slow, afternoon drizzle, reeling from everything Julie had unloaded on me. I hardly felt like a great person now. Some days I wondered if I was even a good person. I'd left every job and every woman the moment I saw them put faith in me. And yet, Julie refused to let go. Like I was the Prodigal Child, she was calling me home.

Maybe she was right about heading back South. Maybe there I would find focus in the culture and landscapes that felt like home. But, could I really go back there? Just a few months ago George W. Bush took over the White House, and it seemed the conservative South was taking it upon itself to be the moral savior of a supposedly wayward nation. I doubted the Welcome Wagon would be rolled out for an out lesbian like me. Even in the South, though, I could find more tolerant places. I heard Austin had a great artist community and an incredible music scene, but Austin was surrounded by Texas. Julie loved Asheville, with its artists and hippies, retired liberals and tree huggers. Asheville seemed a mountain oasis for living out and blending in. But Asheville was too close—to everything.

Prodigal. There was always New Orleans, my prodigal city, and perhaps the right place for the return of a wayward child.

30

Welcome to Mississippi

Need help with my wife. Tractor driving also. Call Preacher Rowe in Onward, MS.

I glanced up to the top corner of *The Vicksburg Post* to make sure I was reading an actual newspaper want ad. After driving for the past fifteen hours, I was bone tired and more than a little punch drunk. I spread the top fold of the newspaper onto my hotel room bed and rubbed my eyes to read the ad again.

Need help with my wife. Tractor driving also. Call Preacher Rowe in Onward, MS.

Over the length of my "Career by Want Ads," I'd never read a Help Wanted ad that was so simple, yet so brilliant. Did Preacher Rowe know when he placed the ad that only serious inquirers would take the trouble to find his phone number, or even find Onward, Mississippi on a map? And what did tractor driving have to do with helping with his wife? Absurd possibilities flew through my mind. I had forgotten that the South was as full of obscure realities as it was blatant stereotypes, and this Preacher Rowe had me curious. I had to know more, maybe even go to Onward, Mississippi and meet the man.

I pulled out my Atlas from my backpack and found Onward after a quick search of Mississippi. Not more than a speck on a state highway, it appeared to be only thirty miles or so from my hotel in Vicksburg. In the morning I could easily make a quick detour to Onward, find Preacher Rowe, and still be in New Orleans by evening. Or maybe I would stick around Mississippi for a while to help Mr. Rowe. I figured a few weeks clearing my mind on the seat of a tractor could do me some good.

The green and white sign planted beside Highway 61 said, "Onward." I slowed down and scanned the territory for some clue about how I might find a man named Preacher Rowe. The parking lot of the African Methodist Episcopal (AME) church at the edge of town was abandoned, as I figured it would be on a Tuesday. A few hundred yards ahead I pulled into the gravel parking lot of the Onward Store and parked beside an island of three gas pumps. The rambling white board building looked a lot like the country stores back in my hometown. Colorful metal signs nailed to the walls advertised RC Cola and Mountain Dew, Camel cigarettes and Remington shotgun shells. Black metal bars covered the windows. I remembered back when the Calera Feed Store had to install bars. Dad said it was a shame that door locks weren't enough anymore.

In the fields, locusts buzzed their springtime chorus. The sound came as familiar as my father's voice as I strolled across the parking lot and climbed the steps to the porch. I opened the screen door and went inside. Two ladies behind the counter turned and greeted me with languid eyes and a lazy "Good morning." I returned the greeting with a tip of my head as I walked by them.

My footsteps on the worn wooden floors took me back to summer days with my father, scurrying to keep up as his Wellington boots pounded down long aisles of feed, tack, metal buckets, and tractor parts in the feed store. There were other reminders, too, like dusty cans of sardines, packages of soda crackers, and Lance peanuts stacked on metal shelves. As in Calera, there was a food counter in the back of the store where I could get a sandwich, fried chicken, or a hot tamale. The tamale was pure Mississippi Delta.

The clerks looked up and slowly straightened their backs as I walked up to the counter with a bag of peanuts and a Coke. "How're you today?" the one at the register asked.

"I'm good." I reached in the pocket of my Levi's for cash. "Beautiful day, huh?" I said, handing her a five-dollar bill.

"Mmm," she hummed in response. Carefully she tapped the numbers into the cash register to avoid chipping the leopard skin design on her fingernails.

"Do you know a man named Preacher Rowe?" I asked.

She looked up at me with a half-grin that could mean a thousand things. She wasn't about to tell me any of them. I wasn't from around here, and she would toy with me if she wanted. She counted my change into my palm and eased the cash drawer shut. "Yeah, I know him. You here about the job with his wife?"

"I thought I'd talk to him about it." The other clerk cut a glance towards at me with a slow, knowing smile. I looked from one to the other and had a sudden urge to haul ass out of town.

The clerk pointed north. "When you go out of here turn left, and then go to the next road on your left. Preacher and Mary live at the end of that road."

"Thanks," I said. I dropped my change into my pocket and grabbed my Coke and peanuts.

"Come back," the clerk said as I walked out the door. I raised my hand and waved to her. The screen door slammed behind me, followed by the faint sound of laughter.

The white cloud of dust trailing behind my pickup blew past and drifted across the front yard. I slid off the truck seat, willing the dust to settle before it hit the gleaming white boards of the house, or the orderly rows of canning jars on the front porch shelves. On the wall between the canning jars and the screen door was a simple wooden plaque that read, *Welcome. Home of Preacher and Mary Rowe.* I walked up the three steps to the front porch, admiring the workmanship of the wheelchair ramp built beside the steps. Pulling in a nervous breath, I rang the doorbell.

The footsteps coming toward the door held the broken rhythm of a slight limp. They stopped at the door and it swung open. The man I had been obsessing about since last night filled the doorframe, looking down at me with curious, pale brown eyes. He looked to be over six feet tall, with broad, square shoulders and a small round belly. A cap of close-cropped white hair starkly contrasted with the brown skin of his chiseled face. "Yes, ma'am, can I help you?" he asked.

"Yes, sir, I came to see about the job in the paper," I sputtered.

He cocked his head back and squinted skeptically. "You're white."

A nervous smile flew to my lips. "Yes, sir, I *am* white."

"My wife is black."

"I thought she might be." I shuffled anxiously under his stern gaze.

"Are you a nurse?"

I swallowed hard and searched for my Alabama manners. "No, sir, I just saw your ad in the newspaper and I thought I'd see if I could help you out."

"So, you're not a nurse, but you came to Onward, Mississippi to take care of an old woman?" His disbelieving stare bore down on me.

"Yes, sir, if you want me to."

"Have you ever taken care of an old woman?" His commanding eyes served up a warning that he did not suffer the dalliances of fools.

"No, sir. I'm not sure what kind of help you need with your wife, but I've driven a lot of tractors."

His gaze suddenly lifted past me. "Is that a '75?"

I followed his line of sight toward my truck. "Yes sir, it's a '75 F-150."

As if in a trance, Preacher pushed the screen door open and walked past me. I followed his slow but purposeful walk across the yard. Together we stopped beside my truck. He lifted his scarred hand to the rail of the bed. "Where did you find it?"

"It was my father's truck. He bought it new." I looked away and swallowed back unexpected emotion. When I turned back, Preacher was watching me, his expression now gentle and compassionate, as if he already knew how to read every line of my face. "The truck survived a tornado. My parents didn't."

Preacher shook his head. "I'm sorry to hear they passed. Has it been long?"

"It was May of 1978."

Preacher nodded. "I remember that day. Some terrible storms hit south of here. One hit a school. We thanked the good Lord it was a Saturday." He looked up and surveyed the sky for a moment, as if he was wondering when the next one would come, and whose luck might run out. He looked at me and said, "You kept the truck up real good. Your father is proud." He said it with such certainty I could almost believe he had a direct line to my dad. "What's your name?"

"Augusta Riley. Most people call me Blue."

"I like the name Augusta," Preacher said. "You don't hear that name much anymore." He patted the rail of the truck and turned for the barn. "So you say you know how to drive a tractor, Miss Augusta?" he asked as he started walking.

"Yes, sir." I caught up to walk beside him. "I grew up on a farm in Alabama, in Calera, not far from Birmingham. It's been a few years, so I might be a little rusty. I'll get it back quick."

"I'll keep you off the row tractor for a while, then."

"So you want to hire me?" The enthusiasm in my voice surprised me.

"I didn't say that. That's up to Mary. If she says okay, then I'll have the Sheriff run a background check on you. I'll need references."

"Sounds fair."

I watched Preacher's ambling gate as we walked in silence toward the barn. The pain seemed concentrated around his right knee, and he hummed softly as he shuffled one leg in front of the other. We stopped under the roof of the barn's open bay. "I keep most of my equipment in this barn. I've got 425 acres in soybeans and beef cattle. Sometime I rotate in cotton. I don't have time to waste on broken-down tractors, so I take care of them. I'd expect the same from you."

"Yes, sir, I understand." In front of us was his row crop tractor, a big John Deere that didn't have a spot of rust anywhere. Parked directly behind the John Deere was the smaller tractor, a blue and white Ford-New Holland he likely used for bush hogging and hay baling.

"If you drive one of my tractors, you check the oil, filter, and hoses every day before you take it out. At the end of the day, sweep it down and hose off the mud, including the tires. On Saturday afternoon I do the weekly maintenance. Nobody drives my tractors on Sunday. That's the Lord's Day."

"I understand." I nodded confidently, though the mention of the Lord's Day again set off my instinct to haul ass. How could a nonbelieving white lesbian work for a Sabbath-observing black farmer named Preacher?

"Do you go to church?" Preacher asked. His somber gaze demanded a straight up answer.

"No, sir, I don't."

"You know about Jesus Christ?"

"I was raised a Presbyterian."

"Church is up to you, then. Are you ready to meet Mary?"

I almost laughed out loud with the thought of how the question would scare me if I had been raised Catholic. Being raised a Protestant, I figured he meant his wife. "Yes, sir," I said.

Squinting into the late morning sun, I walked out of the barn with him. On the porch of the house a woman sat in one of the three rockers. Preacher waved to her. His monotone hum picked up rhythm when she waved back.

That must be Mary.

"Are you actually a preacher?" I asked as we walked across their manicured lawn.

"My given name is Preacher. My folks wanted me to be a preacher, so that's what they named me. It seemed to fit, so I started preaching when I was seventeen. My father preached for more than forty years. He learned how to read on the Bible when he was over in Europe during the First World War. He started preaching when he came back."

"Do you still preach?"

"I quit preaching two years ago when Mary got worse." He kept his eyes on his wife as he walked toward her. "It started with diabetes. Her kidneys quit back a few weeks ago, so now I have to take her to Vicksburg for dialysis every three days."

From her perch on the porch, Mary watched us like a wounded hawk. We stopped at the edge of the porch and looked up at her. A heavy bandage covered her right foot, and a quad cane waited next to her hand. Her small, round eyes squinted together behind her black-rimmed glasses, and the thin ridge of her nose pointed at me like an arrow.

"Mary, this is Miss Augusta Riley," Preacher said with a nod toward me.

Mary nodded cordially and waited for me to speak. "Nice to

meet you, Mrs. Rowe," I said, smiling uneasily. "You have a nice place here."

"Thank you, Miss Riley. Will you be staying for lunch?"

I stared at her blankly as I debated how to answer. I knew that breaking bread together was a serious custom in the rural South, so I figured it best to answer as I would in Calera. "Yes, ma'am, if it wouldn't be too much trouble, I'd like to stay for lunch."

"Good. While we eat, you and Preacher can tell me what you've been talking about." Mary rocked forward and planted her hands on the chair's armrests. Her face showed no signs of pain as she slowly unfolded her frail body and stood up.

Not to be trifled with.

Preacher hustled up the stairs and offered his arm to his wife. She wrapped her hand around the wide girth of his forearm and leaned against him, softly muttering as they walked into the house. I followed them through their front door.

"You can help Mary set the table," Preacher said as he started toward the kitchen.

Mary eased into a chair at the corner of the table. With both hands she reached down for her right thigh, grabbed it close to the knee, and swung it under the table. She stopped for a breath before reaching to pull the other leg around. Fighting back an urge to help—how, I didn't know—I watched her straighten to sit tall. She pointed to a row of polished maple cabinets on the opposite wall. "The plates are over there, if you don't mind; glasses, too."

I opened the cabinet and pulled out CorningWare plates. The pattern in the center sent a shiver through me. It was the same pattern my mother used. My face flushed, I brought the plates to the table and set the first in front of Mary. She looked up at me strangely, and I looked away, avoiding her inquisitive gaze. Over by the stove, Preacher lifted a giant pot roast from the roasting pan. I stared at it when he plopped it on a serving tray. The roast seemed big enough to feed a small army.

"How long have you been working for the county, Miss Riley?" Mary asked.

Preacher froze. He stood at the counter with his back to his wife, though from my angle I could see his wide eyes darting to and fro.

What the hell?

I looked at Mary for a long moment, trying to figure out why she thought I worked for the county. It finally hit me and my words came tumbling out. "Oh, I don't work for the government or anything, Mrs. Rowe. I saw where Mr. Rowe needed help on the farm, so I thought I'd come over to talk to him about it."

Mary eyed me skeptically. "How did you find us? We never have trouble finding farm help. People around here are always looking for work."

I figured what she really meant was why would a forty-one-year-old white woman come to Onward, Mississippi looking for meager farm wages? Mary's eyes were fixed on me, waiting. I looked to Preacher for help. His words seemed stuck in his slowly moving mouth. Thick silence drew around the two of us like an ambush. Then, I suppose in desperation, Preacher squeezed the trigger on the electric carving knife he held in his right hand. Bzzzzz . . .

Mary swung her harsh stare from me and fixed it on Preacher. "Preacher Rowe, what are you doing? Ms. Riley and I are trying to have a *con-ver-sation.*"

Preacher looked down at the knife still churning away. Guilt slumped his shoulders. He put down the knife and walked over to stand by his wife. "Mary, Miss Riley came here to answer an ad I put in the paper. I need more help if I'm going to take care of you and keep up with the farm this summer."

Mary cocked her head. "An ad in the paper?"

"Yes. I put an ad in the Vicksburg paper last week. We've already run through all the girls in Sharkey County. Either they don't want to do this kind of work or you won't let them. I don't know which it is, but all the same, we haven't been able to keep anybody."

Mary frowned. "That's 'cause I taught them all in school. They don't like seeing me like this."

Preacher nodded. "That may be true, Mary, but it doesn't change the fact that we need help."

"Have you ever been to Onward?" Mary asked, turning to me.

"No, ma'am, I haven't. I was heading to New Orleans when I saw Preacher's want ad."

"Are you in trouble with the law or something?"

I shook my head, relieved. At least I could prove that fact. "Oh, no, ma'am, I'm not in trouble with anyone, I promise you. It's like I said, I wanted to talk to your husband about the job."

"I'll get the Sheriff to check her out," Preacher offered, and Mary nodded.

We ate our lunch without much conversation. Preacher seemed preoccupied, and Mary was a careful eater. After swallowing her last birdlike bite, she dabbed her mouth with her cloth napkin and rested her hands on either side of her plate. "Let's go out to the porch, Miss Riley. Preacher will take care of the dishes."

Mary straightened and shifted her legs around. I hustled around the table to help her stand. "Thank you, Miss Augusta," she said as I grasped her elbow. "Sometimes I get dizzy when I first stand up." She set her eyes straight ahead, swallowed, and reached over to grasp my forearm for the walk out to the porch.

"Where are you from, Augusta?" she asked after settling into her porch rocker.

"Originally I'm from Alabama, but I've been living all over the place for the last twenty years or so."

Mary gazed at me thoughtfully. "Why?"

I looked at her, unsure how to answer. The easy answer was that I moved around for the adventure, to explore, to learn more about the country, or maybe because I had a restless spirit. None of those answers seemed true, and I sensed Mary was the kind of woman who could feel deceit in her bones, even if the deceiver did not intend to mislead. "I don't know, Miss Mary. I can't seem to get comfortable, I guess."

Mary tipped her head back, laughing. "I know what you mean, child," she said. "I haven't been comfortable for ten years." I laughed too, and Mary reached over to pat my hand.

For the first time, I relaxed in her presence. "I have pictures from some of the places I've been Out West if you'd like to see them," I offered.

Mary nodded. "I would, but it's hard for me to see much these days. Maybe I could look at a few."

"I'll pull out the best ones," I replied. I went out to my truck and reached behind the seat for the plastic box of photographs I carried everywhere. The envelope of landscapes sat on top of the pile crammed inside. I took the envelope out and flipped through the stack of photographs to check for any wayward party pictures. Satisfied they were all safe enough for a preacher's wife to see, I took them to the porch.

The first picture I offered was of me and Beck standing on the top of a mountain in Wyoming, fully clad in our firefighting gear. Mary held the photograph close to her face and smiled.

"I was a firefighter one summer," I said, and remembered how proud I had been of those days.

"I like to see girls do courageous things," Mary replied. She hummed her approval and held her hand out for the next picture. Before I found one, Preacher walked out onto the porch, carrying a huge, blue Igloo ice cooler in front of his belly. I jumped up to help and caught up at the bottom of the porch stairs. He eased the cooler down at the bumper of his Crown Vic Ford and popped open the trunk, then leaned over the trunk to straighten a mat, leaving the cooler sitting on the ground, just begging me to open the lid and look inside. What was in there, and where the hell would he be taking such a huge cooler in the middle of the day? Preacher pointed to the handle at my end and grabbed the one next to his. Together we lifted the monster into the trunk.

"Thank you, Miss Augusta." Preacher nodded and headed back for the house.

Mary motioned me back to the rocker beside her. "We take food to the poor folks around Onward. We do what we can now that Preacher retired from the ministry."

I settled into the rocker and picked up my stack of photographs. "I wondered why there was so much food cooked for lunch. I halfway expected the 'Bonanza' boys to come strolling in looking for chow."

Mary smiled and then became thoughtful. "Have you ever been poor, Miss Riley?"

My search for an answer surprised me. It should have been an easy question. I was used to living paycheck to paycheck, though I'd never considered myself poor. Even in times when I had no address to call my own, I was never hungry, and at night I always knew I would have a warm place to rest. And yet my answer came slowly. "No ma'am, I've never been poor," I said after a moment.

Mary looked at me as if she weren't so sure. "Well, then, you've been blessed," she said.

It had been a very long time since I'd thought of myself that way.

31

Poor in Spirit

"Mary says okay."

"Preacher?" I pushed my palm against one ear and my cell phone tighter to the other. A yell went up from a gray-haired guy in a leather vest next to me. I turned on my heel and scanned the bar for a place to escape the jumping zydeco beat. Weaving through cocktail tables and clapping drunks, I imagined Preacher's staunch expression of disapproval.

"Can you be here tomorrow?" I heard him ask as I ducked behind the DJ booth.

I looked up at the band and Lindy, the woman who had kept me coming back to this bar for three nights in a row. She was working the guys like some sort of witch queen, mesmerizing them with her wild, rub-board rhythm and her jet black hair draped over one bare shoulder. I had talked her into a date after the band's last set, and her deep brown eyes and voice were enough to keep me in Baton Rouge for a good while.

Preacher waited. I held the phone to my ear and watched Lindy sway on the stage. *How can I leave that?* I thought. Yet, for the last twenty years I had run from one woman to the next, and it had gotten me nowhere. Maybe in Onward, spending days on a tractor working the open fields and listening to my own mind, I could grab onto whatever it was I seemed to be searching for. And, with any luck, the brown-eyed girl on the stage would still be around next time I hit Baton Rouge.

"I'll be there by tomorrow evening," I said to Preacher. I clicked off the phone and hustled back toward the stage.

The humid Delta air had been cooking all day, leaving the sweet, musty smell of the barn hanging in the air like God's own roux. I walked into the barn and rested my arms on the rail of the front stall. Preacher eased around his tractor, blasting mud from the lugs of head-high tires.

"Evening, Miss Augusta," he said after he shut off the water. Methodically, he coiled the hose onto the concrete pad at the base of the faucet. "You'll be staying for supper?"

"I'd like that," I said as I moved toward him. He pulled the bandana from his hip pocket and dried his hands. They were so like my father's, jagged and scarred and cracked from the weather.

"We'll talk about pay after we eat. The Sheriff says you don't have a record," Preacher said as we turned for the house.

"I'm glad you checked. I wouldn't want you to worry. I suppose my life does seem strange."

"Until you prove yourself out there in the fields and find a way to help Mary, I'll still worry." He stopped at the bottom step of his house and motioned for me to go up first.

Mary looked up and closed her large-print *Reader's Digest* when we walked into the kitchen. She pointed to the cabinet that held their dinnerware. "Preacher says you like zydeco," she said as I walked over to the cabinet.

"Yes, ma'am," I replied. I pulled out the plates and took them to the table. Mary's hands moved back and forth on the tablecloth, her mouth pursed in contemplation. I figured her next words would be that zydeco was from the devil, the cousin to voodoo, meant to work folks into a cursed frenzy until they took up all manner of sin and fornication, and God only knows what all. I set a plate in front of Mary and thought about last night with Lindy—and God knows what all.

"I was born in New Orleans," Mary said. "I played a little jazz piano until my hands got bad. I slowed it down after that."

"Do you need a place to stay?" Preacher asked. He set a large bowl of boiled squash and onions on the table and headed back to the counter for the meat loaf.

I glanced over at Mary. Her eyes were fixed on me, expectant. "I wouldn't want to put you out," I said.

"You won't put us out," Preacher replied. He slipped on a pair of oven mitts and reached in for the huge pan of meat loaf. "We have a vacant apartment over the shop. I'll take the rent out of your pay."

"That would save me a lot of time in finding a place," I offered.

"Good," Mary said firmly. "Then it's settled."

I looked into the certainty of Mary's cloudy eyes and knew there was no backing out. I would be spending the summer with two quickly aging farmers in the middle of No-Damn-Where, Mississippi. At that moment there was nothing I wanted more—not even Lindy.

After supper Preacher led me to a metal building sitting a couple of hundred feet behind his house. At a side door, he slid the key into the lock. "The apartment's upstairs," he said as he swung open the door and held it for me. I walked onto the linoleum floor, reeling from the boxed-in heat.

"It's air-conditioned, I hope," I said as I started up the stairs.

"Of course . . . and it's furnished." Preacher's broken footsteps fell heavy on the stairs behind me.

I reached the top landing first and opened the apartment door. A chill ran through me as I glanced around the room. Shelves filled with books, trinkets, and mementos had been left untouched, waiting for someone's return. From the layer of dust I figured that particular someone hadn't been here in a while.

"My mother lived up here until she passed." Preacher now stood behind me. "We took her to Jackson after her stroke. I haven't been up here much since then."

My heart sank. Living in this apartment would be like violating a shrine to a woman of values far different from my own. Beside the bed a finely crafted nightstand held a lamp and a leather-covered King James Bible. On a lower shelf was a modern Bible that swelled with scraps of paper and bookmarks. I spun around to Preacher. "What's downstairs?" I asked hastily. "Is there an apartment down there, too? It smells like sawdust but that wouldn't bother me."

Preacher cocked his head and looked at me in exactly the same way as when he first saw me standing at his front door. "That's good, but you won't be sleeping downstairs, Miss Augusta. This is the only apartment."

"Oh, okay. This one will be fine." I shifted and hoped he would forgive my lack of manners.

Preacher nodded. "Downstairs is my workshop. If you stick around long enough, I'll show it to you." He gave me the slightest smile, like mischief. "The window air conditioner works well. I checked it yesterday," he said as he turned for the door. "There are fresh towels in the bathroom cabinet if you need them. You can pull your truck around front if you want." He stepped across the threshold and looked back at me. "I have a biscuit and eggs at sunrise if you want to join me. Good night, Miss Augusta."

The door clicked shut with his gentle pull. I walked to the bed and sat down. A sharp creak pierced the silence of the room. I shook away an eerie chill and scanned the old lady's apartment.

Why the hell am I doing this? I thought. I should be immersed in zydeco, pinching tails and sucking crawfish heads and watching Lindy's brown-eyed magic from the best seat in the bar. Instead I was sitting alone in a hot, dusty apartment filled with framed pictures of strangers and mementoes exalting the glory of Christ. I sat still on the bed and looked around the room for something to make me feel like less of a stranger. My gaze finally settled on the red cover of the Bible. There was a name embossed on the bottom of the cover. I picked it up and read: *Ella M. Rowe.*

Her name was Ella. Judging by the age of Preacher, she was likely the granddaughter of slaves. I swept my fingers across the gold lettering and imagined Ella's hands opening and closing the book every night. Perhaps she clutched it to her chest when her prayers were heavy. I opened to the page she had marked with the red ribbon attached to the binding and scanned the verses. Matthew, chapter five, verse three was underlined in bright blue ink, "Blessed are the poor in spirit, for theirs is the kingdom of heaven."

Poor in spirit. I knew a thing or two about that. I returned the Bible to the nightstand and looked across the room. Late evening sunlight filtered through the window, its shadow stopping at the base of a bookshelf filled with hardbacks. Outside, a row of tall pines swayed in the late evening breeze.

It seemed Ella was asking me to stay.

32

Infinite Grace

Outside the car window, furrowed rows of early summer cotton clipped by like falling dominos. I glanced over at Miss Mary, who sat straight and tall in the passenger seat of Preacher's Crown Victoria. Looking ahead with alert eyes, she was a picture of royalty in her purple linen skirt and matching jacket. Both hands clutched the patent leather purse she held in her lap.

As I drove toward Vicksburg I wondered if Mary worried, if dialysis hurt, or if she feared her doctors coming in with grim faces to say that her veins could not take any more treatments. If she worried, she did not show it. Mary seemed to be born with dignity, and she wore it like a fresh corsage, always present, beautiful, but never too conspicuous.

"Preacher doesn't like to take me." Mary's words broke the silence of the last ten miles. "I'm glad you don't mind."

The only thing I minded was not being out in the fields. For the last two weeks I had covered endless acres of Mississippi Delta farmland in a truck or on a tractor. In the mornings I was out before dawn, and I came in at dusk with dust and seed clinging to my sweat-soaked skin. After supper and a long shower I fell into bed with Faulkner's *The Reivers* and drifted off to sleep to the hum of the window unit, remembering how peace could feel.

"Why do you say he doesn't like to take you?" I asked Mary.

"Because he doesn't. I know my husband. He can hardly stand it." I kept driving without a response. I'd learned Miss Mary would tell me what she wanted me to know in her own time. "I think it makes him feel helpless, and maybe a little scared, too." She shuffled her back against the seat and settled for a moment before she continued. "I know deep down inside he doesn't want to be alone, and seeing me with all those sick people reminds him how sick I am. After we got married, we learned we couldn't have children, and he's always worried about that. He thinks there won't be anybody to take care of him when I'm gone. I tell him that's nonsense, but he's got his mind set to believe it."

"I can't imagine Preacher ever being alone. Everyone I've met in Onward seems to love him," I offered.

"Not everyone, but that doesn't matter. After I'm gone Preacher needs more than just a friendly face to come by now and then. He's got the heart of an artist, and that kind of heart needs more than most."

"Preacher is an artist?" I asked, holding back the urge to laugh at the notion of Preacher with a paintbrush.

"Yes, I guess you don't know that yet, do you? You'll see his work when he's ready to show you." I looked at Mary. She glanced back and again turned her eyes forward. "I don't know how much longer I have, Augusta. I'm ready to go, but I hang on for him."

"Are you in pain?"

"All the time," Mary said frankly. She looked out her window and said it again, just above a whisper, "All the time."

The tractor's exhaust erupted into a baritone blast as I pushed the throttle forward and headed for the barn. If I hustled, I could be in Baton Rouge for Lindy's last set, cold beer in hand, watching her zydeco magic. I needed her beautiful distraction. Grace again popped into my mind just after sunrise, before I turned the corner of the first row. Spending endless hours on a tractor left the mind free to wander, and lately mine had been wandering back to Grace.

Dust flew across the yard as I rounded the last curve toward the barn. Preacher stood beside the door, his face drawn. "I finished the seed beds in that upper field," I said as I jumped off the tractor. "We're getting a late start planting that one."

Preacher nodded and folded his arms against the top rail of the stall beside the tractor bay. "You like it here, don't you?" he asked after I finished hosing down the tractor.

I wiped my wet hands across my Levi's and nodded. "Yes, I do."

"Come on then, I want to show you something." Preacher pushed away from the railing and began his walk across the yard. "Mary cooked chicken and dumplings today. We had plenty left if you want some for supper," he said as I caught up to him.

"That sounds good, but I'm thinking about going to Baton Rouge tonight. Y'all go ahead and eat."

"We already have."

I nodded and walked silently beside him, trying to discern the tune of his soft hum. He hummed the high note and I remembered; "Rock of Ages," one of my dad's favorite hymns. Did they sing it at the funeral? I couldn't remember.

Preacher walked past the house and headed toward my apartment and his workshop. His hum stopped when we reached the door next to the stairway. I breathed in the familiar aroma of sawdust and waited for him to fish his keys from his pocket.

"So you like the smell of sawdust?" he asked as he guided the key into the bottom lock.

"Yeah, it's such an earthy smell. *Uncomplicated* may be a better description," I replied.

Preacher looked at me with a skeptical rise of his eyebrows. He pushed the door open and held it for me. "What do you think?"

I took a couple of steps into the shop spread out in front of me. It was far more spectacular than I expected. Lumber stacked in three shoulder-high racks lined the wall to my left. Scattered about the room were a table saw and power planer, a drill press, lathe, miter saw, band saw, power sander, and a jointer. Vacuum hoses ran from the power tools, so the floor was free of sawdust. Clamps, hand tools, and cabinets hung on the wall across from where we stood. On the back wall, under a bank of high-set windows, rows of carving tools and several mallets hung over two long benches. I looked over at Preacher. His usually taut frame hung loose and relaxed, and the lines of his face seemed transformed into a much younger man. "Is this all yours?"

"Yes, of course." Preacher smiled in a way I had not yet seen before.

"Why haven't you shown it to me before?"

His gaze swept across his shop. "This is my sanctuary. My *place;* I don't let just *anybody* in here." He chuckled and kept his smile.

"So why are you letting me see it now?"

"Because it looks like you may be here a while, and Mary told me that sometimes you whittle while you're waiting for her at dialysis. She said you have a nice touch, so I thought I might teach you a few things while you're here."

I nodded. "I'd like that."

"Good. I hoped you would. If you're any good at it, you could make a living at it someday." Preacher's smile grew wider. With a tilt of his head toward a door across the shop, he said, "Come on, I'll show you the finishing room."

He flipped the switch beside the door. An exhaust fan on the back wall spun into a steady drone. I looked across shelves lined with stains, dyes, oils, and spirits. He gestured toward a bench beside the table in the center of the room and walked over with me. Preacher sat down first and waited for me to settle beside him before he spoke. "Nowadays, most of my income comes from furniture building, Miss Augusta. I've been selling off the farm for the last ten years. I can't keep up like I could when I was younger. Here lately, I can't keep up with the demands of the shop, either. Arthritis is taking my hands faster than I expected. It would sure be easier if you could help me."

The sincerity in his eyes took me aback, and left me wondering how many people would pay for the opportunity to learn from him. "I work for you," I said, "so I'll do whatever you need me to do. I'm honored that you're willing to teach me. I'd like to learn everything I can while I'm here."

Preacher smiled. "You don't know if I'm any good, yet."

I smiled with him, this unworried and unhurried version of Preacher. "Mary said you are an artist. I figured she was talking about your woodworking 'cause I haven't seen any paintings."

Preacher laughed. "Come on, I'll show you how I make my money."

I followed him to the small shipping room at the front of the building. He flipped on the lights and pulled off the cover of a beautiful cherry armoire he had crafted into a perfect balance of masculine strength and feminine curves. Mary was right; Preacher was an artist.

I walked over to the armoire and ran my fingers across the beveled door. The cheap, particleboard crap I'd been carrying around from one apartment to another hardly seemed worthy of being called furniture when compared to this masterpiece at my fingertips. "How did you get this finish?" I asked.

"That's the part a lot of furniture builders miss," Preacher replied. "Their craftsmanship is solid enough. It's the finish that opens up wallets. I can teach you if you want to take the time. You'll have to start off with restoration jobs. That's the best way to learn about wood and grain."

I nodded as I studied the curved lines at the top of the armoire. "How do your customers find you? It's not like you're advertising or anything."

"Mostly word of mouth. Commissions for jobs in corporate offices pay the most. I've got furniture in boardrooms from Oxford to Nashville, but I like building for folks' houses the most. The look on a man's face when he sees something I carved for him—it doesn't get any better than that."

I know what you mean, I thought, remembering the moment from twenty years ago, when I had pulled a hunk of chestnut from my pocket and offered it to Grace.

33

Do You See the Hope?

The black sky to the south seemed ready to swallow us into its rumbling brutality. I watched lightning splinter the horizon ahead and switched on the Crown Vic's radio for a weather update. At daybreak, the farmer's report, said a late-season tropical storm would hit the Mississippi coast, bringing with it the possibility of tornados.

"You're just like Preacher. You'd rather fret about the weather than talk to a sick, dying woman," Mary said. Her eyes were closed, though as always, she held her head erect and proud.

"I thought you were asleep," I replied, though I knew Mary was right. For the last few weeks our drives to Vicksburg had been burdened by long stretches of heavy silence. But what could I say to her? The lightness of everyday conversation seemed absurd. Being with Mary now, I felt as helpless as watching someone drown. I knew Preacher should be spending time with his wife rather than a reckless lesbian who had ambitions of becoming a master woodworker and furniture builder. There was so much I needed to say to Mary. How should I begin?

"Do you believe in forever love?" I asked, and immediately wondered why I had asked *that*.

Mary looked at me, her cloudy eyes resolute under the thick lens of her glasses. "Of course I do. It's been over fifty years for me and Preacher."

"That's right," I nodded with an idiot smile. "I guess what I mean is, do you believe it's possible to love someone forever, even if you're not with them?"

Mary thought for a moment. "That would be hard on a person. I

221

think it happens, though. Two people are meant to be together, and for whatever reason, it doesn't work out. It could shadow everything for the rest of their lives." Mary turned her purse down against her lap and folded her hands at the clasp. She looked at me with the kind of gentle expression that teases out confession. "Do you want to tell me about it?"

Of course I wanted to tell her about it, but what if she rejected me? She might run me out of Onward by nightfall, and I wasn't ready for that. My hands twisted on the steering wheel and I felt a little lightheaded. *This is what it's like. This is what it feels like to come out when it really matters.* I had spent most of my adult life having to inform people I was gay, yet somehow I had escaped telling anyone I really loved, someone who could reject me. I took a breath, held it, and sucked in another. "Her name was Grace Lancaster."

Fat raindrops popped against the windshield like a drummer's warning. I flipped on the wipers and watched the black blades slam across the windshield, too fast.

"Do you still prefer women?" Mary asked as I fumbled with the wiper switch.

Heat rushed into my face. "Yes, ma'am, I just seem to be made that way."

"I thought there must be something in Baton Rouge to keep you going down there. That's a long way to travel just to hear a zydeco band."

I let out a deep breath I didn't know I'd been holding in. "There's a woman in the band I like to see when I can."

"What's her name?"

"Linda LaRoux, but everyone calls her Lindy."

"Do you love her?"

"Not like Grace," I said without thinking.

The rain came harder now, beating down in a torrent. Mary didn't seem to notice. "But you do love her?" she asked, her expression seeming to say, *Truth child, I want the truth.*

Did I love her? I had given little thought to the question; Lindy didn't seem to want grand gestures or morning promises. It worked the way we wanted, so what business could it be of anyone else? I fidgeted under Mary's gaze and leaned forward to drape my arms across the wheel, searching through the rain for the road's center line. "Yeah, I do love her," I said, because in a way, I did.

Mary nodded, seemed satisfied, and again turned her eyes ahead. "You should never lead someone on just for sex. If you do, you're not respecting yourself or the other person."

I winced, remembering the curious girls, the women who wanted a chance, and the careless nights I barely remembered. But that was before I had a reason to be better. "So you don't mind me going out with a woman?"

"What is there for me to mind?" Mary asked.

I focused on the road to keep stupid words from tumbling out of my mouth. "I don't know. I just thought, maybe you—"

"Because we're Christians?" Mary interrupted.

"Yeah, I guess."

"The Good Book says to love and not to judge. You've been good to me and Preacher, as good as a daughter. You say you love this woman in Baton Rouge, so it's not for me to worry about. When you're ready, we'll talk about Grace." Mary closed her eyes. "Now you drive careful in this rain. I need a nap."

A mother's smile lingered on her lips.

Christmas night I looked up at the compassionate round eyes of the cross-stitched angel hanging above Mary's bed. If the angel could have spoken, it seemed she would have said, "Welcome."

The Shaker chair stationed by the bed squeaked when I sat down. I looked over and studied the collection of pills, monitors, and books on tape scattered across Mary's oversized nightstand. She was growing weaker by the day, and Preacher and I knew that before long our best efforts would not be enough. Right after fall harvest, Preacher had put the rest of the farmland up for sale to pay for nursing home expenses when the time came.

I listened to Mary's shallow breathing and tried to remember if it had always been so rapid. She shifted under her blankets and I

223

reached out for her hand. "Hello, Augusta," she said as I cradled her palm in mine. "I'm glad you stayed with us tonight."

"This is where I should be," I replied.

Mary attempted a smile. "You should be with Grace."

It had been weeks since Mary and I had talked about Grace. I looked at Mary, trying to figure her intent, and how long she had been thinking about Grace and me. "I wish I could be," I replied after a long moment.

"You never told me why you aren't."

"Her parents were wealthy, and they had expectations for Grace. I didn't fit into their plans."

"Is that why you ran away?" She turned toward me and opened her milky eyes. With deliberate, heavy blinks she focused on my face. "That's what you did, isn't it? You ran from school and everything you wanted to become."

I looked into hazy eyes that seemed to see so much. "I suppose I did. When I left, I intended to come back to finish my degree, and maybe get into vet school. Once I started drifting, I couldn't find my way back."

"So when Grace left, you let her take everything else you wanted?"

"I don't think I can blame Grace for that."

"But do you?"

"What do you mean?"

"Are you angry at Grace? If you saw her today, how would you feel about her?"

"I'd be happy to see she was still around, and that she's okay."

"Why?"

"'Cause I care about her. She was important to me, and I want her to be alright."

"Would you want to punish her?"

"No, I would never want to hurt Grace."

"Then you need to find a way to forgive her and let it go. You can't let Grace define your life, no matter how you feel about what happened. You are meant to be something besides a love-scorned drifter. It's beneath you."

It's beneath you. Mary looked at me, certain and waiting. Like Julie, she wanted me to do something with my life, something that would make a difference beyond the next day. Lately I'd started to want the same thing. "What if I want to be an artist—like Preacher?" I asked.

"You'll have to stay put for a while. He's enjoying teaching you, but you've got to stay around long enough to work at it."

"The work I'm doing with Preacher feels important."

"It is important. What about Baton Rouge? Does she want you closer by?"

"I don't know, yet. Lindy doesn't seem to be in a hurry. I think she likes her freedom."

"So do you."

I chuckled. "It works out."

Mary smiled and turned her face toward the ceiling. Her smile lingered as her eyes closed. "Tell me about Grace," she said.

I brought Mary's hand to my cheek and grazed it lightly across my skin. Her breathing slowed. "Grace was beautiful, and not just physically. She was always generous to everyone. She didn't run people down, you know what I mean?"

"Uh, huh." The lift in Mary's hum said she wanted to hear more.

I leaned closer. It felt right to finally be talking about Grace, even though I still held back the flood of painful words that had been dammed in my brain for twenty years. Tonight I would stick with the simple things. "She was a sorority girl who liked to fly-fish, of all things. She was competitive, too. She loved to beat me at anything." Mary smiled again.

I told her about the Christmas Grace had taken me to my parent's graves, about how she wanted to live out in the country, about how she loved horses, about her playfulness and generosity. Mary's jagged breathing slowed as I spoke. After a short while, it became even. She was asleep.

"Merry Christmas, Miss Mary," I said. I tucked her hand under the blanket and touched my fingers to my lips, then to her forehead. "And thank you."

Mary sat on the side of her bed with her foot propped on my knee. I sat across from her on a milking stool worn slick from years of use. I rubbed my hands together to warm the lotion before I massaged it onto her skin. She watched my palms move across her leg with the same expression I saw every morning, her mouth a little worried but her grateful eyes gleaming in the comfort of our morning ritual. "Do you have much feeling in your feet this morning?" I asked her.

She nodded once and said, "About the same as it has been."

I worked the lotion along the back of her calf, warming them as I went along. "Miss Mary, I wanted to thank you for talking to me about Grace last night. I thought about what you said, about finding a way to forgive her."

"Uh, huh," Mary hummed.

"When I thought about it, I realized the first thing I had to do was figure out what I should forgive her for, so I went back in my mind and thought hard about what happened between me and Grace, about why I've been so angry for all these years."

Mary hummed again, this time with a slight, knowing smile.

I moved my hands down her leg, toward the cool, loose skin of her swollen ankle. "Grace really hurt me when she let her family come between us. What made it worse was that for weeks she had known she was going to have to leave before she told me. She pretended we were all good and then one day she showed up at my apartment and told me we were done. Just like that, we were done."

I picked up Mary's foot to check for sores. She watched me without response as I checked her toes and heel and made a quick survey of the sole. Thankful there was nothing new, I moved her right foot off my knee and replaced it with her left. Mary watched silently as I squeezed more lotion into my hand. Over my time with Mary, I had come to the comfort of her silence, warm as a mother's kiss good night. In these moments I knew I could tell her anything.

I looked up at her, my palms turned toward her with the dollop of lotion in one hand. "The thing is, deep down I didn't expect Grace to stay with me. We fought about it once, even though both of us knew we couldn't stay together. But the only thing we wished for was to stay together and live like we wanted, like everybody else does. So when I thought about it last night, that's what I couldn't get settled. Forgiving Grace is one thing, but how am I supposed to forgive the world for being so against us?"

Mary's face softened with compassion. "That's what you've been fighting all these years, isn't it, Augusta? This world kept you from the life you wanted to have, the life you should have had, so all these years you've been fighting this big old world."

I nodded through a surge of hurt. "Yes, I suppose I have. I know you and Preacher went through this, too, and you had it worse than me. How did you do it, Mary? How are we supposed to find peace with a world that says we aren't equal?"

"Honey, if I knew the answer to that, they would be calling me a prophet." We smiled for a moment and Mary reached out to me. "Put that lotion down and come sit up here with me."

I swung around to her side, the puddle of lotion still in my left hand. Mary took my right and cradled it in her lap. "I don't know why the good Lord divided this world into the have's and the have not's. I think sometimes about the things that Reverend King said back in the '60s. I have a dream and we shall overcome. Do you see the hope in that?"

I looked at her, puzzled by what she meant.

"You see, Blue, hope isn't just something you long for, that you wish will happen. Hope is something you do, something you put your best efforts into, even when you don't know what's going to happen."

"But *how*, Mary? What if I don't believe in hope?"

"Oh you do, Blue. You were raised that way, even if you don't realize it. Every year when your father planted his crops, he didn't know what was going to happen by harvest time. There was hope in what he did. Now you've got to find your own way. You've got to find that thing that gives you hope and makes you want to be your best. If you do that, you'll overcome those heartaches you've been carrying around all these years. Life won't be about you against the world. Life will be about you *in* the world."

We sat for a long moment. "I suppose there's hope in what Preacher and I do in the shop," I said. I looked at Mary and smiled. "Every time I put a saw to his lumber, I hope I don't screw it up."

Mary laughed with me. I loved the sound of it; at least for that moment I knew she was happy.

"Let's get that lotion on before it dries on your hand," Mary said.

I hopped off the bed and settled again onto the milking stool. Mary lifted her foot and I placed it on my knee. The skin of her left leg was cooler than the right. She winced from pain when my fingers crossed her ankle. "I'm sorry," I said quickly.

"It's alright, Blue. This old body is winding down. That's all there is to it."

Still smarting from a Baton Rouge New Year's Eve, I slid out of the truck and carefully pushed the door closed. The dull pain lingering at the edge of my skull waited in ambush, ready to launch a full assault against the four Advil Lindy gave me at breakfast. I started up the stairs thinking of nothing but turnip greens and peas, a thick slice of cornbread, watching some football, and falling into bed. Preacher walked out and met me at the top of the stairs.

"How're you feeling?" His tone was free of accusation. For that I was grateful.

"I'm okay, not great, but okay."

"Good," he said. He pushed his hands into the pockets of his cotton windbreaker and looked out toward the fields. "Mary's ready to go."

"Go where?"

"To the nursing home. She wants you to go with us." Preacher glanced at me and took two steps for the door.

"Are you okay with this?" I asked after him.

He stopped and his shoulders slumped. He turned toward me in slow, short steps. Hurt darkened his eyes when he looked up at me. His voice came out coarse. "Of course I'm not, but I can't do right by Mary way out here on this farm, and neither can you. Let's just get on with it before she changes her mind."

I followed him inside, feeling raw and inadequate. Miss Mary sat on the couch waiting, her cane by her side and her red Sunday hat

228

shading her proud eyes. She looked up at me and held out her hand, the way she always did when she wanted me to help her stand. I grasped her ice-cold fingers and swung around to her elbow. Mary rocked forward and stood up between me and Preacher, swaying slightly as she struggled for balance. She held out her cane for me, then made two short steps, stopped, and pulled a ragged breath through her nostrils. The door, just a few feet away, seemed an impossible distance.

The walk would be a process of single steps, steadying, and breaks for breath. Yet it was a walk Mary insisted on making, no matter how long or painful. I held her close and listened to the soft whine of her struggling. The popping corks, sweaty dancing, and lovemaking of Baton Rouge seemed a lifetime away.

34

Recovery

The smell of disinfectant and rubbing alcohol hit me hard when I walked into the nursing home. Even though I had come here almost every day since New Year's, I never got used to the odor. It smelled like a place I never wanted to be; even right now.

In the hallway I passed by Jenny, the Activity Coordinator, taking down St. Patrick's Day shamrocks and leprechauns from the bulletin board and replacing them with rabbits and Easter eggs. A couple of old guys sat in wheelchairs across from her, their eyes fixed on her ass. They hardly blinked when I walked by.

The corridor to Mary's room was quiet except for the orderly picking up breakfast trays. I nodded to him and kept going to the room next to the stairwell. Mary didn't answer my knock on her door. I eased it open and stepped inside. Across the room she reclined in her bed, head-phones covering her ears and a look of concentration creasing her face. She opened her eyes and smiled when she saw me beside her bed. With shaky hands she reached up to take off her headphones.

"What are you listening to?" I asked as I swung my daypack off my shoulder. I sat down on the chair beside her bed.

"*Hamlet*," Mary replied over the electronic buzz of her bed moving her to a fully upright position. "Preacher didn't come?"

"He needed to work on his taxes," I replied, unable to mask the annoyance in my voice. April 15th was more than three weeks away.

"Preacher needs a rest from the drive down here. He has to keep his strength," Mary said.

"He'll come tomorrow," I offered, though I wasn't sure of it.

"If he wants," Mary said. "He likes his time in the shop, particularly since he's teaching you to carve." I looked away from her. She reached over to cover my hand with her soft palm. "I don't want you to feel bad about that, Augusta. When he spends time with you in the shop, he's better when he comes here. He's happier."

But would Preacher be happier if he knew everything about me? I doubted he would be as open as Mary. After all, she was playing jazz piano back when Preacher was first learning to preach. "Miss Mary, have you ever told Preacher anything about me and Grace?"

"No, I haven't. That subject is between you and Preacher. Why do you ask?"

"I've been thinking about carving something special, and I'll need Preacher to help me pull it off. The design I've envisioned is really complicated. I know I can't do it without his help."

"And I suppose this carving has something to do with Grace?"

"Yes, ma'am, it does. I want to do something to celebrate women, and how I once felt with Grace."

Mary looked at me with a quiet little smile. Her eyes brightened. "I'll bet it's going to be a beautiful carving," she said, patting my hand with assurance. I wondered if she knew how good it felt to have someone truly believe in me again.

"It can be, if Preacher will help me," I replied.

Mary squeezed my hand and looked at me confidently. "That grumpy old man loves you, Augusta. You should trust him."

Preacher leaned over my shoulder. Together we peered down a straight gray plank of sinker cypress that had just been delivered from Louisiana. The plank was cut from a cypress log that had been lost long ago on its way to the mill. A couple of years ago, someone dug up the logs from the mud and silt at the bottom of a slow-moving river and gave it a second chance. I figured that man must have been a lot like Preacher—a man not willing to let something go easily.

He straightened and walked over to his rocker. He settled in and set his gaze directly on me, the way he often did when he wanted to tell me something I should remember. "Wood endures many

231

things, Miss Augusta," he began. "If you take care of it, it will last for centuries. Think about that for a minute. All of these things folks think are important now—computers, big screen TVs, fancy cars—all of that will be gone and forgotten. But a hundred years from now, the pieces you're building will still be around. They'll be passed down to someone else, and then someone else after that. If you do it right, your work is going to be around three or four hundred years or more, and someone is going to look at what you did, what you made. They're going to see your name on it, and they're going to know you cared. They're going to know the kind of person you were because of your work."

I slid the cypress plank back onto the lumber shelf and walked over to the bench beside Preacher's rocking chair. I sat down and asked, "So what inspires you to be that kind of person, Preacher?" He nodded as if he liked my question. "What makes you take the extra time to create something beautiful, instead of something ordinary?" I continued. "To make art instead of just practicing your craft?"

Preacher leaned back and rested his head on the back of his rocker. He looked straight ahead, his gaze distant and thoughtful. "I don't know, Miss Augusta. I think it's different things at different times. Sometimes it's for the Lord, or to honor a certain piece of wood that comes from the Lord's creation. Most of the time it's Mary; she makes me want to do things right."

"Then why don't you go to see her every day?" I asked sharply.

Preacher's eyes flew open. He turned to me with an indignant glare, though for Mary's sake, I stared back. We locked eyes for a long moment, and then he bolted up and ambled over to the lathe table. He stood with his shoulders slumped and looked defeated. I wished like hell I could take it back.

"Too much has changed, Miss Augusta," Preacher began softly. He turned around to me. There was pain in his face, but also the calm determination that I had come to rely on. "When you came to help us last year, I had a farm full of crops and my wife at home," he said, his hand raised toward his house. "Now the farm's not mine and she's living in a nursing home in Vicksburg. Every few weeks they cut something else from her body like she was cut-bait. I can tell you, it's hard to watch, Miss Augusta. Sometimes I need a day to collect myself and spend time with the Lord."

I looked away from him. I knew he was watching me, which only compounded my inadequate silence. I had no idea what to say. Since the day I met Preacher, I knew exactly what mattered to him. Mary, the farm, and the Lord. On that he had never wavered. I felt like a fool for ever doubting him. Maybe I had assumed his determination and certainty meant he had it all figured out, that he never felt lost. Or maybe I just thought old people instinctively knew how to handle aging and death. Whatever I had assumed, I knew I was wrong.

Preacher's work boots crunched across wood shavings as he moved back to his rocker. He sat down heavily and tipped the chair into a slow rock. "How 'bout you, Miss Augusta?" he asked. "What's your inspiration?"

I shrugged and watched the toe of my hiking boot sweep out an arc in the sprinkling of sawdust at my feet. "Same as you," I mumbled. "Love."

"That woman down in Baton Rouge?" Preacher asked.

I sat up straight and looked over at him. His clear brown eyes were free of judgment. Still, I let out a nervous chuckle before I asked, "Why do you think it's a woman I'm seeing in Baton Rouge?"

"'Cause if you were going to see a man, I would have heard a name by now," Preacher replied, as if his logic was beyond question. He turned the slightest, knowing smile.

At that moment I couldn't have loved him more. All the times I had held back, not wanting him to know; all the energy wasted in believing he would surely run me out if he did; I should have known country preachers have a way of figuring things out, and he had loved me all along. "Her name is Lindy," I said.

Preacher nodded and looked away. His solemn face sent my heart pounding. After all, suspecting and knowing were different, and the truth had a way of changing things. "Lindy," he said after a moment. He smiled, this time full enough to bring out the dimple in his left cheek. *"Lindy from Baton Rouge,"* he chirped. With a trace of his smile lingering, he asked, "So Lindy's your inspiration?"

Telling Preacher that Lindy was my inspiration was the easiest answer, though if I told him that, I would eventually have to tell him the truth. "No, it's not Lindy." I looked down at the laces of my boots to avoid the compassion of his eyes. "It's a woman I was in love with a long time ago. Her name was Grace."

"Grace," Preacher said softly, as if he liked the way the name sounded on his tongue. We were quiet for a moment, and he reached into his pocket and pulled out a bluebird figurine he had been carving for Mary's bedside table. He held it between his fingers and twirled it slowly as he spoke. "I've seen the way you go about your work, Miss Augusta. The love you had for Grace must have been special."

"It was," I replied. "Or at least I thought so. We were really young; I met Grace in college. In some ways she was so different from me, and in other ways we were very much alike. It took me a while to really fall in love with her, but when I did, she was everything to me. I had lost my parents a couple of years before I met her, and Grace was the first one to bring me out of that hole, to make me feel alive again."

Preacher nodded and rocked. "That was a long time ago, Augusta. You say she still inspires you?" He cut a doubtful glance at me.

I could not blame him for questioning. I had wondered myself why a memory of twenty years ago was now coming back so clear and strong. "I don't know, for sure, if it's actually Grace who inspires me," I replied after a moment. "I think it's more about the way I felt when I was with her. That's the feeling I try to bring back when I'm working in the shop. When I calm my mind just right, I go back to that pure sense of wanting to give, and being held worthy. That's what Grace and I had between us. I try to recall how that felt when I want to be exceptional."

Preacher nodded and stared ahead. He rocked slowly, pondering something for a minute or so. I listened to the drone of the air conditioner as my thoughts bounced from memories of Grace to what he could possibly be thinking, to the design of the trestle table I was building for my third client. I was about to say something lame, just to break the silence when Preacher said, "What you describe sounds like a solid kind of love; rare, in fact. What happened between the two of you?"

"Her parents, for one thing. They were wealthy and well connected, and their plans for their daughter didn't include me."

He nodded. "I suppose it took a lot of courage for you to love like you wanted."

"I don't think it was a matter of *wanting to*," I gently countered. "I think it's just the way it was."

"Did Grace get married?" Preacher asked.

Fuck if I know, I wanted to say. I hated that damn question, although I had asked it myself a million times. "I don't know. It's what her family would have wanted her to do, so I imagine she did."

"Have you ever given men a chance?"

I hated that question, too. "In a way. I had plenty of offers when I was younger. I still do. I like men a lot, only not in a romantic way. As far as romance goes, men just don't do anything for me." Preacher looked at me as if to say, *Me either.* I smiled and said, "Besides, they're too predictable."

Preacher rocked back and laughed. "Well, you know I'm a preacher and I believe in the Good Book, and you know what the Apostle Paul says, so I got to believe it. 'Course, Paul says lots of other things that folks don't seem to have much problem getting around. That same passage says fornication and lying is wrong too, but most folks I know come short of that." Preacher turned to me, his face filled with the loving kindness I had seen when we delivered food to Onward's poor. "So as for your way to love, I don't know too much about it. I *do* know about the strength of your character; we care a lot about you, otherwise you wouldn't be here. What happens on your last day is up to the Good Lord, same as it is with Him and me."

I nodded and said nothing, though I wanted to tell Preacher how much heartache his Apostle Paul had brought on people like me.

"As for you likin' women, I can't say as I blame you there. Women do make life excitin', don't they?" Preacher said. He reached over and gave my knee a playful shake. "Yeah, they have their moods and their ways, so you never know what's coming next. Men ain't like that. They're always pretty much gonna be the same. You know when you see a man what he's gonna say and do, what he'll be like from one day to the next, but women are different. You never know with a woman."

I felt no need to remind Preacher that I was a woman, too. I knew what he meant. Women *did* make life *excitin'*.

"Yeah," Preacher said. He looked at me with a face illuminated by joy. "You want a life, you can find you a man. But if you want to *live*, you find you a woman."

The sound of our laughter filled the shop.

35

Never Ready

Preacher jumped into the passenger seat of the Crown Vic and slammed the door. "Get there as fast as you can!"

I shifted the big Ford into reverse and swung it back across the grass. My pulse racing, I jerked the gearshift down into drive. Tires gripped and shot us forward. I sucked in a breath and tried to swallow back my fear. "Seat belt," I said. Preacher reached over his shoulder and pulled it across his chest.

I tore out of the driveway and spun out onto the gravel road, dust flying into the moonlight behind us. On the blacktop I floored the gas and kept it down until the speedometer hit eighty-five. Across from me, Preacher rocked and hummed, his nostrils flared with determination. "She's not going to die alone," he said through clinched teeth.

I gripped the wheel and accelerated to ninety. I could easily do a hundred on the straight stretch of deserted two-lane highway. The big Ford engine roared as I pushed the gas pedal down another notch. Dark asphalt passed beneath us in a blur.

Vicksburg lights finally appeared on the horizon. Preacher rocked faster and his hum moved to a higher pitch. "We'll be there soon. There's no traffic this time of night," I said, though assuring him seemed absurd. He nodded and stared straight ahead.

At the edge of Vicksburg I slowed to check the intersection ahead. Preacher grabbed his armrest and shifted anxiously. For a moment I thought he would jump out of the car and run. We rolled through the intersection and aimed toward the distant lights of the hospital.

I swung onto the hospital entrance road, glanced both ways, and turned left against the red light. Preacher readied the door handle and held on until I pulled up to the double doors of the Trauma Center. Without a word he swung out of the car and hustled past two nurses smoking near the emergency sign. They casually flicked their cigarettes and watched him disappear inside the doorway.

I kept my eyes on him until he turned down a hallway and disappeared. All of the fear that had been swelling inside suddenly crashed through me. I slumped against the steering wheel and let out a soft moan. I had known this moment would be coming since the day I met Miss Mary, but that didn't mean I was ready. Tears stung my eyes. I swallowed them away and drove around to park.

The first sight of Mary took my breath. An oxygen mask covered her face, and her breathing was as hard and rapid as a winded sprinter. Electrodes and IVs twisted out from her arms and chest. Preacher sat next to her in a gray vinyl chair, holding her right hand. He glanced up when I walked into the room. "Miss Augusta is here, Mary."

Preacher looked as peaceful as I had ever seen him. I took a steadying breath and walked over to Mary. I picked up her left hand and held it between my palms. Her fingers were colder than usual. They gently tightened around my palm and then grew slack.

"Just rest now, Miss Mary," I said.

"You just go when you're ready, Mary," Preacher said softly. "I'll be along before you know it." He started softly humming "Nearer My God to Thee." I thought the tightening knot in my throat would burst.

I looked over at Preacher's giant, battle-scarred hands gently cradling his wife's, his gray head bowed slightly at her chest, his certain eyes, so free of sorrow. He wanted only to be with her when the end came, though afterward, he would need me. "Is there anyone I should call?" I asked.

Preacher rocked and hummed. "Let's wait until daybreak," he said after a moment. "Then you'll know what to say."

LaRonda and Sheri sat behind the counter of the Onward Store, their stools in the same positions as when I first came to Onward over two years ago.

"Hi, Blue," LaRonda said as the screen door slammed behind me. "You doin' okay? You don't look like it."

"Yeah, your eyes are all red," Sheri offered.

I walked over and leaned onto the counter to look past their inquiring eyes. Keeping my gaze on the line of teddy bears on the middle shelf, I forced the words out. "I've been at the hospital all night. Mary passed away a couple of hours ago."

"Oh," Sheri said. We were silent for a moment. "Was it her heart that gave?"

"Yeah, she had a damaged heart valve. The doctor said if they tried surgery she wouldn't be strong enough to recover."

"How's Preacher?" LaRhonda asked.

"He's holding up. Mary's niece, Ruth, is with him right now."

"How are you doing?" Sheri asked.

I wished she hadn't asked. A quiver started at my mouth, and next my eyes filled with tears. I swallowed hard and wiped the corners of my eyes. "I'm okay," I said, willing myself to believe it. I pushed away the flood of emotion and stood up straight. "I've got to go to the house and get some things for Preacher. Will you guys do us a favor and let everyone know?"

Sheri came around the counter and wrapped me in her arms. "It'll be okay," she said. "You go do what you need to do for Preacher. LaRhonda and I will take care of everything in Onward."

I held Sheri close and looked over at LaRhonda. She nodded in agreement, her sincere eyes assuring me that they would.

36

Quitting

"Thank you, Miss Augusta." Preacher took the glass of iced tea I offered. I sat down in the porch rocker beside him. We had just finished a dinner of meat loaf, fresh squash, purple hull peas, sliced tomatoes, and cornbread. It was the first real meal Preacher had cooked since Mary died three weeks ago.

I took a sip of my tea and looked over to the barn at the edge of the yard. The John Deere tractor was still there, only now it wasn't Preacher's. I think he missed the freedom of crawling on that tractor and working the day away as much as I did. I missed watching the heat waves rise from the rows of furrowed ground; the mornings filled with the flitter and chirp of birds that grew still and silent in the day's climbing heat and the drive to the barn at dusk, some days outrunning the thunder and other days surrounded by a chorus of tree frogs and a horizon of fireflies.

"Willa Raintree does spirit faces." The strength of Preacher's voice surprised me. We both had been wounded to silence after Mary's death. When Preacher had spoken lately, his voice sounded vague and broken. "She's up in Memphis. Sometime soon we can drive up so you can tell her about the carvings you want to do. I think she'd do the best job of drawing the patterns you'll need."

"Do you think Willa will understand what I'm trying to accomplish with the carvings? I think it's important to capture the soul inside the faces," I said.

"I know it's important," he replied. His certainty seemed to say he had been thinking about it for a while, maybe since I had described my idea for a relief carving back in the spring. "That's why I wanted to get someone who does spirit faces. She'll understand the need for detail in the expressions. Willa knows how to bring life into her patterns. She can tell a tale by the shape of an eye."

I nodded and thought for a moment. For the first time since Mary's death, I was anxious to start carving again. Lately, my work in the shop had been limited to a kitchen table for a family over in Jackson and a bedroom suite for a young couple in Vicksburg. It took all of the concentration I could find to get the dovetail joints cut correctly. I couldn't find the energy for much else. "Do you think I can do this, Preacher?"

He answered without hesitation. "Yes, I do. You'll need to practice to get the undercuts and shadows right. Carve a prototype or two on basswood before you start on the final piece. It's a fine idea you have. I wish I'd thought of something like it back when I was younger."

I smiled. "Women make life exciting, don't they?"

Preacher let out his first real laugh since Mary died. The sweetness of the sound rang in my ear like a child's first word. "Yes, they do, Miss Augusta," he said. "Yes, they do."

Hardy clumps of grass poked through the gravel parking lot of the Onward AME church. For now, the church grounds were deserted. Preacher had been here earlier, as he had been every morning since the funeral. Today, I waited until he was gone. I needed time alone with Miss Mary.

I grabbed my paperback copy of *Harry Potter and the Sorcerer's Stone* and got out of my truck. The cemetery was located adjacent to a white, one-room church building, and was shaded, in part, by the far-reaching limbs of a Nuttall oak. In the woods behind the church, tangled saplings and vines begged for a drenching afternoon storm. The July heat had burnt the life out of everything.

I walked across the dusty parking lot and onto the grass of the cemetery. Mary's grave was a couple of hundred feet away, on the north side under the shade of the oak. The sun had not yet reached its peak, and I was thankful for that.

241

I stopped at the edge of the shade and looked down at the spot where we had buried Mary. Sprigs of grass were growing over it now, though I could still see spots of bare gray soil from the digging and filling. As on every day I visited, I read the name on her stone: Mary Burns Rowe. February 2, 1933 – June 14, 2002.

"Sixty-nine years you lived on this earth, Miss Mary. I only knew you for a little more than a year of it. I wish it could have been more. You taught me so much."

I moved into the shade and settled onto the grass beside her. "Do you remember that *Harry Potter* book I was reading to you? Well, after you passed I haven't been able to finish it." I opened the book and flipped through the pages. "You know how you can be looking at words and not really reading? That's what happened every time I tried to finish. But lately I've been curious to know what happens to Harry and Ron and Hermione, so I thought I'd come over here and see if I could finish it with you."

A nickel-sized black carpenter ant crawled across the top of Mary's gravestone. I leaned up, swept it off, and sat back down. "We left off after chapter seven. We can start there."

I opened the book and began reading. The sun broke from behind a cloud, and Mary and I took off into a world of magic and potions, of boys and girls and good and evil, and things that were not always as they seemed.

"Crap!" I pulled back my gouge and looked down the carving I had been working on for most of the afternoon. A minute ago she looked like a sweet-faced schoolgirl, until I angled my tool incorrectly and popped out her pupil. Now she looked more like a hollow-eyed demon.

Preacher leaned across the carving table to take a look. "Woo, woo," he said as his belly began to shake with laughter. "See what happens when you go a little too far?" He laughed heartily and tapped his palm over his chest. Laughter still twitching his cheeks, he said. "The eye looked fine until you made that last cut. There's a lot to be said for knowing when to quit."

"I know, I know." I took out my bandana and wiped the sweat from my forehead. August in the Delta was as miserable as wearing a fur coat in the Congo, and our air conditioner hadn't been able to keep pace since June. Even after sundown my sweat would splatter onto my work like fat drops of rain. I grabbed my glass and sauntered over to the water cooler. "Knowing when to quit seems to be my main problem. I either quit too soon, or I don't quit at all."

Preacher nodded. He seemed to know I wasn't talking about carving. Or maybe I was. If I knew when to quit, I wouldn't be trying to carve such an intricate piece to honor women—a piece particularly inspired by my love for Grace. If I knew when to quit, I would have stayed at college—and I would have quit thinking about Grace years ago.

"Do you remember a while back when you asked me about inspiration?" Preacher asked. "You asked what it is that inspires me to do something exceptional, rather than something ordinary."

"Yes, you said it was mostly Mary who inspired you to be exceptional."

"That's right. It will always be Mary for me. It's important to keep your inspiration with you when you want to give up. You could quit working on that carving right now if you want. No one will ever know you decided that the work you dreamed of was just too hard to finish. People never know about the things you dreamed of and decided not to do. They'll only know about the dreams that you made happen."

"And they'll know what kind of person I was, and that I cared," I said, repeating Preacher's words back to him.

"You got it, Miss Augusta. I'm gonna care about you no matter what you decide to do. It's up to you to decide who else will care."

37

Closing the Book

I closed the cover of *Harry Potter* and looked up to the clear October sky. "That's the end of the first book, Miss Mary." I shifted in my lawn chair and looked down at Mary's grave, now covered by browning grass and a scattering of crisp rust and yellow leaves. "There are two more *Harry Potters* we could read together. I hear she's working on the fourth, and every book is getting longer. I suppose we could read all of them together, but I'm trying to learn how to quit when the time is right. I know you could have helped me with that."

I held up the front cover of *Harry Potter* and looked it over. Mary could hardly see the cover when I first showed it to her months ago in the nursing home. Still, she grasped the book with both hands and held onto it, an IV dangling from her left arm. She loved books more than anything. I remembered an October Saturday a year ago when we sat together on the porch, sipping coffee in the morning sun while I read to her. The morning turned into a glorious afternoon, and Mary and I spent it driving through the Delta National Forest. Tall trees and dense vines shaded the dirt roads as we drove through the forest, listening to football games and CDs of ladies singing jazz. We'd both loved that day.

I stood up and looked around. The Onward AME church gleamed white in the bright autumn sun. Through the window, I saw the pulpit where Preacher delivered hundreds of sermons. I would like to have heard one or two of them, even though I was still a nonbeliever.

"Preacher is still delivering food around Onward, and he's helping me in the shop," I said to Mary. "I'm working on that carving I told you about, the one with the women's faces. Preacher and I got Willa

Raintree to design the patterns, and I'm working hard to get it right. I told Lindy I wouldn't be coming down to Baton Rouge for a while, so we decided to break it off. I'm ready to take a break from dating, anyway. I need more time in the shop."

A breeze swept through the cemetery, pulling the leaves into a swirl that settled at the edge of the woods. I reached into my pocket for a carving of a boy's face with a lightning bolt slicing down his forehead. "I made this for you." I bent down and put the wood figure on the corner of her headstone. I straightened and looked at it perched against the granite. "It's supposed to look like Harry Potter. I made it so you'll know I think about you a lot. That's not going to change, Mary, no matter where I am. You and Preacher changed my life because you helped me remember who I was a long time ago, and who I want to be again."

From the back of my mind, I heard an echo of her voice. "You've been good to us, as good as a daughter," she had said. Maybe they knew what I was looking for before I did.

"See you again soon, Mary," I said aloud. I turned from her grave, folded up my chair, and walked back to my truck.

Preacher settled his back against his chair at the kitchen table. The Burl Ives version of "Rudolph the Red-Nosed Reindeer" was on the television in the den, and the gray drizzle outside was getting darker and colder. An hour ago, we had finished delivering the last of Thanksgiving dinners to the poor and old folks in Onward. Now our own bellies were full, and Preacher seemed happy.

He picked up his fork and dabbled with the bits of cranberry sauce left on his empty plate. His contemplative face said he was ready to tell me something he had been thinking about for a while. "Miss Augusta, in the last bit of my life, the Lord has called me to feed folks. Onward depends on me to make sure nobody goes hungry, and I know that's got to be my final mission. I'm getting older now, so it takes more out of me to cook everything and make sure it gets delivered on time. Eventually our time in the shop is gonna dwindle down, so I figure you should start thinking about what you want to do when you leave Onward."

Preacher put down his fork and looked at me. I knew, by the tone of his voice and his relaxed, unhurried expression that he didn't intend for me to leave right away. "You've got a life of your own to lead now. Mary is gone and there's no farm work to worry about. Onward is mine and Mary's place in the world. You've got to get out there and find your own place."

I looked at him with an easy smile. "I've been thinking about that, too, Preacher. I'll stay around as long as you need me. In the meantime, I'll think about where I want to go and what I want to do."

"You could have your own shop one day, you know. More folks are calling to commission your work, and you're building the reputation you need to stay in business. You've got enough skills already to make a decent living. If you stay around here for another year or so, I can teach you more. Finish your carving and make it your showpiece. Your work will demand a higher dollar if people can see what you're capable of."

"I'd love to have my own shop. The thing is, I don't know if I could ever afford the start-up costs."

"Don't worry about that. I'm giving you my tools and equipment."

I rocked back, my eyes wide and jaw slack. I stared at him, hardly able to believe what he'd just said. "You'll give me your tools and equipment?"

Preacher shook his head and picked up his fork. "No, I'm not going to give them to you." He met my gaze, gently waving his fork toward me. "I'll sell it to you for a dollar. That way, no one can ever contest it, if they had a mind to."

The whole lot of it, power planer, the joiner, the drill press, the lathe, the saws, the hand tools, the vacuums; I could hardly imagine how much Preacher had paid for it all, or how much he could get for it now. I wasn't sure I was comfortable with such a gift. He had known me only a little over a year and a half now.

Preacher twirled his fork and watched me, waiting for some kind of answer. "Preacher, I can't buy your shop from you like that. Let me figure out a way to pay a decent price for it. It's worth thousands."

"I know that, Miss Augusta, and I've decided I want to give it to you one day." Preacher folded his arms on the table and leaned toward me, then narrowed his gaze on me in a way that said he wanted no more of my nonsense. "I'm selling you my shop for a dollar, Miss Augusta. You know better than to argue with an old man."

That much I did know, particularly about *this* old man.

Preacher picked up his plate and took it to the sink, humming "Silent Night" as he walked.

I used the Sunday comics to wrap Preacher's birthday present. The paper was as practical as the gift. I had bought him a Cuisinart electric knife, complete with two stainless steel blades, one for carving meat and one for bread. Preacher's old electric knife, the one he'd used the first day I met him, finally quit in the middle of a ten-pound ham. With his slowly worsening arthritis, he needed a new one to carve the huge ham, turkeys and roasts he was cooking for his friends in need.

At a Hallmark in Vicksburg I'd found a funny birthday card with a grinning donkey on the front. The card seemed perfect for what I wanted to say—I love you, but let's avoid the sentimental B.S. I signed the card and headed over to Preacher's house with his gift and the card. I found him at the kitchen table, cooking up an industrial-sized pot of gumbo and reading his Bible. The smell of Cajun spices filled the house, making me instantly hungry.

"Happy Birthday, Preacher!" I said as I walked toward him. He looked up with a bashful smile and closed his Bible. I pulled out a chair across from him and plopped his gift on the table. His smile grew wider when I scooted the box toward him.

"So how old are you today?" I asked.

Preacher looked up at the ceiling. "Let's see. I was born in March of '29, so that makes me seventy-four, I guess. Yes, that's right, I'm seventy-four today." He looked down and clasped his present between his two great hands. "Can I open this now?"

"Yes, absolutely, and I've got another surprise for you."

Preacher tilted his head and looked at me curiously.

"This afternoon I finished the last face on the prototype for the vanity. As soon as we find the wood, I'm ready to start building the actual piece."

He meticulously unfolded a corner of the comic paper and took out his pocketknife to cut the tape. He smiled and said, "Sometimes I think building that vanity is the only reason you stayed in Onward. It's going on two years that you've been living in this hot, humid, speck on the map, and that's a long time for a restless spirit like you."

Preacher was right. I had been staying in Onward until I finished the vanity, though I wouldn't tell him *all* the reasons I stayed. I wouldn't tell him about coming to terms with the wasteland that twenty years of unanchored living had left behind. I wouldn't tell him of the good women who tried to save me, of the worldly women who wanted a new experience, of the drunks and druggies, the executives and bored housewives, and the women I almost loved. I wouldn't tell him that the long days in the fields on his tractor and the nights in his shop had brought me back to something I had lost a long time ago. And, I wouldn't tell him of all the ways he reminded me of my father, or that I loved him.

I let the grinning donkey do that.

38

Going Home

Preacher stood up when he spotted me turning into the driveway. Steam rolled out from his coffee mug and swayed in the cool November breeze. By his eager smile I wondered if he had spent the whole afternoon on the porch waiting for me. "How was your trip?" he asked as soon as I got out of my truck.

"It was good. And long," I replied, shaking the road miles out of my bones.

"Come on in and tell me about it," he said.

Inside, the fine aroma of chocolate chip cookies pulled us toward the kitchen. Preacher settled into his chair at the head of the table and waited for me to pour a cup of coffee. I sat down at my place at the corner of the table. He pulled the plate of cookies toward us and handed one to me. "So, how is your Aunt Julie?"

"She's doing well." I bit into the cookie and chewed for a moment. "She took a long weekend off so we could go backpacking. She's not the hiker she once was, but she can still cover a lot of miles carrying a backpack. We hiked almost twenty miles in two days."

Preacher raised his eyebrows and nodded his approval. "Did Julie talk you into going to see your friend from home?"

"Yeah, while we were camping, Julie asked me about Susan. I realized it had been a while since I saw her, so I gave her a call. I had no idea I would end up staying with her and Cory for three days. I hope it wasn't a problem, me being gone that long."

Preacher waved a dismissive hand and looked at me with certainty. "I was fine, and I don't want you thinking I need someone to look after me. As soon as you finish the vanity, I want you to be moving on."

"Yeah, about that." I picked up a cookie and broke off a bite. "Susan asked me if to build a bedroom suite for one of her girls. Her daughter's birthday is in February, so it may stretch my schedule out for finishing the vanity."

Preacher eyes brightened, seeming to be pleased with the prospect of a new project. "Anything special?"

"Nothing out of the ordinary. Probably something in red oak or ash," I replied.

Preacher nodded and sipped his coffee. He dropped his chin in his hand and looked over at me, so much like a father. "Have you given more thought about where you want to go after you leave here?"

For long stretches of the last few hours I had thought of little else. I rolled out of Tuscaloosa on I-20, past massive pine plantations and endless horizons of pastures and fields; through towns with names like Boligee and Epes, and over the flat, broad flood plains of the Black Warrior and Tombigbee rivers. The landscapes and towns and rivers were those of my youth, places I still loved in a way, yet I knew I couldn't stay tethered to them for long. The zeal of the God-fearing, flag-waving natives would eventually wilt my spirit. The solitary hours and endless, deserted horizons convinced me that my place was in the mountains.

"I think I'm going back to North Carolina," I replied. "That's where people go when they're looking for furniture and craftsmanship. Julie wants me to move closer to her, too, and so do I. Sometimes she makes me angry, but I love my aunt more than anything."

Preacher nodded. "North Carolina makes sense to me. I can't see any good reason not to go there, can you?"

A couple of weeks ago I would have said yes. North Carolina never felt right when I had gone back before. This time felt different—like possibility. "I can't, really, though it's a long drive from here, and—"

"There is no *and*," Preacher interrupted. "I've told you I'm not having you stay around here to babysit an old man."

I looked at him sincerely. "Not a day I spent with you or Mary has been wasted, Preacher."

"And you're not about to start now," he replied. His gaze bore down on me with certainty.

"Yes, sir," I said, straightening like a soldier. We smiled at each other and I reached for another cookie. Preacher sat back and drummed his fingers on the table. I watched his fingers move and thought about the journey they had made; the pulpits they had gripped and the plows they had guided. And now they were teaching me his craft, and showing me how to tell the world that I cared. One day I would teach someone the same way that Preacher had taught me. He would expect it.

"Did you go to your parents' graves while you were home?" he asked.

"Yes, I did. I took them some flowers and stayed for a while. They said they'd be there next time I wanted to stop by."

Preacher chuckled and then fell silent. I knew something serious was coming. After a moment, he looked me in the eye and said, "I wish you would find your way back to the Lord, Miss Augusta. I'd feel better about things if you would."

"I know you would, Preacher, but the way I see it, if the Lord is out there and all powerful like you say, he sent that storm right at my folks. So I think it's best I don't believe in a god that would do something like that. If I did, I'd be too angry at him. I'd never get over it."

"Aren't you angry, anyway?" Preacher asked sincerely.

I thought about his question for a long moment. "Not anymore, Preacher," I replied, meeting his gaze.

Preacher studied me, his eyes shrewd and pondering. "I believe you, Augusta," he said. "I've seen your heart open up since you've been here. That's all the more reason for you to go."

39

I Thought About Grace

"It's as beautiful as I thought it would be," Preacher said.

I savored the gentle admiration in his voice as I stood at his shoulder, looking down at the mahogany vanity I had finished after nearly two years of planning, practice, and construction. The piece stretched about three feet across, with a drawer for makeup and hair clasps on each side. There was a flat surface for hairbrushes and crèmes, and attached to the back was a domed mirror with a relief carving of tangled honey-suckle vines. At the base of the mirror was my feature carving, the design I had created to honor the life of a woman.

The carving was a series of faces; the one on the far left was that of a young girl, about six years old. The next was the same girl in her teens, and then in early adulthood. To the right of the center was the woman at middle age, and at the end, the mature woman. In each of the faces was a letter, so subtle as to fade almost imperceptibly into each carving: G-r-a-c-e. I had wanted her to look happy, and Willa Raintree's patterns and Preacher's guidance on shading and detail helped me pull it off.

"There were days when I wanted to quit, Preacher," I said. "But I was determined to make something extraordinary."

Preacher turned to me. He wasn't the kind of man to be overcome by sentiment, yet his deep brown eyes seemed to be gleaming with a film of tears. I figured I must be imagining it. "This is extraordinary, Miss Augusta."

I didn't know how much I had wanted to hear those words until I heard him say them. I knew all of the ways we had grown to love each other. We laughed easily and disagreed respectfully. We shared daily meals and occasional confidences. We shared hardships and helped each other cope with the loss of Mary. And yet, I never knew if he saw me as his peer, his equal in the labor that moved our souls. "Do you think other people will see the letters?" I asked, quickly moving past our sentiment.

"Some will," Preacher replied. "Those who do will likely wonder if your letters represent a person or the grace of a woman as she ages. What will you say if they ask?"

"I think I'll say that Grace was my inspiration and leave it at that. That will leave room for their own interpretations."

"Do you still plan to use it as the feature of your store?"

"Yes. I think it's too close to my heart to sell it. I'm not a frilly girl, so I don't have much need for a vanity at home."

Preacher smiled and stepped up to run his fingers across the finish of the wood. "I guess you'll be leaving soon."

"Yes," I said over my shoulder as I headed for the refrigerator and a chilling bottle of champagne. "I've been talking with a realtor in Highlands. She knows of a space downtown that should be coming vacant in a couple of months." I lifted the champagne bottle up for Preacher to see. "Will you join me in a toast? I thought we should celebrate finishing the vanity and our three years together."

Preacher nodded from his rocking chair. "A little wine before dinner won't hurt, I guess."

"The space the realtor showed me will need some work, and I'll have to expand the back to accommodate a workshop, but the location couldn't be better." I rustled through the bag I had brought down from my apartment and pulled out the two champagne flutes. Working the cork out of the champagne bottle, I rattled on. "I think I have enough of an inventory to stock the showroom. The vanity will serve as my showpiece." I poured the champagne into the flutes and took one to him. "I have something else for you," I said, hustling back to the bag on the counter. I pulled out a gift bag and walked over to sit next to him.

"What's this?" Preacher asked as took the gift bag from me.

"That is a gift made especially for you by the second-best wood carver in Onward, Mississippi."

Preacher smiled and set his champagne on the workbench and reached down into the blue tissue paper. Inside the paper he found a Nuttall oak picture frame I had made for him. Along the sides I had carved a series of irises, Mary's favorite flower. Centered in the frame was the wedding day photograph of Preacher and Mary.

Preacher stared at the photograph for a long moment. He wiped the corners of his eyes, and this time I knew I wasn't imagining the tears. He studied the photograph for a minute or so while I fretted over his reaction. Had I gone too far with such an intimate gift?

Preacher rubbed his thumb across the crown of Mary's veil when he finally spoke. "I guess it is time for you to go, Miss Augusta. I can see by this gift that I've taught you everything I can teach you about carving. And about love."

His sentiment was more than I could take. I quickly lifted my glass high and caught his gaze. "To love, in all the forms it takes," I said proudly.

Preacher picked up his champagne and raised it to meet mine. "To love, in all the forms it takes." His tears were gone as quickly as they had come, as if dried by the hand of an angel.

Part Four

The Vanity

Spring 2005 – Winter 2007

40

Mountain Home

The screen door popped shut behind me as I walked onto the front porch. Hot coffee warmed my hands and my breath came out in delicate white puffs. Mist still hung in the hollows below, and last night's late spring frost had not yet given way to the morning sun. In the forest surrounding my cabin, only the hemlocks and white pines were fully green; the poplar leaves had not yet filled out beyond the size of a squirrel's ears. That was how the locals knew spring had come to stay—when the poplar leaves were bigger than a squirrel's ear. Such local wisdom was one of the things I loved about my new home. Once I had thought these Appalachian Mountains slow and thick, but now they wrapped around me like the arms of a familiar lover.

I sipped my coffee and looked out to watch the sun rising on Whiteside Mountain. In the distance a car door closed, followed by the roar of an engine. Driveway rocks went flying as Marty, my neighbor and landlord, rounded the corner and headed toward my cabin. She stopped beside the porch stairs and hopped out of her truck.

"Good morning," she said as she hustled up the stairs. "I was just on the way to check the water tanks and saw you standing out here. How are you?"

"I'm doing fine. Just getting ready to go to the shop."

"We haven't seen you much since that article in *WNC Magazine*. That was a good story, by the way."

A couple of months after opening, a writer from a regional publication called *WNC Magazine* offered to feature an article about my shop in their upcoming issue. The magazine covered Western North

Carolina and catered mostly to the rich folks chasing a promise of heaven on earth in the mountains.

"Thanks," I said. "I was pleased with the article, too."

"I thought the way they brought the name of your shop into the title worked really well. "Original Blue," in bold blue print along with that great picture of you sitting in your shop. It gave the story a real intimate feel to it."

I nodded as a flush of heat rushed to my cheeks. "Yeah, I've got to get used to the marketing aspects of the business. It felt a little embarrassing to see my picture plastered across the feature page."

Marty cocked her head back and looked at me over the curve of her hawklike nose. "Embarrassing? I don't know why you'd feel embarrassed. That was a beautiful picture of you, kid. And the photographs of the shop, the article captured it all so well. I loved the pictures of the ceiling beams you guys salvaged from the original building, and the stained glass window in the transom. Some people will want to come by the shop just to see the architecture, and while they're there they'll see the incredible work you do."

"I hope so. Cory did a great job with the remodeling."

Marty shook her head. "You won't take a compliment from a silver platter. As I recall your hand has been in every aspect of building that shop, not to mention the inventory."

"Yes, let's *don't* mention the inventory. I don't have enough on the floor right now. Since the article ran, my orders have nearly doubled, and the hits to the website have quadrupled."

"If you need more help in the shop, I know a couple of kids who could use the work." Marty crossed her arms over her chest and tapped two fingers on her forearm, the way she often did when she was thinking.

"I'll keep that in mind. Right now, I'm waiting to see how business is once the effects of the article tail off. I've got Sarah Jackson coming in on the weekends and a couple of days during the week to help with the office work, so the three of us are still managing to get the most of the work done. Nat is helping a lot with the orders. She's learning fast."

"Natalie is a good kid," Marty said. "She had some trouble in high school because of her sexuality, but she's smart as a whip. She was in my English class the year before I retired."

"She's been great about working extra hours. I'm sure she'd rather be out climbing with her girlfriend."

Marty grinned. "She adores you. Maybe one day you can talk her into going to college."

"We'll see," I replied after another sip of coffee. "I really don't think college is necessary for a person to be successful. Nat's one of those people who learns quickly through experience. She has the kind of skills that college won't help."

Marty eyed me skeptically. "She could always benefit from a formal education. College never hurts anyone."

"It didn't do me any favors," I replied.

Marty clicked her tongue and grimaced. "Now that's a heck of a thing to say. Where would you be if you'd never left Alabama to go to college?"

"I like to think I'd be fine. A person can learn plenty without getting it from a professor."

Marty's hands flew up and she shook her head. "There's no use in arguing about this. Neither of us is going to change our minds and I've got to check those water tanks. *Farmer's Almanac* says we're in for another drought this summer."

"You got close to drying up last year, didn't you?" I asked.

"I always worry in August," Marty replied.

"I can help pay for another tank," I offered.

"No need," Marty said. "The rent you're paying is fine. If you want, you can give me a discount on that bed frame you've promised." She winked and turned to go. "See you later," she said over her shoulder. "Joyce and I will be home tonight if you want to visit." She bounded down the stairs and opened her truck door. "Don't forget, my grandkids will be here in a couple of days. They can't wait to see you again."

After a quick wave, she jumped into the truck and backed out. Gravel flew as she zoomed toward the spring. I shook my head with a smile and went inside to put on my work Carhartts, white t-shirt, and faded denim shirt—the attire that seemed to draw the approving attention from the guys with money, as well as their wives. I was learning the way to bring top dollar for my work was to present myself as an artist and an individual, as well as a craftsperson.

Preacher once said the demand for his work was as much about it being produced by a black farmer-preacher from the Mississippi Delta as it was his impeccable workmanship. Now, the image of a self-assured, blue-eyed, *independent woman* living in the mountains was becoming a part of the Blue Riley mystique. I figured I might as well get used to it.

Nat appeared at the workshop door and leaned against the frame, her hands shoved deep into her pockets. "Some hot-looking woman is here to see you," she said. "I told her I could help her, but she insisted on talking to you."

I looked up at Nat with an aggravated glare. By now she should know I was in my zone, carving an intricate bluebird design on the headboard for Marty. Interruptions were as annoying as working with a dull edge.

Nat casually shrugged off my rebuke. "I can tell her you're not here."

I laid my chisel on my workbench. "No, if she specifically asked, I'll assume she needs to see me. It better be important, though." I tossed my carving glove onto the workbench and walked out of the shop. Nat turned and followed at my heel. "I swear I'm never going to get that headboard finished in time for Marty and Joyce's anniversary," I grumbled as we sauntered through the hallway toward the show-room. "Marty's going to kick me—" The words stuck in my throat. I stood frozen still and staring, for the moment too shaken to speak.

Though her back was turned to me, I knew it was Grace. She turned and looked at me with a hesitant smile. Searing blood raced through me, and my legs suddenly felt like lead. Still unable to move, I stood there and hoped Grace could not see the blood rushing to the surface of my skin.

"I told you she was hot," Nat whispered as she passed by me on her way back to the workshop. Her voice jerked me back to reality. I walked over to the counter, keeping it as a barrier between Grace and me.

"Hello, Grace," I said calmly, though my mind was swirling. "It's been a while."

"Too long," Grace said. She moved toward me, but then stopped, her expression becoming uncertain. Her gaze darted away and back to me, seeming to be searching for words. "It's good to see you again."

"You, too," I said coolly, though I feared Grace could surely hear the pounding in my chest. She had always been so good at reading me, of knowing what I was thinking and feeling. But that was twenty-four years ago.

Grace's nervous smile faded and she looked away, her eyes zooming everywhere except at my face. After a moment she dared another look at me. "I read the article about you and the shop in *WNC Magazine,* so while I was in town I wanted to come by and wish you well."

Wish me well? She comes crashing back into my life to wish me well? Grace was never that naïve. "Don't you think you should have called first?" I asked. I stared at her, stone-faced and cold.

Grace nodded, emotion twitching the corners of her mouth. "You're right, I should have called. It was wrong of me to disturb you like this. I apologize." She stood for a moment, seeming to waver in confusion, and then she said, "Take care of yourself, Blue."

"Yeah, you too, Grace," I said bitterly. I needed more than an apology. I wanted to jump across the counter and grab her to shake an honest confession out of her bones. I gripped the edge of the counter, my knuckles going white as I glared at her. She flashed a nervous smile and turned away.

Grace took a step to go, and Mary Rowe's voice suddenly rang clear through my mind. *If you saw her today, how would you feel about her? Would you want to punish her?*

And then I recalled my reply, *I would be happy to see her, because I cared about her. She was important to me, and I would want her to be alright.*

You're meant to be something more than a love-scorned drifter. It's beneath you. You have to find a way to forgive her.

"Grace, wait," I said as she took a step to leave. She turned around. Her face was pale and drawn. She looked as confused as I felt.

I took a deep breath and tried to think clearly. "If you want, you can come back around lunchtime. We'll get some coffee or a bite to eat if you like."

Grace's face lightened when she answered, "Lunch would be nice, Blue. Thank you."

"I usually eat early. Come back around 11:30."

"See you then," Grace said. She looked at me with a quick smile and turned for the door. I watched her leave and walked back to the workshop, trying to shake the thick stupor from my brain.

Nat looked up at me from her work stool, holding a hand plane as if she had actually been doing something with it. "Who was that? You look like you've just seen a ghost or something," she said.

"That was Grace," I replied, still trying to shake away my fog.

"The Grace you carved the vanity for?"

"Yep, that was her."

"Killer," Nat said with a sly smile.

"You could say that," I replied. I walked to the lumber rack and stared at the piled stacks of wood. For the first time in years, it all looked like nothing but planks and boards. No hint of possibility seemed to be waiting in any one of them. My thoughts were stuck on Grace; the way she moved, still so familiar, yet now in a way even more controlled than in our time on campus. There was no flirtation now, only a woman aware of the need to project a proper image. How had things turned out for her? Had she lived up to her father's expectations? And was she married? She must be, yet I hadn't looked for a ring. How could I not have looked for a ring?

"So what did she want?" Nat asked, again bringing me back to the moment.

"She said she had seen the *WNC* article and wanted to say hello."

"She'll flip when she sees her name in the vanity," Nat said.

"Maybe, or maybe she won't see it," I replied. I hoped she never would.

Grace stood in front of the vanity, closely studying the carvings. She looked up and caught me watching her. Her left hand, along with the wedding band and diamond solitaire, slipped into the pocket of her navy blue Capri pants. I glanced down at her pocket and pulled in a deep breath. "Are you ready, then?" I asked.

Stepping outside of the shop reset my mind. Only a slight chill lingered in the sun-kissed air. Streets along the downtown blocks were filling with early summer tourists. Rock climbers in their deadhead grunge wear, golfers in their neat, Callaway Golf ensembles, affluent forty-somethings showing off their oversized SUVs and Wall Street successes, relishing their day in paradise. Highlands was fully awake from its winter siesta.

I looked over at Grace as we started down the sidewalk. "So, are you living in North Carolina now?" I asked.

Grace nodded and looked at me with the kind of polite, practiced expression that comes from years of meeting strangers and trying to win them over with the first hello. "Yes, we live in Winston," she said with a faint smile. "Both of the children are out of college, thankfully. Katie is in law school at Georgetown and Brian received his officer's commission with the Marines after graduating from VMI. They're twins. In some ways, that made things easier."

I stepped toward Grace to slip by an older couple holding hands as they shuffled down the sidewalk. "And your husband?" I asked as indifferently as I could manage.

"George is an attorney, and also a state senator, which keeps him very busy. He spends a good deal of time in Raleigh."

I looked over at Grace, hoping to find a hint of something left unsaid in her expression, yet I found no hint of malice.

"How about you?" Grace asked without looking at me, I hoped because of apprehension for my answer.

"You pretty much saw it all back there," I said, nodding back toward the shop. "I have the shop, some great friends scattered across the country, and a cozy little cabin up the mountain. My landlords are a fantastic lesbian couple who treat me like family. Life is pretty good right now."

Grace nodded politely and looked at me with the warm smile that once took my breath away. We stopped at the edge of the block to wait for a cluster of Harleys to ease by, their thunderous engines prohibiting conversation. "So, no partner, then?" Grace asked as we stepped onto the street behind the Harleys.

"No, not right now. My work is keeping me busy." Grace again nodded politely. Her graciousness was beginning to irritate me.

"Yes, I hear you are in high demand. The vanity piece you have featured in the shop is just incredible, though I noticed there was a *Not for Sale* sign in front of it. Any chance you would change your mind? I would love to buy it." Grace stopped at the door of Sully's Restaurant and looked up at me, waiting for my answer.

Still pushing, aren't you? You're not having everything you want this time.

I grinned through my annoyance and pulled the door open for her. "Nope, the vanity is the best example of my work. I can't sell it."

"If you ever change your mind . . ." Grace said.

I nodded and looked around for someone who could seat us. "Hi, Blue. Table for two?" Tina asked as she rushed toward us with a stack of menus. She glanced around the restaurant without spotting an empty table. "We have some tables outside or you can wait a few minutes."

I looked at Grace with a shrug.

"Outside is fine," Grace said. Tina led us through the main dining room and out to a table in the corner of the patio. She took our drink orders and left us sitting across from each other at a table that felt as big as Texas. I glanced over at Grace. The light breeze tossing her blonde hair across her shoulders sent an unwelcome twist to my gut. Quickly, I picked up my menu.

Grace finished scanning the lunch selections and put the menu down beside her napkin roll. She smiled and leaned a shoulder toward me, her hands clasped in her lap, positioning her body the way society women do for polite conversation. "So how did you get into wood-working? Did you finish vet school?"

I closed my menu and cocked my head back with a callous grin. "Grace, I never even finished college." She blinked and stared blankly at me for a moment, then looked down at her hands folded in her lap. The hurt in her face seemed honest. "I left Chapel Hill that summer you went to Europe. I intended to come back and finish, I just never did."

Grace looked up at me. "Was it because of what happened between us?"

Of course it was, I wanted to say. I knew it wasn't true. I shook my head and leaned toward her. "It was a lot of things, Grace. I needed to get away that summer, so I went up to Kentucky to look for contacts in the horse industry. Things got fouled up after that."

Grace moved her hand toward me and rested it on the table. She spoke softly, "Blue, I never wanted to hurt you. You know that, don't you?"

I turned away from her and sat back, wanting as much distance as possible between us. Out on the street I spotted a young father helping his daughter out of his truck cab. The little girl looked to be about six or seven and already walked with a kind of tomboy swagger. I kept my gaze on them as I answered. "A lot of things hurt me, Grace. I can't lay the fact that I never finished school at your feet." I looked back at her with a cutting glare, hoping she wouldn't see the hurt in my eyes. "Besides, I think I ended up where I need to be—and you ended up where you need to be."

Grace studied me for a long moment. A fire began to blaze in her eyes and for an instant I thought she might snap back at me. Grace was far too polished for such dramatics. Her voice again became politely measured. "Yes, I suppose we did. Your work is simply incredible. Who knows if you would have discovered that talent had you become a veterinarian."

Tina stepped between us holding two tall glasses, each topped with a lemon wedge. "Two waters. Now what else can I get ya?" She reached to her hip pocket for her notepad. She looked at Grace first.

I watched Grace politely nod and smile at Tina's enthusiasm for all of the salads, or trout if Grace wanted an entrée. This restaurant and a casual lunch was not the place to burn through more than two decades of emotional baggage. I thought I had forgiven Grace for the way she left me. Now I knew I had not. Yet I was the one who wouldn't let her turn around and walk away. I had asked her to lunch, and I now needed to hear the answers to years of questions, whether or not I was ready to hear them.

Tina left with our orders. I fidgeted with my silverware and searched for words of truce. After a moment I looked at Grace and said, "So you have two children. They must be very important to you."

Grace smiled. "I adore my children. They're such good kids. Living in a political family has not been easy for them. Sometimes they were under the microscope, and sometimes they had to take care of each other. We tried to spend as much time with them as we could, but with my job and George's schedule, there were too many nights they went to bed without seeing us."

"It sounds like they're doing well. You must have done something right."

Grace grasped her water glass and slowly slid her fingers up and down. "I suppose," she said softly.

I watched her fingers move on the glass—those soft, elegant, long fingers, the way they had once felt on my skin. I flushed and looked away. "So you mentioned your job," I said, turning back to her. "What do you do for a living?" The question sounded strange when asked of a woman who had never *needed* to work to live.

Grace shifted into her polite pose. "I'm the director of philanthropy for the C.L. Lockley Foundation. We provide grants for medical research in the U.S. and Europe. Right now we're focusing on funding stem cell research."

"It sounds like important work."

"It is," Grace replied soberly. "I'm proud of the work we do, though not so much for where the money comes from." I looked at her curiously, imagining ties to the mafia. "The foundation is made up primarily of wealthy tobacco families," she continued. Her gaze became distant and drifted out toward the street. "I think contributing large sums of money to medical research helps them feel better about killing people," she said. She fell silent, then straightened and looked at me again. "I try to focus on where the money is going rather than where it comes from."

I nodded but said nothing. Grace Lancaster was still a knot of contradictions.

When lunch came, Grace mostly pushed her food around the plate. She said she had had a late breakfast, though I sensed it was something more, something she was still holding back. I decided not to push her. The Grace I remembered held back her emotions, then spilled them out in rush when she could no longer keep them in.

I cleared the plate that had been covered with trout, potatoes, and asparagus. Tina dropped by the table to ask if we wanted dessert. I surprised her by saying yes. She was back in a few minutes with coffee, hot tea, and a huge double fudge brownie. She set the dish in the middle of the table and placed a fork on each side. I picked one up and held it out to Grace. She shook her head. I shrugged and plunged my fork into the brownie. "So how long do you plan to stay in Highlands?" I asked as I pulled away my first bite.

Grace winced from the heat of her tea and lowered the mug to the table. "Probably three or four days. I'm here to do some fishing and shopping, and yes, in that order."

"So fishing to get dirty and smelly before an afternoon in the boutiques?" I looked at her with a teasing smirk and dipped the fork in for a second bite.

Grace grinned. "No, I meant I'm here to fish unless the weather doesn't cooperate. Shopping is the alternative."

I nodded and reached for my coffee. Tilting my mug toward her I said, "Here's hoping for good weather."

"Why? You don't want me in town?" Grace propped her elbows on the table. She tucked her chin on her hands and looked at me with a coy little smile.

"Don't go putting words in my mouth," I warned her.

Grace frowned and looked out to the street. She glanced back at me, her face wary as she reached for her tea. "Can you believe neither my kids nor my husband like to fish?" Grace asked after another careful sip. "I taught the children when they were young, but once the teen years hit, forget it."

"That's too bad," I said with more sarcasm than I intended. A part of me wanted to push on, to tell her that her life was a result of her own choices. For the moment, I chose for the peace to stay between us. "So do you go alone?"

"Not totally alone." She looked into her mug and bobbed the teabag. "I usually take Madge with me."

"Madge? You have a fishing partner named Madge? Seriously?"

Grace replied with a slow smile easing onto her lips. "Well, sort of. Madge is the .38 I carry in my waders."

I stared at Grace for a moment, trying to reconcile this polished, gun-toting, society mother of two who just happened to fly-fish alone. Mischief flickered in her eyes to match her smile. At the same time, we both started laughing.

Neither of us said much on the way back to the shop. We reached the door and stood facing each other in awkward silence. Grace reached out for my hand. Her light touch pulsed on my skin with the weight of the last twenty-four years. I looked at her warily and pulled back my hand. Grace blinked for a moment and looked up into my eyes. Her perplexed expression turned apologetic. "I know I should have called before I dropped in, Blue. The truth is I was afraid you wouldn't want to see me—but it was good to see you again. I'm so glad you are doing well." She reached into her shoulder bag and pulled out a small leather wallet. "Here's my business card." She took a card from the small stack tucked inside a silk crease. "My cell number is listed in the corner. That's the best way to reach me, if you should ever want."

I looked down at the card. Grace L. Marshall. The last name caught me like the nick of a thorn, an irritation that could fester for weeks. "And obviously you know how to find me," I replied.

"Take care of yourself, Blue," Grace said.

"You too, Grace," I replied. She waved once as she turned to walk away. I watched her for a moment, until I couldn't any longer, and bowed into the store.

41

Damn Grace Lancaster

Goddammit! I swung the covers off and got out of bed. The alarm clock on my nightstand read 2:41, forty minutes since the last time I checked. I clicked on the lamp and looked over at my dresser. Grace's business card sat there on the edge, drawing my eyes like a junkie to a fix. I grabbed the card and held the corners, my hands taut and ready to rip the card into pieces.

Grace L. Marshall. In the right corner was the cell number I could call anytime. Her voice would be on the other end; the voice I feared I would someday forget. What would she say if she knew how often I'd thought of her? How often I would let my gaze drift through a crowd, wondering if I would see her face? Why had I never let her go?

Shivering in the chill, I pulled on my flannel robe and walked through the dining room and into the kitchen. The bottle of Woodford Reserve bourbon sat on top of the refrigerator waiting for me. Sweet Kentucky whiskey hadn't failed me on nights I couldn't sleep, a quarter lowball glass for some nights, for others a third. I poured a generous third and headed to the den and my rocker.

The sting of the first sip streamed through my chest. Grace was somewhere close, maybe just over the rise of the ridge, or at the crook of the creek, or maybe too many miles away to matter. Was she alone? Was she sleeping next to George? Maybe she was awake, too, and thinking of me.

Why the fuck did I care? Grace was one woman, and she had fucked me over worse than anyone else. Mary said I needed to find a way to forgive her. She never said I should invite her back into my life. Why would I do that? To be friends?

Her smile was the same. And, oh God, that body.

I took another sip and the numbing started. Thank the gods for bourbon. Why was I up at three o'clock in the morning drinking bourbon, anyway? I had so much shit to do at the shop. Would Grace pop in again and screw up my whole day? No way, she wouldn't do that again. She knew how I felt, didn't she? What if it rained and I saw her in town? It always rains in Highlands. Grace knows that. Goddamnit.

Another sip.

Did her children look like her? Was Katie as generous and observant as Grace had been at that age? My God, Grace had two grown children. She had said once she wanted children—she meant with me. Had I been a coward, too, when I said she was dreaming? No way. I was realistic. What did it matter, anyway? Grace wouldn't have done it. She could never see past her mother's ego.

A full swallow streamed through my body.

Ego. Is that why Grace's leaving had hurt me so bad? Was it my ego? Was she simply the first lover to break my heart? No, we'd had something special. I'd let her memory come back fully to me while I was in Mississippi. I had forgiven her for falling short of what we wanted, and then the good came back. I remembered Grace to remember love, and let the memories guide my work. Today she was more than a memory. Today Grace was real again. What would I do with that? When I thought of her now, I would see the woman I saw today: a woman with two grown children and a husband. A woman I barely knew. Did I want to know her again? If Grace and I were to become something else, something besides lovers, would I lose the inspiration that came with my memories of her? Maybe I already had. Maybe I lost it in the moment I saw her standing in my shop. But, God, the way she affected me when I saw her standing there, when I watched her eyes and the way she moved, still so familiar.

I took the last of the bourbon down in a huge swallow and let it fill my cells. The engine in my brain finally slowed, and then switched off. I moved over to the couch and pulled the blanket tight around me. In a minute or so, I was asleep.

The next morning I woke up late and called Nat to open the shop. It was almost ten when Marty drove up and found me on the porch swing, still in my robe and cradling an oversized mug of coffee.

"You okay, kid?" she called out as she climbed the porch stairs.

"Yeah, I'm fine. I just couldn't sleep last night."

Marty sat down on the porch rocker beside the swing and started a slow rock. "I know the feeling. It gets worse with the change."

I chuckled. "It's not that. Not yet, anyway. I got a bit of a shock yesterday. Grace Lancaster dropped by my shop."

"Grace Lancaster?"

"Yeah, Grace Lancaster. The one from college. I told you and Joyce about her."

Marty slowly nodded and her eyebrows furrowed as she tried to remember. "Oh, her. She just dropped in out of the blue?" Marty crossed her arms over her chest and looked at me curiously.

"Apparently. She said she saw the article in WNC magazine and wanted to stop by while she was in Highlands to 'wish me well.'"

"Seems odd," Marty said. Her index finger started tapping her forearm and her eyes narrowed in contemplation. "So if you were up half the night, the meeting must not have gone well."

"Well, we got by without any theatrics. In fact, we were very cordial to each other. The whole thing was surreal, really, like I was walking through some sort of strange dream."

"How so?"

"I don't know. I think it was because I've tied a lot of stuff to Grace. Dreams of how I wanted my life to be, and how I should feel when I was with someone. Nobody could be Grace. When I started carving, I knew I needed something that would take me to the next level, something that would make me want to learn more and get better with technique. Then I had the idea for the vanity, and I knew to pull it off I was going to have to get much better. I wanted so badly to bring my vision to reality. I worked long and hard to develop my skills, just to create a carving that celebrated a woman I once knew."

Marty nodded thoughtfully. "And yesterday she comes walking in the door."

"That's why I was up half the night drinking bourbon."

"Did it do you any good?"

"I finally got some sleep, but this morning when I woke up the first thing I thought about was Grace. Not the memory, but the woman she is now, with a state senator husband and two grown children."

Marty blew out a sigh. "I see. So do you think you'll stay in touch with her?"

"She gave me a business card, but I'm not going to call her. I can't risk letting her get into my head and messing things up. With any luck she'll stay in Winston and let it go. I can live my life just fine with Grace Lancaster being nothing more to me than a memory."

42

Disappearing

I barely heard the knock on the door. Dropping my book onto my bed, I listened closer. The knock came again, this time louder and more demanding than the first. I slipped on my moccasins and pulled on a sweatshirt on the way to the door. Opening it a crack, I peeked out onto the porch. The faint glow of the porch light washed Grace's face with a golden hue.

"Grace," I said softly as I slid past the screen door and quietly pulled the door closed behind me. "Are you okay?"

Grace shuffled uneasily, arms crossed tightly across her chest. She glanced at the door, and then back at me. Her hushed words spilled out, "I'm sorry, Blue. I know I shouldn't have come out here like this. I should have called first. I keep doing this to you, don't I? I'd better go."

Grace spun around to leave. I grabbed her arm. "Grace—wait a minute. I think you'd better tell me why the hell you're here." I dropped her arm and waited.

Grace looked away. In the expectant silence I watched her struggle for an answer. She took a deep breath and said, "I don't really know. I was packing to leave tomorrow morning, and I kept thinking I wanted to see you again. I know I should have called, but I didn't know what I would say if I did. So I grabbed my keys and drove out here. I sat in the car until I got the nerve to knock on your door."

I looked at her with an incredulous smile. "So let me get this right. You take the time to find out where I live, and then decide to drive out here? Why would you do that, Grace? Did you want to wish me well again?" I watched her struggle beneath my glare, and I almost gave in and reached out to her.

"No, of course not," she replied, her eyes turned down. She shuffled, then gathered her nerve and said, "Can you say good-bye that easily? You'll never want to talk to me at all?"

Never want to talk to her at all? I thought I would not—convinced myself, in fact. Yet, now she was standing in front of me again, challenging my resolve. I could not let her. "I'm not going to answer until you can honestly tell me why you're here."

Grace replied with a blank stare. Her face flushed and she looked away. She huddled her body close, shivering in the night air. "Can we sit down for a minute?"

Reluctantly I raised my hand toward the patio table in the center of the porch, "Go ahead. I'll get you a blanket." I slipped into the cabin and grabbed the fleece blanket off the back of the couch. Grace draped it across her shoulders as I sat down across from her. Still she shivered; I sensed it wasn't from the cold.

Grace pulled the blanket tightly against her chest and said, "Blue, when I saw your picture in that magazine article, I felt like my breath had been knocked out of me. Suddenly there you were, looking right at me, with this huge caption that read, "Original Blue." I stared at that picture, and then I read the article, twice. When I finished, I couldn't get it out of my mind. I wanted to know more, to fill in the gaps of all the time since I'd seen you, but I didn't know how to do that. No one had heard from you in years. Finally, I said to hell with it and found your shop. Now I don't know if I can know where you are and simply ignore you."

I leaned in so she could see the sureness in my eyes. "Well, you're going to have to. What is it you want anyway, Grace? A second chance to screw up my life?"

Her mouth twitched. "I didn't know I screwed it up the first time."

I fell back and looked at her with a cynical smile. "Well, you sure didn't help it any, did you?" She looked away. Anger boiled up and filled my voice. "What's next, Grace, an invitation to Sunday dinner with the family? Maybe we could have tea with your mom. That would be lovely, don't you think?"

Grace's eyes narrowed on me. "Leave my mother out of this. This isn't about her."

"Isn't it? I think it is exactly about her. Come on, Grace, one day I walked into my apartment and found out I meant less to you than your mother's fucking ego!"

"Oh, come on, Blue. You know damn well I cared about you. I loved you."

"Is that why you married George and had two kids with him?"

Grace looked away and raised her hand to disguise the quiver of her mouth. I watched the pain deepen in her face. For the moment, forgiveness replaced the anger. I leaned in closer and spoke softly, but firmly. "Grace, after we broke up, I just took off. The way you left was hard on me, Grace, really hard. I ended up going from one place to another, one woman to another, without any anchor or direction. By chance, I met some people who changed all of that. Now I'm here, and my life is where I want it to be. I can't say right now if I want you to be part of it or not, and until I figure that out I can't allow you to drop in whenever you feel like it to tell me about your kids, or ask for my vote or a campaign contribution, or whatever it is you want from me. Do you understand that?"

In the silence I heard a gathering gust of wind begin its march toward my porch. When it reached us, Grace pushed her hair away from her face and turned to me. "So that's it? After I leave tonight I may never speak to you again?"

I looked at her, and in that moment I knew I wasn't ready for another forever good-bye. I shook my head. "I don't know Grace. I only know you're asking too much of me right now."

She blinked and looked as if she finally got it. "I think what you mean is you're not sure you'll *ever* want me in your life again."

"Maybe so, Grace."

"So what do I do until you decide?"

"I think you can start by learning to respect my boundaries. First you showed up unannounced at my shop, and now you're out here in the middle of the night. This place is my home now, and I'm not sure I want you here. Or coming into my store."

Her vacant eyes turned down. "Okay," she said softly. She stood up and reached to her shoulder for the blanket. "Thank you for this," she said, holding it out to me. "Have a good night."

Grace walked away with long, sure strides, her arms swinging freely by her sides, the same unrestrained gait I remembered from our days exploring the woods. Her footsteps bounded down the stairs, and then crunched on the gravel drive. When she reached for her car door handle, I called out. "Grace!"

She turned around and looked at me curiously.

"Never mind," I grumbled. "Good night"

"Good-bye, Blue." She opened her door and got in without a look back.

I slipped into the cabin as the taillights of her Land Rover disappeared down the drive.

43

Look for the Beautiful

Marty bustled through the door of my workshop and took a look around. "So this is where you make the magic happen," she said. I put down my bench plane and walked next to her. The smell of product lingered in her freshly cut, salt and pepper hair.

"Are you and Joyce going out tonight?" I asked, looking over her newly coiffed 'do.

"No, our anniversary isn't until next week. I told you I wanted the headboard today 'cause I wanted to be sure it was ready."

I laughed. "I'm not one to miss deadlines."

"I know. I also know how hard you've been working lately. We haven't seen you around much."

"We've been busy trying to stay on top of the orders coming in. I expect things will slow down eventually." I nodded toward the storage room that housed all of our outgoing orders. "Come on, I'll show you that headboard."

Marty followed me into the storage room and grabbed the opposite end of the quilted blanket draped over the headboard. Together we lifted it off. She shuffled over to the center of the carving and blew out a low whistle. "Wow, kid, I knew it would be beautiful, but I wasn't expecting this." Marty had generally described a headboard with a center carving that featured interlaced tree branches and flowers, accentuated by a couple of birds huddled in the middle. The exact design she left up to me. "Joyce will cry when she sees this," Marty said.

I smiled and grasped her shoulder as her face beamed. "Actually I'm pretty darned happy with the way it turned out, too. How about a glass of wine? We'll toast your years together."

"You know I can't turn down good wine," she said, grinning up at me.

Marty followed me to the lunch bar at the back of the shop and slid onto one of the stools at the counter. She watched as I looked over the wine selection I kept in a well-stocked cabinet. A few minutes of wine and conversation were always offered to my customers before I took their multithousand dollar checks.

"Are you sure nothing else is going on besides work? Joyce worries, you know." Marty looked at me with single eyebrow cocked.

"Tell Joyce I'm fine." I checked the wine label and reached in a drawer for a corkscrew.

"Maybe so, but I agree you haven't been yourself lately. Joyce noticed it weeks ago, about the time I found you hungover on the porch, right after you said Grace Lancaster dropped in on you."

I looked at Marty with a smirk and pulled out a couple of wine glasses "I was not hungover. I just hadn't slept well." I poured the wine and walked over to the stool beside Marty. She took her glass and I sat down with mine. "Can you believe she dropped in again? Totally unannounced, I might add. It didn't end well."

"How so?"

"I made it clear she can't keep showing up whenever she feels like it, and I asked her what she wants from me. She didn't have an answer."

"I think it's obvious what she wants from you, and I think you know it, too." Marty took a sip of wine and leveled her knowing gaze on me. That gaze, along with her finely calibrated bullshit detector, had a way of blazing a route right into my unexplored truth.

"Yeah, I suppose I do know."

"I think a part of you wants the same thing, or else we wouldn't be having this conversation, would we?" I gave Marty a sour look, but I didn't say anything. "How much do you know about Grace now?" Marty asked.

"Not much, I guess. It sounds like you know a bit, though."

"I do." She set her glass down and looked at me earnestly. "My Joyce is a curious one. When she wants to know something, she finds the answers, so she did a little Internet search on Grace."

I nodded. "So what did she find?"

"She found Grace's name attached to quite a list of nonprofits in this state—everything from the Nature Conservancy to Norton Center for the Arts, to local school charities and food banks. Grace Marshall's address book probably contains the name of every millionaire in this state."

I suppose Marty thought this information should impress me somehow. It didn't. "She's a state senator's wife. I guess that's the kind of thing they do."

"Not really," Marty replied. "Not like your Grace does."

"She's not my Grace," I snapped.

"Hit a nerve, did I?" Marty cradled her wine against her chest and watched me. She was making me crazier than my own thoughts. I sipped my wine to avoid meeting her eyes.

"So what *is* it you want from Grace? Why can't you tell her to get lost?" Marty asked.

I had been asking myself the same question now for days on end. "I don't know." I looked down at the wood shavings clinging to my pants and thought about it. "The last time I saw Grace Lancaster, Ronald Reagan was president and Gloria Vanderbilt jeans were in style." I looked up to find Marty still watching me closely. "And you're right—I don't know a damn thing about her now. I do know we're not two girls in college anymore. Grace has this whole society wife thing going on, and I have a business with employees who depend on me to keep it together." I paused and looked around the shop. "Everything about Grace is in the past, so part of me wishes we could keep it there—but, to be honest, another part can't accept the thought of never seeing her again."

"*Now* we're getting somewhere. So, which part is bigger?"

"I don't know. Sometimes I want to call her. Then I think, what happens next? We become friends, have lunch together when she's in Highlands, maybe meet for a drink now and then? That doesn't sound so bad. Grace could be a good friend, and maybe she can still read me like she did when we were younger. She helped me cope with losing my parents, and we could talk about anything. I wouldn't want to lose the chance to have someone like that in my life. And then this little voice in my head says, 'Get real, Riley. It will only lead to all kinds of problems, no matter what happens.' So here I am, stuck between taking a chance with her again, or playing it safe and keeping Grace as only a memory."

Marty nodded slowly and grabbed her knee to rock back, thinking for a long moment before she asked me, "Do you think you could live with that memory now that you've seen her again? It seems you both feel you have some unfinished business."

"I'm not sure I have any unfinished business with Grace."

"Oh, you don't think so?" Marty said with a smirk. "You took months and months out of your life to design and carve a tribute to her and you don't think you have unfinished business?"

I sipped my wine, thinking about her question before I answered. "Carving the vanity was a cathartic experience for me. I closed the book on my relationship with Grace the day I finished it."

Marty looked at me, unconvinced. "Well, I wish I knew what to tell you about your Grace. All I can say is, if you keep your head about you, you can take some risks. I would never have met Joyce if I hadn't taken some big chances. It wasn't always painless, but we got through it." Marty's face lightened and she reached over to pat my forearm. "It's a crazy path we walk, kid, and nobody has a map."

I slammed the lid of my laptop down and stared out at the ageless face of Whiteside. The mountain didn't seem to care that I was being an idiot; that I'd spent the last hour surfing through random website articles and photographs of Grace. I thought it would help to see her in the present, to know that she wasn't the same person she had been at twenty. My Google search only made it worse. Everything I read made her life seem so full and complete, yet she had ended up at my cabin door, searching for something that ribbon cuttings and ballroom galas couldn't give her. After the Internet search I knew the Grace-fueled commotion in my mind could be settled in only one way, and it pissed me off.

The screen door slammed behind me as I stormed down the cabin stairs. I headed down the hollow in long strides, the angry energy building inside me like liquid fire. Of all the women, of all the women, why wouldn't Grace Lancaster ever leave me? Grace wouldn't even admit who she was, who she still is. Her life seemed nothing more than a series of half-truths, and I was in imminent danger of landing there again.

I walked on as darkness fell over the cove. Moonlight lit the gray-white gravel on the road ahead of me. The woods were quiet now; the birds at roost and the frog and insect chorus not yet at its fervent nightly pitch. Who was I fooling? Marty was right. Grace had crawled under my skin the first day I saw her at that damn car wash, and she hadn't left since. I thought I'd put her safely away, forgiven her and secured her memory in the bittersweet confines of could-have-beens. Now she was busting through like a wrecking ball.

I circled back around to my driveway and ambled up my porch stairs, sat down on the top step, and looked out into the night. I knew what I was going to do, and I knew it was brave and foolish all at the same time. I turned to the stars and talked to Mary. "I wish I could call you right now. I could really use your advice."

The stars looked back, brilliant and clear over the shadow of Whiteside. *Just keep yourself when you give to her.* I recalled the day Mary said that to me. We'd been working in the kitchen preparing collard greens for canning when I casually asked Mary the secret to a long and happy marriage. She had surprised me with her answer. Mary never stopped teaching.

Just keep yourself when you give to her. If only it could be that easy.

I went inside to find Grace's business card.

44

Stubborn Grace

The headlights of Grace's Land Rover pierced the orange hue of morning's first light. Grace slid out of the driver's seat to open the back hatch. "Good morning," she said with a gentle smile. I slid my fly rod into the back of the Land Rover and ambled around to the passenger's side. She pulled over her seat belt as I got in. How could she look so damn put together at this hour of the day? She shifted into first gear and turned down the drive.

"Grace, about the night you came over," I said as we turned out onto the gravel road leading to Cashiers.

She broke in before I could continue. "Can we wait until we're more awake to talk about that?" She glanced over at me with a quick smile and I nodded. She turned on NPR to fill the silence. Still, the hurt hung over us like a hornet's nest.

Ten minutes up the road, Grace turned down the radio and turned left. She rolled her window down and rested her arm on the door. A content smile turned on her lips and stayed there as we drove down the gravel road. It seemed Grace still loved to listen to the forest.

We crossed a one-lane bridge and she stopped for a moment to listen to the stream flowing beneath us. After another half mile or so, we slowed to turn onto a red dirt road scratched through the woods. Leaning up to the steering wheel, Grace slowly picked her route up and over the ruts and boulders of the washed-out road. The Land Rover swung from side to side, bouncing our shoulders against the doorframes until we reached the high bank of a small rocky stream. She stopped there and killed the engine. "This is it."

I stepped out of the Land Rover and looked around to take in the mountain morning. Bird songs echoed out in full chorus, and thick dew hung from a spider's masterpiece spun at the edge of the tree line. Below us was the creek: beautiful, but unremarkable for western North Carolina.

Grace stepped around to the back of the Land Rover and pulled out our gear. She handed my fly rod over and slipped her arms through her daypack. "You ready?" she asked. She didn't wait for an answer. I followed her to the edge of the creek's steep bank. Dirt and rock tumbled from beneath our feet as we scrambled down to the stream. "Don't worry, this isn't it," Grace said when we reached the water's edge. I stood on a narrow shoal and watched her jump from one rock to the next without a wobble. In that way, she hadn't changed.

Grace waited until I reached the other side, and then took off down a path I couldn't see. She walked like she was in a hurry, and I followed her without talking. A quarter mile up the path we reached a small stream, only a few feet wide. She turned there and headed upstream. Steep terrain challenged our lungs as we followed the stream's course, picking our way through the rocks and rhododendron on a slow and careful climb. In the distance I could heard the rush of a waterfall.

Grace glanced over her shoulder, "We're almost there." The path closed in, forcing us to hug the sandstone cliff at our right shoulders. She ducked around a boulder that jutted out across our path. "Here it is," I heard her say.

I swung around the rock and stood next to her. "What do you think?" she asked.

I looked around. The sandstone cliffs now surrounded us like a cathedral, rising forty feet above the rocks and boulders at the base of the forest floor. All around hemlock, beech, poplar, and white pine limbs dissected the rising sun into a veil of soft light. Rich ferns mixed with the jack-in-the-pulpits and trillium to form an endless mosaic of green. Ahead, the stream surged from the edge of the rounded rim of the hollow, tumbling down onto the solid rock below. Grace standing there, lost in the stillness, looked as strong and handsome as I'd ever seen her. "Incredible," I said.

"Isn't it?" she replied. We stood for a moment, listening to the water and wind and letting our hearts slow.

"There aren't many places like this around here; at least not many that aren't overrun with people," I said.

"I've been coming here for years, and I've never seen another soul." Grace looked at me sincerely. "I never thought I would share this place with anyone, until I saw you again."

I looked at her, clueless for what to say. "Come on," Grace said with tilt of her head. "There's a great spot at the top of the waterfall where we can eat breakfast."

She led me past the bottom of the falls and around to a break in the rocks. Swinging our fly rods out of the way and grabbing onto rock and saplings, we scrambled up to the top of the rock rim, then doubled back to the edge of the waterfall. For a moment we stood there, watching the stream race to the lip of the rock and disappear. "Are you hungry?" she said. "I brought some bagels and coffee."

"Yeah, that sounds good."

She took a few steps upslope, set her rod down, then kneeled to the ground and slipped off her daypack. I sat down beside her, close enough to catch her light scent in the morning breeze, for a moment taking me back to the days when I woke up next to her.

"The coffee's black, medium blend," Grace said. She held a stainless steel thermos out to me and again reached into her pack. "I brought sugar and creamer if you want," she said as she pulled out two stainless steel coffee mugs. "I've got two blueberry and one plain bagel, and jelly, cream cheese, and honey."

"I'll take a blueberry with honey," I said as I poured the coffee. I handed a cup to Grace and leaned back onto the ground covered by fallen leaves and evergreen needles. "I love these mountains," I said after a careful sip of steaming coffee. Grace handed me the bagel with a contented smile. "I spent a lot of time in the mountains Out West and I loved it, but when I came back here it was like coming home."

"I'm glad you're back." Grace flushed and turned away when our eyes met. She looked down into her pack and fumbled around inside. "I don't know what I did with the honey." Her face filled with color.

"Grace, it's okay."

"Here it is." Triumphantly she pulled out a small plastic bag filled with honey packets. She passed it over to me and licked her fingers. I had to look away.

We settled in with our bagels and watched the life of the woods as we ate. Grace swallowed her last bite and her eyes suddenly brightened. A dab of jelly clung to the corner of her mouth as she spoke. "Wouldn't it be great to put a yurt up here? Right here on the stream bank, next to the waterfall."

"A *yurt*?"

"Yeah," she reached over and pushed my knee. "Don't laugh. You should see the custom yurts they're building these days. I bet you could even get one with a sauna." She smiled as if she meant it.

"A yurt sauna—that sounds rather exotic for Macon County, don't you think?" I laughed, and Grace laughed, too. "I think I'll pass on the yurt. This place doesn't need humans, but maybe we can visit now and then."

She looked at me with a guarded smile and shifted in the expectant air surrounding the word *we*.

I studied her for a moment, trying to determine if her restless face was self-satisfied or anxious. "Grace, why did you want to bring me out here today?" I looked at her sharply and hoped for an honest answer.

She pulled her knees to her chest and wrapped her arms around them, as if to guard herself. "You really surprised me when you called, especially after being so angry when I showed up at your cabin. And you were right to be angry. I had presumed way too much. The last thing I wanted was to blow it again." Her gaze drifted out toward the forest. There seemed to be honesty in her faraway stare. "I didn't want to just go for coffee when you asked if we could meet somewhere. I remembered how it felt to be out in a beautiful place like this with you. We connected so well out in these mountains. I knew if I only got one chance to see you again, I wanted to make the most of it. So I offered this suggestion and hoped you'd say yes."

Morning sun fell across her profile, moving the shadows away from her face. In the light I saw the subtleties of change, the trace of crow's feet and worry lines that had not been there before. I thought of the time that had passed, of the seasons I had missed because she had been afraid. Back in Mississippi I had forgiven her for that, yet I needed to know how much of her fear was still in her. "So, what is it you want from me?"

Grace shifted and pulled her legs in tighter. She turned to me and said, "I really don't know. Do you know what you want from me?"

Her evasiveness stirred a latent pool of anger that had been simmering inside me since the day she came into my shop. "Right now, I want your honesty," I said crossly.

She flinched and thought for a moment. "More than anything, I'd like for you to know that I never meant to hurt you, and I know I did." She paused and turned away from me. "I should have told you what was going on with my parents. I was being selfish, or maybe stupidly hopeful that something would change before the summer came. I've regretted the way I treated you since the day you left. When I saw you were back in North Carolina, I hoped to find a way to tell you, maybe make it up to you somehow." She pushed a heel of her hiking boot hard against the ground. "Once again, stupidly hopeful."

In the blinking of her eyes and the twisting of her mouth I saw her emotions were churning inside her, much the same as my emotions were churning inside of me. This moment can be a true catharsis, I thought, if she will let it. "What else do you regret, Grace?"

She looked at me again.

I waited, my heartbeat growing stronger against my chest as I watched her eyes grow calm and steady.

"That I didn't fight for us. You deserved that from me. The truth is I didn't even try." Grace shrugged and picked up a fallen branch, holding it on one end as she studied the crooks in its form. She tapped it on the ground, lost in her own thoughts. After a long moment, she took in a deep breath and her body relaxed. Her confession came spilling out in a voice barely above a whisper. "I was so lost when I went to Europe that summer. Every time I looked around, there was something I wanted you to see, something I wanted to experience with you. I even called once, but your phone had been disconnected, so I tried Julie. Her answering service took the call. I freaked out and didn't leave a message. After that, I pulled myself back to reality, knowing that I was the last person on earth you wanted to hear from. Then, toward the end of the summer I met George Marshall. I didn't really love him, nowhere close to the way I loved you, but he was exactly the kind of man my mother wanted me to marry. So that was it—I married him. We had the twins soon after we graduated. They kept me busy and out of George's way. He was obsessed with his work and building his political career, and I was the kind of wife he needed. My family loved him, probably more than I did. We shared his career, but not much more than that. After a while, I let George know I wouldn't mind if he had affairs. George took me up on my offer. I think that's how we've managed to stay together all these years."

Grace would not look at me. Her gorgeous vulnerability was now everywhere, in the narrowing of her eyes, in the tight control of her lips, in her slight lean toward me. I watched her struggle and tried to process her confession.

"Why did you stay with him if he was not what you wanted?" I asked after a moment.

"I had the twins to take care of, and George let me do as I pleased."

"Do you mean you had affairs?"

"I did for a while—with men *and* women. Early on, I slept with a couple of men, mostly to see if I was missing something with George. With the women, it was more complicated; the attraction was more intense."

"Did you love them?" I asked, not sure I really wanted to hear the answer.

"Yes, in different ways," Grace began. "After a while I realized affairs are too difficult, so I learned to live without them."

"So what do you do instead?"

She looked at me with a sad smile and leaned back to rest on her hands. "I guess you're asking how I distract myself from the need for sex."

"Yeah, I suppose so," I said as an awkward heat rose up my neck.

"I find other things to do. Right now, I have Katie's wedding coming up. She moved the date up after we found out Brian will be deploying overseas soon. That put us behind with all the planning, so we've got some catching up to do. There's George's politics and the causes I'm working on. I get out here as much as I can." Grace looked toward the stream, and then out into the thick forest surrounding us. "It is beautiful, isn't it?"

I watched the stream rush to the edge of the waterfall, tumbling over in a delicate spray of color and light. "Yes, it is. I've always loved the streams here, and all the life they bring. They're different from Out West. The streams here seem more intimate."

Grace was smiling when I turned to her, I supposed because of the unexpected way I described how I felt. We were silent for a moment, and then I said, "Maybe this place gives you the intimacy you're looking for. That's why you carve time out of your schedule to come out here."

She did not respond right away. "Actually I think you're right," she said after a pause, her eyes set on the woods around her. "When I'm out here there are no demands on my time, no one wants anything from me." Grace got up and walked over to lean her back against a giant beech tree. She tucked her hands behind her hips and raised one foot to rest on its trunk. Her face turned up to the sun, soaking in the warmth for a moment. I didn't expect the jolt that hit when as I watched her; her shaggy morning hair loose and wild, shoulders relaxed against the tree bark, her boyish stance that came natural to her out here.

I stood and walked over to join her. "Grace, for what it's worth, I admire the work you do for your foundation and time you spend with your children, but most of all, I admire that you still know the importance of a place like this."

She looked at me but didn't say anything. For a moment a quiet peace of understanding fell between us. Something inside me shifted, like a distant battle that suddenly fell silent. In that moment I knew Grace would not break through my walls with force and fury. She would dismantle them one brick at a time.

She pushed away from the beech and said, "So, enough of this. Are you ready to catch some brookies?"

"Are you ready to get your ass kicked?" I answered, grinning.

Grace shook her head and started toward her fly rod. "Still at it, huh, Riley?"

"Some things never change."

She looked over her shoulder at me and smiled.

Grace drove up to my porch steps and shifted to park. "I hope I haven't made you too late for work," she said.

I tapped my fingers on her dashboard and glanced over at the clock. I expected to be back almost an hour ago. "I asked my assistant to open the shop this morning. I'll make up the missed time tonight. That's one of the advantages of being the boss. The disadvantage is that I have to work all the time to keep up."

Grace shifted around to face me. "Will we be able to get back together anytime soon?"

"Maybe. I thought this morning was nice. Thank you for being honest with me. It couldn't have been easy for you."

"It wasn't, but I owed you that much." Grace paused as I started to fidget. The day was wearing on and I needed to get to work. With another discussion of our past, I'd be out until noon. "Do you ever see Trish Youngblood anymore?" she asked.

I smiled with a memory of Trish. "No, I haven't seen Trish since the summer I lived in Kentucky. I thought about calling her a few times, but I just never have."

"Would you like to see her?" Grace asked.

"Sure, I guess so," I replied, though I wondered where the hell the conversation was going. Grace and Trish were never exactly close in college, and I couldn't imagine they were still in touch. "Why are you asking me about Trish Youngblood?"

"I'll probably see her in a couple of weeks. There's a benefit gala in Atlanta, mostly lesbians with money from the Atlanta area and along the I-85 corridor. Trish and her partner are there every year." Grace paused and looked at me guardedly. "You could see Trish if you went to the benefit."

Disbelief ran through me first. A few good hours in the woods and she thinks we should go away for the weekend? Grace knew what she was asking, and bringing Trish into the mix was nothing more than sweet manipulation. "Grace, come on. If I want to see Trish, I'll look her up myself. I don't think I need to go to Atlanta with you."

"Then don't go with me. I'll make a reservation for you at the hotel. You can come and go as you like."

"I don't see the point, Grace."

She stiffened. I wanted her to give up, to see the madness in what she was proposing—and then I realized I didn't. I didn't want her to give up. I wanted her to keep trying, and she did. She looked at me, her gorgeous green eyes full and sure. "You came back here, Blue. Was it only for the mountains? Or is there something else you're looking for?"

I couldn't say. I supposed I had missed something about the people here. Trish had been my best friend back then, my confidant for all that mattered. Susan had forgiven my absence. Maybe Trish would, too. I wondered if she could still make me laugh so easily.

Grace didn't wait for an answer to her question. She moved her hand toward me, but stopped short of a touch. The last time she'd tried, I'd pulled my hand away—and saw the traces of hurt and doubt when I did. This time, her eyes were bolder. "There are people here who've missed you. Don't shut them out."

I reached for the door handle and held it. "I'll think about the benefit, Grace."

"Just let me know," Grace said.

I nodded and got out.

45

Possible Grace

Preacher once told me that carving is the art of knowing what to take away, and what to leave. We cut, pound, and chip until we find the possibility waiting underneath. Resting my shoulder against the mahogany column of the Buckhead Ritz Carlton ballroom, I watched Grace glide about in her knee-length black silk dress, wearing a smile and moving through the room with three finger waves over her shoulder and quick handshakes, charming her way through the crowd with the ease of a politician's wife. Could I ever carve away enough of her layers to find the possibility waiting underneath?

Lost in my thoughts, I didn't notice Trish Youngblood walking up beside me until her palm slapped my shoulder. "Blue Riley! Goddamn, it's you!"

I swung around to the voice I still knew. Trish looked up at me with a huge smile. "I heard Grace Lan—Marshall walked in tonight with some blue-eyed wonder. I thought it might be you. How in the hell are you?"

"I'm doing well! Jesus, it's good to see you!" I grabbed Trish for a tight hug. When I pulled away, I grasped her shoulders, holding them tight as I scanned the length of her fit body. "You look great for an old woman," I said. I let her go and stood at her side. "So this is the pack you run with now, huh?" I asked with a tilt of my head toward the crowd.

Trish nodded, still smiling. "Yeah, this is my tribe. It's a little different from Chapel Hill days, huh?"

"Just a bit."

"Maybe not too different—you are here with Grace, aren't you?" Trish's smile slipped to a sly smirk.

291

I looked at her warily, "Not in the way you're thinking. We're friends. Well, not really friends, more like—hell, I don't know what we are."

"Well, at least that hasn't changed." Trish elbowed my ribs and I looked down at her with a we-may-be-friends-but-I-still-might-kill-you glare. "I'm just sayin'," Trish shrugged.

I nodded. "I know, I know. You're right. If I were you, I'd be confused, too." I smiled when I realized what I had just said. "Hell, I'm confused myself. At least we're not sleeping together."

"Why not?" Trish looked at me as if she truly had no clue.

"Among other things, she's married."

"That hasn't stopped her before," Trish replied. She turned toward Grace and I followed her gaze. The couple standing in front of Grace leaned forward to listen close, their serious expressions matching their understanding nods. "She's broken a couple of hearts in this room, I can tell you. 'Course she's been out of that scene for quite a while now. She hasn't brought anybody to this benefit in years. That's why all the jaws started flapping when she showed up with a date."

I leaned in close to Trish. "I'm not her date. I came here to see you, crazy woman."

Trish gave me a doubtful glance. "Yeah, whatever Riley," she said. She grasped my elbow and gave it a tug. "Come on, I'll buy you a drink and you can tell me what you've been up to for the last twenty-odd years." We started toward the bar in a slow shuffle, twisting and sliding our way through the crowd. Trish went straight to a thirty-something bartender with black hair and dark eyes.

"What can I get you ladies?" the bartender asked as she wiped her hands on her bar towel.

"Bud Light," I said, sticking with beer. Being with Grace, that dress she was wearing, the way her diamond pendant necklace framed the small hollow at the base of her throat, I needed to keep my wits.

Trish grabbed the drinks and threw a twenty on the bar. "Over there," she said, lifting my beer toward an empty table tucked against the wall.

"So what are you doing now?" I asked Trish after we sat down.

"I'm a financial analyst for Fellows Trust Bank. I went back to get my MBA and came to Atlanta after that. How about you? Did you ever finish school?"

"No, I never did. I design and build furniture now. I've got a shop up in Highlands, North Carolina."

"No shit!" Trish replied, nodding approvingly. "We'll have to come up and see you sometime."

I gave Trish a card listing my website and insisted she make good on her offer. We sipped our drinks unhurriedly, swapping short snippets of the last two decades of our lives. Trish told me how she stumbled upon the love of her life, an ob-gyn, at a funeral, and though she knew how wrong it was to approach a woman at such an event, she just couldn't help herself. "It was till death do us start," Trish said. She grinned and watched me laugh, pleased with the line she must have used a thousand times.

The band returned to the stage at the far end of the room. Drumsticks clicked a beat over the buzz of voices, and then a cover of "Don't Tell Me" drifted through the room. Trish scooted closer and leaned in. For the first time all night, she looked dead serious. "So how *did* you end up here with Grace Marshall?"

"Like I said, I came to see you." Trish cut her eyes up at me. She wasn't buying it. I picked at the label of my beer bottle to avoid her Sherlock Holmes stare. "I guess I'm trying to figure out what Grace is all about now. A couple of months ago she showed up at my shop, totally unannounced, like nothing ever happened. I was pissed, but I gave her a chance and had lunch with her. A couple of nights later, she shows up at my house. That really pissed me off. I basically told her to get lost." Trish nodded, transfixed in the newest round of Grace–Blue drama. It seemed her fascination with us hadn't waned over the years. "Grace stayed away like I asked, but she wouldn't leave my mind, just like always. As soon as I think I'm past her, something brings her back."

"So this has happened before?" Trish asked.

"No, not in the physical sense. When I was in Mississippi, I started thinking a lot about Grace. I told Miss Mary about her and she convinced me to forgive her. I realized Grace really didn't do anything other girls in her place wouldn't have done. It was just the times back then. There weren't a lot of lipstick lesbians around. It took a little testosterone to tell the old bastards to go to hell like we did."

Trish laughed. "And the world's a better place for it." I laughed and nodded in agreement. "So you forgave Grace, and then?"

"And then I got this idea for a carving. It's a series of a woman's face depicting the span of her life, and one letter of Grace's name is incorporated into each of the faces. The letters are subtle and really hard to detect, but it's right there for all the world to see."

Trish's gaze was glued on me. "Damn, Riley, you've still got some deep shit going on in that head of yours."

"Deep or stupid," I replied. "The thing is, I still like Grace, and I think about her more than I should. Not the memory of back then, but the woman she is now."

Trish nodded. "Grace carries a lot of baggage like we all do, but she's a good woman at heart. She helps a lot of people through her connections."

"Yeah, she told me about her work with the foundation."

"It's not her work I'm talking about. It's what she does behind the scenes for benefits like this, and for individuals having trouble. Even some of the women here have called her for help. She's careful about it, but she usually comes through."

Careful Grace. She had always been so maddeningly careful, and so full of possibility underneath her façade. "So if Grace comes to events like this, how does she stay out of the political gossip columns?" I asked.

"For one thing she would never go to an event like this in North Carolina. Grace knows how far out of state she needs to go to stay under the radar, and these women won't talk outside their circles." Trish scanned the women standing in close clusters around the ball-room and continued, "Families like the Marshalls and Lancasters have been all about knowing how to play the game for a long time now, and frankly, the private lives of state politicians like George Marshall don't get much media attention. That will change if he ever runs for national office."

"Any chance that will happen?"

"Right now I don't think so. George doesn't seem to have the stomach for it, and I think Grace would strongly object."

Trish suddenly sat up straight and held up an index finger. She reached to her belt for her phone. "Hey, baby. You ready? Okay, I'll see you in a few." She slipped the phone back into the case and hopped up. "It was great to see you again, Blue, but I've gotta go. My wife is waiting." She took a last sip of Scotch and nodded toward Grace. "So is yours." She smiled and turned away before I could reply. I watched her slip through the crowd, making her way toward the stage. She stopped there and waved the emcee over, said something into her ear, and headed for the door.

I sat back with my beer and looked around the room. Nothing but women, some holding hands or standing close, couples dressed in designer suits, or both wearing dresses, or one in a stunning dress and her partner in a suit. On the dance floor women held each other as their bodies moved together. All around, beautiful and striking women stood close, dressed and moving just for each other; a lesbian's dream. My gaze lingered on a few of them, and eventually drifted over to Grace.

Her head was thrown back in laughter and her hair fell down her back in light waves, her shoulders, tanned and firm, rolled with her joy. I remembered, as I watched her lightly touch the arm of the woman next to her, the nights I had looked up at the stars with haunting thoughts of her, the miles I had logged running from her memory, the hours of carving fueled by the memory of how it felt to hold her in my arms. Grace turned and looked at me. Her lips turned a slight smile and her eyes lingered for just a moment before she turned back to her conversation.

Screw it. I left my beer and headed through the crowd. When I stepped next to Grace she took my hand, as natural as a morning kiss.

"This is the woman I was telling you about," Grace said to the couple now standing across from her. "Blue, this is Elisha Duncan and Willow Wheeler-Duncan." I briefly shook each of their hands while Grace continued, "Blue designs and builds furniture. She has a shop in Highlands."

"One of our favorite getaways," Willow said. I'd seen her affected smile before on the faces of haughty customers who walked into my shop expecting my instant adoration. They pulled out their wads of cash or gold cards, trying to impress me. "It's beautiful up there," Willow was saying. "Do you design for individuals or businesses?"

"Both," I replied. "I work with clients to build custom pieces or suites to fit their needs. Most of my work is for individuals, but I've done a few boardroom pieces as well."

"Grace mentioned you are a carver, too." Elisha said. Her honest eyes seemed absent of her partner's conceit.

"Yes, I am. Most of my clients want a personal feature, so I usually add a carving." I reached into my pocket, pulled out a business card, and slipped it between Elisha's fingers. "Drop by next time you're in Highlands. I'll show you around the shop."

"It will be worth it. Her work is amazing." I looked over at Grace. It felt good to hear her say so.

The music, which had been more background than overwhelming, faded to silence. The emcee stood at the center of the stage and reached into her tuxedo pocket to pull out a note. She held it out as she spoke into the microphone, "This next song goes out to Blue Riley from Trish. She said you'll know what to do."

Grace turned to me. I shrugged, clueless. Together we look back to the stage. The lead singer stood quite still in her sequined silver dress, her eyes closed in concentration. She reached for the microphone, caressed it like a delicate flower, and began to sing, "Unforgettable— that's what you are."

Heat rushed up my neck and filled my face. I turned to Grace with the heat still rushing in. "I think I've been set up."

Grace squeezed my hand. "I think you have." She looked at me with a delicate little smile and watched me squirm.

I took a deep breath and moved in front of Grace, standing very straight with my hands clasped behind my back. "Would you like to dance, Grace Lancaster?" I said formally.

A wide smile broke onto Grace's face. She gathered herself as if we were at a cotillion. "Why yes, Ms. Riley, I would."

I nodded once and took her hand to lead her to the dance floor. We moved past a row or two of swaying couples before I squared around to offer her my left hand. We stood for a moment in awkward indecision, not sure exactly how close to bring our bodies. Grace decided. She took my hand and tucked it in to where our shoulders met, then wrapped her arm around my neck and leaned fully against my chest.

A rush of fear came first, but in the next second, exhilaration. I moved my hand to the small of her back and pulled her closer.

Grace swiped the key card across the hotel room lock and pushed the door, opening it just a crack. She paused, seeming to be caught in a moment of indecision, and then looked at me as if she still wasn't sure. "Would you like to come in?"

I leaned my shoulder against the wall and looked at her with an ambivalent smile. "It's been a wonderful night, Grace, but I can't."

She nodded as if she understood. "How about breakfast?"

"I'd like that. Maybe an outdoor brunch?"

"Yeah, I'd like that too." Grace looked at me with a dim smile, and then touched two fingers to her lips and placed them lightly on my cheek. "I'll see you in the morning." She slipped around the door and turned the security lock.

I walked down the hall toward the elevator, my mind filled with imaginings of what could have happened if I had walked through her door; unbuttoning, unsnapping, pulling up and pushing down; heated, electric bodies desperate for connection; familiar moans of pleasure, ecstasy, collapsing with exhaustion and finding the spark again before finally giving over to the simple peace of caressing her body while we slept. And then?

You're not going to get out of this one alive, sister, I whispered to myself, and then I kind of smiled.

46

Returning to Grace

I pulled my cell phone out of my pocket and flipped it open. Grace's number lit up the screen. "Hello, Grace," I said. The faint disco beat of "Knock on Wood" drifted through the receiver. "Are you listening to *disco* right now?"

"I know. It's a crazy thing I do when I'm stressed. Listen, is there any chance you can meet me tomorrow? I'm driving over to Asheville for a fundraiser tonight and I thought I'd see if you were free tomorrow for lunch."

Amii Stewart's disco lyrics mixed with the roll of Grace's car engine, *"the way you love me is frightening."* I smiled with the thought of Grace cruising along I-40, tapping her steering wheel to the beat. "Here in Highlands or Asheville?" I asked.

"Wherever—it doesn't matter. I just wanted to see you while I'm over that way."

"If you're stressed enough to listen to disco, I guess I'd better take time to meet you," I teased her.

"Hey, don't knock it till you've tried it," Grace teased back. "So, how about lunch in Highlands?"

"Okay, sure. Give me a call when you get in town. I'll see you then."

I hadn't seen Grace since the morning after the benefit. We had breakfast together, and then parted for home. Since then, she had been busy with Katie's wedding and had called only a couple of times for a quick chat before rushing off to a bridal shower or another dinner party. Each time I hung up with the sound of her voice lingering in my mind for hours. "Sweet lord, where are we going with this?" I muttered to myself. I grabbed my chisel and started back to work.

"So what do you think, will you come to the lake sometime this summer?" Grace asked. Her mood lifted for the moment. She had been distracted through lunch; checking her phone in ten-minute intervals before setting it back down with a frown. She leaned toward me with her arms crossed on the table. Her white cotton button-down shirt was open just enough to expose the curve of her breasts. I couldn't keep my gaze from wandering there. "I'd love to show you around the lake. We've got a ski boat if you're still into that."

I returned her smile with a doubtful look. "It sounds nice, Grace, but I think Lake Norman is a long way to go over and come back in one day."

"You can stay the night if you like. The lake house has plenty of room."

She shifted and her bracelet clicked against the table; two diamonds set in white gold to match her engagement ring. Grace was married, like too many other women I'd been with. I thought I was done with that. "Look, Grace, I don't know if it's a good idea for us to keep seeing each other right now," I said, as much to convince myself as to convince her. "I've thought about it a lot since that night at the benefit. I don't know if we can spend time with each other like this, like we're only casual friends. And I don't want an affair."

"I wish you wouldn't think of it that way, Blue," Grace replied. She paused and tucked her hair behind her ear, searching for the right words and how to say them. "What I mean is, I don't think we have to figure it all out right now. Everything in my life seems to be consumed by plans. It doesn't feel that way when I'm with you. Life seems more organic when you're around. I want more than anything to trust that and see where it leads."

I felt it, too, when the world was only Grace and myself. We still knew each other. Through the pain and denial, through the harsh words and bluster, we were connected. In unguarded moments she could still pull me to ease, and I relished her laughter and decency, and that she saw the world, in so many ways, like I did.

"I understand what you're saying, Grace. My concern is that I've done this before; we've done this before. The things that pulled us apart are still there, only now it's more complicated. I thought I was through with the complications of being with someone who's married."

"But I told you about my marriage," Grace cut in. "It's more of an arrangement than a marriage."

"Yet, you're still in it, so where does that leave me?" I asked curtly.

Her eyes sharpened and focused on me with the intensity of a woman who was certain of what she was about to say. "It leaves you wherever you want to be. Tell me to get lost like you did that night on your porch. I'll do it, Blue. I'll stay away forever if that's what you want. That doesn't mean I won't think of you every day. It only means I'll go back to my planned life and leave you to yours."

I turned away from her. The room around us buzzed with the hustle of waiters and lunchtime patrons. The whole stinking busy world swirled around us, and still I couldn't find a distraction from the tug of her presence. I was here with Grace because I wanted to be. I had answered her calls and danced at the benefit and come here today because that's what I wanted to do. I could have stopped it all the day she walked into my shop, but I didn't. I'd drunk and walked and cursed the sky to keep from doing it. And then I'd called her.

Grace was calm when I turned back to her, ready to hear whatever I was going to say, including, it seemed, good-bye.

"So what's got you stressed out enough to listen to disco?"

She returned my thin smile and gathered herself again, swallowing back her rising emotion before she answered. "Brian finally got his orders. He's going to Iraq." Fear twitched in the corners of Grace's mouth. "He said he'll send a message when he knows more details." A film of tears covered her eyes. I knew she wouldn't let them fall. Her mother would say it was poor form to weep in public.

"Grace, I'm so sorry. You did know this could happen, didn't you?" I asked.

She pulled in a deep breath. "Of course I did—intellectually. I know how these things go. Brian's a Marine officer up for deployment and we're in a war, and if he wants to further his military career he needs combat assignments. I learned that much from my father. As Brian's mother, the whole thing terrifies me." Her twitch came harder.

"Have you talked to your father about this yet?"

Her face flushed and went pale. "My dad passed away three years ago."

I wondered, for a moment, what her relationship had been with him at the time. I knew it didn't matter in the end. "I'm so sorry, Grace," I said earnestly.

"Thank you, Blue," Grace said, and for a moment I thought she would reach for me. Instead, she looked away and composed herself.

She hadn't mentioned her mother, who I supposed was still around to rule her family according to her own will. I doubted Grace would talk to her mother about anything too close to her heart. "What about George? Have you talked to him about this?" I asked.

Grace shook her head. "Not so much about how Brian's deployment worries me. George and I are very cerebral when we talk about things like military conflict. Feelings aren't much discussed if it has anything at all to do with politics, which is about the only thing we talk about." She looked away and very deliberately straightened her napkin across her lap. Control in public places had been driven into her head since the time she was born into the Lancaster family.

"So how do you feel about the war?"

"How do I *feel* about the war?" Grace bitterly repeated. "I feel like it's not worth my son's life, or any other parent's child for that matter," she snapped. She paused for a moment and straightened her shoulders. I could almost hear her mother telling her to watch her manners.

"As for what I *think* about the war, that's a different matter. I grew up surrounded by the military and I understand that sometimes war is necessary. I don't think this one is. We should be focusing on Afghanistan and Pakistan instead of invading Iraq. Politically, George and I have to show our support for any and all military operations. He's a Blue Dog Democrat, so that's what we do. If George ever runs for national office, his positions on these things will come up."

Trish had been right about the possible run for national office, which scared me as much as my growing desire to be alone with Grace, if only to hold her and let her tears fall as they should. I reached my hand toward her and let it rest by her arm. "Does Brian know how you feel about all of this?"

She shook her head as regret slipped into her eyes. "No, he doesn't. I can't let him know, either. I won't do anything to bring doubt into his mind. He has to think he's doing the right thing for the right cause."

"But you don't think it's the right thing, or the right cause?"

Grace drew up, tense as a coil. "What cause? Iraq is Bush's war, that's all it is. I can't stand the thought of losing my son for that son-of-a-bitch's war."

I let her seethe for a moment. It didn't seem necessary to say I agreed with her. "Do you know when Brian's unit leaves?" I asked after the hard lines eased from her face.

"Soon—about a week after Katie's wedding. He'll come home on leave for a few days, and then they ship out. He could be gone a year or more—if he comes back at all."

"He'll come back, Grace. The odds are in his favor."

"The odds don't mean a damn thing to me." Grace's bitter voice cut through the air between us. "Thinking about the odds is not going to help me sleep at night."

"Of course not," I stammered. What did I know of all that Grace was feeling? What did I know of loving a child more than your own life? What did I know of welcoming them into the world, and watching them learn and grow? What did I know of teaching him to drive, or the pride that came when he said he wanted to serve his country? Knowing that Grace had experienced being a woman in those ways made me want her all the more.

"Grace, I'm sorry I said that," I said earnestly. "I didn't mean to be flippant, believe me. I don't know what it's like to have a child, much less watch him go off to war."

She forced a smile that quickly disappeared. The ache hiding in her eyes drew me in deeper. "I know you didn't intend to be dismissive, Blue," she said after a moment. "This was a lot to drop on you all at once. I shouldn't have lost it like that. I thought I was better with it—until I started talking."

"I really didn't mind, Grace. I know this is difficult for you." I reached across the table for her hand. "How about I come over to the lake after Labor Day? Things will have slowed down at the shop by

302

then, and the stress of the wedding and Brian's deployment will be over. We'll go out in the boat and have a bit of fun and talk all night if you want. I'll consider it my support to the war effort."

She nodded. "If you're sure you want to come. I'll be okay if you don't. Really, I'll be fine."

"I want to come, Grace. I'm sure of it."

47

Like I Remembered

After three miles of driving down twisting narrow roads, I came to the driveway. A small, light blue sign nailed to an oak spelled out *Marshall Landing* in black, routed letters. I took a deep breath and turned off the blacktop.

Grace answered the first ring of her cell phone. "Hello, Grace. I'm here."

"So am I," she said brightly, and hung up.

My fingers drummed nervously on the steering wheel as I eased down a driveway surrounded by tall pines and scores of dogwoods. The winding drive was lined by a strip of deep green grass on either side; a luxury that indicated the work of a landscape service. After the final curve, I spotted Grace standing on the front porch under a huge powder-blue and black Carolina Tar Heels flag, the same colors as the trim and shutters of the sprawling white house.

"Did you have trouble finding me?" She now stood at the edge of the porch, her hands wrapped over the railing. A white tank top hung loosely from her shoulders, revealing the sleek lines of her tanned, fit arms.

"Not much," I called up to her as I slid out of the truck, pulling my leather bag out behind me. I took a quick look around. Downhill the lake formed a semicircle around the manicured grass lawn. A boathouse and pier sat in a secluded nook, away from the main channel of the lake. The back entrance of the house spilled out onto a stone patio. Marshall Landing looked to be the perfect place to relax, or for a wealthy and well-connected family to entertain. I sensed from the inconspicuous sign at the entrance that this was not the place George and Grace used for the latter. I wondered if George used it for his little hideaway, too, and if there was a calendar to prevent unexpected cohabitation.

Grace strolled over to the stairs to meet me. After a quick embrace, she slipped her arm into the crook of my elbow and walked with me across the wooden slats of the porch. Inside, a Chesapeake Bay retriever watched us closely from the front window. "I love that you still have that truck," Grace said.

"I thought you might like to see it again," I replied.

"It brings back a lot of memories." She held the door open for me, her smile steadying my jumpy mood. Inside the entryway the retriever ambled up to my side, eagerly wagging her tail and checking my scent. "Her name is Murphy," Grace said. "This is her favorite place. She's always happy to share it. Come on and we'll show you around."

The hallway opened into an expansive great room with cathedral ceilings framed by red oak timbers. The open kitchen anchored the back wall, and a long bar lined by six stools separated the kitchen and den. Floor-to-ceiling windows along the front wall overlooked the lake, and a stone fireplace centered the right wall. The furniture was lightly colored leather and well made, but definitely high-end factory stuff. Three bookcases overflowed with an assortment of hardbacks and a few paperbacks. A well-worn chair draped by a quilted throw sat in front of the bookcases.

"This is the room where all the action happens," Grace said as we walked into the great room. "The master bedroom is through that door," she said, pointing to the door behind her reading chair. We moved farther into the great room as Grace continued, "The room I have set up for you is on the other side of the house." I followed her across the room and down a hallway. We turned into the second door on the left and I looked around. The mission furniture and earth-tone décor was far too masculine for a guest room.

"This is Brian's room. The guest room and Katie's room are still full of wedding gifts, I'm afraid," Grace said with a sigh. "The bathroom is through there," she said pointing to a pocket door on the left side of the room. "I'll leave you alone to get settled. We'll go out on the boat whenever you're ready."

Grace left and I tossed my bag onto the bed. On the dresser across the room was a photograph of a closely shaved young man standing next to Tar Heels Coach Roy Williams. I walked over and picked up the picture frame. Inlaid on the bottom corner was the Marine Corps insignia; Brian. I couldn't quite discern the color of his hair because of the Marine Corps cut. He looked to be about six feet tall and as handsome as I expected. Though it was hard to gauge from the picture, his eyes and nose seemed to resemble Grace's. I set the photograph down and turned away. If Brian knew the history of his mother and me, he would probably run me out at the tip of his bayonet. Or maybe he would understand. His generation looked at things differently than mine, and he was raised by Grace.

I sat down on the bed and looked around the room. Brian's unit was now in Iraq, and a month ago Grace was playing mother of the bride for her daughter Katie. Everything about the Marshall family seemed so normal and forthright. The truth of George and Grace's life was so very different. I wondered if Katie and Brian knew, and if they did, how did they feel about it?

Ahead of us the smooth water of the lake reflected the deep orange and purple of the evening sky. The distant sun perched at the rim of the lake, set to take its nightly dip. I stretched my legs out in front of me, relaxed after the full afternoon of boating and swimming. Warm sun and miles of beautiful shoreline had put me at ease with Grace. Watching her navigate through the land markings of islands and coves reminded me of the woman she was when she was left to be herself.

Grace got a beer from the patio bar cooler and brought it over to me. She sat down in the chair next to mine and looked over. The amber patio lights accentuated the golden flecks in her eyes. "So, you've never told me how you learned woodworking," she said. She picked up her wine from the occasional table beside her and took a sip.

"Quite by accident," I said, smiling with the recollection of Preacher and the crazy way I met him. "I was living on the West Coast, and one day—my birthday actually—I got a letter from Julie.

She wrote to light a fire under my ass, and said since I wasn't doing anything with my life I might as well live closer to her. So I decided I'd try New Orleans for a while. I never made it, though. On the way there, I happened to meet a man named Preacher Rowe. Believe it or not, that man changed everything for me. He taught me how to design and build furniture and how to carve. The rest, as they say, is history."

"Was he actually a preacher? I know you were never too keen on religion." Grace looked at me with her subtle smile, the one that still drove me to the edge.

"That hasn't changed. Preacher and I agreed to disagree on religion. Although, if anyone could have convinced me, it would have been Preacher."

"He sounds like a special man." Grace rested her chin in her hand and looked at me with quiet contentment.

"He is. He reminds me a lot of my dad. At first he seemed like a straightforward, no-nonsense man. Turns out, he's really a romantic at heart. He was absolutely devoted to his wife, Mary. She was sick with diabetes for years. In fact, that was how I met them. Preacher was looking for someone to help him with Mary and farming, and I could do both."

"*You* were someone's nurse?" Grace looked skeptical, and then amused.

"What? You don't think I could do it?" I looked back at her, feigning hurt. "I was going to be a veterinarian, you know." Grace cocked her head back, still unconvinced. "Okay, maybe I couldn't be a nurse, but I did help Preacher take care of Mary, mind you." I smiled and tipped my beer bottle towards her.

Grace returned my smile and asked, "What was Mary like?"

"Fierce—Mary was courageously fierce—and incredibly perceptive. She was ill for years, but she met all of her challenges with dignity. Preacher and I made sure she kept that until the end."

"She changed your life, too, didn't she? I wish I could have met her."

"She knew about you," I said without thinking.

"You talked to her about me?" Grace looked at me curiously.

"Eventually, I talked to both of them about you. I lived at their place for over three years, so we talked about a lot of things."

A frown furrowed Grace's eyebrows. "I hope you weren't too rough on me."

I shook my head. "No, I wasn't. They knew you once meant a lot to me. That was enough for them."

A gentle breeze blew in from the lake to greet our silence. Grace had turned away from me, seeming to be struck for the moment that I had used past tense to verbalize my feelings for her. I wanted to take it back, but I wasn't sure how. I let the moment be and watched the sun dip lower.

"I'm glad you found Preacher and Mary," Grace said, breaking into our silence. "It's hard, not having someone to talk to about important things." Her distant tone implied she was not really speaking of me.

I nodded. "It took me a long time to talk to them about that part of my life. After I did, I learned people's reaction to finding out I'm gay isn't really about me at all. It's about their personal baggage. Preacher and Mary didn't have baggage. They were clear with who they were and what they believed. I was never a threat to any of that."

"People live in fear," Grace said softly. Again she fell silent.

"Have you heard from Brian?" I asked after a few moments.

"Not in a few days. He said he would be on patrol so not to expect any communications for a while. I'm hoping for an e-mail, but who knows when it will be."

"Would you like to go up and check? I think you should." All I could offer was an understanding smile, though I wanted to wrap her in my arms and let her release all she was holding back.

Grace nodded and touched my arm. "Come inside with me? Just in case?"

"Sure." I took her hand and stood up beside her. She looked up at me and said, "Thank you, Blue. I hate this part of it all. Having you here right now makes it a bit easier." She turned toward the house and walked away without waiting for me.

In the den, Murphy and I took our post outside Grace's bedroom door. One hand scratching Murphy's ear, I scanned the titles on the bookcase in front of me—*The Earth in Balance* by Al Gore, *Silent Spring, Cradle to Cradle,* and then, *Howling Wind.* A hardback edition of the book I'd helped Cecelia write now sat on Grace's bookshelf.

The absurdity almost made me laugh. I pulled out *Howling Wind* and looked at the photograph on the back. Cecelia looked fantastic. Curiosity led me to the well-worn crease at the acknowledgments page. Instantly I found my name, "To my southern girl, Augusta Riley, thank you for everything."

"She's one of my favorite authors." Grace's voice startled me. She stood with shoulder pressed against the doorframe, watching me. "I'm guessing you read that one," Grace said, pointing to the book.

"Not since it was published." I turned the book over and again looked at Cecelia's picture. "I saw it in the bookstores when it came out. I decided to wait for the paperback since I already knew the story. After a while, I sort of forgot about it."

"Do you know her well?" Grace asked with a hint of insecurity.

"A long time ago I did." I slid the book back onto the shelf and looked over at Grace. She had changed into her lounge clothes: a loose fitting pair of white cotton pants and jacket with a scooped neck t-shirt underneath. Her hair was pulled back into a loose ponytail and she had washed off her makeup. She was stunning.

"Did you hear anything from Brian?" I asked, wanting to move off the subject of Cecelia before we wandered into the details of my first affair.

Grace's face fell into a deep frown. "Not yet. I know I shouldn't worry like I do. It's not as if everything goes according to plan over there."

Murphy sauntered over to stand by Grace, the tip of her tail wagging. Grace kneeled and held Murphy's head between her hands, "Your brother is going to be fine, isn't he?" Murphy stretched her nose to lick Grace's chin. "Oh thank you, sweet girl. He'd want me to give you a big cookie for that kiss."

With light, bare footsteps Grace walked to the kitchen and fished a dog biscuit out of the Marine Corps bulldog cookie jar on the counter. Murphy took the biscuit across the room to her bed by the fireplace. Grace watched her settle in, and then turned to me. "Would you like some cake and coffee?" she asked with her brave smile.

"Sure," I replied. I settled on a stool at the kitchen bar and watched Grace move around the room, slicing cake, making decaf, and asking me if I wanted ice cream, doing anything to avoid talking about Brian.

She worked her way to the bottom of her ice cream glass, rattling on about other things—Katie's wedding and the healthy toll it took on the family's bank account, the board of directors of the C.L. Lockley Foundation, her sister's first granddaughter. I listened and sipped my coffee, though I wanted to ask why she was avoiding talking to me about Brian. Instead we kept our distance from each other, acting as if it were all so fucking normal that we were together and behaving like we were nothing more than friends.

"You're not saying much," Grace said after I finished my coffee.

"I know. It's been a while since I spent a day in the sun. I'm a little tired." I stood and stretched my arms back. I wouldn't tell her what was really going through my mind—that she was not being candid, and I hadn't come here to talk about society weddings or her job. I had come to give her the safe space she needed to talk about the difficult things, like her fears about her son. Tomorrow morning I would tell her that perhaps it was too complicated for us to be open with each other about the hard stuff, and maybe we should stop trying to see each other.

I picked up my plate and coffee mug and took them to the sink. "Thanks for everything, Grace. It was a good day."

"It was. Sleep well, Blue." Grace looked at me with the saccharine smile I'd seen her use with her sorority sisters back in college.

The bedroom was dark as pitch when I woke up from a fitful sleep. I flipped over in Brian's bed and kicked back the covers. I should not be in his bed. I should be across the house, in another room, another bed, my body pressed against Grace, holding her while we slept. I turned on the lamp and looked over at the alarm clock—thirty minutes past two a.m. I sat up and rubbed my eyes.

Murphy raised her head when I went into the kitchen. "Your mom won't let you sleep with her?" I glanced over at Grace's bedroom and saw a light coming from underneath the door. Grace was probably still awake, maybe reading while she waited for a message from Brian. I wanted to go to her—or else to grab my keys and drive away without looking back. I grabbed a beer from the refrigerator and headed outside. Halfway down the walkway, I saw Grace's shadowed form sitting near the shoreline. I walked down and stopped at her shoulder. Her hair was wet and tucked away from her face. She sat on a towel, wearing the cotton pants and jacket she had worn earlier, only now the jacket was zipped up to her chest. She wore nothing underneath it.

"Hey, you," she said as I sat down. She looked at me with a thin smile. "It's beautiful out tonight, isn't it? Sometimes on nights like this I take a swim to help me sleep. It usually works."

I draped my arms across my knees and looked out to the open waters of the lake. "What's keeping you from sleeping?" I asked.

Grace was silent for a long moment. When she spoke, her voice was composed and even, though she wouldn't look at me. "Brian's unit was in a firefight. I think he may have killed someone. He didn't say he had, but his message wasn't like they have been. Something was different."

"But he's okay?"

"Yes, for now. I can't think of how he'll be when he comes back home. I know what a good, solid young man he was when he left. Will he still be when he comes back?" Grace picked up the wine glass that sat by her side. She took a sip and returned her gaze toward the lake. "Do you know they won't let the press take pictures of the coffins when they bring their bodies back?" Her soft, reflective voice held an edge of venom. "Young men and women give their lives for this egotistical war, and we won't even give them the dignity of acknowledging their sacrifice. If Brian dies over there, I will want everyone to know, I will want to scream it from the rooftops that my son is gone. That wouldn't be proper according to the Pentagon. They want everyone to go about their lives, oblivious to the fact that my son, like so many others, died in some bloody hell—and for what?" Grace rocked the tight coil of her body and clinched her jaw.

I reached over to cradle the back of her neck in my palm. "Grace, I know this is hard for you, and I want to help you through it. I don't know how if you won't let me. I knew you were avoiding talking about Brian earlier tonight. I can see the worry in your eyes, but you won't talk about it."

"I know. I know. I wanted to talk to you earlier tonight." Grace raised her hand to her chest and softly tapped her breastbone. "It's just too close, you know." In the moonlight I saw a glistening in the corner of her eye. She straightened her back as if to pull herself away from her heavy thoughts. "It's safer to come out here and swim myself to exhaustion. If I started talking I know where it would lead, and it wouldn't be fair to fall apart in your arms."

I rubbed my hand across her neck but didn't say anything.

"I suppose you were right about us, Blue. Everything that has happened makes this far too complicated. I have to learn to let you go."

"What if I don't want you to?"

"What do you mean?" She looked at me in a way that held as much uncertainty as hope.

"What if I said it's a farce for us to be sleeping in separate rooms? What if I said my instincts are screaming to be with you tonight, and I know you feel the same way?"

Her eyes filled with tears, though the corners of her mouth twisted into a ragged smile. "I'd say you are right, though I'm not sure what we do about it given your reservations."

I dropped my hand away from her neck and looked out to the silver moon hanging high above the lake. My reservations about us were right. I knew that. I also knew that Grace would always have been my life if she had been given the liberty to choose. She had followed expectations rather than the truth of her own spirit. Eventually she had found ways to make her choices her own. For us, I knew the trouble would start again when our choices crashed into the lives of her children. "Do Katie and Brian know about your arrangement with George?" I asked after a moment.

Grace chuckled and said, "My *arrangement*. Doesn't that sound so very proper?" She shook her head and her voice became delicate. "They know our marriage is different, that there are more *understandings* between me and George than there is love. George has been less careful with his liaisons than I was, so they figured him out. I think both of the kids sense there is something much deeper that I keep from them."

"Do you want them to know what that is?"

"Someday, yeah, I do want them to know exactly who their mother is. I'm not ready to go there yet, not with Katie being a newlywed and Brian in combat."

I leaned in close and wrapped my arm around her shoulder. The tension between us dropped and she let out a soft breath. My fingertips swept the line of her neck. "So what do we do now?" I asked.

"I don't know. Whatever it is, I want to be true to you this time, Blue, whether that means staying with you until we figure it out or letting you go when you've had enough."

Though I had tried to deny it, it seemed I could never have enough of Grace. Not in this lifetime, or the next. "Do you want us to be together tonight?" I asked.

"More than anything," Grace replied at the base of my ear. Her breath sent a charge through me that I wouldn't deny. Our lips moved toward each other and met in a way that seemed familiar and unhurried. I don't know long we kissed. Neither of us felt the need to quell the urgency coursing through our bodies. I lingered on her lips and the soft skin of her throat, tasting her again. My hand moved down to her hip and slipped under her jacket. I stopped, pulled away from her mouth, and looked into her eyes. "Are we ready for this?" I asked.

Her face became bold and sure. "Yes," she said. She stood up and reached her hand to me. "Let's go inside."

I grabbed her hand and held onto it as we walked toward the house. At the patio shower we washed the grass and dirt from our feet, then climbed the stairs to her bedroom. "Can we leave the lamp on?" I asked, closing the door to the room. Grace stood at the bed, turning down the sheets. "I want to see you," I said as I took her in my arms.

"And I want to see those damn blue eyes," she replied.

I unzipped her jacket as I pulled her into my kiss. My blood rushed hot and almost took me over when I pushed the jacket away from her shoulders. My fingertips moved across the skin of her chest, soft and warm and moving with the quickening rhythm of her breath.

Grace kissed me deeper, her tongue and lips becoming urgent as she reached down for the hem of my t-shirt. She pulled it up and dropped it to the floor. I stood in front of her, struck still by the beauty of her body. She took my hand and pulled me into her bed.

Her hair was still wet from the lake, leaving her face bare as she looked up at me with her gorgeous eyes. I brushed my fingertips across her forehead and down the line of her jaw. I wanted to study every inch of her body, to know it again like I had known it before. My fingertips moved slowly down her neck, down the hollow of her throat, across her shoulders, over her breast. Grace's breath came quicker, and I heard a soft moan as my fingertips teased her nipples. The skin of her stomach was the softest, and there were stretch marks from the twins. I started my kisses there, letting my lips linger over the length of her scars. Her hips stirred anxiously as my mouth moved down, slowly caressing each inner thigh. Grace's familiar taste filled my mouth as I parted her lips with my tongue and moved up. She moaned deep and low, her back arching with my first touch. She reached for my hands and I laced her fingers in mine, squeezing them lightly as my strokes quickened. Her hips rose and fell rapidly now, increasing their thrust with my rhythm. I wrapped my arms around her legs and held her tightly to take her fully into my mouth. The taste of her came sweet, like the lake, like the ocean, like I remembered.

48

The Vanity

Nat stood with her hip pressed against my workbench, one arm tucked across her chest and the other hand on the stick of the Tootsie Roll Pop she twirled in her mouth. She was staring at my face rather than watching my hands, and I was getting a bit annoyed. "Something's been different about you the last couple of days," she said thoughtfully. I kept shaving wood and ignored her. She pulled the lollipop from her mouth and narrowed her eyes. "You've started seeing someone, haven't you?" She paused and kept watching me, waiting for a reaction. I didn't give her one. "That's why you've been going in the office to talk on the phone," she said, as much to herself as to me.

"Jesus, Nat," I leveled a warning glare at her. "Don't you have anything better to do than keep tabs on me all day?"

Nat shrugged. "I'm just sayin' something's different. Sarah's noticed it, too." She sauntered to the table saw and propped her hips against the bench. For a few seconds there was blessed silence and I went back to my carving. Before I could make a cut, she spoke again. "Come to think of it, you've been acting kinda different for a while now, ever since Grace dropped by the shop that day. I'd probably be acting all monkey shit, too, after seeing her again. She's one hot woman."

"She's not a 'hot woman,'" I replied, too fervently.

Nat cocked her head back and looked at me. She seemed to be pleased she had struck a nerve.

I laid down my carving knife and walked over beside her. "Look, Nat, maybe I should have told you, I went to Grace's lake house last weekend."

"You spent last weekend with Grace Lancaster?" Nat cut her eyes at me with a pleased little grin. "As in *spent the weekend*?"

"Yes, as in *spent the weekend*."

"Holy shit, no wonder you've been acting all weird the past couple of days. That woman would definitely spin my head around. So when are you gonna rent the U-Haul?"

I chuckled. "I don't see that happening, Nat. She's married."

"That's too bad." Nat thought for a moment. "But are you gonna start seeing her now?"

I shrugged. "I don't know what we're going to do. For now, we're taking it slow and trying to figure it out."

Nat nodded and swept her fingers over the arc of the table saw guard. I wasn't sure if her expression registered disappointment, or worry, or simply contemplation. After a moment she looked up at me. "Do you think you'll ever give her the vanity?"

"Why do you ask that?"

"I noticed her staring at it that day she came in the shop. Do you suppose she saw her name in it?"

"I doubt she did. She said she wanted to buy it, but she didn't mention seeing her name. I would think she would have mentioned it if she had."

Nat smiled proudly. "Most people don't see it right off like I did." She popped her sucker in her mouth, gave it a couple of pondering twists, and tugged it back out through closed lips. "So if Grace is married, does she have kids?"

"She has two; twins about your age."

"She's bi-?"

"She says she prefers to be with women."

"But she's married to a man?"

"Yes, she's married to a man."

"So now she's back on our team," Nat said, grinning up at me like a conspirator.

I returned a sour glare. "Come on, Nat, this isn't about 'teams.'"

"Alright, settle down, boss. You take shit so serious sometimes." Her mouth twisted with the sting of my reproach, though only for a moment. When she looked back to me her face had become sincere. "So if you're not trying to settle a score, why are you seeing her?"

Her question hit with the accuracy of a sage counselor. I had asked myself the same question and quickly dismissed it as dabbling in the dangers of thinking rather than the business of living. "I don't *know* yet," I said.

"Do you love her?" Nat asked. She crossed her arms and waited for my answer.

"Yes. I don't know. It's complicated, Nat."

Her eyes narrowed. "Did you think it wouldn't be? I didn't ask if it was complicated. I asked if you love her."

I shrugged and turned away.

"You don't have to answer," Nat said as I walked back to my bench. I picked up my carving knife and swung my leg over my stool. "You've always loved her," she continued. I looked up and she nodded toward the showroom. "That vanity says so."

Through the large front window of their cabin I saw Marty and Joyce settled in their chairs, their eyes trained on the TV in the corner of the room. I walked to the door, wine bottle in hand, and knocked.

Joyce looked up and motioned me inside. "We wondered when you'd be by," she said as I walked through the door. Marty's attention was glued to the story on the evening news. She raised her hand with a quick wave and kept watching Diane Sawyer's report.

"I brought Cabernet," I said, raising the bottle up.

"You *are* a dear," Joyce said. She moved the tuxedo cat out of her lap and rocked herself up from her easy chair. "I'll get the glasses." She grabbed the wine on her way to the kitchen. "We haven't seen you since you went to the lake to meet Grace," she said as she inspected the wine label. She nodded, pleased with my selection, and opened the cabinet for glasses. "And it didn't get by us that you weren't at home Sunday night."

"Or that you've been walking the woods every night since you got back," Marty offered.

"Yeah, I suppose that's why I'm here. I figured I could walk holes in my shoes and I'd still be right where I am now. I think I need a bit of advice."

"I'd imagine us old birds can help you, then. We have about a hundred years of lesbian experience between us." Joyce turned a corkscrew into the top of the bottle and popped the cork out easily. She poured two-thirds into each of three glasses, grabbed the bottle stopper I had made for them, and pushed it into the bottle. With ease her large hands worked around the stems of the glasses. I stepped over and took one, and Joyce motioned me toward the couch. As I sat down, the evening news went to a commercial.

"How's your heart?" Marty asked. She muted the television and took the wine glass Joyce offered. "This stuff's good for it, you know." She leveled a look at me over the top of the glass and took a sip.

"My heart's fine," I replied. Truth was, since I had left the lake house my heart seemed to have a mind of its own; racing, pounding, jumping, and annoying the hell out of me every moment I thought of Grace.

"All those walks since last weekend seem to indicate otherwise. I'd say you have heart troubles, my dear," Marty said.

"You're right." I took a sip of wine and rolled the glass between my hands. "I'm in a bit of a conundrum. What do you do when the cosmos leads one way, and reality leads another?"

Marty swiveled her chair around to face me fully. "How much wine have you had, kid?"

Her startled face made me chuckle. I supposed I didn't usually talk about the ways of the cosmos. Not out loud, anyway. "What I mean is that everything is natural and easy when it's just me and Grace. It's like we're in another world or something. Then we go back to the real world, and it feels like everything is pulling us apart."

"Things like her marriage," Joyce looked at me with a wary grimace. "It worries me that you're getting involved with this woman. I can't see anything but trouble if you keep seeing her."

How well I knew. Trouble seemed everywhere except in the rare moments when we were alone. "I know, I know. I've been fighting with myself since I left the lake. I can't get around the fact of her marriage, and the fact that she lives three hours away, and she has children, and a high-profile job, and she's this society figure in central North Carolina, and her manipulative mother is still around."

"It's a lot to take on, kid. What would make it worth getting wrapped up in all of that?" Marty asked.

"And risking the damage it will do when she lets you down again," Joyce added.

I looked out to the bird feeder attached to the window. A couple of birds fussed over the seed, blustering about before they settled in for a moment. I watched them fuss and settle, fuss and settle, thinking before I answered Joyce. "Having Grace will make it worth everything," I said with my eyes on the birds. "I'm getting to know her in a new way, and I'm seeing she could still be the woman I want, maybe more than ever."

"And what if you end up without her? What will you have lost?" Joyce asked.

I turned to her perceptive eyes that reminded me of Mary's. "I've already lost some of the peace I found in Mississippi. I thought I was done with affairs, but here I am in another one. Now I find myself rationalizing that Grace should never have gotten married in the first place, that she should have been mine all along. But, my rationalization doesn't change the fact that she is married and has two children."

"What else would you lose?" Joyce asked.

"I don't know." I looked down and tilted my wine glass, as if swirling around fermented grapes would produce all the answers. "When I left Mississippi and came back to North Carolina, I had an idea of the person I wanted to be. In the past I hadn't always lived up to my own expectations, and then I was given a chance to change that. Being with Grace while she's married means I will have to compromise my own principles, at least for a while."

Marty furrowed her brows skeptically. "You think all you would lose is a little self-esteem? You don't think there'd be heartache?"

"I've had heartache from Grace before, and I was just a kid then," I replied, a bit too defensively. After all, heartbreak over a lover was a sentiment I had conquered and put away. I knew how to survive it. "If that happened, I have enough to keep me grounded now. I've got my shop, my friends, Julie, you guys."

319

I turned back to Joyce, as if she were the judge and jury of my own doubts. Thoughtfully she pulled at the edge of a hand-tatted lace cover draped over her armrest. "Just considering yourself—what's the worst that could happen?" she asked.

"I find out Grace isn't capable of being the woman I need her to be." I sat back and turned up a healthy sip of wine, surprised at how quickly I had answered.

49

Coming Out

November chill settled into Horse Cove with the certainty of an old man heading for his nap. I pulled our fleece blanket around Grace's shoulders and rested my chin in the curve of her neck. On my cabin porch I could hold her close, nestled in the chaise lounge Nat built for me. In our hidden nook we were secluded from the world.

Grace settled into my chest and dropped her head to my shoulder. "The fall colors were so beautiful this year. Just once, I wish I could be here for the entire season. I spend the best mountain days running around the Piedmont in Winston or Raleigh."

I had missed Grace, too, on so many clear October days, when the forests of the cove had reached their height of red and golden yellow. I'd sat on the porch, drinking my morning coffee, looking out to the mountain, and wondering what it would be like to have her beside me, making mundane plans for the day; or holding her in the evenings like I was holding her now. "You could, you know. You could be here on this porch with me all year," I said.

Grace stiffened. "What do you mean?" she asked hesitantly.

I pulled her in tighter. "I mean you could live here, with me, all year."

"Don't tease me, Blue Riley. I may take you up on your offer." Grace glanced at me with a sly smile that was meant to end the discussion.

I pushed on. "I'm serious, Grace. I've been thinking about this for a while now. It's what we both want, isn't it? We've got to start making moves if it's ever going to happen." Grace let out a deep sigh and pulled away. She sat for a moment and then swung her legs around to face me. As well as I knew her, I wasn't sure if her expression was disbelief at my innocence or my audacity. All I knew for certain was that we were about to argue. I had to make my point quickly.

"Grace, the timing is perfect. George was just reelected by a land-slide, and you said yourself you didn't have to do much campaigning this time. His reelection will give us two years. If you start now, you can begin to hint publicly at problems in your marriage. It could be about anything, too much time apart, differences about the war, your straying politics—anything George wants to say. You quietly slip into divorce and there is no major political scandal to overcome. After a couple of years, you'll be more obscure and you and George can get on with your lives."

Grace listened patiently, though her patronizing expression suggested I was being wildly impetuous. "Blue, my hesitation isn't about George's political career. It's about you and my children. George and I know how to handle rumors and innuendo. It's going to be another thing entirely when we step out there and verify that it's all true. And it won't be about Grace and George Marshall anymore. You will be dragged right into the middle of it. I can't see you taking that kind of scrutiny very well."

Her disparaging tone pushed my anger deeper. "Why don't you let me decide what I'm ready for, Grace?"

"Okay, then, let's suppose you're ready to take it on," she replied evenly. "What about Brian and Katie? Do you think I can simply drop Brian an e-mail to let him know his parents are getting a divorce?"

"I've never suggested that," I replied crossly.

Grace drew her back up straight and eyed me keenly. "You knew the complications we were taking on when we got back together."

"Yes, I was fully aware of the complications. What I'm seeing now is your reluctance to do anything about it. We aren't talking through any solutions. Instead we live with this ultimatum that we either keep seeing each other, or we never see each other again. How long is that supposed to last? It seems pretty damn convenient for you right now."

Grace glared at me. "Those were your terms, Blue," she snapped.

"Oh that's bullshit, Grace! You show me where there's anything in between."

Our eyes locked for a moment. Grace turned away and closed her eyes. She bit her lip to stop the trembling of her mouth and pulled in a deep breath to gather her emotions. When she looked at me she wore the calm mask of tightly harnessed anger. "You're right. There is nothing in between." She paused, gathered herself and continued, "I need you to understand how difficult it will be for my children when I tell them I want to leave their father to be with a woman. With Brian in Iraq and Katie settling into her marriage, I don't think the time is right."

I dropped against the hard back of the chaise lounge, done with her endless loop of complications. I knew telling her kids would be difficult. I knew finding the right time was as important as finding the right words. But was Grace using her kids as another excuse, another closet to run into? Would she do it again, pull me in for as long as she could and then walk away? She leaned forward and touched her fingertips to my cheek.

I turned away from her, wanting none of her apology, if that was what she intended. "Grace, why the hell are you doing this to me again? If you aren't willing to go through with it, why did you ever let it get this far?"

"I *am* going to go through with it. I need you to trust me for a while."

"Trust—that's an odd word for you to use with me," I said tartly.

Grace's stunned expression slowly morphed into anger. Her jaw clinched tight and she bolted up and stormed across the porch. The slap of her hands on the porch rail scattered the autumn birds gathered on the ground below. She seized the rail in a death grip and rocked back and forth like she was finally ready to blow.

I watched her. Her misery was of her own making as far as I was concerned. She could blame the gods or the fates or whomever she wanted, but the choices were hers. And my choices were mine.

Grace spun around to face me. "You're acting as if I'm in control of all of this, Blue—like I'm some sort of bitch who manipulates you whenever I want. Don't you think I have more respect for you than that?"

I didn't answer. Twenty-four years ago I thought she had more respect for me—until the day she walked out.

"I don't know what you want from me right now." Grace's shoulders dropped in exasperation, like she had no fucking clue.

My head began to pound and I wanted to scream. I clinched my jaw and bored in. "We've been seeing each other for months, and you haven't even talked to George about us. Now I get up the nerve to mention someday living together and you laughed it off as if it isn't even a possibility. What the hell am I supposed to make of that?"

I waited, cursing the cold wind. The crackling swirl of fall leaves filled a silent minute while I waited for her answer. Grace spun around and started walking away. I sprang to my feet. "Oh, now you're walking away? Maybe that's what you should do. Go back to you mother—or better yet, go back your husband. Go renew your fucking vows for all I care!"

Grace stopped dead still. She turned back to me, her face crimson. "I'm not going anywhere, Blue. I'm going for a walk—a long walk. And when I get back maybe we will have calmed down enough to talk about this rationally."

Her angry steps pounded across the driveway. She stormed out across the field and beyond the pond. I watched the breeze move her hair into a golden dance across her shoulders. The sight of her was maddening. I took off for the garage and found my ax.

The blade came down on the first blow with the force of all my anger. Quarter sections of the log went flying, and I grabbed another one to split. I burned through split after split, sending the pieces tumbling around me. Sweat poured and my heart pounded as the wood scattered.

"Blue, stop," Grace said.

I turned around. She stood at the edge of the drive, her hands resting at the seams of her jean pockets. She took a couple of steps toward me. "Do you know I'm scared of what will happen every time I see you?"

I stood there, ax at my side, trying to catch my breath.

"You can tell me to go to hell if you want, and right now I won't blame you if you do. I don't want to lose you again, and I know I'm in real danger of that happening. The thing is, I can't bear the thought of my children turning away from me, and I can't bear the thought of you turning away from me, either. I can live without seeing you every day. It's not what I want, but I can live with it to avoid hurting to my children. You can't live on those terms, and you shouldn't have to. I realize I have to make a choice now."

Would it be her children that came between us this time? As mad as I was, I wasn't ready to find out. Not yet. "You don't have to do anything right now, Grace," I said, trying to disguise my fear in the coolness of my voice.

"No, it's time, Blue. Just tell me one thing: if you don't trust me, why did you give me another chance?"

I drove the ax into the splitting stump and sat down on a fat section of a log. Grace came over and sat down beside me.

I rubbed my hands together to work the sting out. "When you first showed up, I didn't know what to do about you," I began. "I tried to put you out of my mind, but I couldn't stop thinking about you. After a while I began to think we might have another shot at what we lost before, and I had to admit to myself how much I wanted it. When I lost my parents the only thing I really wanted was to have a family again. Back then I thought somehow you would become my family. It was all I wanted for my life, and then I found out you didn't feel the same way. When you left me, I felt like I didn't belong to anyone. I drifted around for a long time, restless and refusing to be attached. I wasn't sure what I was looking for until I happened upon something that felt like home. I found it in Mississippi first, with Preacher and Mary, and then I found it here. Then one day out of nowhere, you walked into my shop. When I couldn't shake you from my mind, I began to think you were meant to be part of my life again. I couldn't turn away until I found out."

Grace nodded and stretched her legs out in front of her, thinking about what I'd said. So many times we had sat beside each other under a rich blue sky, talking about what we wanted. The stakes had never seemed this high before. "When we do this," Grace began, "we have to be together every step of the way. That means you'll have to trust me. A lot of people are going to see you as the enemy, the selfish home wrecker, and my family may be the hardest on you. That's going to be tough when we can't see each other every day. I won't be able to see you, to reassure you that we'll get through it, and that I still want it. Your friends, Marty and Joyce, even Nat, they can help us through it. If we decide this is what we want, we'll need to ask them for support."

"You know Joyce has reservations about us," I said.

"Just as you do," Grace replied. She reached around my waist and leaned in to kiss me. Her mouth covered mine with soft reassurance, enough to make me believe we could be possible.

Marty leaned back from my dining-room table and glanced around the room her father had built. The memories settled gently on her face. She rested her arms on the table and turned to me. "So, you and Grace have something you want to talk to us about?"

I realized all eyes were on me. Joyce, ever the keen one, scooted to the edge of her chair. She let out a sigh, as if she knew what was coming. "Yeah, yeah we do." I began. "Grace and I have decided we want to be together, and we're going to start taking steps to make it happen."

"When?" Joyce asked. I looked over at her, expecting to see her frown of skepticism. It wasn't there.

"Soon," Grace replied. "George and I will have some down time during the holidays. While we're together, I'll tell him I'm ready for a divorce." Grace blinked and turned from them. I reached for her hand, squeezing it to pull her away from the tug of failure that hit every time she said the word *divorce*.

"It sounds like you two have given this a lot of thought," Marty said.

"It's all we've been talking about since yesterday," I replied.

"We've both been thinking about it for a while, although we hadn't said anything to each other until Blue brought it up yesterday," Grace added. "Now that we've made the decision it's what we want, we need friends like you to support us."

Marty nodded and turned to Joyce. Her partner raised her eyebrows with an acquiescing shrug. They looked at each other for a moment, as if reading each other's thoughts. Marty turned to Grace. "Let's go for a walk," she said.

Grace stood up with Marty and followed her outside. Joyce tilted her head toward the closing front door. Together we walked out and stood at the edge of the porch. Marty stopped a couple of hundred feet from the cabin. Grace beside her, they looked toward Whiteside.

"I thought you'd be against this," I said to Joyce as we watched them talk.

"I'm cautiously optimistic," Joyce replied. "Seeing you together, I can see how much she loves you." She looked down at me. At nearly six feet tall, Joyce was one of the few women who could. "She *does* love you. I hope you see that." Joyce's commanding stature led me to believe she was always right. I sure wasn't going to argue with her about this.

"What do you suppose Marty wants to talk to her about?" I asked.

"Marty has been where Grace is right now." Joyce wrapped her arm around the center post of the porch and leaned against it. "Marty was just a few years younger than Grace when she divorced her husband. She was the mother of three kids and the wife of a school superintendent in Raleigh, so she's been through some devastating times with her family. Marty may be able to help Grace in ways you can't."

The sun was quickly fading on the horizon, and Marty and Grace now stood in the long shadow of the tree line, their bodies a silhouette in the evening's gray light. Grace took a step toward Marty, listening intently to whatever she was saying.

"Grace was raised to stay in line, no matter what," I reflected.

"Do you think she can do it?" Joyce asked. I looked at her, not sure what she meant. "You do realize how tough this is going to be for her, don't you? Marty had to have such strength to get through those years. The scrutiny of the local community was almost unbearable, and *her* mother was sympathetic. Grace won't have her mother with her, and her social profile is much larger than a superintendent's wife."

Grace bowed her head and Marty reached out to take her wrists. For a moment they stood still, and then Marty spoke again. Grace suddenly looked up, her shoulders relaxing as she stepped into Marty's open arms. They held each other tightly, Grace nodding against Marty's shoulder in response to what seemed to be confident words.

"I know Grace has regretted some of the choices she's made. I hope this won't be another one," I said.

"Marty says she never regretted her decision," Joyce replied. Marty kept her arm around Grace's shoulder as they walked toward the cabin. We watched them draw closer as Joyce continued, "Marty says, looking back, it was better for everyone. Her ex found the woman that was right for him, and her children no longer had to suffer the consequences of their parents' misery. As Marty says, there is no better way to tell people you love them than to quit lying to them."

At the top of the porch stairs, Marty waved Joyce over. Grace came to me and slipped her arm around my waist. The smile on her face was the brave one; the one that hid her nagging fear. We stood together with our arms around each other, watching Marty and Joyce walk home, their hands occasionally touching as they walked.

"Marty said that not going through with this would bring the greatest pain to everyone in the long run," Grace began as we watched them saunter up the drive. "The pain will get worse for all of us if I can't find a way to do it." She pulled her arm tighter around my waist and looked up at me. "Brian and Katie deserve to know who their mother is. And they should know the woman I love."

50

The Gift

The lazy effects of a Christmas noonday feast slowed my steps as I walked home to my cabin. Behind me, the squeals and laughter of Marty's boisterous grandsons echoed from her porch and filled the woods with the same delicate ease of last night's snow. Nat was on her way over with a Christmas present that she promised would be "intense." Later, Julie was coming for dinner, accompanied by her new girlfriend Olivia, who seemed already to have my aunt wrapped.

Snow crunched beneath my feet as I climbed my porch stairs, and then came the sound of an approaching engine, complete with music. Nat's truck slipped through the wall of vegetation at the end of my drive. "Jingle Bell Rock" pounded from the truck's speakers as she passed by the porch. She stopped in front of the steps and hopped out. A long white package filled the bed of the truck, one end leaning onto the tailgate. I walked over for a closer look. By the shape of it, I knew what was under the wrapping.

"A door—you're giving me a door for Christmas," I said as I peered over the truck rail.

"Not just any door." Nat scurried around the side of her truck to lift one side of the long, white package topped with a giant red bow. She nodded to her girlfriend Kris and together they lifted it from her truck bed. Slowly and carefully they eased one end onto the ground and rested the other against the tailgate. Nat planted her hand on the top of the package. "This, O Great One, is a very special door."

I pulled away the bow and tore down the wrapping. It *wasn't* just any door. It was Honduran mahogany, lightly stained, with an exquisite carving of a warrior woman centered at eye level. Eyes wide and jaw slack, I stared at the carving.

"It's Brighid. She's a goddess in Celtic mythology. She's supposed to be a warrior and protector. I thought she could be a protector for you and Grace."

"Some of the facial features look a little bit like you," I said, recovering from my astonishment before I lost all my cool points. I stepped in for a closer look and turned to Nat with a wry smile.

"Well, nobody knows what Brighid looked like, so I took some liberties. I only altered the pattern a little bit."

I leaned in to study the carving again. It was a hell of a generous gift. The wood itself would have cost more than Nat could really afford, and even with her rapidly developing skills, it must have taken countless hours to carve.

"I'm pretty good, huh?" Nat said.

"More like pretty cocky." Nat gave a shrug and we both grinned. "But, yeah, you'll be good one day."

"Better than you?" She shifted and looked at me with careful bravado.

"Probably. But only because you started earlier." I smiled and put my hand on her shoulder and held it there for a moment. Nat couldn't know how good she was just yet. As Preacher taught me, complacency kills ambition.

The ring of my landline shook my contentment away from the fireplace and hot chocolate. I looked over to check the number. Grinning, I picked up the receiver and headed toward my bedroom. "I'll be taking this one," I said to Julie and Olivia as I slipped out of the den.

"Merry Christmas, baby. How was your day?" I plopped a couple of pillows at my back and settled in for a long conversation.

"It was wonderful, actually. We got some exciting news from Katie and Neil today. They're expecting!"

The joy in Grace's voice was infectious. "That is wonderful news, Grace. How far along is she?"

"Ten weeks. She wanted to wait until we were all together to tell us, although I suspected the minute I saw her. We had Brian on video, so we all heard it at the same time."

I imagined the moment: George, Grace, Katie, and Neil anxiously waiting for Brian to pop up on the video feed, and then the grand announcement. One day I would be in the middle of those family moments with Grace. I took in a deep breath and tried not to dwell on yet another complication that we would be facing. "I'm sure Brian was thrilled," I said heartily.

"He was, and so am I, except the part about becoming a grandmother. I'm not sure about that."

"I am. You've got nothing to worry about. You'll still be the sexiest woman on the beach this summer."

"I'm glad you think so."

"I know so," I replied.

"Hmm," Grace hummed skeptically.

"So, Katie will be pregnant while she's finishing law school. She has another semester, doesn't she?" I asked.

"Yes, she does, and I'll have to admit I have some reservations about the timing. I'm not surprised by it, though. Neil is a devout Catholic and he talked Katie into going natural until they have three. Katie said once that happens they're going with science instead of religion."

I laughed. "I didn't know Neil was Catholic."

"Yes, he is. You should have seen my mother's face when she found out."

Sarcastically I said, "Speaking of your lovely mother, where is she tonight?"

Grace chuckled. "She's in Rome, thank God. She hasn't spent Christmas in the States since Dad died."

"With any luck, she'll stay there," I joked, though I really couldn't think of anything that would be better.

"No, she won't stay. She wouldn't have anyone to dictate to." A silent pause fell between us. "I'm going to tell her soon, Blue. I think she already knows I'm involved with someone. She just doesn't know it's you."

"I wish I could be there. I would love to see her face when you tell her." I smiled with the thought of it, and then my heart began to pound, anticipating the question I had to ask. "So have you talked to George yet?"

"We're going out for dinner and drinks at a club outside of Raleigh the day after tomorrow. I told him I wanted to go someplace where people wouldn't know us. George seems as anxious about it as I am. I'm sure he knows what I want to discuss. We'll settle on the timing and how we want to go about it while we're there. Of course, Katie's pregnancy will have to be considered now."

The miles between us fell silently over the phone line. "It's not going to change anything, Blue. You have to trust me on this."

51

A Change of Seasons

Springtime surrounded Grace. Red geraniums and pink and purple petunias hung in wrought-iron baskets from the edges of her porch, and white dogwood blooms graced the yard below. She moved along the porch railing with her powder blue water-wand, giving each pot and planter a long soak. I stood in her lake house driveway and watched, wanting to burn this image of her into my memory.

"Are you going to stand down there all day or come up here and join me?" Grace asked.

"Here's good," I teased her.

"You'll get hungry eventually," she replied. Her smile faded too quickly.

I stood my ground and watched her. There was a kind of restlessness in her movements, and a worry in her face that I'd never seen when she tended her flowers. On the phone Grace had mentioned Katie was continuing to do well with her studies, and she thought George had a new mistress. There had been no word lately from Brian, but Grace knew his current mission wouldn't allow home communications for a few more days to come. She had told me these things not more than an hour earlier when I turned south on I-77. Watching her now, I remembered sensing a lack of joy in her voice. With Grace there usually would have been joy, at least when she talked about Katie, but today she sounded as if she were reporting the news of some distant cousins.

I grabbed my leather bag out of the truck and climbed up the stairs of the porch. Grace flipped off the water and I walked over to wrap my arms around her waist. "Are you okay?"

She moved her palms over my hands and pulled them in tighter. Her head dropped onto my shoulder. "I'm a little tired, I think. I didn't sleep well again last night."

I nuzzled my face into the soft tucks of her neck. "How about a nap?"

"I was hoping you would ask," she murmured.

Inside, a breeze flowed through the open windows of the den, and the house held a hearty scent of fresh-growing pines. In Grace's reading chair, a book lay open across one of the arms; on the table next to it a spent teabag draped over the side of an empty mug. Murphy stood up and sauntered toward us, her tail in a helicopter spin. I kneeled down and wrapped my hands on the sides of her head. "I think she's as tired as I am," Grace said.

Grace led me into the bedroom and sat me down on her bed. She stood in front of me and pulled my shirt over my head, let it fall to the floor, and crossed her arms in front to pull off her own. "I thought you wanted to sleep," I said. I watched her hair fall onto her bare shoulders and took her hips in my hands to pull her close. Looking up past the swell of her breasts, I saw the weariness in her eyes.

Grace's cool palms caressed my face. A faint scent of lavender lingered at her wrists. "I do," she said as she swept back my hair. Her eyes brightened a bit when she looked down at me. "I don't want anything between my skin and yours."

Stepping out of my hands she grabbed the bed covers. I waited for her to crawl underneath and then I slid in beside her. She rolled toward me and propped on an elbow. The exhaustion was back in her eyes. "I couldn't get my mind to turn off last night. One minute I'd be thinking about Katie, and then Brian, and then work, and then you." Her gaze drifted down to the top of my breastbone. She moved her hand to rest it there. Her voice filled with weariness, she continued, "It's been happening a lot, lately. I go to bed and the mind race begins."

"Did you get any sleep at all?"

"I don't know. Maybe an hour or two. Murphy and I went outside and sat by the lake for a while. As soon as we came back, I started worrying about Brian."

I brushed her cheek and left my fingers there. "How are you feeling now?"

"Better, especially since you're here." She lowered her head to my shoulder. "With Brian halfway around the world and Katie trying to finish law school while she's pregnant, it gets too much sometimes."

"They say it's a mother's job to worry."

"If that's true, I'm doing a fantastic job of it."

I trailed my fingers through her hair and let silence settle over us for a moment. "How are things with you and George?" I asked.

I felt her take in a deep breath. "Cordial, like always. I think he wants to go through with this divorce as much as I do. We both know the time is right. For us, anyway."

"And your mom?"

"Demanding—she wants to get together to plan our trip to the Caribbean. We'd talked about going this spring but I don't see that happening. It will have to be this summer, or next fall."

"How about not at all?" I teased.

"How about you take her for me?"

"They'd be calling the authorities before we got off the plane."

Grace smiled. "That's probably true, and I don't need an international scandal on top of everything else." She pulled me tighter. "Right now all I want is to feel you next to me."

I rolled to my side, facing her. "I'll be here."

Grace kissed me once and twisted around in my arms. Nestling her back against my chest she said, "I love you, Blue." She kissed my fingers and fell asleep almost instantly.

We woke to gray twilight filling the room. Grace moaned softly when I reached out and pulled her close. Her lazy eyes focused on mine. "You feeling better?" I asked

"Yeah, I am." She brushed her fingers across my face. "Waking up with you always makes me feel better." I leaned forward to kiss her. Before my lips reached her forehead, her Blackberry jumped into its annoying ring. She grabbed it and looked at the number. "It's George." She sat up to answer. "Hello, George. Yes, I'm at the lake house. George, is something wrong?" Grace swung toward me. The color had drained from her face and her eyes moved nervously back and forth. She bit her bottom lip and grabbed my hand. I sat up next to her, my heart now pounding as I knew hers was. "Katie's in the hospital?" She squeezed my hand and again bit her lip. "And the baby?" she asked faintly.

"I'm going up there," Grace said with strength rising in her voice. "Can you arrange it?"

Grace listened, then said, "Yes, I am. Blue is here." She looked at me and gave me the Blackberry.

I held it to my ear and watched Grace slip on her robe. "This is Blue Riley," I said as calmly as I could.

"Hello, Blue. Can you drive Grace to the Charlotte airport?" George asked. The caring in his voice surprised me.

"Yes, of course," I replied. Grace stood at her dresser now, efficiently gathering underwear from her top drawer to pack.

George went on, "My assistant is working on arrangements for a flight to D.C. I'll call back with specifics soon."

"No problem. Will she be meeting you there?"

"Yes. We'll be flying up together."

"Okay. I'm so sorry about Katie. I'll do everything I can to help you guys."

"Thank you," George said and hung up.

I tossed the Blackberry on the bed and went to Grace. She stood now in the threshold of her closet, staring at her clothes. I touched her shoulders and she turned to face me. I pulled her in close and held her. "They're going to be okay, Grace. All of them." She nodded into my shoulder. A warm tear dropped onto my neck.

Out of the corner of my eye, I caught a glimpse of Marty strolling through the gap in the lush wall of rhododendron at the edge of my yard. "Hey, kid," she called out when she got closer.

I waved her over and looked back to the roof of my cabin. Marty stopped beside me and looked up, too. "What're you studying?" she asked.

"I had a leak in the roof last night and I'm looking to see if I can tell where it's coming from. Maybe we should have a roofer take a look at it." I checked Marty's reaction. Even if Nat and I helped, she would have to pay for a roofer and all the supplies. I wasn't sure she could afford it. Marty only nodded and continued her scan of the roof. "If you know a good roofer, we can help out with the labor. I'll pay Nat and Kris to help. We know they're not afraid of heights and Nat loves to learn how to do things."

Marty nodded. "Have things slowed down enough to give you time to do it?"

"Not really, but I'll have more time on my hands when I'm not working at the shop."

"So Grace is still up north with Katie, I take it."

"Yep, she is. The accident caused some complications with Katie's pregnancy, so her doctor put her on bed rest for a while. Something about the placenta pulling away from the uterus, I think."

"Probably placental abruption," Marty said. I looked at her curiously. "Joyce did some research into pregnancy complications that can happen from an auto accident."

I nodded and watched the frown deepen on Marty's face. I wondered what else she knew. I hadn't taken ten minutes to research Katie's condition. I reassured myself it was because I had been talking to Grace at least twice a day, and that worry wouldn't change things.

"What's the prognosis?" Marty asked.

"Grace said Katie should be able to carry the baby to term if she minimizes her activity. Her doctors are monitoring her and the baby closely."

"Are you going up there?"

"Ha!" I blurted out. Marty had obviously lost her mind. "Are you kidding? Grace's mother is circling around like a pit bull on patrol. I'm the last person Grace needs hanging around up there."

"You're exactly the person Grace needs right now."

Marty was as right as the certainty on her face. Every night when I heard the growing strain in Grace's voice, I knew should be helping her through it, propping her up so she could remain the strong and stable Grace everyone was expecting her to be. "Maybe so, but that doesn't mean I'll go," I said.

"You two have got to get this stuff cleared up, kid." She tilted her head and looked at me as if she wondered if I'd ever get my shit together. "It's not good for your relationship, being apart during times like this."

"I couldn't agree more, but Grace says she wants to wait until the baby is born and Brian comes home before she talks to them."

"That seems reasonable." Marty's face soured. "Those young soldiers are having enough of a tough time of it as it is."

"I never thought I'd be waiting for a soldier to come home," I said. Marty looked at me strangely, until I couldn't hold back my playful smile. She grinned with me, and I returned a wry smile.

Grace stormed into the cabin and came straight for me. She kissed me hard and pushed her body into mine, moving us toward my bedroom. Our tangled, swiftly moving feet tripped across the room until my back crashed against the bed. Grace topped me and reached down for my belt. Unbuckling and unbuttoning, she pushed her hand down past my waistband and into the wetness between my legs. Her eyes closed tight as two fingers pushed against me and slipped slightly in. I reached down to her. A low shuddered cry came from her mouth as Grace rocked her hips against the sweep of my fingers. She came in an instant and collapsed against my chest.

"Well hello, nurse," I said after a moment.

Grace's muffled laugh fell into the folds of my shirt. She made a loose fist and lightly punched my shoulder. "Was it as good for you as it was for me?"

"It's hard sayin,'" I teased. "I mean, I'm all for efficiency, but some things do get better with time." I wrapped my arms around her and pulled her up to my shoulder.

Grace moaned and rolled off of my chest. "I hate time," she said in exasperation. She slipped her head back onto my shoulder and stared up at the ceiling. "Lately I've been either rushing through it or waiting for it to pass. Waiting for time to pass so the baby will grow, waiting for time to pass so Brian can come home, waiting for time to pass so I can see you again and barge in to attack you like a horny teenager." She raised her arm in frustration and let it drop back onto the bed. "I want it to be tomorrow, Blue. I want Brian to be home and I want the baby to be born and I want to start our life together. I want us to be there now."

I fingered the tips of her hair. "What does *there* look like?" I asked.

Grace turned and curled her body into mine. "*There* looks like here. Our place will be in the mountains somewhere, like we wanted before. We'll finally have it, Blue, in a few more months we'll be there."

"I can't wait to get there, Grace," I said in a voice as blithe as a dream.

52

A Phone Call Away

Nat blew the dust out of her carving and studied it for a moment. She seemed satisfied with her work for the day. "So how long will Grace be gone this time?" she asked as she slid her hand tools into the slots of her carving kit.

"At least three weeks. After the baby is born, she'll stay on for a couple of weeks or so," I replied. Through the window of the office, I watched Sarah Jackson shutting down her computer for the night. Sarah's smile and bouncing energy usually bolstered my mood on rainy Highlands afternoons. Today even Sarah couldn't lift my spirits.

Nat pulled up a stool beside me and reached into her pocket for nail clippers. She sat down and started inspecting the edges of her nails. "You mind if I take off tomorrow? Kris is off and we want to get in some climbing."

"No, go ahead. You've been putting a lot of time in lately. Maybe you should take a week and go camping or something," I said, rather dully.

Nat stopped her inspection and turned to me, the clippers still at the edge of her fingers. "A *week*? I asked for a day, not a week."

I nodded, wondering why the hell I said a week. "Right, sure, go ahead and take tomorrow off. It's fine."

Nat dropped her hands into her lap. Her perplexed look hadn't left her face. "Something eatin' at you?"

"Yeah, I suppose. I think it's all of this stuff going on with Grace and her kids. Katie's baby will be here soon and Brian will be coming home before long. There's also the fact that I don't trust Helen Lancaster for a second. That woman is all about protecting her precious family name and she still has a grip on Grace. I'm not sure where I'll end up when the dust settles."

Nat stuffed the clippers back in her pocket and jumped off her stool. "I swear, you'd borrow trouble from a beggar," she said, heading for the refrigerator. "Grace is crazy about you. You don't see the way she watches you when you aren't looking. She's *not* going to cave to her mother."

"Helen Lancaster is a formidable woman. She's used to getting her way."

Nat took a beer from the six-pack of Fat Tire. "So talk to Grace. Tell her how you feel about it." She sauntered from the refrigerator and climbed back on her stool. "I don't get you sometimes, boss," she said, twisting the cap off her beer. She flipped the cap across ten feet and into the center of the trashcan. "You act like Grace should be able to read your mind and know what you want without telling her."

"You would be surprised how often she has done just that."

"So you expect it every time?" Nat looked at me, exasperated by my pigheaded gloom. "In case you haven't noticed, Grace has a lot going on at the moment. Her focus probably isn't on you. You need to tell her the shit going on in your head or get over it."

Her youthful, blunt advice could be refreshing or aggravating, depending on the day. Today it was aggravating. "Maybe so, Nat," I replied. The distant ring of my cell phone turned our attention toward the office. Sarah leaned out the door, holding the phone out toward me. "You left this in here. I think it's Grace."

I hustled over and took the phone. Sarah waved and closed the office door on her way out. "Hey, baby. What's up?" I said to Grace.

"Can you come up here for a few days?" Her voice sounded weary, almost defeated.

"Yes, of course. What's going on?"

"I finally heard from Brian this afternoon. He was injured by an IED explosion a couple of days ago." Her voice trailed off into silence.

"Grace, is Brian okay?" I asked as calmly as I could.

"He will be. He had a concussion and his eyes and cheeks are black and swollen. He's got a row of stitches on his face that looks—" Grace paused, and I cursed the distance between us. She took a deep breath and continued, "The good news is the hearing he lost in one ear is coming back. He'll be in Germany until he comes home."

"Good, that's good, Grace." I turned on the computer to check on flights to D.C. "Is the day after tomorrow soon enough? I'll only be able to stay a couple of days."

"I know. Just come, okay?"

Grace pulled back the sleeves of her silk houndstooth jacket and propped her elbows on the white tablecloth in front of her. Late evening sunlight filtered in through the slats of the plantation shutters behind her, highlighting the loose waves of her hair. "Did you enjoy your dinner?" she asked.

I looked down at a plate that had been covered with scallops and asparagus. "Yes, it was delicious, but you didn't have to bring me to a place like this," I said, though I hoped she would see the appreciation in my eyes when I raised them to meet hers. "A hamburger would've been fine."

"I like to see you dressed up once in a while," she replied with a smile that quickly faded.

"This is rare," I said, tugging at the lapel of my navy blue blazer. Though I was beat from the day's travel, the time with Grace was worth it. The way we were dressed, our attention only on each other, we were like all the other couples around us—loving and grateful for the evening. Tonight, away from North Carolina, I could finally be out with her in a way that didn't feel like hiding.

Grace put her palm over my hand and kept it there. On her ring finger she wore the sapphire ring I had given her a few weeks ago. "Baby, thank you for coming up on short notice. I know you're busy in the shop with summer tourist season starting," she said.

I rolled my hand into hers. "It's fine, Grace. You wouldn't have asked if you didn't need me here. Nat and Sarah can handle the shop for a couple of days." Probably longer, I thought, although I wasn't ready to find out the hard way. "So tell me how you're feeling about Katie and the baby."

Grace sighed. "I'm worried, even though Katie is really doing well, and the baby seems to be developing as she should. There is so much that can happen, so we won't know everything until she's born."

"It must be nerve-wracking for all of you."

Grace drew in a worried breath. "Sometimes I think Katie is holding up better than I am." She paused. Her gaze drifted down to our interlocked hands. "I lost it a little bit after Brian called. I don't know what I would have done if you hadn't come up here." She looked up at me and continued, "I hope you don't mind spending the day alone tomorrow. I'll leave as soon as Neil gets home after work."

"Don't worry about me. I knew this wouldn't be a vacation," I said with a thin smile.

Grace nodded and tapped my hand with two fingers. I could see her mind had moved on. "I want you to meet my children soon," she said. "George and I are planning a family gathering when Brian comes home at the end of the summer. If you can come by, I'll introduce you to them. I think it's important that you meet them before I tell them about us. I believe this could be a good opportunity."

"Won't it seem strange for me to drop in on a family gathering?"

"A lot of people will be there. I'll figure out a good reason for you to be invited," Grace replied.

I looked at her cautiously. "Is your mother coming?"

Grace straightened her back with defiance. "The hell with my mother. She had her say when I told her I was seeing you again, and there's no way she's keeping us apart this time."

53

Oorah!

Perfectly spaced rows of miniature American flags lined the drive to Marshall Landing. A sign lettered in bold red and blue type stretched across the driveway near the house.

WELCOME HOME BRIAN
WE'RE PROUD OF OUR MARINE
OORAH!

My stomach flipped again. The place would be swarming with a lot of Lancasters and Marshalls. I wished I'd taken time to shop so I wouldn't be strolling around in my river sandals and fishing shorts. I kept rolling down the driveway, though a big part of me wanted to run. In the graveled loop at the end of the drive, I saw an assortment of cars, some of the luxury models probably worth more than my cabin. There was a Lexus sedan, a Lincoln Navigator, a Mercedes convertible, BMW sedan, and closest to the lake house, Grace's Land Rover.

Tension constricted the muscles of my neck as I eased out of my truck and looked around. Adults holding drink glasses talked in groups or in pairs, and a few kids chased through the yard playing tag or something. I spotted George standing with a small group gathered on the patio. Right away, the woman next to him caught my attention. She wore a flowing white cotton pants and a hip-length matching shirt that perfectly complimented her summer tan. Her gray hair was swept back into a thick wave that ended with a fine point at the base of her neck. In her right hand she loosely held a wine glass in exactly the same way as Grace. Even from my distance I could see she was a striking woman—and that she was Helen Lancaster. My senses heightened like I had heard the cock of a gun.

"Bloody hell," I muttered to myself. At least I had met George. I hoped he would be as gracious as he had been when I met him back in April. That day, he had been anxious to get to his daughter and still he had taken a few moments to thank me for helping Grace and driving her to the airport.

George looked relaxed now. His Levi's fit his tall, trim frame as if they had been tailored for him, and his red polo shirt nicely contrasted his dark hair. Next to him was a man of almost exactly his height, who wore a gray crew cut and stood ramrod straight. The resemblance to George was uncanny, and I figured by his age he was George's father. The man rested his hand on the back of a slightly pudgy woman with a glowing shock of auburn hair that fell pleasingly onto her blue and gold blouse. The clutch of thin gold bracelets on her right arm slipped toward her elbow when she turned up her cocktail glass. I figured she must be George's mother.

I looked past the four on the patio and down to the group gathered in the seating area near the lake. The Adirondack chairs were clustered only a few feet from the spot where Grace and I had kissed on our first night here. Grace looked up from the group, waved once, and started up the hill. I waited at the edge of the patio.

"How are you doing?" Grace murmured when she reached me. By the stiff way she held her shoulders, I knew she was anxious, too.

"Nervous as a cat," I replied. My gaze darted about, unable to rest on anything. I glanced over at Helen. She broke the dismissive glare she had locked on me and turned back to George.

"I am, too, but it will be okay," Grace said. She turned towards her mother and husband. "They may as well get used to it," she added, too flippantly to sound secure. "C'mon, Brian and Katie are down here."

We headed down the hill toward the lake, avoiding the looks from the four on the patio. Still, I felt the cutting stare of Helen Lancaster on my back. I looked out to the water and considered running into it and swimming away as fast as I could.

Grace walked around and stopped in front of the semicircle of chairs. I stopped beside her, now fully on display in front of her children.

I focused on Brian first. He looked up with ice blue eyes and flashed an easy smile. His dark hair seemed to be about the same color as his dad's, although it was hard to tell for sure because of his Marine Corps buzz cut. I knew from Grace's photographs that the young woman sitting to his left was Katie, and next to her was her husband Neil. I wasn't certain of the woman to Brian's right. I assumed her to be Whitney, Brian's new fiancée.

"Don't get up." I held my palm up to Brian as he started to stand. He hopped up anyway and stood with his hands straight down and curled into loose fists, ready to move into a handshake or salute.

Grace stood beside me, ready to introduce me in the proper way she knew so well. "Brian, this is Blue Riley. Blue, this is my son, Brian Marshall."

Brian's arm pivoted to a crisp, sharp angle when he offered his hand. I grasped his palm firmly in mine and held his gaze. "It's nice to meet you, Brian."

"Pleasure to meet you, ma'am," he said. His voice came in a softer tone than his practiced, military officer movements. "I've seen some of your work on your website. I'm looking forward to seeing more of it soon."

I glanced at Grace for a hint of what he meant. Grace moved on without acknowledging the glance. "And this is my daughter, Katie Frazier."

Looking at Katie's face struck me still. The green and gold irises were the exact colors of Grace's. Her hair was darker, more the color of her father's, though as I looked into her face I felt I'd been transported back in time. Her smile came as easy as her mother's. Katie glanced away when I grasped her hand, and in this way she seemed more cautious than her mother. Neil stood on the other side of Katie, waiting for Grace to introduce him. His languid eyes and pale face held the exhaustion of a new father and a young man who had been through quite a lot in the past few months. He gripped my hand for a solid shake, and then dropped his arm lethargically by his side.

"Is the baby here?" I asked.

Neil pointed up to the house. "She's up in the house with our sitter," he said. His tired smile dropped back into a blank face.

"This heat's too much for a newborn," Grace offered.

Whitney stepped closer to Brian's side when Grace turned to her. Going by her looks Whitney seemed a typical fresh-faced, sorority-type girl. Her deep brown eyes set on me with genuine enthusiasm when she reached for my hand. I held on for an extra moment with Whitney. In a way I figured she felt as I did, wanting to make a good impression on the new families surrounding her. I gave her a confident smile and turned to Brian.

"I made this for you, Brian," I said holding out the box I'd brought for him. "It's a little something from me and the folks in my shop to thank you for your service."

Brian took the box and looked down at the lid, Katie and Whitney at his shoulder. I'd carved the Marine Corps insignia in the center, using a pattern Sarah found online. Nat did the finishing work, smoothing down the cherry wood to a glass-like finish.

"Wow, this is beautiful, Ms. Riley," Brian said. "I'm honored, ma'am."

Whitney leaned into him and added, "Brian and I are hoping to own more of your work soon. Brian's mom suggested one of your pieces as a wedding present, so we thought we'd drive over one day and take a look around your showroom."

"Good, I'll be looking forward to it," I said, though it was the first I'd heard of it. Grace said she would figure something out when I had asked her how she would explain my presence at their family gathering. The suggested wedding gift must have provided her with the excuse, though at the moment it seemed a thin one. "I'll be happy to custom-build something if you prefer."

Whitney beamed, "I would love that."

I smiled at her joy and remembered what Preacher said, "The look on a man's face when he sees something I carved for him—it doesn't get any better than that." Indeed it did not.

"I'll look forward to talking about your ideas for a piece when you come to Highlands," I said.

"We'll look forward to it as well," Brian said earnestly. "Mom said I may be able to talk you into showing me around your workshop, if you wouldn't mind. I've always had a curiosity about making furniture by hand. It seems to be a dying trade."

"I wouldn't mind at all, Brian," I replied with an easy smile. In spite of his Marine Corps mannerisms, there was a welcoming gentleness about him.

Neil's cell phone buzzed and took our attention. He looked down to the screen. "The sitter says the baby's awake," he said.

"We'd better go up, Mom," Katie said. She looked at me in a way that said she was trying to understand something, though her mind was not yet clear on what it could be. "If I don't see you again, it was nice to meet you, Blue."

"You too. It was nice to meet you both," I replied.

"Nice to meet you, Ms. Riley," Neil said. He took his wife's hand and we watched them walk away, their slow footsteps drained by fatigue.

Grace touched my elbow. "Come on, let's get you something to drink," she said with a nod toward the house. I followed her gaze up the hill. George was walking toward the boathouse with his parents, leaving Helen alone on the patio, watching us. Grace's eyes narrowed on her mother for an almost imperceptible moment, and then she lowered her gaze to Brian and Whitney. "We'll be back in a bit," she said.

Grace returned her mother's stare as we moved up the hill toward her. We stopped on the patio directly in front of Helen. "Mom, this is Augusta Riley. Most everyone calls her Blue. And Blue, this is my mother, Helen Lancaster," Grace said.

"So I finally get to meet you," Helen said. She stuck out her right hand, expecting me to take it. "At least George knew better than to introduce his mistress at a family gathering," she added. Helen looked directly at me as I grasped her hand, though her last comment was clearly aimed at her daughter. I glanced over to Grace. She held a defiant chin up, but I knew there was hurt beneath her bravado.

Part of me wanted to reach out and throttle Helen until she turned blue. Over the past twenty-five years it was one of the responses I'd imagined if I ever came face to face with the woman. I decided against jail time and settled instead on the smart-assed option. Moving my hands behind my back, I made a slight nod to Helen. "Mrs. Lancaster, it's easy to see where Grace gets her good looks. You are even more beautiful in person than in your photographs."

Helen cocked her head back with a disdainful frown. Out of the corner of my eye, I saw Grace raise her hand to her mouth to conceal a smile. Grace looked at me and touched my shoulder. "Shall we get you that drink?"

Everything in the house felt foreign when I followed Grace inside. The reading chair, the bookshelves, the kitchen bar, everything I had become familiar with over the last year seemed to be the claim of someone else, of George and Brian, and Katie, and even Helen Lancaster. Grace was behaving no differently than when we were alone here. She breezed about the den and into the kitchen, taking a moment to touch my arm and my back when she walked past me. Yet something felt different. I supposed it was because Grace's children were an absolute reality to me now. From the day she walked back into my life, I had heard about Brian and Katie, and I had known they were a fact of her life. For months our lives had revolved around them in ways that were both small and monumental, and yet they had never known of me. Today I looked into their eyes and touched their warm flesh, had seen the legacy of Grace's genes, and George's too. Was I the outsider or were they? If Grace had never left, Brian and Katie would have never happened. Looking into their eyes, the thought of it didn't seem right.

Grace's voice brought me back from my thoughts. She was looking out the window toward the pier. "It looks like Whitney is going out for a boat ride with George and his folks," she said. She opened a cabinet and took a tall insulated tumbler from the bottom shelf. "That will give us a chance to talk with Brian a bit more."

"What have you told him?" I asked, not sure if she had mentioned anything of me other than my woodworking skills.

"Not much, really. I mentioned I knew a woman who built some of the most sought-after furniture around, and that one of your pieces could make a wonderful wedding present. Once I showed them your website, they were sold on the idea. Brian asked if I thought you would show him around the workshop. I said he would have to ask you, so I'm glad you agreed to it. He really needs a distraction." Grace finished putting ice in the tumbler and took the lemonade pitcher from the refrigerator. "Whitney and I are worried about him. He hasn't been sleeping as well as he used to, and he's already talking about wanting to go back to Iraq. Whitney teases him that he's trying to escape planning the wedding, but we're both worried. I can't imagine what another deployment would do to him."

"Do you think he's depressed or something?" I asked.

"I don't really know. He hasn't been diagnosed with anything as far as I know, but something is going on. So, I've been reading about ways to help soldiers recently back from deployment. Most of the articles suggest finding interests outside of job and family. They say something creative is often helpful."

"Woodworking, for example," I said.

Grace nodded. I took my lemonade from her and looked out the windows. The pontoon boat was pulling away from the boathouse.

"Come on then, let's go talk to him," I said.

Brian sat alone with his face toward the sun. His head rested against the back of the Adirondack chair and a trace of a smile lingered on his mouth. I sat down on his right and Grace to his left.

"Grandmother said to tell you she had left, Mom," Brian said without opening his eyes. He lazily turned his face to me. "You shouldn't worry about my grandmother. She can be nice, but some days she finds us all rather distasteful."

I grinned. "Today must be one of those days."

Brian shrugged with a lazy smile. "Looks like."

I shifted around to face Brian more fully. "Brian, I've been thinking, how would you like to spend a day or two with me and my assistant in the workshop?"

Brian sat up straight and his face brightened. "I think I'd like that," he said.

I glanced at Grace. Her eyes flashed a glimmer of hope. "Then let's do it," I said to Brian. "Have you done any woodworking before?"

"Not exactly," Brian replied. "I had a buddy in college whose father was a builder. I worked for him a couple of summers."

Grace put her hand on his shoulder. "You should have seen some of the things he built with Lincoln Logs when he was growing up. He's always been good with his hands."

"Whenever you're ready, give me a call."

Brian nodded. "I'll do that."

"Good, I'll look forward to having you work with us." Brian nodded again. It seemed we'd said enough for our first day, and I didn't want to push it. I stood and said to him, "See you soon, then."

Grace walked me back to the truck. "Thank you for driving all this way to meet them, sweetheart," she said as we walked. "I know it wasn't easy, especially with my mother here."

"Your mother should work on her hospitality," I said with a smile more forgiving than I felt.

Grace returned my smile, though I knew she still felt the sting of her mother's insolence. "True. At least she knows about us. After I talk with Brian and Katie, George and I will file for the divorce."

We reached my truck and I opened the door. "You will talk to them soon, won't you?"

Grace stepped in closer, though the glare of the sun kept me from seeing her face. "Yes, as soon as I find the right time." She paused. The certainty had left her voice when she continued. "Brian needs a little more time to adjust to being home. I know the things he's going through are to be expected, but that doesn't make it any easier to watch him deal with it."

"Maybe a few days in the mountains will help," I offered.

"Maybe," Grace replied.

The doubt in her voice scared me.

Brian stood in my shop in the same spot where I had first seen his mother almost seventeen months ago. He held his hands clasped behind his back as he glanced around his surroundings. For a moment I watched him from the hallway. His manner was so much like Grace had been at his age—curious, confident, and at ease with the world around him.

"Hello, Brian." I walked out of the hallway and reached out my hand to him. "It's good to see you again."

Brian took my hand firmly and glanced up and down my body. I wore the unstained workpants and white t-shirt I often wore on days

I planned to meet with customers. For most of the morning, I had worn my apron to keep it all clean. Brian seemed to be taking a mental note of my appearance, right down to my sand-colored work boots.

"Did Whitney come with you?" I asked.

Brian frowned. "No, she couldn't make it. She had to go over some things with our wedding planner."

"I'm sorry to hear that," I said, stepping beside him. "Have you had a chance to look around the showroom yet?"

"Not yet," he said, his eyes making a quick sweep of the room. His gaze stopped on the vanity. He walked over to it and leaned down. "Tell me about this," he said. His eyes squinted together as he focused on the carving of the young girl. He studied it intently for a moment and then moved on to the carving of the teenager. "You've never considered selling it?"

"No, I haven't. I carved the vanity to honor the women in my life. Some works are too close to the soul to trade for cash." Brian stood up straight and looked at me peculiarly. I returned a polite smile and quickly moved his attention to the next piece, a cherry writing desk I had finished two days ago. In the center I had carved a simple quill and ink well. "Pieces like this writing desk are selling well, and they don't take a fraction of the time a piece like the vanity takes."

"Success through mass production?" he asked amicably.

"Or working her assistant to death," Nat said from behind me. She walked toward us, a straw dangling from her mouth and her faded workpants covered with various shades of stain. Nat had been psyched about meeting Brian. "Our Marine" had taken on a bit of acclaim in the store. I wasn't sure if it was because he was Grace's son or because he was our link to a war that seemed vague and too far away to otherwise be real. Maybe it was both.

Nat stopped in front of Brian and took the straw from her mouth, shoving it in her back pocket as she stuck out her other hand. "Natalie Clark. You must be Brian Marshall."

"I am," Brian said as he took her hand.

Nat turned to me. "Sarah said you need to call Bill Winters right away. He's going out to do some logging this week and needs to talk to you."

I'd been waiting for a week for Bill Winters to call. Bill was a forester from down in Swain County, who had started up a pecker-wood mill after retirement. I got most of my local wood from him. He was an opinionated old bastard who did exactly as he pleased in exactly his own time, which meant we got along great. It also meant that when he was ready to talk I had to respond. I looked at Nat, now standing beside Brian. "Why don't you show Brian around the work-shop while I call Bill back," I said.

Nat nodded her nonchalant agreement to cover up the fact that the call from Bill had come at a most opportune time for her. She looked at Brian. "Come on, all the fun stuff's back here."

For almost an hour I discussed my order with Bill. After I hung up, I caught up with Brian and Nat in the shipping room, standing in front of two bookcases I had built for Grace.

"These are beautiful, Ms. Riley," Brian said. "My mother is going to love them."

"Thanks; and please call me either Blue or Augusta." I stood next to Brian and looked up at the carvings at the top of the bookcases, one carving of hemlock boughs and cones, the other of a brook trout rising toward a fly in a stream. "I built them for the lake house. I'm contemplating the carving for the third one. I'm thinking either the profile of Grandfather Mountain or a Tar Heel. Right now, I'm leaning toward the Grandfather profile. The Tar Heel seems out of character with these two."

"I agree," Brian said. "Does my mother know about them?"

"No, I want to surprise her," I replied.

"That's very generous of you," Brian said.

"Your mom has helped me make a lot of connections," I tried to explain, although I couldn't stop the heat and color from rushing up my neck.

Nat jumped in to my rescue. She put her hand on Brian's shoulder and said, "You haven't seen any of my stuff yet. Come on, I'll show you some of the doors I carved."

Brian followed Nat to the section of the showroom that held her doors. They stood in front of them, looking up at Nat's carvings. "I'm thinking of specializing in doors. That way I won't have to compete with Blue's furniture. I wouldn't want her to feel bad when I get better than her."

"I heard that," I said, and then I thought, *This might work.*

"You were supposed to hear it," Nat replied.

Brian looked at her and grinned. I supposed the bond forming between them was natural. They were about the same age and both smart, athletic kids, and although their life experiences had been so different, their early view of the world had been seen from the same prism of events.

Brian reached out and swept his fingers down the mirror smoothness of one of Nat's doors. "If I can learn to make something as beautiful as this, maybe I won't think as much about the things I've destroyed."

Neither Nat nor I could find a proper response. Brian sensed our unease and leaned toward us with a teasing, crooked smile, "And the drill sergeants here will be way better looking."

Our ease returned with our laughter. Brian stepped toward us and held his hand out to Nat. "So I'll see you tomorrow morning, Nat," he said, looking at her with a sweet smile. He turned to me, a bit more sincerely. "I'm looking forward to working with you tomorrow, Ms. Riley—I mean, Blue."

As we watched Brian walk into the flow of tourists moving along the sidewalks of Highlands, Nat said, "I knew I'd like him." She leaned her shoulder against the door and pushed her hands in her pockets. Her muscles' definition popped out along the length of her arms. "He is a good guy."

"I agree. I think we'll enjoy having him around for the next couple of days."

"He knows about you and Grace."

I spun around and stared at Nat. She looked at me like it was no big deal. It was a very big deal, and Nat had no business getting in the middle of it. "Did you *tell* him?" I demanded.

"Hell no, I didn't *tell* him," Nat replied incredulously, her shoulders hunched up and her gaze on me like I'd gone mad. "When we were in the workshop he started asking a lot of questions about you. Then he asked if you were in love with his mother. I didn't say anything, but then he said he could tell right away when he saw you two together."

I shrugged my acquiescence. Brian would be a hard man to fool, if I ever felt the need. Nat relaxed and continued, "He said he had to learn to read body language really well in Iraq. He had to see the little things most people don't see, because sometimes that was the only way to know who was going to kill you, and who just hated you."

"Did he say how long he has known?"

"No, but I figured he must have suspected before he got here."

Nat watched me process everything she'd said. I wanted to do things right for her, to be someone she could look up to. I knew she loved Grace, too. She had always wanted us to make it. Maybe it was the romantic in her, or maybe she wanted her elders to have some guts.

"Are you going to tell Grace he knows?" she asked.

"I don't know, Nat."

"You still don't trust her, do you?"

"I didn't say that."

"You don't have to," Nat said. She gave me a reproachful shrug and walked back to the workshop.

54

Looking for Grace

"Hey, baby," Grace stepped out of her bedroom door, toweling off her hair. Her white bathrobe hung loose around her body, revealing the soft skin that stretched below her neck. "Give me a minute to get dressed. I'm really hungry, if you can believe that. After everything I ate for Thanksgiving I shouldn't be hungry for a week. I'll make us a sandwich and then we can do whatever you want." She stepped back into the bedroom and tossed her robe onto the bed as I walked by. She looked so gorgeous that for a moment I forgot to breathe. I wondered if I would react the same way six or seven years from now, when I was with her every day.

Grace seemed happy. I hoped that meant she had talked to Brian and Katie and that it had somehow gone better than she had expected, particularly with Katie. I sat down on the arm of her reading chair and listened to the sounds of her getting dressed. "I didn't get a chance to talk to Brian and Katie yet," Grace said so casually I almost missed what she said. A drawer closed and there was the sound of her white, down comforter rumpling when she sat down. "Katie and Neil wanted to get home with the baby and Brian and Whitney were out visiting friends today."

Disappointment washed over me. The weeks since Brian's Welcome Home celebration were now stretching into months. I understood that telling Brian and Katie would be a difficult issue, yet it had to be done before we could move on. I looked up to the ceiling and tried to shake my growing doubt that Grace would go through with it. "I had hoped you would talk with them while Brian is home for Thanksgiving. You may not get another chance for a while," I said calmly, trying to keep the evening from going sour.

Grace walked out of her bedroom rubbing lotion into her hands. She went into the kitchen and opened the pantry door. "I'm spending the little time I have with Brian trying to talk him out of volunteering to go back to Iraq. He seems to be doing much better lately with adjusting to life back in the States. If he goes back there, he'll be right back where he was when he first came home. Maybe worse." Grace shook her head and pulled out a loaf of whole wheat bread and a couple of paper plates. She brought them to the counter and set the plates side by side.

I moved over and sat down on the kitchen barstool across from her. Grace pulled four pieces of bread out of the bag and put two each on the plates. She gave me a cautious glance that hinted she recognized the reason for my silence, and then continued. "Do you think he can come over to the shop tomorrow? He could use a distraction while he's home. He still talks about how much he enjoyed it when he came over to work with you guys last summer."

"Sure, he can come over if he wants. I'll call Nat if he decides to come. They really enjoyed hanging out with each other."

"Good, I'll text him tonight." Grace went to the refrigerator and pulled out the mayonnaise and mustard, a plate of turkey, and a zip-lock bag of lettuce. She brought it to the counter and dipped a spreader into the mayonnaise. Her busy work with the sandwiches covered her reluctance to look at my face. "You're being quiet." Grace put down the spreader and looked at me. "I've disappointed you again, haven't I?"

I nodded. "Yes, you have. I don't understand what's holding you back. Brian has already figured us out, and Katie is not some naïve child. I was hoping we could move forward soon."

Grace planted her palms on the counter and looked at me with the confidence of someone who had wrestled the same doubts in her mind. When she spoke, she seemed to be using the assurance she had used to convince herself. "I know, and we will, baby, as soon as I know I've done all I can to help Brian make the right decisions. I want him to apply for a transfer of his commission to the Reserves. Whitney's ready to start a family, and George and I want him to begin building his civilian career so he'll be fully ready when he gets out of the military."

I listened to her excuses, dissatisfied and silent.

Her mouth tensed and she let out a deep sigh. "Okay, you have to talk to me. I have to know what you're thinking."

I shrugged, as if it were really a simple answer. "First of all, you're pressuring him on the wrong things, Grace. Brian needs to make up his own mind on what he needs to do about the military and you need to support him. Otherwise, he'll end up resenting you like you resent your mother."

Grace shook her head. "I don't think that's true at all. Even if Brian resents it now, someday he will realize I only want the right thing for him. It's not the same as what my mother did to us. I mean this is real life we're talking about now."

Real life. Did Grace realize what she had just said? Had I learned in this off-handed comment exactly how she saw us in the world? If we weren't *real life* to her, then what was our relationship about? What was my entire life about? Was I something less to her than her pretend husband and the mother she nearly despised? Over the last year, Grace had convinced me that I had been her real life, and everything that she had done before was the farce. My anger began to storm inside me. I wanted to believe I was wrong.

"So, do you think when your mother helped break us up she wasn't interfering with real life? Were we just some disposable college romance to you?" I asked, controlling the anger in my voice with every measured word.

Grace shook her head and looked away. "That's not what I meant."

"I think that's exactly what you meant. How else could you justify what you're doing now with Brian as being different from what your mother did to us back then? This is real life too, Grace, yours and mine," I said, pointing back and forth between us. "This is real life—only you refuse to live it!"

Grace's face instantly burned crimson. "What do you mean? I'm with you right now, aren't I?"

"For tonight, yeah, but you belittle us all the time, Grace, as if we aren't important enough to matter. You're still stashing us in a corner and pulling us out when it is convenient for you, when you need me to prop you up. Whether you see it or not, we're as real life as you and George, as Katie and Neil, and Brian and Whitney. What we have is real life, Grace. Or at least I thought it was!"

She stared across the room, her eyes squinted and fierce as she gathered her emotions. Maybe she was counting to ten the way her mother had taught her to do when she was angry. She had become so good at that, keeping in the anger, measuring her words to keep from saying too much. It only pissed me off more. I wanted all of the fire and passion that I knew was boiling inside her.

Grace looked at me cautiously and said, "Give me another month, that's all I'm asking—until the new year. I'll talk to Brian and Katie when they're home for Christmas. And there are some things I need to finish with the foundation before the end of the year. I'll give them my notice after I talk to Brian and Katie. Then we'll be free to do whatever you want."

I shook my head and turned away. Her body was tense and anxious when I looked back at her. "In a month it will be something else, Grace. The baby will be christened, and I won't be included because we can't have Neil's family knowing grandma's a lezbo. And then Brian's wedding will roll around, and there will be the in-laws and how do we explain it all to them? Real life will always be waiting, Grace. Every week and every month you'll have to decide whether you want to meet it honestly or not, and I can't live like that."

I stood there, wanting her to fight back. The fact that she didn't, that she stood there looking at me in distress, or indecision, or whatever it was that was holding her back, told me more than a thousand pleas ever could. I looked at her, my beautiful Grace; the only one I ever really wanted. "This life can't be lived in the bedroom. I thought you understood that. Maybe it was all just words." She looked at me, saying nothing. "I've got to go."

Her low, resigned voice burned into me as I turned to walk out. "Where are you going?" Tears welled up in her eyes.

For a second they almost drew me back. I shrugged. "I don't know."

"We can't work this out if you walk away. Tell me when I can see you again."

"That's up to you. You know what I want." I looked at her one last time and walked out the door, her silence boring through me with the sting of a winter wind.

55

Merry Christmas

White Christmas lights draped along Highlands' light posts and store fronts couldn't shake away the dullness of my mood. With December's piercing cold invading my bones, I accepted a long-standing offer from an Australian client to sponsor me on a work visa. It would be summer there, with plenty of warm skies to reinvigorate my work. Nat and Sarah could run the store while I was away over the slow season. I would leave sometime after New Year's.

I looked up at the clock centered on the back wall of the workshop; a few minutes after five. The gray skies had been spitting snow most of the afternoon, and it was almost dark outside. Sarah walked into the workshop carrying two shiny green gift bags topped with red tissue paper. Her dark green appliqué sweatshirt spelled out J O Y in a collage of sparrows and finches. On her left collarbone a Rudolph pin pulsed with a tiny red light.

"I flipped the closed sign and locked the front door," Sarah said as she breezed through the shop. She hoisted the two gift bags onto our lunch counter and sat down. "Time for a little celebration, girls. Come on now, your fruitcake is waiting."

"I'll get us a beer," Nat said to me. "Sarah, what do you want?"

"Bring me a Pepsi. Pete and I have to go to Wal-Mart and then I need to wrap presents before we go to Momma's. I'll be up half the night."

I moved beside Sarah and playfully pulled at the edges of the red tissue paper in the gift bags. She swatted at my arm. "Wait till Natalie gets back, missy." She straightened her back and smiled at me, her eyes wide and full of childlike expectation. "What'd you get me, boss?"

"The usual. Nothing."

"Nothing but a big ole check," Sarah replied. Her fantastic white smile contrasted perfectly with the gleam in her dark eyes.

"Maybe. We'll see. The size of the check depends on what's in here." I rattled the gift bag and Sarah swatted me again.

Nat returned with the Pepsi and a beer for me. "Okay, go ahead, boss," Sarah said.

I dug through the red tissue paper and found a fruitcake at the bottom of the bag. Tied to the fruitcake was a five-inch, hand-knapped knife. The stone blade was wedged into an antler handle wrapped by a leather cord. "Oh my God, it's beautiful," I said as I pulled the knife from the bag and checked the knapping along the cutting edge. "Thank you, Sarah."

"You know, Pete's friend Jack Knowles makes those," Sarah said. "I thought you'd like it."

Lightly I plucked my thumb along the edge. It was sharp enough to split my leather apron with a single stroke. Beside me Nat pawed her way through the tissue paper of her bag.

"Holy shit, that's sharp," Nat said as she checked the knife's edge. "I think I could even cut this fruitcake with it."

Sarah threw a hand up, "Okay, enough with the fruitcake jokes."

I chuckled at them. In a few weeks they would be in charge of my store, my livelihood and the best thing I had done in my life. They would step up, I knew they would, and yet I had to wonder about the decisions they would make without me. The thought was unsettling, though I had to believe in them. I needed a break from North Carolina.

"This is for you." Nat opened the cabinet door at her knee and pulled out a neatly wrapped box. She handed it to Sarah. "If you don't like it, you can sell it and use the money to buy some high heels or something."

"Oh honey, I haven't worn high heels in years." Sarah unwrapped the package and pulled up the flaps on the box. Inside was a rosewood jewelry box Nat had been secretly working on for weeks. Delight filled Sarah's eyes. "This is so beautiful, Nat," she said. She lifted the top tray and fingered the scarlet red felt lining the bottom and sides of the box. "I'll treasure this." She gave Nat a quick hug and turned to me. "Okay, boss, what you got?" She smiled and clapped her hands together.

I pulled out two envelopes from my back pocket. "I guess you're waiting for these." I handed the one holding a check for $600 to Nat and the one for $400 to Sarah. "This year I have a couple more surprises." I took out the box I had hidden under the counter and pulled out two store-wrapped gifts. "After you open these, I have something I need to talk to you about."

Nat eyed me warily. I had told her about walking out on Grace. I had been moping around the store, distracted and uninspired, and she kept asking until I had no choice but to tell her. Pushing through to finish Christmas orders took everything I had in me.

They ripped through the wrapping paper in an instant. Inside their packages Sarah found a GPS unit and Nat an iPod. Nat looked at me with a cool kid smile and raised her hand high for me to meet it. Sarah held up the GPS and tapped Nat's shoulder. "Look what I got."

Nat smiled. "Now maybe you'll get to places on time."

Sarah playfully punched Nat's shoulder and turned to me. "Okay, boss, what do you want to tell us?" Rudolph's nose pulsed on her shoulder like a warning light.

Nat focused fully on me now. I couldn't look her directly in the eye. "I'd like to ask both of you to do something for me," I began. Sarah shifted on her stool and became as serious as Nat. I took a moment to steady my nerves and continued, "I've decided to take a commission for a job in Australia. I'll be gone for a couple of months and I'd like for the two of you to keep the store going while I'm away."

Sarah looked stunned and Nat looked pissed. Nat grabbed her beer and walked around to the other side of the counter. She stood with her shoulder to me, staring across the shop, her jaw clenching and unclenching.

"Is this about Grace?" Sarah asked. "'Cause if it is there's no need in heading off to Australia. We'll find you another woman. One that's not married, this time." Sarah looked at me, her eyes critical. "She's not worth all that."

Nat jerked around to face Sarah. "Grace is so worth all that," she snapped.

Sarah planted her palm on her hip and leveled her eyes on Nat. "You're just sayin' that 'cause she's straight, and I know you've got a thing for straight women."

Nat shrugged and held Sarah's eyes. "Grace isn't straight."

Sarah's eyes narrowed. "Well, what's that other thing you call us. Oh yeah, breeders. Grace is a breeder."

"Okay, okay! It doesn't matter what Grace is." I looked from one to the other until I knew I had their attention. They were smart and responsible enough to keep my store going, though the last few minutes had not done anything to bolster my confidence in them. "The fact is I'm going to Australia for a while and I want you two to keep things going while I'm gone."

Sarah opened her mouth to say something and the doorbell rang. I looked at Nat and nodded toward the door.

"Probably somebody running late," she said as she started across the shop. She unlocked the deadbolt and we looked outside. Grace stood there waiting.

"Grace," I said, dumbfounded and staring. I had expected she would be in Raleigh, working the room with her understanding smiles and patient nods at some family or social function. Her face was pale as I walked toward her. Nat stood by the door, shifting and searching for some place to look other than at me. I stepped outside and closed the door. "Let's go out to my truck."

Neither of us spoke as we walked across the thin coat of ice covering the alleyway. I fished my keys from my pocket and unlocked the truck door. Grace crawled inside and moved across the seat. She huddled her body close inside her wool coat. She hadn't worn gloves, and that wasn't like her. I started the truck and turned on the heater.

"So why are you here, Grace?" I asked. I hadn't taken the time to grab my jacket, and I started to shiver from the cold.

"I came to ask about the night you walked out. You said I belittled you."

I shook my head. "I said you belittled us, Grace. Us."

She looked as if she still did not understand. I swung around to fully face her. "It's been over a year now since we talked to Marty and Joyce about what we had to do to have a life together. A lot has

364

happened since then. You've had me with you during all of those rough times, but I wasn't really with you, not like partners should be." Grace lowered her head but said nothing, so I continued, "When you were in D.C. with Katie and you called me, I came up in a heartbeat because that's what people in a relationship do. Only no one knew I was there—no one. Not Katie, or George, or even your mother. I stayed in the hotel room or walked around the city. It felt like we were just two people who happened to be in the same town, except at night when you came back to the hotel. And with Brian, you asked me to help him get past Iraq, but we couldn't be honest about who I was to you. We've acted like we are friends and nothing more. That doesn't feel like an honest relationship to me, Grace. It feels like an affair, and I told you a long time ago I'm done with affairs."

Grace nodded and turned away from me. I could see the anger and frustration building up inside her. Would she push it away again to be the cool, calm Grace who looked for an easy way out? Her hand suddenly slammed against the door. "Goddammit! Why does this have to be so fucking hard!" She brought her fist to her mouth and let her tears fall down her cheeks. Finally I had honesty. I wanted to reach for her, even as I would reach for a friend. I didn't do it, for fear of being caught up again.

Grace dropped her fist from her mouth and looked over at me. We sat in bewildered silence, the dismay surrounding us like a jailer's stare. I watched her gather herself, as she always did, until she became steady. She looked at me and said, "You're right. Everyone should know about you and who you are to me. You deserve that and I still want to be the one to grow old with you. I want to give you everything you want, but something keeps coming up that stops me from making it happen. I tell myself I'm waiting until the time is right. Maybe the truth is I'm still too afraid."

I wanted to tell her to be brave and fight for us, but she already knew what she had to do. "I've told you what I want, Grace," I said.

She looked at me, nodded once, and got out of the truck. I watched her quick footsteps pick through the icy alleyway until she turned the corner. She was gone.

Nat sauntered through the back door of the workshop, rubbing the painful effects of a New Year's hangover out of her eyes.

I chuckled when I saw her. "Morning, Sunshine. It looks like you had a good time last night."

"Ughhh," Nat groaned. "Tell me again why you wanted us to come in today?"

"We need to go over a few things before I leave. It's easier if the shop is closed." I walked over and wrapped my arm around her shoulder. "Come on, let's get this done so you can get home and back in bed."

Nat groaned again and followed me down the hall to the showroom counter. Sarah was there, perched on her stool reading Danielle Steele. Nat pulled herself onto the stool beside Sarah and dropped her chin in her hand.

"You had fun last night." Sarah's fully awake eyes beamed at Nat. "Is that a hickey?" She smiled and reached over to lightly touch a purplish bruise on the side of Natalie's neck.

Nat leaned away and grimaced. "No—Kris doesn't do hickies. I'll tell you about it when I feel like laughing."

Sarah rubbed Nat's back and looked at her adoringly. "Y'all are so sweet." She turned to me with her smile still wide. "Okay, let's go boss. I've got turnip greens to cook this afternoon."

I leaned against the counter I had built over two years ago. I'd paid a small fortune for the salvaged chestnut wood. Every cut I'd made as carefully as a jeweler would a diamond. Against the wall behind where Nat stood was the first table she had built. It wasn't quite good enough for the showroom, though we all loved it. It was part of us. I looked around the shop, to my name on the transom window, to the vanity. The place would be different when I came back. For two months the place would be theirs to run, without me.

Nat and Sarah leaned against the counter, their shoulders almost touching. I looked at them and said, "First off, I want you to be careful with the inventory. You'll only have Nat's stuff coming in, so keep the showroom as full as you can. Volume generates interest from the walk-ins. Don't panic and let anything go too cheap. There's enough money for payroll and other fixed expenses, so you should be okay with the bills until I get back."

"You *are* coming back, right?" Nat looked at me warily.

I understood her worries. She had heard plenty of stories from my life of drifting around, and she was smart enough to figure out the catalyst that came from my being hurt. "Yes, Nat, I'm coming back," I said sincerely.

"You shouldn't let women troubles make you leave. I've done told you that," Sarah said.

I held up my palm. "Okay, girls, let's give it a rest. I'm not leaving because of *women troubles*," I said to them, even though they knew it wasn't true. "Think of it more as a long vacation. I've always wanted to go to Australia and now may be as good a time as any."

"Have you called all of your clients about their orders? 'Cause I don't want them calling me." Sarah's face scrunched into a wary grimace and she chuckled nervously.

"Yes, I called them all and I only had one cancellation. Everyone else said they'd wait."

"Rich people are weird," Sarah grumbled.

"Money complicates everything," I replied.

"So does a husband and two children," Sarah quipped.

I didn't need that. I looked at Sarah, somewhere between anger and disbelief. She sat up straight and ran her hands across the golden chestnut wood in front of her. "I'm just sayin,'" she said, glancing away from me. I knew she had meant well. The world was still simple for Sarah. She was one of the lucky ones. The ring on her finger and the right to say *I do* was all she needed to show the world her love was worthy.

56

G-R-A-C-E

Sarah Jackson said it was women troubles that pushed me to consider going to Australia. I argued it was my desire to see a place my father had never gotten the chance to visit. As much as I had packed into my life so far, I didn't want to leave the world knowing I could have done more. That had been the hardest part of standing up to Grace, too. We had the potential to be so much more than she had ever let us. I'd begun to wonder if giving her more time could have gotten us there.

I thought about my decision to go as I stood on my porch with my second cup of coffee. I would miss my mornings with Whiteside. Even on the coldest days, I would find a few minutes to spend with her, watching the sun reflect off her face, or the fog move up and around her crest. She had anchored my days with something constant but ever changing. I knew I would miss her while I was gone as surely as I knew I would come back to her.

Through the quiet of the morning I heard Marty's truck engine start. In less than a minute, her truck bounced along my driveway. "Morning, kid," she said as she got out of the truck. "Beautiful day we've got going, isn't it?"

"Yeah. Cold, though," I replied as I watched her climb the porch stairs. Her movements were slow and stiff, and I wondered if she was up to the task of helping me move my front door. "Are you sure you want to help me? I can call Nat."

"Nonsense," Marty replied. "It won't take us ten minutes."

"Come on, then, I'll take the pins out of the hinges and we'll get 'er done."

I slipped the pins out and squatted beside Marty's feet, grabbing onto the bottom of the door. "Okay, back it off easy." Marty wrapped her hands around the top and backed up. Together we shuffled over to the wall and carefully set the door down. I stood up straight and looked at the gift Nat had given me a year ago. She had been so proud, and I knew when I saw the carving that Nat and I were bonded in the same way as me and Preacher.

Marty stood beside me admiring Nat's work. We had seen Nat come so far. For Marty, Nat had grown from the struggling kid in high school to a gifted craftsperson, and for me she had grown from the girl at the Dairy Queen to the young woman I was entrusting with my shop. "You've made a lot of difference in her life. You know that, don't you?" Marty asked.

"I hope I have," I replied.

Marty crossed her arms over her chest. "Still, she's awfully young to be leaving her with the shop," she said. Her finger began tapping on her forearm, and I knew she had more to say. "You don't have to leave you know. Spring will be here soon enough to clear away your winter doldrums."

"C'mon, let's hang the old door before everything in the house freezes," I said, turning the conversation from wherever Marty was heading next. I picked up the old door and brought it over to the frame. It was much lighter than the one Nat had built. "Watch your fingers," I said to Marty as we twisted the door through the open doorway. Marty grunted when we lifted it to the hinges. I set the pins and Marty straightened. She grabbed her hip with a wince and slowly twisted from side to side, working out the muscle ache.

"So, you're not going to talk to me about your decision to leave?" she asked.

"Let me make some hot tea and get you a couple of Advil," I replied.

She followed me to the kitchen and pushed her shoulders flat against the wall. "You know you wouldn't have to fool with storing that door if you weren't leaving. The only time things get stolen is when nobody is around."

I loved Marty, but sometimes I wished she'd give it a rest. I turned on the faucet and held the kettle underneath. "Marty, I know you and Joyce don't think I should leave right now. To you it probably looks like I'm leaving because of what happened with Grace, and to some extent that's true. I wouldn't be going to Australia if Grace and I were moving forward." I put the kettle on the burner and flipped it on. "But it did happen, and I need some space to put it past me. I've got this great opportunity to go to Australia, and I'm going to take advantage of it."

Marty nodded. "Have you ever been there?"

"No, but I've always wanted to go. I shipped a piece there last year. My client said if I ever wanted to come Down Under she would sponsor me on a work visa. She wants me to build a bedroom suite for her and her wife, and she said they'd like for me to come down so I can get a sense of their space. I suppose she'd rather pay for workshop rent and expenses than for shipping costs."

"Interesting," Marty said. For a moment she drifted away in thought, and then she looked at me again. "What does Julie say about you going half a world away?"

"She's okay with it. Not thrilled, but okay. She has Olivia now. She'll be fine without me." I worried more about leaving Marty and Joyce. Winter was hard in these mountains, and they would be alone through some of the worst months. A heavy snow could strand them at home for days. "Marty, I know you and Joyce have some apprehension about being here without me. I've asked Nat to help out while I'm gone. She and Kris will be staying here at the cabin some nights and weekends. I'll ask them to stay here when snow's predicted."

Marty nodded. "Joyce and I can help with the store if they need us. Be sure to tell them that."

A faint trail of steam whistled out of the kettle. I moved it from the heat and gathered a couple of mugs from the Hoosier cabinet by the door. "Let's go talk by the fire," I said. In the den, Marty sat down on the couch close to the fireplace and looked around. Her memories of this room ran deep. I could see her body relaxing as she sat there. The room had the same effect on me, now. The low ceilings and round, stacked timbers soothed like a warm cocoon.

I sat down in my rocking chair by the fire and caressed my mug to let the heat seep into my palms. Marty leaned forward on her elbows, the steam from her tea rising up to her eyes, which were focused directly on me. "Blue, Joyce and I have been talking, and we'd like to know if you'd be interested in buying this cabin."

I smiled at her. "Marty, I am coming back from Australia. You don't have to sell me your property to make sure I do."

Marty looked at me, undaunted. "This has got nothing to do with you going to Australia. Horse Cove is your place in the world. This is where you belong, kid."

Her insight astounded me. Horse Cove *was* my place in the world. I had never felt it as strongly in any other place I'd ever lived, including the farm where I grew up. "Wow. I'm not sure what to say, Marty," I said after a moment. "I'd like nothing more than to buy this cabin and a few acres or so. You know how much I love it here."

"I do," Marty said. "When you get back we'll take a walk around the place and figure out where we want to put the property corners."

I returned a broad smile that said yes and sat back. Someday soon I would have my name on a deed. Augusta Blue Riley would own a small piece of land in the Appalachian Mountains in a place called Horse Cove. Until then, I needed only a change of scenery, some days in the sun, and maybe a nice, uncomplicated woman to pass the time with me.

Nat sat next to me, sulking. Outside a cold, dry wind blew through the streets and alleyways of Highlands. The strongest gusts howled against the walls and windows of the shop. Inside it was eerily quiet without the whine of saws or sanders, the tapping of chisels, or the burr of spinning lathes.

Nat watched me place my carving mallet in a shipping crate and cover it with a layer of bubble wrap. "What if the crate gets lost?"

"I'll buy more tools," I said. I closed the crate and straightened to stretch my back.

"They won't be the same tools," Nat mumbled. "You've got some of Preacher's stuff in there."

I looked at her and wrapped my palm around the back of her neck. I remembered a long time ago when Julie would do the same thing before she told me something important. "I'm coming back, Nat, really I am. I'm leaving you to run my shop, for chrissakes."

Nat shrugged. "I know you'll be calling and all, but it's not the same as having you here every day."

I understood why Nat was worried. She was so young, only twenty-three, and I would be leaving her and Sarah with a hell of a responsibility. I had considered closing the shop while I was gone, but it was the slow season, and I decided keeping the shop open would give them both the best sense of normalcy. Most of all, I wanted Nat to know that she could do it without me, if she ever needed.

"Come walk with me," I said with a gentle squeeze to Nat's neck. We walked into the showroom and stopped in front of the vanity. I traced my fingers along the polished surface, remembering my days with Preacher, how we had worked on the design, and then the hours of conversation and coaching needed to get the carvings right. It was my best and most deeply inspired work, and I knew I would never create anything like it again. I kept my fingertips moving across the surface as I spoke to Nat. "While I'm gone I want you to sell this piece, but you have to promise me something. I want you to use the money to go back to school."

Nat rocked back on her heals and bit her bottom lip. Her brooding gave way to thoughtfulness. "You've always said the vanity wasn't for sale, so how come you want to sell it for me to go back to school? Shouldn't we use the money to keep the shop running or something?"

I shook my head. "Don't worry about that. I've planned enough money to keep the shop going and for you and Sarah to get your paychecks. The main thing is I want you to go back to school. It doesn't matter to me if it's college or trade school, but I want you to get more education."

"But I'm learning a trade here in the shop. Why waste money on school?"

"Because an education can give you a lot more options. I want you to know some basics about business, how to read an income statement and a balance sheet, how to manage finances and people. At least get an associate's degree, Nat."

Nat shoved her hands in her pockets and looked at me with a trace of defiance. "Sarah can teach me all that bookkeeping stuff. I don't need to go to school."

I nodded. "She can, but you may need the piece of paper to be competitive. You never know what might happen. One day, people may not be able to afford these high-end products we're selling. You need something to fall back on."

Nat gave me a wary glance and said, "How will I have time to work if I'm in school and having to study all the time?"

"You don't have to go to school full time. Take one class a semester if that's all you want. The money from the vanity will give you the financial leg up you'll need to keep from borrowing."

Nat turned to me, chin up and arms crossed. "So, do you care who I sell it to?"

I knew who she meant. "I'll make a list of clients who've expressed an interest in it. Just do me a favor and don't sell it to Grace."

Brian Marshall's Chevrolet pickup pulled into my driveway. He got out and looked up at me. His face was solemn and drawn, and my heart began to pound with wild imaginings that something had happened to Grace. "I heard you're leaving," he said.

I nodded, relieved. "That's right, I am," I replied. I looked over and noticed Whitney sitting in the passenger side of the pickup. She waved and went back to texting. "How did you find out?" I asked.

Brian rested his foot on the first step of my porch. "Nat told me when we went by the shop to see our wedding gift."

"I see." I crossed my arms and shivered in the evening wind. "Since you drove out here to see me, I take it there's a reason." Brian nodded. "Let's go inside then. I've got a fire going." Brian started up the porch stairs without his fiancé. "Doesn't Whitney want to join us?" I asked.

"No. She thinks it's best to keep this between you and me. She doesn't want to leave her heated seat, either."

Brian followed me inside. He walked over to the fireplace and stood with his back to me, his hands stretched toward the fire. "Can I get you something, coffee or tea?" I asked.

"No, thanks," he replied over his shoulder.

I leaned against the wall by the door and watched him, waiting for him to talk when he was ready. He lifted one arm to rest on the mantle. The other hand slipped into the pocket of his blue cargo pants. His face, and whatever expression it wore, was turned toward the fire. "Mom told Katie and me that she's in love with you. She's filed for a divorce from Dad."

Two weeks ago I had wanted so much to hear those words from Grace. Hearing it from Brian, I wasn't as sure. Maybe it was because of the matter-of-fact way he said it, as if it wasn't something that would change his family forever. Brian looked at me, expecting some response. The fire popped and we both flinched.

"How's your family doing?" I asked from across the room. The tension between us suggested we keep our distance.

"Katie cried about it for a couple of days. I talked to her, and I think she's doing better. Neil says she's still upset, mostly about the divorce. She puts on a good face for Mom. I pretty much knew about you and Mom the first time I saw you together."

"What about your dad?"

"He's fine with the divorce—kind of happy about it, actually. He says if Mom won't wait until after the election, it's best to keep it low key. I asked Mom if she was going to tell you. She said she wasn't right away. She needs to work out some of her own stuff first."

We were quiet for a moment. The tension between us subsided and I walked over to stand across the mantle from Brian. The glow of the fire lit the profile of his face. The scar on the right side ran from the corner of his eye to the base of his jaw. Grace said it had taken over twenty stitches to sew up, and he almost lost his eye. Their family had been through a lot. Maybe they all needed time, too.

"When are you leaving?" Brian asked.

"As soon as possible; I'm waiting for my passport. There's a back-up in processing at the State Department."

"So are you going to call my mom before you leave?"

I thought about it before I answered. "I don't know how much your mother told you about us. We've got a lot of history to work through. I think we could both use some time apart to figure things out."

Brian looked at me as if he could see right through. "You're itchin' to run, aren't you, Ms. Riley? You're itching to run to someplace far away from here."

I stared at him, clueless for what to say. The intensity of his eyes demanded an honest answer. I couldn't find one, so he continued, "See, I understand that itch to go someplace where you don't have to deal with all of this, where no one has a hold on you, and you can do your thing. Whether it's your art, or your mission, or job, you just do it, you get to focus on that one thing, and if you do it better than anyone else, you'll be rewarded. But, the problem is you and I don't get to do that anymore. We've asked somebody to love us, so we don't get to run. You're not standing up if you do. I'm done with trying to run, Ms. Riley. That itch is no longer mine to scratch."

Brian had his mother's ability to perceive the deep-seated emotion living beneath the surface of people, and in spite of his Marine Corps persona, he was a gentle man. I wanted to argue with him, to convince him he was wrong about me. He wasn't, and I knew he felt the need to move around as strongly as me.

"Do you know how difficult this could be for your family?" I asked him.

"Our family is strong, Ms. Riley, and a lot of that is because of my mom. So long as she's strong, we'll be okay." He paused and studied me for a moment. "I don't understand everything that has gone on between the two of you, you're right about that. I'll never understand my parents' marriage, either. But I do know that my mom's a good woman, and if you're the one who can make her happy, I think you should be strong enough to try."

I let him leave without telling him how hard I had tried.

"This place looks great, especially now that you've got a few boxes unpacked and a couple of pictures on the wall," I said, scanning the kitchen of Julie and Olivia's house in New Bern. They'd wanted a place on the water, and looked for several months before finding the right one.

"We've been spending a lot of time on the boat since we moved here," Julie said. "We haven't taken time to do much in the house, so I appreciate you coming over to help us get everything in shape. I don't feel too bad about it, especially since I helped you figure out how to move all of that shop equipment from Mississippi." Julie grinned, and then she asked, "How's Preacher doing, by the way?"

"He's good. I'm glad I took a few days to go over and see him. I took him up to Memphis one day. We had a ball on Beale Street. We had some of the best ribs I ever tasted at a restaurant across from BB King's." I sat back and ran my hands across their kitchen table. It was plain Shaker style, beautiful dark walnut and sturdy. "Preacher would love this table." I looked across its wide width to Julie. "Did you buy it recently?"

"It was Olivia's grandmother's. It's original Shaker from Kentucky," she replied.

"It's been in storage for a couple of years," Olivia offered. She stood at the counter across the kitchen adding spices to a large bowl of shrimp and cheese grits. "I was afraid it would have to be refinished. Turns out, a bit of polish was all it needed."

"We got it out of storage when we moved here," Julie added. She picked out a walnut from the bowl centered on the table and picked up the nutcracker. Her hands, still steady and strong, effortlessly squeezed the handles to break open the shell. "So how long are you planning on staying, Blue?" Julie asked. She picked out a piece of walnut meat and popped it in her mouth.

"I figured a week or so, depending on when my passport comes. I'll go back to Highlands for a couple of weeks to tie up loose ends and check in with Nat and Sarah."

"When do you fly out for Australia?" Olivia asked. She set the bowl of shrimp and grits on the table and returned to the counter for the bread. "That's a very long flight, you know."

"I fly out of Charlotte on the fourteenth," I answered.

"So you're flying out of the country on Valentine's Day to get away from a woman." Olivia's displeasure hung in the air.

I shook my head with a weak smile. "I keep telling everyone I'm not running from my trouble with Grace. I don't know why nobody believes me."

Julie eyed me with a smirk and reached into the bowl for another walnut. "Because it isn't true, that's why. Have the two of you talked at all?"

Their discerning eyes were on me. I listlessly pulled the edge of my cloth napkin to avoid them. "No, we haven't talked since she came by the shop around Christmas."

Julie grabbed another walnut and cracked it between metal jaws. She turned it once and cracked it again. In a way I felt like the walnut, ready to crack from the squeeze of expectations. It seemed daily I was pressured by someone to call Grace, as if I hadn't thought about it myself for hours. In a moment of clarity I decided I needed assurance that she would be the complete Grace; that she could walk through the world in the same way I did, without apology or secrets.

Julie picked out walnut meat as she continued. "Why won't you talk to her? Grace has done what you wanted her to do. I'm sure this has been hard on her family. She could use your support right now, I'm sure."

Everyone seemed sure but me. Still, I went on pleading for someone to see it my way. "See, that's just it. I've always been the one to compromise," I said to Julie. She returned a doubtful gaze and waited for the rest of what I had to say. It seemed whatever it was, she wasn't going to agree with me. "I know Grace took a big step telling her family and filing for divorce, but that was only the first step in going from an affair to the possibility of a real relationship. I'm giving her all the space she needs to figure out if an honest life with me is what she really wants. I don't want to compromise again. Ever."

"So why don't you tell her that?" Julie asked. "Go get your damn phone out and call her." The solid resolve I saw in her eyes still made my stomach flip.

Olivia sat down beside Julie and popped out her napkin. "Let's talk about something else, shall we? I didn't spend all this time in the kitchen to have you two fighting through dinner."

Morning sunlight beamed into the bathroom window upstairs. It felt warm on my bare skin, like an assurance that something was about to change. I stepped into the shower and stood close to the nozzle, absorbing the heat of the water. Olivia and Julie were downstairs in the kitchen with the morning paper and their coffee. In a while, when the sun had warmed the morning, they would take me out to see the work they had done on the boat.

After the shower I bounded downstairs to find Julie. She stood at the living-room window, the drape pulled back between two fingers, looking outside. "Someone's been waiting for you," she said when she turned to me.

She quietly slipped out of the room. I walked to the window and pulled back the drape. Grace's Land Rover sat in the driveway. "Oh fuck." The drape dropped from my fingers and I turned away from the window, my heart pounding, annoying as ever.

I walked out onto the veranda, as far as I would go toward Grace. She got out of her car and moved around to the end of the hood. She wore black slacks and a light blue cardigan, and her hair was gathered up in the back. The corners of her eyes were red and droopy like she hadn't slept well. Still, she looked as beautiful as the day I met her.

Grace folded her hands in front of her hips. I glanced at her fingers and saw her wedding band was gone. "I told Brian and Katie," she said, her voice controlled.

"I know, Grace."

"George and I have agreed to the divorce terms."

"I know."

"Who told you?"

"Brian."

A neighbor's car backed out two driveways away. We watched until it passed and drove away. "How did you know I was here?" I asked when our eyes returned to each other.

"I called Julie late last night. I didn't want to call your cell. I thought we should speak in person." She shifted, and looked uneasy. "Can we talk, Blue? I'd rather not do it out here."

"Julie and Olivia are in the house. We can go out to the boat if you want."

Grace nodded and climbed the stairs to the veranda. She pressed past me in the doorway, and her perfumed scent stirred my instincts for her. When we walked into the kitchen, Julie lowered her newspaper and peered at us over the top of her reading glasses.

"If you need a place to be alone, the keys to the boat are by the back door," Julie offered without my asking.

I grabbed the keys on the way out. Side by side, Grace and I walked down the planked walkway and out onto the pier. I held the galley door open and waited for Grace to duck inside. I followed behind her and grabbed a couple of blankets from the bin by the door. I handed the blankets to Grace and closed the door. "Let's get some heat going in here," I said, slipping by her to get to the heater. Her breath drifting across my neck set my nerves to attention.

Grace wrapped a blanket over her shoulders and sat down on the bench near the bed. She looked up at me and said, "I hear you're leaving for a while."

I sat on the cramped double bed next to her and swung my blanket over my shoulders. "Yes, I am. A client has invited me to work in Australia for a bit."

"You are coming back, aren't you?" Grace asked in a way that seemed more determined than hopeful.

"Yes," I said with no intention of telling her how long I would be gone.

She nodded and looked away from me. I watched the thoughts gather in her mind and considered how I would respond to a plea to stay and come back to her. I knew she would argue that things would be different now that she was out to her family. Different was still a long way from what I wanted.

Grace looked down at her folded hands, focusing on the bare ring finger of her left hand. "I know about the vanity, Blue," she said.

My eyes snapped up to her. "What do you mean?" I asked.

She looked at me in a patient way that said she could explain everything. "Last Sunday, Natalie and Brian brought over the bookcases you'd built for my birthday. They brought the vanity with them.

Nat told Brian she had your permission to sell it, so he bought it from Nat for a wedding present for Whitney. He asked if he could keep it in my room until the wedding. When he left that night, he thanked me for keeping the vanity for him, and he said if I wanted to feel close to you, maybe it would help to have your best work close by."

Grace's face now twisted with emotion, and I wondered if her heart was pounding as hard as mine. She straightened her back and drew in a deep breath before she continued. "The next morning, I was lying in bed, looking at how you had interpreted the life of a woman in the faces you carved. It was the A I saw first. Then I looked at the face to the right, the woman at middle age, and I saw the C. I sat up to look closer, and it suddenly popped out at me; G, R, A, C, E, right there, a letter of my name woven into each of those beautiful carvings. For a minute I could barely breathe. I sat there, staring at those carvings and crying my eyes out. The rest of the day I barely remember."

A part of me wanted to reach out to her. The rest was holding out for what I wanted.

Grace scooted up on the couch, closer to me. Now I could see the sadness in the golden flecks of her eyes. "Blue, I know you designed and carved the vanity while you were in Mississippi, before I barged back into your life. Will you tell me why you did it?"

"Because I always came back to you, Grace. No matter how hard I tried with other women, my mind kept coming back to you and the way we had loved each other. I never loved anyone else like that. When I started woodworking, Preacher told me that if I did it right, the pieces I was building would be around for a long time, maybe a hundred years or more after I'm gone. And so I had this idea that if I couldn't be with you in this life, somehow I could still bond us together; your life and my life together in one beautiful creation. I hoped that two hundred years from now someone would see my signature on the vanity, and they would see your name in the faces. When they see it all, they'll know how much I loved you."

Grace nodded as tears began to glisten in the corners of her eyes. "Was the series of faces meant to embody the lifetime you wanted to have with me?"

"Yes. You were the one I wanted to move with me from one stage in life to the next. I wanted to be with you in every day of every year."

"But you were so angry when you saw me again."

I nodded. "I was. I thought I'd forgiven you, and I suppose in some ways I had. I thought when I finished the vanity I could move on. I had done what I needed to do to deal with my feelings for you, and I thought I'd never see you again. When you showed up, you pulled me right back to where I'd been before, still drawn to you, but angry that you had left me, and pissed at the world for taking you away from me in the first place."

Grace wiped her tears away from her cheeks with her fingertips. She tried to smile, and I saw the familiar twitch at the corner of her mouth. She took a moment to pull herself back from her tears, and then she said, "Sweetheart, I've never been worthy of those carvings. It may as well have said 'stupid idiot' for the ways I've hurt you. There are no excuses for what I did, any of it. I can only move forward and tell you that I want to be worthy of your work one day. More than anything, that's what I want."

I wanted it, too. I wanted to know that Grace could give me what I needed: a life that was fully open, for better or worse, for richer or poorer, in sickness and in health. Anything less was a compromise I wasn't willing to make. "And I've told you what I want, Grace. Are you willing to give it to me?"

She gave me a little smile and reached for my hand. I looked down at our fingers laced together. The beauty of our hands melded as one sent a charge of joy rushing through my body. Grace covered our hands with her palm. "I told the board of the foundation I'm getting a divorce from George and I'll be living fully out now. They surprised me and said they hope I'll stay on."

At that moment I knew we could be possible. My Grace Lancaster had finally shed the skin of deceit, and she had done it for me. "Grace," I said, smiling with all the joy inside me, "Have you ever been to Australia?"

Her face became a mixture of laughter and tears. "No, but I've already got a passport."

I laughed and pulled her onto the bed beside me. The moment our lips touched, I knew the hundreds of nights before had never been quite right. There had always been something between us, a veil of doubt, a holding back to avoid becoming lost in the caverns of trust. And now the veil was gone. This time when our bodies met, our spirits came out to dance.

Epilogue

**Original Blue Annual Charity
Furniture Auction**

You are cordially invited to the
Original Blue charity furniture auction

Presenting the Works of Brian Marshall

Saturday, June 2

3 to 6 in the afternoon

Wine and Beer reception provided by
Brian's mentor, Blue Riley,
and his mother, Grace Lancaster-Riley

10% of all proceeds to be donated to
The Wounded Warrior Project

ORIGINAL BLUE GALLERY
HIGHLANDS
NORTH CAROLINA

About the Author

Wynn Malone grew up in Alabama, surrounded by dairy farms and good people. She bounced back and forth from central to north Alabama, until changing one number on an application resulted in a job offer and a move to Kentucky. Wynn fell in love with the people and the landscapes of the Bluegrass Country, and she remained there until another career move took her to western North Carolina. Once again, she was surrounded by good people and beautiful landscapes, but the pull of the Bluegrass Country took her back to Kentucky once again. She now lives in Lexington, Kentucky with her partner and their assortment of dogs and cats. Wynn invites you to drop on by her website at wynnmalone.com for the latest goings on.

Acknowledgments

Many people joined me along the journey of writing this story. I want to thank everyone who walked the path with me, whether for the entire length or just a few steps. I have been truly blessed by your support.

There are a few people I would especially like to thank. First and foremost, I would like to thank Bett Norris for your belief in my writing and for your friendship. Your feedback on early drafts of this story was invaluable. I would also like to thank Marcia Finical, my fellow Bywater author, for your support and encouragement, and for helping me make sense of it all.

To Julie, Embry, Nancy, and Michal, thank you for your time, advice, and the perspectives you offered along the way. To Patti, Karen, and Melissa, thank you for your open hearts and your hospitality. To Sharon Speegle, thank you for time and attention to early edits, and for keeping me honest. "Eighty-five words, Malone!"

I am most grateful to the women of Bywater Books for sharing your time, skills, and treasure. To Marianne K. Martin, for your patient shepherding; Kelly Smith, for your extraordinary insight; Caroline Curtis for lending a sharp eye to the final editing task, and for pulling it all together; and to Michele Karlsberg, for keeping me moving forward.

And most of all to Brantley, thank you for walking beside me every step of the way.

Bywater Books

SHAKEN AND STIRRED

Joan Opyr

"What a great read! Character, story, dialogue—it's a trifecta of a page turner." —Kate Clinton, author of *I Told You So*

"Opyr is a master of mixing light and dark—of telling a story about family dysfunction, alcoholic rage, and life without a lover with laugh-out loud panache." —*Book Marks*

"It's a wonderful novel" —*Out in Print*

Poppy Koslowski is trying to recover from a hysterectomy, but her family has other ideas. She's the one with the responsibility to pull the plug on her alcoholic grandfather in North Carolina. So she's dragged back across the country from her rebuilt life into the bosom of a family who barely notice the old man's imminent death.

Plunged into a crazy kaleidoscope of consulting doctors, catching fire with an old flame, and negotiating lunch venues with her mother and grandmother, Poppy still manages to fall in love. Because nothing in the Koslowski family is ever straightforward. Not even dying.

Print ISBN 978-1-932859-79-9
Ebook ISNBN 978-1-61294-018-2

MISS McGHEE

Bett Norris

"Any reader will love this intelligent, richly detailed, altogether satisfying portrayal of a resourceful woman's struggle for love and self-determination in 20th century small-town America. *Miss McGhee* signals the arrival of an impressive, gifted story-teller." —Katherine V. Forrest

World War II is over, and like millions of others, Mary McGhee is looking for a future. A new start, a new job, a new place. But in the small Alabama town she's chosen, she soon finds it's not so easy to leave the past behind.

There's the old problem of being an unwelcome woman in a man's world when Mary takes on the challenge of returning a neglected lumber empire to profitability. Then there's Lila Dubose, the boss's wife, who stirs up desires Mary can't escape, fears she can't control, and reminders that she is surrounded by threat.

Set in the shadow of the civil rights movement, *Miss McGhee* is a sweeping tale of forbidden love in a turbulent time. First-time author Bett Norris portrays one of the darkest and most troubling times in American history with exceptional skill and sensitivity, giving us a unique insight into our own recent history.

Print ISBN 978-1-932859-33-1
Ebook ISNBN 978-1-932859-805-1

Available at your local bookstore
or call 734-662-8815
or order online at www.bywaterbooks.com

At Bywater Books we love good books about lesbians just like you do, and we're committed to bringing the best of contemporary lesbian writing to our avid readers. Our editorial team is dedicated to finding and developing outstanding writers who create books you won't want to put down.

We sponsor the Bywater Prize for Fiction to help with this quest. Each prize winner receives $1,000 and publication of their novel. We have already discovered amazing writers like Jill Malone, Sally Bellerose, and Hilary Sloin through the Bywater Prize. Which exciting new writer will we find next?

For more information about Bywater Books and the annual Bywater Prize for Fiction, please visit our website.

www.bywaterbooks.com

9 781612 940458